ARCTIC OCEAN

FINLAND

UNION OF SOVIET SOCIALIST REPUBLICS

Genghis Khan's Tomb, amazing!

MANCHUKUO

INNER MONGOLIA

Jarvis Hancock, Istanbul

Armageddon!

IRAN

AFGHANISTAN

???

Shambhala

CHINA

JAPAN

White Russians

Simcha Golan—don't trust him

INDIA

NEPAL

BURMA

SIAM

PACIFIC OCEAN

PHILIPPINE ISLANDS

Yamashita's Gold

ANGLO EGYPTIAN SUDAN

ETHIOPIA

KENYA

SOMALILAND

EAST INDIES

BORNEO

SUMATRA

NEW GUINEA PAPUA

BELGIAN CONGO

TANGANYIKA TERRITORY

MOZAMBIQUE

MADAGASCAR

SOUTHERN RHODESIA

TRANSVAAL

UNION OF SOUTH AFRICA

AUSTRALIA

NEW ZEALAND

Written By
Chris Lites

Additional Material by
CS Barnhart,
Benn Beaton

Line Manager
Chris Lites

Interior Artwork By
Giorgio Baroni,
Dust Studio

Edited By
Scott Woodard

Graphic Design By
Rick Hershey
Michal E. Cross

Cover Artwork By
Giorgio Baroni

Cartography By
Giorgio Baroni

Photography By
Nick Fallon

Miniatures By
Dust Studio

Publisher
Chris Birch

Art Directed By
Giorgio Baroni

Proofreading By
Benn Beaton,
Chris Lites,
Peter Holland,
Steve Hanson,
Morgan Swiers,
Michael Fulks,
Philip Campanaro,
Gilles Tremblay,
Matthew Dixon,
Benjamin Koch
And thanks to the rest of our fans!

Community Managers
Zarina Kadylbek,
John Dodd,
Steve Hanson

PAOLO PARENTE'S DUST ADVENTURES

***Dust* Created By**
Paolo Parente

Published By
Modiphius Entertainment Ltd. 35 Turneville Road, London, W14 9PS.
info@modiphius.com

Modiphius Entertainment Product Number: MUH050045
ISBN: 978-1-910132-34-0

Find out more about *Dust Adventures* at
www.modiphius.com/dust-adventures
www.facebook.com/groups/dustadventures

TABLE OF CONTENTS

CHAPTER 1: WELCOME TO THE APOCALYPSE

Welcome to the first campaign for ***Dust Adventures***. Herein you will find thrilling chases, lost cities, epic battles you can play out with your ***Dust*** miniatures, artefacts rare and priceless, and secrets the ***Dust*** universe has not, to date, given up.

Players find themselves on a quest to retrieve the Seven Seals written of in the Bible. Along the way, they uncover secrets even the Vrill feared, and organizations long thought dead.

All three blocs want to unlock the secrets of the Seven Seals and whoever does so may gain knowledge that will win them the war. In the background, working against everyone involved, are the remnants of the Nazi *Ahnenerbe* and a cult called the Sons of Belial. Only by their wits, prowess, and more than a little luck will the PCs prevail and prevent Armageddon.

This campaign is a follow up to the adventure Operation: Apocalypse found in the core rulebook. It is not necessary to have played that to enjoy this adventure, but it does provide some interesting backstory. This text is for the GM only. If you plan to play, stop reading now! There are secrets inside this book best discovered by the players during the course of play.

A SECRET HISTORY

10,000 or more years ago, a war raged between two alien races: the Anunnaki and the Vrill. They vied for control over the Earth. Anunnaki bases were the first to be established. Following a protocol of total war, the Vrill launched an asteroid at the planet. The result destroyed almost all remnants of the Anunnaki as well as the human civilizations they had been guiding and manipulating. This story has been all but lost to time, surviving only as the great flood myths of civilizations around the globe.

To preserve their knowledge and culture, the Anunnaki created seven tablets or "seals" which would allow their civilization to be re-established in the future. Each tablet was taken to a different corner of the Earth where they would be safeguarded until the Anunnaki could return. The Seals were also keys to a great Anunnaki secret resting deep beneath the birthplace of human civilization in the Fertile Crescent. This secret augurs the end of the world. When the Seven Seals are brought together once more, the Apocalypse may be unleashed.

Operation: Apocalypse follows a globetrotting quest to recover these Seals. The PCs find themselves searching from France to Shanghai, and Tibet to Alaska, to recover the Seals and unlock the greatest secret mankind has ever known. Fighting against them are the Axis and SSU who both want the secret for themselves. In the shadows lurk the last Nazis who have long been seeking the Seals. Standing against everyone are the Sons of Belial, a cult which has passed down the culture of the original human civilization destroyed in the Great Deluge, and who worship the Anunnaki as gods.

Whoever gathers all Seven Seals will unlock the secret beneath the ruins of Megiddo, the city also known as Armageddon...

OUTLINE OF OPERATION: APOCALYPSE

EPISODE ONE: THE ARK

Following the events in ***Operation: Apocalypse*** (see core rulebook), ASOCOM is determined to find the other Six Seals mentioned in the Book of Revelation. The team is either fresh off that previous mission or recruited specifically to pick up where the other unit left off. Temporarily reassigned to Clio, the mythological and archaeological wing of ASOCOM, team members follow a lead indicating the tablets, upon which the Ten Commandments were inscribed, were actually one or more of the Seals said to presage the end of the world. This inspires a search for the lost Ark of the Covenant, brining the characters face-to-face with an ancient cult as they make their way from a medieval Cathar stronghold in France all the way to the United States in pursuit of this rare antiquity.

EPISODE TWO: THE NEW WORLD

Following clues provided by a tantalizing image discovered while looking for the Ark, the team travels to the American Southwest for further information. With enemies hot on their heels at every step, the bold Rangers then travel north to Alaska and the front of the SSU invasion. If the Seal is in Alaska, only the native Tlingit know where. Seeking them out, the Rangers search for the next Seal in an abandoned experimental facility once run by Majestic 12 and Howard Hughes.

EPISODE THREE: REVOLUTION

The trail leads south, as the Rangers pursue a lead in Rio de Janeiro, currently in the midst of an SSU-backed coup attempt. A mystic guides the team to her granddaughter, while the Nazi *Ahnenerbe* is close behind. Pursued by the SSU and the *Ahnenerbe*, the team discovers the location of the legendary lost city of gold—El Dorado. Can they beat their enemies to this ancient wonder and the next Seal?

EPISODE FOUR: THE CHINTAMANI STONE

Buddhist texts speak of a wish-fulfilling stone that fell from the heavens. ASOCOM believes this stone is one of the lost Seals. The Rangers are sent to the hedonistic "open" city of Vladivostok where gangsters and gamblers, as well as a former Russian aristocrat, vie for a map leading to the next Seal, but the map only leads them to another mystery, dragging the team deep into the Gobi Desert where they uncover the tomb of Genghis Khan. From there, they are off to the mythic city of Shambhala, better known as Shangri-La.

EPISODE FIVE: RONGORONGO

India, a land of mysteries both ancient and occult—here the Rangers pursue a lead found in the previous episode, discovering uncomfortable truths about the history of planet Earth. From there, they plunge into the intrigue that weaves through the Free French City of Saigon. Insurgents and an AWOL American soldier lead the team into the jungles of Cambodia. With both the SSU and the Axis making gains, the Rangers soon find themselves back on the front lines of the war during the Battle of the Philippines. Finally, their mission draws them to Easter Island and the truth behind the catastrophe that befell that civilization.

EPISODE SIX: THE TOMB OF ALEXANDER

In the espionage war dominating Istanbul, the PCs search for clues to the location of Alexander the Great's tomb.

RUNNING OPERATION: APOCALYPSE

Operation: Apocalypse is a long campaign with a complex backstory. It integrates theology, legend, history, and outright fiction to form a pulp style adventure buttressed with grand, Dust Warfare/Tactics battles. As GM, you not only have to familiarize yourself with the material, you also need to be prepared to improvise.

While many of the encounters are pegged to specific events or decisions the characters might make, there is also enough player agency afforded that the GM needs to keep up with what each faction is doing. This is not a static campaign—events change and the path forks as the players make decisions to which the NPCs react. While the general overview is probably the way things will play out, a great many things can go wrong. No plan, it is said, survives contact with the enemy. Likewise, no adventure survives contact with the clever minds of a veteran gaming group.

Most Secret: Eyes Only

The following reveals some of the intricate threads woven into the Dust universe. This is by no means the totality of secrets hidden behind the public face of the war, but there are deep secrets contained herein. You have been warned.

Dust begins with the Nazi discovery of an alien spacecraft, and its occupant, in 1938... or so we have been told. We must peel back that page, and the one before that, and the one before, as we plunge into the remote past. We are still on Earth, but some 12,000 years from when we started. It is near the end of the last Ice Age, and the great glaciers that cover vast portions of the globe recede only because of inadvertent alien interventions.

To understand the whys of this intervention, we must scroll further back and farther away. Somewhere out among the stars that primitive men attempt to decode in the dark of night, two races war. How long they have warred, and over what, is not for humanity to know. We know only that their war stretched across light years and eventually reached Earth.

Like the weapons man has made based on VK technology, the two races—the Vrill and Anunnaki—powered their destructive conflict with VK. Earth was a rich source of the element, and it is little wonder the two races fought over this tiny, otherwise insignificant planet.

VK was mined in vast amounts, and there are those who say that man toiled as slave labour under the whips of these aliens. This cannot be confirmed. What is known is that one of the species deployed a terrible weapon. Its power illuminated the night sky, and these images are recorded in petroglyphs the world over. The weapon caused the glaciers to melt and the seas to rise up against the constructions of man. We know this as the Great Deluge, Deucalion's Flood, the Flood of Noah, and many, many more stories passed down through the ages.

Here now, in 1947, the three blocs continually search for any hint of what the alien soldiers left behind. In so doing, archaeologists have discovered a human civilization wiped out during the Flood that lives now only in legend. Off the Northern Coast of France, a strange tablet was recovered, and according to the writing on this tablet, there are six more. Together, they make up the Seven Seals written of in the Bible. The Book of Revelation warns that opening these Seals will bring about the end of days. To most people living in the war torn world of Dust, the end has long since come and gone. What more does the world have to lose?

The PCs may soon find out.

For two thousand years, treasure hunters have killed and died trying to find Alexander's treasure. From Egypt to Libya, the Rangers seek the tomb only to find that the great conqueror wound up in the unlikeliest of places.

EPISODE SEVEN: ARMAGEDDON

From one corner of the world to the other, the team has pursued the Seven Seals. They have fought Nazis and Axis agents, as well as SSU *Spetznaz* and cultists, all of it leading here to Armageddon. Also known as Megiddo, this site is prophesized to be the location of the final battle bringing about the end of the world. That battle has begun, and the Rangers are in the middle of it, trying, with everything in their power, to unlock the greatest secret mankind has ever known! Where civilization first climbed its way up from barbarism, that civilization may now come to an end. Is this really Doomsday?!

THOSE WHO SEEK THE SEALS

Five distinct groups are after the Seven Seals including the Allies. Each of them is briefly described below along with their goals. In many of the individual episodes, you will find sections outlining the function of each faction in that episode. ***Operation: Apocalypse*** has a lot of moving parts, so quick notes like these are provided for reference in each chapter.

THE AXIS

The villainous former SS officer Colonel Orbst represents *Blutkreuz* and, for most of the campaign, the Axis. The SS know about the Seven Seals through documents taken from the *Ahnenerbe* before the fall of the Nazi Reich.

The Axis also knows that there is a great storehouse of energy left by the Anunnaki somewhere in the Middle

East. They believe the two things are connected and will stop at nothing to find all Seven Seals and unlock their secrets.

THE SSU

The SSU is divided in this campaign. One section is the party-faithful SMERSH (intelligence agency), while the other sections are those agents loyal to Rasputin. Rasputin wants the Seals for himself. He has some idea what they may lead to, while SMERSH only knows rumours.

The SSU is also the closest thing the PCs are likely to find to an ally. While their respective blocs are enemies, neither side wants to see the Axis, or especially the Nazis, possess all Seven Seals.

THE *AHNENERBE*

The remnants of this Nazi ancestral and archaeological SS organization still exist in the world. Currently headquartered in Argentina, the *Ahnenerbe* possesses the original documents that speak of the Seven Seals and the energy in the Middle East. For more information on this, see *Dust Studio's* ***Operation: Babylon***.

The Nazis have continued to pursue occult and alien artefacts all over the world. They dream of restoring the Third Reich and, possibly, even using VK to somehow resurrect Hitler. In their mad schemes, the secret energy of the Anunnaki and the Seven Seals figure prominently. While the Nazis do not have the numbers necessary to directly combat the other blocs, they believe that alien technology will position them to seize power once again.

THE SONS OF BELIAL

The Sons of Belial trace their roots to Antediluvian times. While the current organization only bears the name of that ancient group, the Sons of Belial are dedicated to preventing the powers of the world from recovering Anunnaki technology. They believe they alone are heirs to this technology and await the return of the aliens they see as gods.

Venerating this second alien race perverts their agenda. They are less concerned with gaining the tablets than preventing others from doing so. Ironically, their goal of bringing the Anunnaki back may come true no matter who emerges victorious. The father of a major NPC in ***Operation: Apocalypse*** is currently a member of this cult. The Sons of Belial believe the return of their masters heralds the end of this world and the beginning of a new age.

THE ALLIES

The Allies are represented by the PCs, ASOCOM, and Clio—ASOCOM's archaeological and mythological branch. Following the discovery of a tablet on Mont Saint-Michel in the first part of ***Operation: Apocalypse***, Clio examined it and determined it might be one of the Seven Seals spoken of in the Bible. Clio also came to the conclusion that the tablet was not Vrill, but the product of another, unknown race. This has, of course, complicated the entire backstory of planet Earth as understood by the Allies.

While many of the tablets are located inside enemy territory, the Allies have both the resources of ASOCOM and the financial backing of the United States, to throw at the problem. While they cannot afford to divert whole battalions in pursuit of what may turn out to be mere legend, the Allies can send their most elite operatives—the PCs.

THE HIDDEN HISTORY OF THE WORLD

The following is an overview of the as yet unrevealed history of the ***Dust Universe***. Coupled with the introduction, this serves to illuminate the entirety of the plot for the GM. However, the campaign is written so that the GM, too, might enjoy some of the revelations along the way. This section is one of advanced spoilers. The GM is free to read this section (and the introduction) later, after having read through the adventure and seen the plot reveal itself much as the players might during the course of the campaign.

Still there? Then here we go.

This is a significant bit of backstory. If you are familiar with ***Operation: Babylon*** from *Dust Studios*, some of this ties directly into that narrative. If not, don't worry, as things are explained for those who have not read that product.

What most ***Dust*** players generally know is that the Germans discovered an alien ship in Antarctica prior to the war. The Germans also discovered an alien, who called himself Kvasir in honour of his rescuers. The alien was a member of a species called the Vrill who came to Earth in prehistory in search of VK.

Less commonly know is why the Vrill would travel so far away from their home system for VK. The reason was to fuel an interstellar war between themselves and a race called the Anunnaki. Both races fought for VK, but the Anunnaki developed a secondary source of energy stored in the Middle East and that is what the Axis seeks in ***Operation: Babylon***.

Operation: Apocalypse concerns itself with the pursuit of the history and artefacts of this second alien race. Some 12,000 years before the start of World War II, the Anunnaki came to Earth and established colonies.

They used human beings, possibly even helped genetically modify them, to mine gold. As time went on, these humans developed a complex and highly technological society of their own. This civilization predates those we know of as the first to appear in the Fertile Crescent.

The gold held no aesthetic value to the Anunnaki, but it did serve as shielding against the powerful radiation their new energy emitted. In time, the actual value of gold was forgotten by man. All of our conquests for it can be tied to the original, technological purpose for which the Anunnaki sought the element.

For some time, the Anunnaki colonies flourished, as did the human civilization under them. That continued until the war between the Vrill and the Anunnaki reached Earth. Their war is recorded as a war between Heaven and Hell in the Bible, a war between gods in the Hindu tradition, and the revolt of the gods against the titans in Greek mythology. In every case, the real story has been obscured by time and legend.

Over the course of centuries, the two races sought dominion over the Earth and the energy found here in plentiful amounts. At this point in their war, both sides suffered enormous casualties and all their resources were turned to feed the war machine (not unlike the current war man wages across the globe). Long since had the civilian populations of both species become mere tools in the unending conflict. On Earth, the war resulted in the Vrill employing a devastating weapon.

Powered by giant deposits of VK, the Vrill created the means to use meteors as weapons against planet-bound targets. The first test of such a weapon was on Earth, circa 10,000 B.C. The meteor was aimed at the Pacific Ocean so it might wipe out the Anunnaki colonies along with their human counterparts while leaving the rich deposits of energy intact. This ultimate weapon worked. The comet struck the Pacific and tsunamis of such scale as to be nigh unimaginable swept over the land. These all live on as the Great Flood myths of various cultures. The Anunnaki knew such a weapon was being developed and sought to preserve their culture and those of the humans that followed them.

The information they wished to preserve was hidden in nine vaults under Tel Megiddo in what would become Judea. The codes for unlocking the vaults were stored in seven tablets which later became famous as the Seven Seals. When humanity reached a point where it was technologically able to understand this—long after the Great Flood—the Anunnaki wished them to return to the Middle East and activate The Tower of Babel. The tower was a space elevator used by the Anunnaki to move gold and energy off-world. The reactivation would mean humanity had regained a certain level of technological development and were thus again worthy of the Anunnaki's attention. Why they are so interested in mankind is unclear and a secret for another book. Whatever their interest, the Tower of Babel is the ultimate goal of the operation, though this is not apparent until well into the campaign.

Whether the Anunnaki receive the signal and return, and how the Vrill respond, is left to other books and other operations. Surely, with two alien races invested in Earth, the Second World War could drag on for decades—just as the alien war has raged for millennia.

CHAPTER 2: THE ARK

GETTING UP TO SPEED
Here is a brief recap for those who did not play through the adventure in the ***Dust Adventures*** rulebook.

A team of Rangers (the PCs) was dropped over occupied France with the mission of snatching a former Nazi scientist for the Allies. The Rangers were shot down and crash-landed in France. Without transport out, they made their way to the ambush spot chosen to nab the scientist.

They managed to reach their target, but he refused to help unless they rescued his daughter from a castle nearby. The team had little choice, as the scientist had poisoned himself. He would be of no use to anyone dead, and the antidote was inside the castle.

Reluctantly, the Rangers infiltrated the castle and found the girl, only to encounter a giant Ubermensch and an experimental Nazi rocket. They put the scientist and his daughter in the rocket and programmed it to fly to Allied territory. The Rangers were now stuck in France.

This adventure begins in one of two ways. In the first, the PCs continue on from the adventure, ***Operation: Apocalypse***, in the core rulebook. In this case, you will not need to generate new characters. The current PCs return to England, which is currently under siege. At a base in Scotland, they are put under the command of Clio, ASOCOM's historical and archaeological research division. The stone recovered from the monastery on Mont Saint-Michel was analyzed and found to be of extraterrestrial, but not Vrill, origin. In working with the stone, researchers uncovered references to six other stones, or tablets, related to the first. The PCs are partnered with an archaeologist working for Clio named Dr. Jessa Carter. She assists the team in their retrieval of the remaining pieces and plays a major role in the campaign.

The second way to begin the adventure involves fresh characters that never went through ***Operation: Apocalypse***. These characters are assigned, or hired (depending on the make-up of the team) by Clio to perform the same mission listed above. They are briefed on the backstory of ***Operation: Apocalypse*** (see sidebar), and paired with Dr. Jessa Carter.

THE MISSION

All PCs are briefed on the mission at ASOCOM headquarters in Glasgow. The base itself is located in the Kelvingrove Art Gallery and Museum. The building is a fury of activity with decoders and clerks running reports to and fro and huge crates being loaded for shipping to the United States. England has gone to great lengths to ensure all her cultural artefacts that can survive, will survive. When the PCs arrive, the scene looks chaotic at first, but patterns of rigid, military discipline soon reveal themselves.

TELEGRAM

From: General Leslie Granger, Commander of ASOCOM Operations, England.

To: (The highest-ranking character's name)

You are hereby temporarily transferred to Clio under the command of Lieutenant Colonel A. Wallace Stone. Your mission is to retrieve six stone tablets secreted around the globe. This mission is of utmost importance. Blutkreuz and SMERSH may already be ahead of us. Expect their involvement. Lt Col. Stone will brief you on the specifics of the mission.

Good luck, men.

Signed,

General Leslie Granger, Commander, ASOCOM England

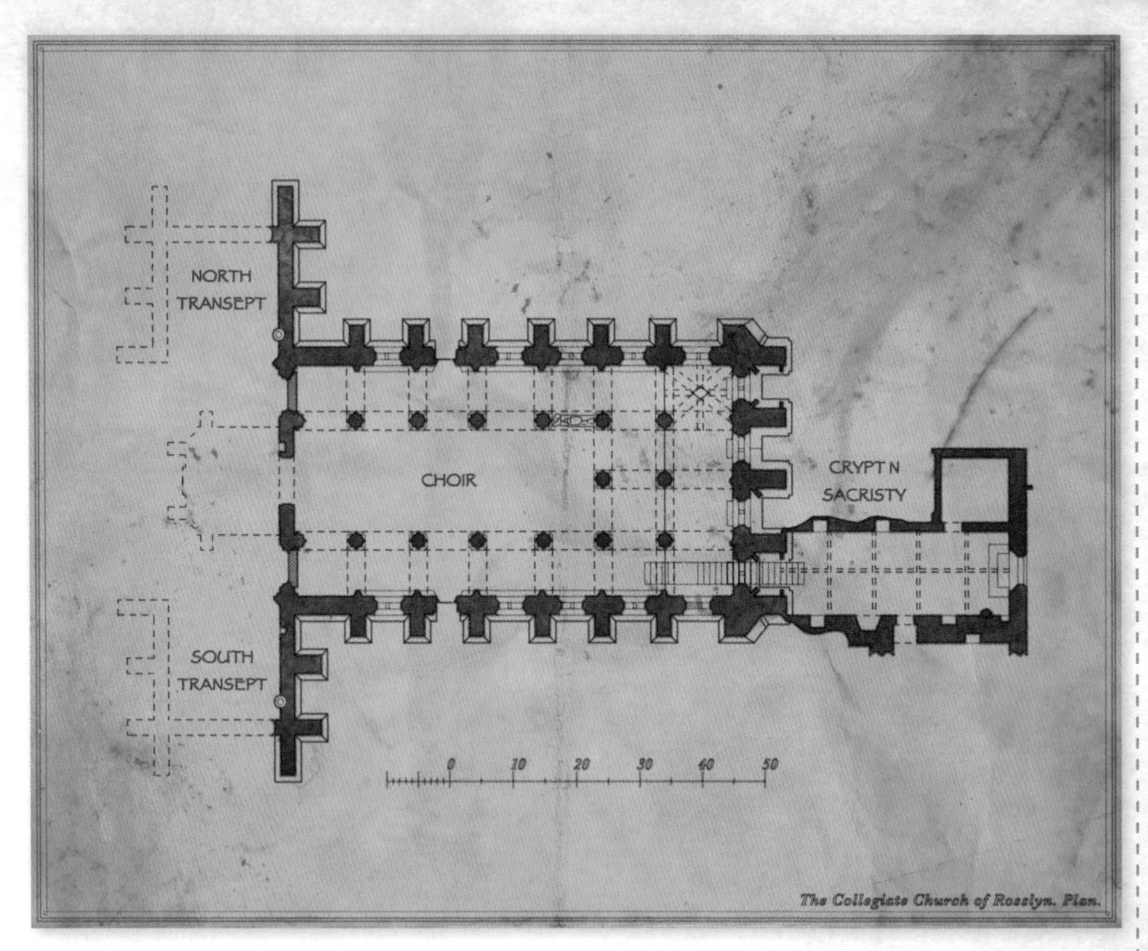

The Collegiate Church of Rosslyn. Plan.

The PCs should be read or shown the telegram presented on the opposite page.

You are lead by a clerk through the clacking of typewriters and telexes inside what was once the main lobby of the museum. Rectangular spots, free of dust, show where art once hung along the walls. Down a long hall where pedestals sit empty of their busts you arrive at an elevator. The clerk closes the cage, and the elevator whines down to the basement level. Here, much looks like the offices of academics of one stripe or another, but everything has been commandeered by the military. Where the names of these professors and experts were painted on the frosted glass of each office, masking tape, with military ranks and names written in black felt pen, now list who works within. The tape suggests the building is expected to be temporary. If this is ASOCOM England's current HQ, they must not expect to hold out for long.

The clerk stops them at the largest office, that of Lt. Col. Stone. He knocks once. A voice says, "Come in." Seated behind the desk is a man younger than one would expect to find heading up ASOCOM England. He looks a bit overwhelmed, though he is squared away like the soldier he is. He has replaced the previous commander, who Rangers from the first adventure likely remember. That commander was killed in action during the current siege of London. He stayed behind to help despite orders to pull out.

Leaned against Stone's desk, smoking a cigarette is the breathtaking Dr. Jessa Carter. She looks the team over, apparently unimpressed. Stone stands and introduces himself and Dr. Carter. The doctor, an American, is a graduate of Oxford and the University of Chicago.

Her tone is professional, and she appears rather devoid of emotion. She explains the mission to the team.

She personally examined the tablet that was recovered in France and explains that it is most likely an alien artefact, though not Vrill. She does not elaborate. She explains she has reason to believe there are six others like it. It is her belief that this is one of the Seven Seals spoken of in the Bible. Incredulity from any PC gets an eyebrow raise and a comment such as, "Oh, really and where did you do receive your PhDs in archaeology and comparative theology?"

She also does not appear to have a sense of humour. She reminds the PCs exactly what the Bible says about the Seven Seals: that, when opened, they bring about the apocalypse. Dr. Carter also points out that apocalypse, in Latin, refers to an unveiling, not necessarily the end of the world:

"When the Lamb broke the seventh seal, there was silence in heaven."

— Revelations 8:1

The six remaining tablets are key to a vital piece of technology, or so she believes. Any further inquiry is met with, "You do not, at this time, need to know that."

Their only way out was to rely on the Resistance. Travelling to meet an important member of that organization in Paris, they dodged Nazi agents and managed to get a route out of France. Unfortunately, it led to the island of Mont Saint-Michel that had been besieged since France was recaptured by the Axis. What's more, ASOCOM wanted an object inside the monastery atop the island and the Rangers had to retrieve it.

They reached Mont Saint-Michel just as the Axis prepared a final assault to claim the island. During the fight, the Rangers discovered the monks were not what they seemed, but part of an old cult called the Sons of Belial. The object they found inside the monastery was the first of the Seven Seals. With the Seal in hand, the PCs escaped Mont Saint-Michel, leaving many people behind to an uncertain fate.

This campaign picks up where that initial adventure left off—with the PCs looking for the other six tablets.

***HAUPTMANN* KLAUS ORBST**

Orbst was handpicked from the surviving ranks of the SS by Sigrid von Thaler. He is uncompromising, amoral, and a skilled commando. Sigrid herself has personally assigned Orbst the mission of recovering the Seven Seals. He takes this as a badge of honour. Orbst, while a former Nazi, was always more interested in personal power than the Nazi ideology. Joining the SS was merely a way to rise more quickly to prominence. With the death of Adolph Hitler, Orbst was one of the first to disavow the Nazi's goals and beliefs.

Orbst is out more for himself than for the Fatherland. It is likely von Thaler knows this, as little escapes her watchful eye, but she chose him anyway. Perhaps she believes he is the right man for the job or perhaps she believes he will eventually betray her, but she plays along for her own, convoluted reasons.

Orbst has a scar running like a gorge down the left half of his face. He earned it in Stalingrad. He dislikes Americans, but hates Russians.

Orbst's stats are found on pages 123-124 of this book.

Right about then, Lt. Col. Stone coughs politely and explains that the team is technically under the command of Clio now. As such, they take their orders from Dr. Carter. No one is likely to be happy with that arrangement, and it is designed to cause running tension throughout the adventure. A note to GMs, in the practical "real world" of combat and play, Dr. Carter has only so much authority. Her butting heads with the team, in particular its leader, should be fun to roleplay.

Their first stop is Rosslyn Chapel in Scotland. She believes members of *Blutkreuz* are already on the trail of the next tablet. She offers nothing further right now.

WHAT'S REALLY GOING ON

Dr. Carter believes one or two of the Seals described in the Old Testament are the tablets received by Moses on Mount Horeb. They are the Ten Commandments and, therefore, were placed inside the Ark of the Covenant when Moses smashed them. Dr. Carter doesn't believe the Ark still exists, but she does believe that the Knights Templar (see ***Dust Adventures***) found evidence of the tablets. Dr. Carter is a sceptic in many ways. Only because she has personally seen recovered Vrill technology does she believe that aliens and such exist. Her father, who comes into play later, is much more the believer.

Rosslyn Chapel is not far away.

ROSSLYN CHAPEL

Built in the 15th century by William Sinclair, the chapel is a splendid example of Gothic architecture. Dr. Carter is happy to rattle this off along with other historical titbits. She knows the original chapel was designed as a cruciform, which is typical of such places, but was not completed as such. Rumour holds that the Temple of Solomon stood as a model for Rosslyn. She scoffs at this, as no one really has any idea what the Temple of Solomon looked like.

Outside the chapel is a sandbag emplacement and an anti-aircraft gun. Curiously, it is unmanned. This should seem strange to any military characters. Orbst's men killed the three-man crew and dragged their bodies inside.

While the team is outside the chapel, they hear an unmistakable explosion. *Blutkreuz* agents have just used a charge to blow open what is known as "The Apprentice Pillar," a twisting column that is unlike any of those that surround it. If the PCs rush in, they see the *Blutkreuz* agents digging though the ruins of the pillar. One says, in German, "It is gone!" He appears enraged. This man is Hauptmann Klaus Orbst and he is a recurring villain in this campaign. See the appendix for Orbst's stats.

Whether the team arrives in time to hear Orbst or not, the rest of his men, five in all, immediately open fire if any of the characters are in uniform. If not, they pretend to be part of the Cultural Recovery Project, an offshoot of Clio trying to save as much of England's treasures as it can. Of course, they claim some miscreants attempted to loot the chapel and were just now chased off. They take no responsibility for the pillar.

This devolves quickly into a firefight. While the characters are under the jurisdiction of Clio, they have not sworn an oath to uphold the primacy of cultural artefacts—in other words, they are free to shoot the place up if they wish.

Orbst is already convinced someone got to whatever was inside the pillar before him. His tactics are to fall back in a two-by-two formation to escape. The Germans have a fast car waiting in the back. If a chase ensues, Orbst radios for assistance. A Messerschmitt arrives and strafes the PCs. Orbst escapes, for now.

Of course, the plane wasn't there only to assist Orbst. After all, this part of Scotland is still mostly in British hands. The plane's job is to destroy Rosslyn Chapel. The PCs see the plane bank for the chapel and must get to the AA gun in time to shoot it down.

The Messerschmitt's initial run is a strafe. On the second, the pilot drops a bomb on the chapel. The PCs must use the AA gun to take out the German plane. If they miss, the GM may decide the first bomb also missed. The pilot tries again. The plane is modified to carry two such bombs. The AA gun is a Quad .50 Cal Victory. See ***Dust Adventures*** for the weapon's stats.

AFTERMATH

With Orbst and any German survivors having fled and, hopefully, the chapel saved, the PCs are free to explore Rosslyn Chapel. Inside, Dr. Carter takes out a notebook and directs one of the lower-ranking characters to use her camera to take pictures of whatever she indicates. Most of these subjects are meaningless to anyone other than an academic type. Dr. Carter directs the PC, rather condescendingly, to take photos of the destroyed pillar, a couple of stained glass windows, the carved head of a wild man, and various other carvings along the walls. Some of these objects look a lot like corn, or maize and the GM should tell the players this.

If the chapel was built circa 1450 A.D., how does corn appear on the walls? There is also another plant native only to the Americas on some columns. Dr. Carter makes notes of all this, but says they would need a botanist to be certain. To the PCs, it really does look like corn.

A wardrobe closet contains three dead soldiers who were assigned to the AA gun.

Should the PCs (on their own or following the orders of Dr. Carter) reassemble the broken pillar, they find that it clearly once featured a hollow recess. Whatever was in there is now gone. However it could not have been one of the tablets, as the space is too small.

Once she is done taking notes, Dr. Carter demands they return to Glasgow. If pressed to answer questions, she reluctantly reveals that "crusaders" may have hidden a treasure at Rosslyn, but someone beat both the team and the Germans to it.

BACK IN GLASGOW

The team returns to the museum/HQ where Dr. Carter has a private meeting in Lt. Col. Stone's office. The PCs wait outside. At first, the two seem to be having a normal conversation, but it quickly becomes heated and voices are raised. The PCs overhear Dr. Carter demanding that the colonel arrange passage to Jerusalem. He protests that they do not have available resources, until she loudly invokes her position in this matter. "What did ASOCOM tell you to do when I asked for something, Colonel? What?!"

Stone sighs and relents.

Carter exits the office with a smug look on her face. The colonel looks angry, but he has too much on his plate for it to be of concern for long. She explains to the team that they are going to Jerusalem. Right now, that's as dangerous, if not more so, as being in England. Well, at least they aren't in London.

Of course, Dr. Carter says, they have to stop at the British Museum in London first. Not all the artefacts made it out. She needs one in particular before they journey to the Holy Land. With that, the characters have to go into a very volatile situation. London is in the midst of being captured by the Axis.

While at HQ, the PCs can get questions answered about Orbst and his men. They learn it is a *Blutkreuz* team, and that Orbst often works directly for Sigrid von Thaler.

LONDON FALLING

The city of London is besieged. Trafalgar Square is occupied, and the Axis Knight's Cross hangs over the statue of Admiral Horatio Nelson. Curiously, Dr. Carter specifically mentions this. If the PCs ask why, she reveals that Napoleon's men found the artefact they're seeking during his campaign in Egypt. He and Nelson first squared-off there, and Nelson won. One of Napoleon's men came back with a copper scroll that purports to be a copy of a Babylonian account of a lost treasure found after the fall of Jerusalem in 586 B.C. Sadly, the scroll is encoded. She meant to get a look at it prior to now, but had other priorities until the tablet was discovered in France. This is what she is after. Of course, *Blutkreuz*, likely led by Orbst, is after it as well.

While the city is falling, there are still roads that the Allies control. Getting in is not a problem, but no one can guarantee how long those roads will remain open. It has come down to an hour-by-hour shift in the lines surrounding the city. Further, the British Museum is in occupied territory.

DR. JESSA CARTER AND THE TEAM

While Dr. Carter is designed as an antagonist, she is not a villain. The GM can misdirect the team with all the secrets she keeps, but she does not betray Clio or ASOCOM. She keeps secrets because very simply she thinks the team is stupid.

Carter also exists as a potential romantic interest. Pick a PC, preferably one who argues with her the most, and let the tension build. There is something crackling between their conflicts. The PC probably doesn't fully trust her, which adds to this dramatic tension.

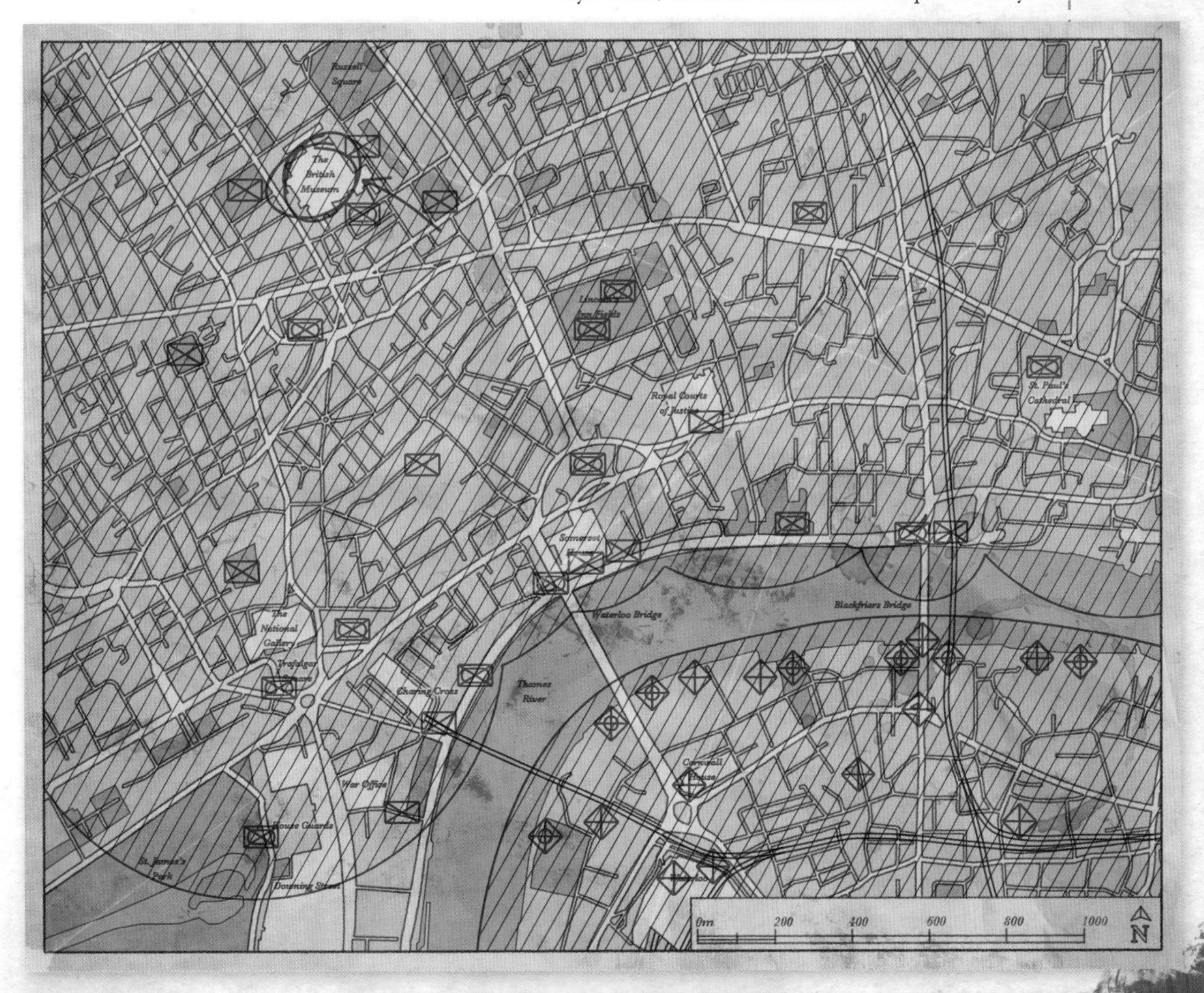

Getting in and out is going to require a delicate touch or a big can of firefight.

If the PCs suggested it in Glasgow, ASOCOM can outfit the team with Axis uniforms. It helps if one of them speaks German. If none does, Dr. Carter does, but she is not accustomed to fast-talking soldiers. This is an area where the PCs need to step up and deliver better plans. Dr. Carter gives orders and illustrates on a map how they ought to get in, but her plan has little practical value. She isn't purely an academic, but she certainly isn't a tactician. Should one of the PCs question her plan, it escalates into an argument.

Below is a map of London as it sits when the PCs arrive. Sections are divided into Axis Occupied and Allied Occupied.

However they choose to proceed, the team is moving through enemy territory. The GM should decide how much trouble he wants to throw their way. Remember, the city is in the midst of a siege, so characters not in Allied uniforms have a decent chance of being ignored. One or two "close calls" with a patrol or advancing unit, should suffice. You may read or paraphrase the following to the players to set the mood. Stealth rolls at Difficulty 2 may also be employed.

The city is falling. Since it was called Londinium when originally founded by the Romans, the city has had a series of disasters—plagues, fires, revolution, but it has not been occupied by enemy forces in hundreds of years. The results are devastating. In London, one sees a real possibility that the Allies could lose this war. Great monuments blaze against the darkening twilight sky. Whole neighbourhoods are reduced to the powdery ruin of cities like Zverograd. A child's bicycle, warped by fire, lays abandoned in the street. People's suitcases lay cracked open next to their corpses on the ground, victims of pounding artillery or dropped bombs. Even in the relative quiet of a dead street, one hears the popping of artillery and small arms in the background. Such noises have become a permanent feature of your world.

Things are dire. London will not hold for more than another day or two. The roads north are thick with refugees. Inside the city, resistance holds out in small pockets, but the Allies' main task is getting as many civilians out as they can. They have abandoned all hope of keeping the city.

The team witnesses various violent acts. Anything from house-to-house fighting to executions on the street (both sides) against suspected traitors or armed partisans. *Blutkreuz* squads are prevalent and the GM must decide if the team encounters one.

BLUTKREUZ SQUAD (6) TROOPERS

Use stats for Axis Grenadiers on p. 144 of ***Dust Adventures***.

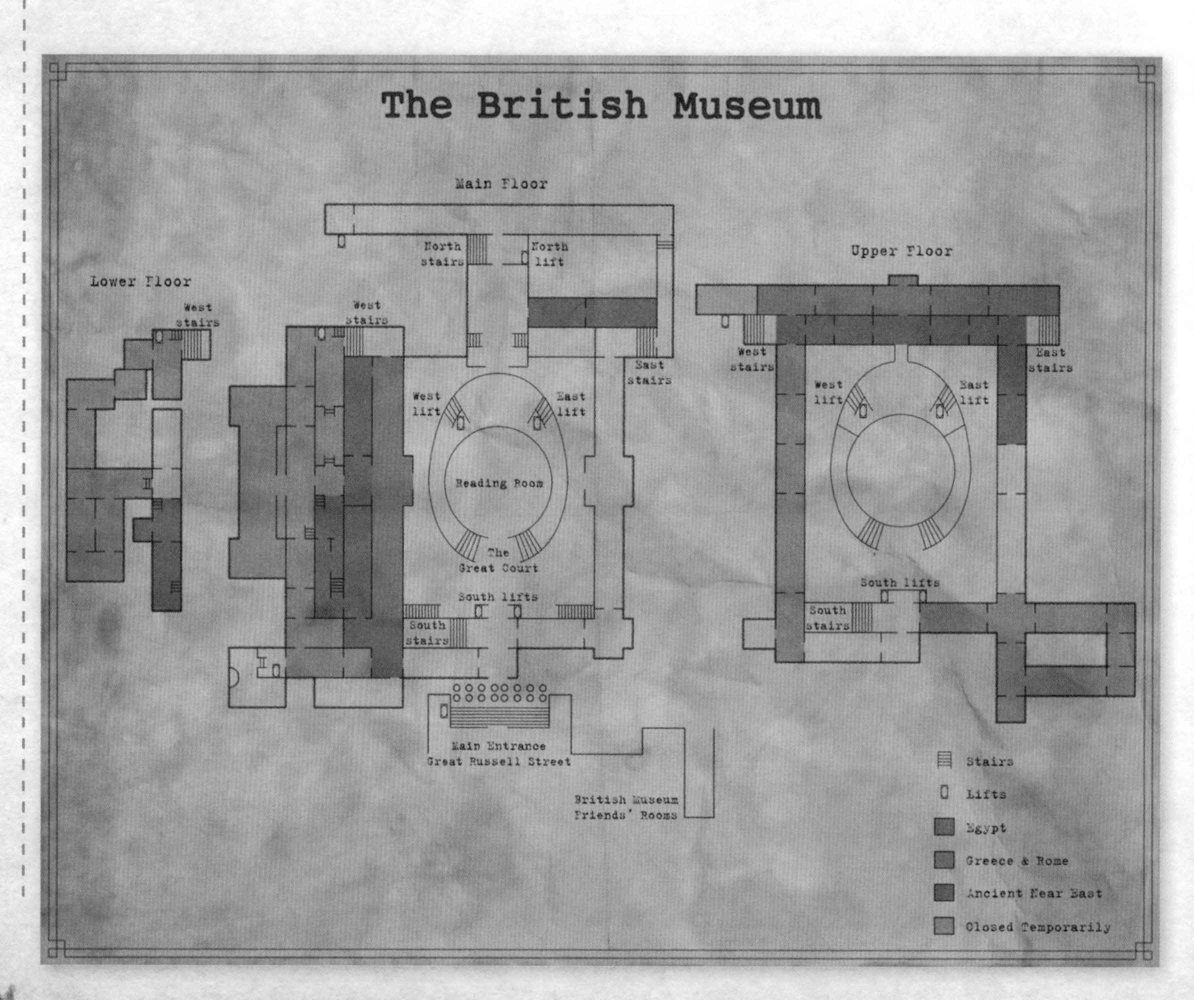

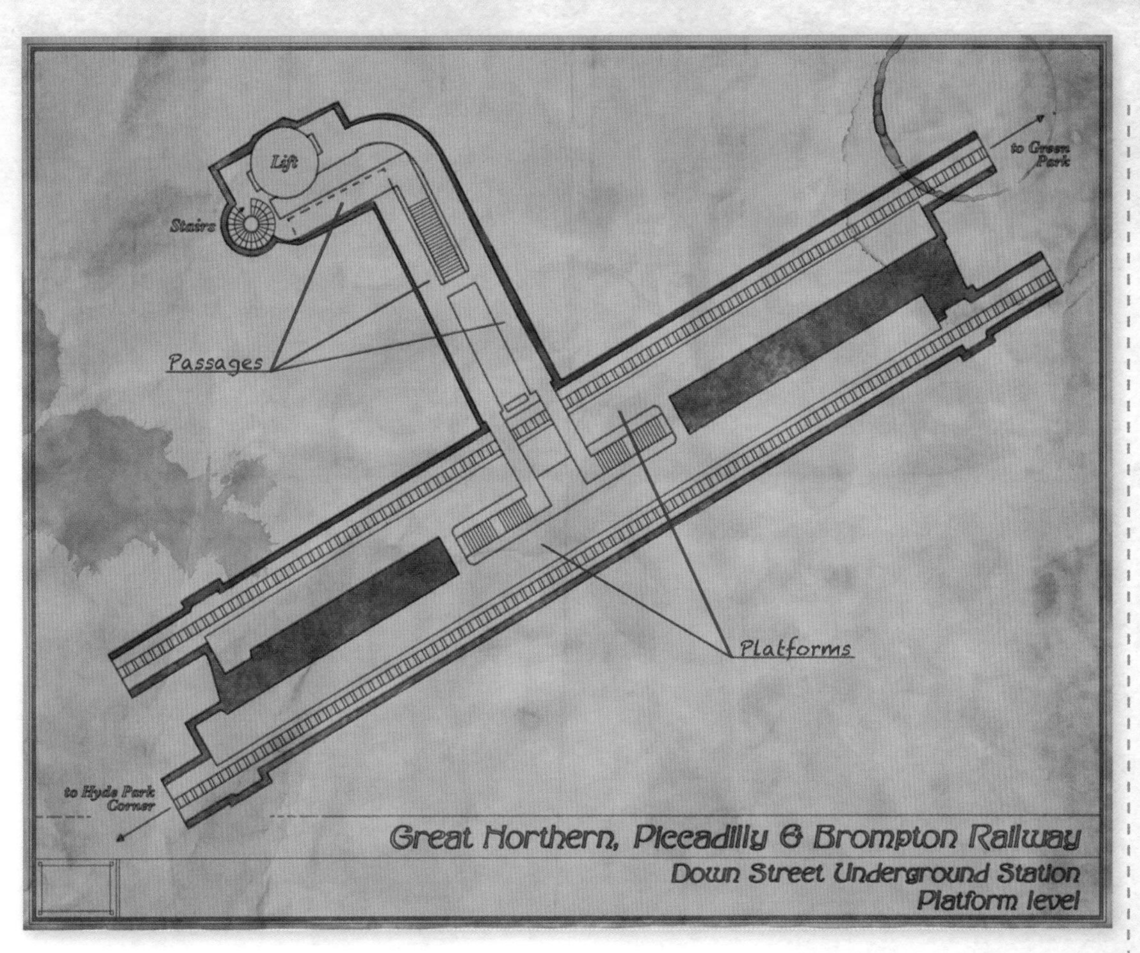

THE COPY OF THE COPPER SCROLL

This rubbing is made from the original copper scroll. It is similar, but not identical, to one of the Dead Sea Scrolls that were discovered between 1946 and 1956. One of those scrolls lists all the treasure the Babylonians looted from Jerusalem in 586 B.C. The Ark of the Covenant is not listed on the scroll, though it certainly would have been the most significant item.

It is not listed because the Babylonians returned it as accounted for in the copy of this copper scroll. Much like the Philistines before them, after the Babylonians captured the Ark, tragedies befell them. People died of a strange disease, crops failed, and like the Philistines, the Babylonians brought the Ark back to the Temple of Solomon. It was then hidden away by priests who wanted it to never fall into enemy hands again. They hid it among the water tunnels beneath the Temple Mount.

The scroll describes the tablets. Writing in the form of glyphs covered one side. The stones were made of an unfamiliar rock or crystal. There is no translation on the rubbing, but it does prove the Ark was extant after 586 B.C. This inspires Dr. Carter to follow up on a map offered to her from an untrustworthy antiquities dealer some time ago. She telegrams him, but he insists they meet in person. Dr. Carter requests that the team handle it personally. She has reason to suspect Majestic 12 is keeping tabs on the military as it pertains to this mission.

THE BRITISH MUSEUM

Once the largest building site in Europe, the British Museum has always been one of the jewels in the now collapsing British Empire. It is in rough shape when the team arrives. Bombs have hit the venerable neoclassical design. The steps are carpeted in ash that floats down from the sky like snow.

Getting in is difficult, as *Blutkreuz* seized control over this sector specifically to guard the museum. Characters will be challenged. If they speak fluent German, and appear to know German military behaviour, they are sent away. One must have papers to get inside the museum.

If the team tries to bluff their way through with the requisite knowledge, they are going to get into a gunfight. There are only three guards at ancillary access points, but six on the stairs in front of the main entrance. There is a 20% chance another guard unit responds to the shooting (roll one die, on a Target, the unit responds). This is a war, after all. The guards do not yet have radios.

Once some of the guards are killed, their absences, or bodies, are noticed. The PCs do not have a great deal of time to dawdle in the museum. Dr. Carter knows where the copper scroll was on display and takes the team there.

BLUTKREUZ SOLDIERS (3-6)

Use stats for Axis Grenadiers on p. 144 of ***Dust Adventures***.

Inside the museum, the team finds a scene much like the one at Glasgow HQ—many of the displays are empty, and *Blutkreuz* personnel are collecting and packing up what is left. The trouble comes when the team gets to the copper scroll display. There, they run into Orbst who definitely recognizes them. One of his men is prying open the display case now. The item is listed as being of "Egyptian origin" but written in an unknown cipher.

The team needs to get their hands on the scroll, but it is a difficult task. A shootout starts as soon as Orbst identifies the team. Shooting inside the museum definitely alerts other soldiers. The team could soon be overwhelmed. In the midst of the firefight, at a dramatically appropriate time, Dr. Carter says, in a eureka moment, "A rubbing!"

She means that whoever studied the scroll would have made a rubbing or clay impression. These items would not be on display but stored in the basement, assuming they survived at all. They certainly were not catalogued with other items rescued during the evacuation. The team needs to fight their way out of this situation on the first floor, and then head to the basement. Again, Dr. Carter has a good idea where the copy is located.

Of course, this all happens while they are being pursued by the Axis. The only saving grace is, in a city under siege, resources are not yet properly allocated. *Blutkreuz* does not have infinite troops in the museum to track the PCs down.

The Map

The map dates to 1307, specifically August of that year. The back appears blank, but heat and limejuice combined reveal a letter. It is addressed to one Jacques de Molay, Grandmaster of the Knights Templar who are referred to here as the Poor Knights of Christ and the Temple of Solomon.

The letter reads:

Grandmaster De Molay,

I am on my way to Montségur to secure the treasure most sacred. As agreed, we shall move the Ark from its current resting place and take it to Avalon Across the Sea. I hope this letter finds you. We here, wish you had fled when alerted about the King's plans. The Pope no longer protects us. Your capture is not necessary. We respect your stand. The Templar organization will be dead in the next year, but we will rise again as plans dictate, in other places and other times. The great project cannot be stopped by the efforts of mere kings.

May God have mercy when you face the rack. We will remember you always.

W.E.

The map itself is of Montségur circa 1244 A.D., during the Albigensian Crusade in which Crusaders, who put Cathars to the stake and the sword, invaded the South of France. The castle fell, and rumours held that a great treasure was removed. This is not so. The great treasure was hidden away in caves beneath the castle, which rests on an enormous rock formation. Whoever W.E. is, he appears to have ventured there to move the Ark. The map shows a cave system beneath the castle where the Ark was supposedly kept.

Dr. William Carter

Formerly with the British Museum, William Carter has taught at the University of Chicago, Oxford, and Harvard. A rising academic, it was not until he became obsessed with the Knights Templar that his career derailed. His daughter was already in college and fought hard to overcome the stigma of his name. She tried to get her father to see reason, that this obsession was ruining his career, but he refused to stop. After losing his position at the University of Chicago, and with Jessa's brother killed in action on D-Day, William Carter apparently took his own life.

This is the official story. The reality is quite different. William was obsessed with the Templars, but he made more headway in his research than his daughter, or his colleagues, ever knew. The more he looked, the closer he got to the Sons of Belial, an offshoot of the Templars dedicated to protecting the secrets of the Anunnaki. By this time, William's obsession was evident to the cult and, rather than killing him, they recruited him. William has worked for them ever since. His "suicide" was cover for his indoctrination in the cult. Once one joins the Sons of Belial, one forsakes their old life including friends and family.

William's obsession has turned toward a belief that the Sons of Belial are the saviours of the human race. Only they can protect the Anunnaki's secrets and prepare for the day they return. He is, to an outside observer, not in his right mind.

Make it tense for them, keep them guessing, and throw a few soldiers at them now and again. Once in the basement, they are led to a room with shelf after shelf of tagged objects—those deemed expendable. The copy of the copper scroll is among these. It takes a few tense minutes for Dr. Carter to find it. When she does, the team needs to bug out. If the GM wishes, a small three-man unit stumbles upon the PCs while Carter searches for the scroll.

On the way out of the museum, the team finds good fortune for the first time. A group of insurgents is fighting for the city. These are former gangsters. They are not letting "Jerry take their bloody town without a fight" when they went to so much effort to take it for themselves. The gangsters are in the midst of a firefight when the PCs leave, regardless of which exit they take.

One of the gangsters recognizes one of the PCs, perhaps an English member of the team. Sort this out as you wish. They can be old friends, friendly rivals, or even enemies who now find themselves on the same side. This is an Expendable Resource as outlined in ***Dust Adventures***.

The man who recognizes the PCs is Robbie "Mad Dog" Corrigan.

Corrigan and his gang allow the PCs to get safely out of the museum. After a few under-fire pleasantries, Corrigan tells the team to follow him. They do not have any better options offering themselves. Dr. Carter vehemently disagrees with trusting "an obvious thug," but quickly relents when a bullet takes a chip out of the old Victorian brickwork next to her head.

Corrigan pulls them through an alley while his men unleash their Tommy Guns. The whole group retreats to a tube stop in the Underground, Holborn Station. Getting there takes them down several streets, and *Blutkreuz* is in pursuit. British troops are stationed at Holborn Station, holding it for refugees. Corrigan guides them down and they talk on the way. Corrigan is interested why the PCs are in London now of all times.

When the PCs explain that they need to get out of the city, Corrigan, who has his ears to the ground, tells them that the road they came in on is now closed and the Axis has the city all but encircled. The team needs a new way out and Corrigan can help.

He has connections all over the city, and can offer to get the team out if he believes it's for a good cause. Originally, Corrigan and his mates were going to try to loot the museum or, as he puts it, "protect our cultural heritage." There happened to be a dodgy Irishman who was going to take the items off his hands for better "protection." Since Corrigan did not get any items, he is willing to introduce the team to the Irishman.

They meet up with him in the East End and while he can help, he does demand a fee for his services. He has some Axis soldiers greased on a road out. They won't ask questions, but the Irishman—and that's how they keep referring to him—expected valuable antiquities. In other words, he needs "proper compensation, like," he says.

The PCs may or may not have spare cash. If they asked for it, ASOCOM provided up to three thousand pounds. If not, they have what they have. It is up to the team to make arrangements with the Irishman. Once they do, they make it out of the city. Along the way, the lorry the Irishman loaded them into is stopped. Have the Axis soldiers walk around the truck. Make the PCs feel the tension: boots in the mud, a barking German Shepherd, and a suspiciously long wait while papers are examined. None of it amounts to anything. It is there for window dressing. The team gets past the checkpoint and smuggled back north to an airfield in Scotland.

If the GM wishes to throw something more substantive in their way, the team can always encounter a group of Axis soldiers who have not been paid off.

JERUSALEM

How the PCs get to Jerusalem is up to the GM. Submarine is probably the easiest method. A convoy with destroyer escorts may be headed for Operation: Babylon. You only need to "Indiana Jones" this part. Imagine a red dot. A line extends from it and leads toward the Atlantic Ocean, turns around Spain and makes for the Mediterranean and Jerusalem...

The area around Jerusalem is still under Allied control. Operation: Babylon has shifted control of parts of the Middle East and North Africa, but it has not hit here yet. PCs have a chance to breathe, acquire fresh gear, and recuperate. Dr. Carter is very impatient, and rushes them in any way she can.

Her goal is the investigation of the Templars (see p. 104 of ***DUST Adventures***). According to legend, the Templars found a great treasure on the Temple Mount, the foundation that remained from the Temple of Solomon. While the Dome of the Rock is now there, no one is exactly sure where the Templars may have dug or what they found. In 1307, the Templars were arrested, tortured for heresy, and ultimately disbanded, though many Templars escaped the fate of their brethren.

This is why Jessa Carter wanted to come to Jerusalem. She believes the antiquities dealer has information she requires to find the tablets that supposedly made it into the Ark of the Covenant. The dealer has also been involved in scandal and possibly fraud. She does not trust him, but she has no other option available to her. He would not talk by phone or telegram but insisted on meeting her in person. When the PCs hear this, they may become suspicious.

Jessa Carter knows something about the Templars because her father investigated them years ago. He had been an outstanding academic, but his work on alternative theories outside mainstream peer review eventually caused him to be ostracized. In July 1944, he took his own life. Or so Jessa thinks. In reality, he is very much alive.

The antiquities dealer, Simcha Golan, lives and works in a narrow shop off the Mahane Yehuda market (aka "The Shuk.")

A brass bell tingles as you enter. The shop is cramped. Narrow walls clogged with the detritus of millennia. Small oil lamps, carved idols, fragments of pottery, and more are arranged according to no known system. The air is stale. Simcha, comes out from a back room, mopping his brow with a rag. He is a heavyset man, his waistcoat straining against an ample belly. He holds a hand out to you as another bead of sweat rivers down the right side of his face before finding his thin moustache.

Simcha Golan is not just sweating because of the heat. He is in serious trouble. In the back room are four assassins who have come to get a map from him. He claimed not to have it, but they began to threaten cutting off fingers and then limbs. Simcha is not a brave man. These assassins are from the Sons of Belial. They pushed him out here to get rid of the visitors.

Simcha is nervous, but he is trying to hide this. He tells Jessa that he did have possession of the item in question but sold it. He is fairly convincing here. The PCs have a chance to sense the danger in the shop. At some point, whether Simcha slips up or the PCs look in the back, the assassins attack. Each is armed with a pistol and a curved dagger. They dress like the locals. While talking

ROBBIE "MAD DOG" CORRIGAN

Robbie inherited both his position as a top East End gangster and his moniker from his father. Robert Corrigan Sr. fought for the Royal Army in India. There is a saying that comes from those days, "Only mad dogs and Englishman go out in the afternoon sun." Mad Dog got his name by being madder than a dog in that same afternoon sun. When he got back to London, he started his criminal career. His son now runs the firm. Corrigan is wild, flamboyant, and a tough sod to break. He speaks with a heavy East End accent and takes no guff.

with Simcha, the PCs may make an Interaction test at Difficulty 3 to determine he is lying. After years of working in the Shuk, he is a veteran liar.

The cramped space makes melee combat difficult. There isn't much room to fire a weapon, and the assassins are very close. As the action scene plays out, Simcha tries to sneak off to the back room, collect his map and money he has stashed there, and exit through the rear. PCs who spot him have a good chance of catching the rotund man.

He squirms and complains but eventually hands over the map. It is written in Latin and appears to date from the Middle Ages.

Montségur is the next likely stop. It is possible they translate "Avalon Across the Sea" as "America," and they would be correct. However, they have no location to start with, though player knowledge about Oak Island may well trump character knowledge. Hopefully, they do not make the connection now. If they do, you may allow them to skip to Oak Island.

MONTSÉGUR

The team finds themselves back in France and in enemy territory. They must reach Montségur and get back out of France. Unfortunately, U-Boat patrols make submarine extraction in the Mediterranean all but impossible. The team has one other option, but it is potentially as dangerous as being sunk by a U-Boat—enter the Forbidden Zone and cross into Spain. There, they can link up with ASOCOM agents who can get them back to Allied territory.

Easier said than done.

The first task is to get to France. As it has been reoccupied by the Axis, there is no legal way to get inside. From Jerusalem, the PCs can get a lift via cargo plane to Egypt. From there, they can get an ASOCOM stealth plane to drop them off the coast. They then raft in and climb the cliffs of the southern coast. It is rough going, but it beats being killed or captured by the Axis.

Appropriate Athletic checks should be made as required, but this part of the episode should move very quickly. Any tests should be made at Difficulty 2.

CHÂTEAU DE MONTSÉGUR

From where the PCs come ashore, they must make a 140km journey to Montségur. That is two days journey by foot or a couple hours by car. Of course, there are checkpoints along the roads. The PCs must decide which option they feel is best. Because they may very well come

up with something different, the GM must exercise and reward their imagination here. What the PCs encounter along the way is up to you.

Once they reach the castle, the PCs need to get inside. *Blutkreuz* guards have secured it. Even now, Orbst is inside looking for the cave where the Ark was allegedly taken. The castle lies atop a 1200m rock formation at the end of the Pyrenees. Scaling the rocks at night is the best method of access, though the team might find an alternate route. Getting past the guards on the ground is not too hard, given that they believe the great height will stop most intruders. Most of the men stationed here think of it as a babysitting job.

Once atop the rock formation, the PCs encounter spotlights and guards. The guards stand alongside the lights in the tower. The castle itself is largely in ruin, but was rebuilt in the 1800s. That later construction has also been brutalized by the war.

Two guards man each tower. Another ten wander the inside perimeter of the castle. The PCs may enter wherever they choose. Once inside, they need to move quickly. The entrance to the caverns lies in the castle's former dungeons. Once they reach the cavern system, they should be able to follow the echoing voices of Orbst's men. They are currently breaking through a wall that seals off the resting place of the Ark. Orbst himself is in the castle-proper trying to work out what was inside the secret chamber in the Apprentice Pillar.

How the PCs approach the situation is entirely up to them. They have the element of surprise. If they take out the men, three in all, they see that the group was using pickaxes to get through what appears to be a natural rock wall. It is not natural, but was made by expert masons to hide the chamber beyond.

The *Blutkreuz* men did not get through the wall. The PCs have to finish the job. Fortunately, this far below ground, there is no one else to bother them. Once the team makes a hole through which they can see, they find an empty room. On the back wall are rune-like glyphs. Inside the room itself, they see a raised stone dais in the center of the room where the Ark once rested. It is there no more, and has not been for 700 years. The glyphs were left as a message to other Templars, who would seek the Ark. It is coded, and appears to be a map of the coast of Europe and the east coast of America. Of course, America was not visited by Europeans until 1492 and this carving dates from at least 1307.

Dr. Carter orders the characters to shine their flashlights on the map and code, while she takes pictures. She then makes several notes. Flipping through her notebook, she frantically searches for entries. Then she laughs in a self-congratulatory manner. "Oak Island! Of course!"

She declines to explain anything until they are out of the castle. "If we were captured," she says, "it's better you do not know."

Now, the team has to get out of the castle. As they do, Orbst goes to check on his men's progress. He finds the team took them out. Approximately three rounds later, an alarm sounds inside the castle. The Germans now actively hunt the team using two experimental helicopters based on captured SSU designs.

The helicopter is the team's best method of escape. They may decide to blow up the other one, so it cannot pursue them. This is feasible if they are armed with explosives or come up with another way to detonate the craft. A Pilot skill is required to fly the helicopter. No rolls are needed for normal operation.

The GM needs to adjudicate just how many *Blutkreuz* soldiers make it into the courtyard as the PCs attempt escape. If the second helicopter is not destroyed, the team is pursued by air.

Spain is the closest border. The *Luftwaffe* can scramble fighters to intercept the chopper over the Mediterranean Sea. Problem is, once the PCs cross over the threshold of the Forbidden Zone, the helicopter's engines immediately fail, and they are in for a very bumpy landing. Make some falling rolls for damage (see Falling pp. 35-36 of ***Dust Adventures***), but do not knock them around too badly. The Forbidden Zone will be difficult enough.

THE FORBIDDEN ZONE

Little to nothing reliable is known about the Forbidden Zone. Few have come out, and those who have are loath to discuss the experience. For more information on the Forbidden Zone, see p. 102 of ***Dust Adventures***. As far as the heroes are aware, they are the first Allied agents to enter the Zone. In truth, another Allied agent working for ASOCOM entered in 1945 and he is still inside. The PCs encounter him as they traverse this strange terrain along the border of France and Spain.

TRAVELLING IN THE FORBIDDEN ZONE

The Forbidden Zone is full of anomalies that prevent compasses and traditional navigation methods from working. The sun may appear in one part of the sky when you look to track it, but then suddenly appears in another the next time you look up. Shadows don't behave correctly in the Forbidden Zone, at least not in conjunction with the angle of the sun. It is maddening to look at, shadows creep out in the wrong directions. A man walking finds his shadow remains behind him for several seconds before it catches up. Days or weeks can be spent lost inside and there is no proven way out. The players may spend a good deal of time here, subjectively, but only twelve hours will have passed when they emerge.

Things are not right in the Zone.

ENCOUNTERS IN THE FORBIDDEN ZONE

The following are a handful of encounters found in the Zone. The list is just a sample of what might happen inside. An entire campaign could be set in and around the Zone, as PCs attempt to unlock its secrets.

BLUTKREUZ SOLDIERS

The PCs encounter 1-10 Blutkreuz troops. They have been in here since earlier in the war. They look ragged, hungry, and barely holding it together. Even if the PCs are dressed in Allied uniforms, they do not necessarily shoot at the team. They have been here for far too long, and desperately want to find a way out.

Use stats for Axis Grenadiers on p. 144 of ***Dust Adventures.***

TOWN

The team comes across a mid-size town that appears abandoned. As noted above, unspoiled remains of food and drink sit on tables. There are canned goods in cupboards and beds appear to have just been made. A bicycle leans against a cafe on a cobblestone road. The team can find any normal item here that reasonably could be expected in a French or Spanish town circa 1940 A.D.

MEDIEVAL VILLAGE

This village disappeared without a trace in 1199 A.D. and scant records remain. Like the modern town above, it appears as if all the citizens simply stepped away. A blacksmith's shop is lit with a still-burning forge. Smoke rises out of the hearths in the public house. The players can find any normal object from that era here.

COMMANDER DONOVAN BONNEVILLE

Commander Bonneville was a member of the SOE before the Allies officially became a bloc. He has been inside the Zone for two years. In that time, he has seen no one. No fauna, no people, nothing. Bonneville is on the edge of sanity. Whether it is an effect of the Zone, isolation, or a combination of both is unclear. He does have theories on the Zone.

When he was briefed before his mission—explore the Zone and report back—the Zone had just appeared. That was July 16, 1945. He has been in the Zone ever since. His briefing consisted of a decoded Axis communiqué that tipped the Allies off to the appearance of the Zone. Reconnaissance flights either disappeared, or saw nothing but cloud cover. When they tried to dive under these clouds, they found they did not end.

Further, several academics from various English universities approached MI5 citing references to the Zone in old texts dating back the Roman Empire. According to the academics, none of these entities were there previously.

Bonneville believes the Zone is an intelligence. Somehow, it is alive and toys with those who enter. Whether this is true or not matters little to him. Talking to him, one can see the obsession behind his eyes. He tells the team that he cannot leave. The Zone has become used to him. It wants him. If the PCs stay too long, the same happens to them.

Bonneville can show them a way out. He has done calculations based on the oddness of shadows and stars. He has a theory that the Zone operates in a discernible cyclic pattern. Based on this, he believes there are specific times the Zone "allows" people to leave. He shows the PCs one of these exits in two days. In the meantime, they can stay in an abandoned school that Bonneville calls home.

In the classrooms of the school, scrawled on chalkboards, are complex equations. When asked about them by Dr. Carter, Bonneville insists he did all his work on paper. The equations were there when he arrived.

LEAVING THE FORBIDDEN ZONE

At some point, the GM should have the PCs encounter Bonneville. He is their most likely way out. Otherwise, roll four ***Dust*** dice each day. If all four come up the same, the team finds their way out that day. This could obviously take a good deal of time.

Depending on how wild the GM wishes to get, the team could also encounter Germanic tribes, Celts, or a lost battalion who fought in World War I. The Zone is an enigma. Perhaps the entire area is nothing more than a shared hallucination. Its secrets will not be revealed here.

When the team leaves, they find themselves in Spain. Only 12 hours have passed regardless of how much time they spent inside the Zone.

SPAIN

The GM can hand wave a lot of Spain. Spain is a Neutral Nation but sympathetic to the Axis cause. Americans tend to stand out. Word could get back to *Blutkreuz* very quickly and therefore Orbst. *Blutkreuz* agents have been planted in Spain and can be called up quickly to intercept the team. That is left to the GM. There is no reason they need to encounter them. In fact, it may be wiser to merely follow them for now.

The Sons of Belial, formerly a branch of the Knights Templar, also have members in Spain. They, too, are tracking the PCs. Most of this is via a network of informants, but either group may follow the PCs directly. That is up to the GM. Remember, large intelligence apparatuses exist in World War II. Many have moles inside them, and intel is often leaked in one way or another. Perhaps there is even someone plotting against the PCs inside ASOCOM?

Physics Inside the Forbidden Zone

Natural laws are only suggestions in the Zone. You cannot count on anything to act the way it should. Some areas exhibit irregular gravity. Certain objects such as trees and walls have variable density and can be passed through. No wildlife appears anywhere. At night, the stars come out, but they are not the stars they should be. Dr. Carter observes that, at least on one occasion, the stars appear to be in a configuration that would place them in roughly 12,500 B.C.

The towns and villages that existed along the border remain, but none of the people do. Vines and flora crawl over abandoned buildings, personal objects are left where they sat last, cups of coffee and tea are set out on tables, but there is no one there to drink them. Further, they may be cold or warm depending on the GM's whim.

Nothing the team can expect to happen will necessarily happen. Guns might fire normally, or the bullets may exit the barrel and float straight up. This makes a firefight extremely unnerving. Every time the PCs (or NPCs) attempt to use a mechanical device (including a gun), roll 4 *Dust* dice:

- **0 faction symbols (20%)—The item functions normally.**
- **1 faction symbols (39%)—The item does not operate.**
- **2 faction symbols (29%)—The item performs the reverse of the intended action. (Firinga gun causes it to unload and kick out its ammo, for example).**
- **3 faction symbols (10%)—The item operates as if gravity were reversed.**
- **4 faction symbols (1%)—The item disappears and is replaced by something random from throughout the ages.**

Obviously, this is going to make things difficult. The GM is encouraged to improvise. There isn't any rhyme or reason in the Zone. The players should not expect to have something occur the same way twice.

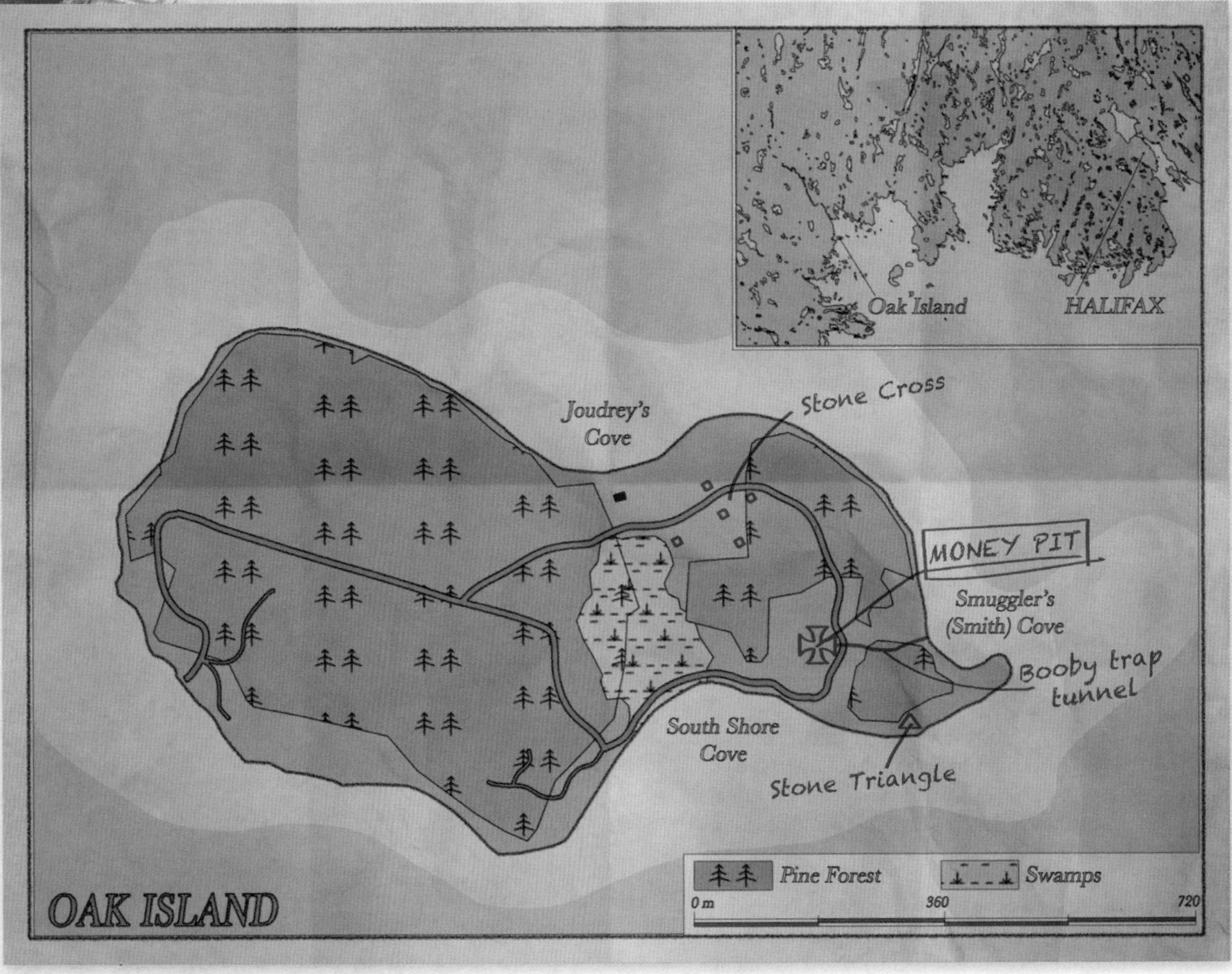

OAK ISLAND

Leaving Spain is not difficult, but getting from Spain to Scotland is. Even in the short while the PCs have been gone, London has fallen, and the Axis is nearing Hadrian's Wall. The Axis Navy has closed the English Channel and patrols the waters along the Spanish coast. ASOCOM has no way to get the PCs to their next destination—Oak Island.

Sometime while in Spain or the Zone, the PCs may have pushed Dr. Carter to reveal more about Oak Island. See the sidebar for details.

GETTING TO OAK ISLAND

Players have to arrange transport to Oak Island. ASOCOM wires them any funds they need, but it is up to them to book passage on a merchant vessel. The trip takes a few days and leaves the team in New York. From there, they can drive or take a train north to Nova Scotia. Allied authorities control all territory they pass through, so they have no worry of being swarmed by Axis soldiers. That does not mean Orbst and the Sons of Belial aren't keeping their eyes on them, though.

The team does not encounter either until they reach Oak Island. There, the PCs see Orbst and his men have set up an excavation of the money pit. Orbst is there with 10 *Blutkreuz* agents, half of whom speak perfect English. They are armed with StG 47s and Mauser pistols. There is a U-Boat waiting for them in deeper water off the island in Mahone Bay.

A firefight ensues, and the team drives Orbst and his crew from the island with little resistance. The Germans escape by boat, which takes them out to the sub. The team is now free to finish the excavation, but the pit is empty. Two days worth of digging, with the help of the Army Corps of Engineers, reveals a tunnel system below the island along with another empty chamber. This one, unlike the last, offers no clues as to where the treasure went. Like the last chamber in Montségur, a raised stone is carved into the floor upon which the Ark once rested.

WHAT DO WE DO NOW?

The team finds themselves at an impasse. All their clues have lead to another empty chamber. The Germans left the island, and the Sons of Belial, who they likely do not know by name yet, remain elusive. Dr. Carter orders them to go to Kansas where ASOCOM headquarters is located in a building known as the Octagon.

The PCs probably haven't been here before.

The Oak Island Legend

Located off the south shore of Nova Scotia, Oak Island it a treasure hunter's paradise. For about a century and half, people have tried to uncover its secrets. The legend arose when two boys found flagstones buried in 1795. Digging further, the boys found a series of log platforms every ten feet. A professional team came in eight years later and dug to a depth of 27m in what would become known as "the Money Pit." Allegedly, they found a stone with a code inscribed on it that, when decoded, read, "forty feet below, two million pounds lie buried."

Coconut fibres, not native to North America, were also found. Each attempt to dig further resulted in flooding of the pit. Apparently, a system of tunnels extends out to the sea. When tripped, these tunnels flood any attempts to uncover the treasure. Rich and famous folks, including former President Roosevelt, have invested in trying to find the secret treasure they believe lies buried within. Rumours suggest everything from the Holy Grail, to pirate treasure, to the lost manuscripts of William Shakespeare are buried on Oak Island. So far, no one has found anything.

In the *Dust Universe*, the Ark of the Covenant was indeed buried on Oak Island. Taken from Montségur in 1307, it rested for a long time in Scotland. At one point, the Ark was kept at the current location of Rosslyn Chapel. That is why the church is modelled on the Temple of Solomon. The Temple of Solomon contained the Ark in the Holy of Holies. When William Sinclair built Rosslyn to house the Ark and its secrets, he had already travelled to America following old Norse routes passed down in oral tradition. By the time his son, Prince Henry Sinclair, took the chest from Scotland to America, the Templars had split into several groups. Among them, the Freemasons, the Bavarian Illuminati, and the Sons of Belial. It is the latter that buried the Ark in the New World. The Templars sought to make a paradise of free thought and democracy in America. Some say they succeeded. An interesting historical note: many of the Founding Fathers, as well as FDR, were Freemasons.Nothing here should otherwise be considered historical in any way. It is based on supposition and imagination but so is an alternate World War II augmented with alien technology. This is pulp adventure, not history.

WHO SENT THE COMMUNIQUÉ?

Dr. William Carter sent the communiqué as an encoded cable knowing full well it would be intercepted and decoded by ASOCOM. He sent it to alert his daughter to the location of the Ark. Carter has decided he wants his daughter on board with him. This is a test he lays before her to see how she reacts. He believes her loyalty lies with logic and science over the Allies. He also has his own agenda. The Allies getting their hands on this part of the tablet serves his needs. Where the Sons of Belial do not want the Seals to open the secret spoken of in Revelation, William Carter does. There still remains too much of the curious archaeologist inside him. Also, he thinks he's fighting for a larger goal.

The Octagon is the largest manmade structure on Earth. The sheer size is overwhelming. Inside, the octagonal design revolves around an open central hub where well-tended gardens grow. Every inch of polished marble corridor in the entranceway shines with a gleam. American flags hang next to Allied flags, making no mistake who really funded the building of this stone behemoth.

The building itself is quiet, with sound baffling having been built into the walls. When the team does come upon a busy area, the noise is likewise reduced to a dull hum. IDs are checked thoroughly as the team is screened upon entrance. They are then screened again as they enter one of any of the eight areas the Octagon is divided into. One such section is partially occupied by Clio and that is their destination.

Following his work on the Manhattan Project, General Leslie Grove was put in overall command of ASOCOM. He is expert at managing the conflicting goals, egos, and techniques of this huge intelligence machine. Dr. Thackery Schliemann is in overall command of Clio. He holds the rank of Colonel, but rarely wears a uniform. His appearance is that of a man less concerned with how he looks than what he does. He and Grove often fail to see eye-to-eye.

At Clio headquarters, the team is again debriefed—getting to be routine for them. Grove shows up during the debriefing. Schliemann is already there. Two men in suits, not uniforms, do the debriefing. If asked, they decline to say who they are.

Elect one player to tell the story. As Grove and Schliemann listen, a knock comes at the door. A non-com clerk enters the room. He holds a recently decoded telex, which he hands to General Grove and then whispers in his ear. Grove's eyes shift to Jessa Carter.

"Apparently," he says, "it is addressed to you."

It is, prompting some suspicion from Grove. Schliemann vouches for Carter, and Carter, through gritted teeth, vouches for the team. She has begun to give them grudging respect, but only just. Even still, Majestic 12 is known to have infiltrated ASOCOM, so paranoia is a carefully cultivated asset these days.

The secret communiqué names Dr. Jessa Carter followed by what looks like a series of coordinates. There is no other clue offered, though a listening station in Ireland intercepted the cable.

Schliemann reads the coordinates and clicks his tongue as if he's discovered something. Grove rises, straightens his uniform, and says, "Well, doctors, you apparently have this well in hand. I have other business to attend to. Good luck

with the recovery of the second tablet." On his way out, he gives Jessa a microsecond of suspicion.

The PCs notice this. At this point in the campaign, they should be unsure whether or not they can trust Dr. Carter too.

Schliemann's recollection of an article that appeared in a local Colorado newspaper back in 1909 caused his epiphany in the debriefing room. The article, and another following the next month, alleged The Smithsonian sent an archaeological team to the Grand Canyon where they found a network of tunnels and caverns collectively known as Isis Temple. Inside, the team found statues in Egyptian style, something akin to hieroglyphs on the walls, and mummies. They also claimed the room was filled with other treasure including a golden chest. Schliemann saw the coordinates and realized they mark a point in the Grand Canyon.

Quickly, Dr. Carter snatches a map from someone's desk—the person using begins to protest until silenced with a harsh look. She spreads the map on a large table in the huge Clio comm room. She takes the coordinates, a compass, and a T-Square. With them, she pinpoints the location.

"But who would have brought it so far? If it was there in '09, surely it was moved prior to that? The Templars died out centuries ago. Just who are we dealing with here?"

THE GRAND CANYON TREASURE

Getting to the Grand Canyon is relatively easy. In the United States, the team has access to a good deal more of ASOCOM's resources. A military transport takes them to an airbase in Colorado and they journey overland to the canyon from there (about 400km). The plan is to rappel down 300m to a cliff ledge. There, they find a small opening—large enough for one person at a time—leading into the tunnels.

They have to crouch to get inside. Once past the main tunnel, the corridor opens, and the team can stand. A military escort remains at the top of the canyon awaiting their return. Spider webs are thick in the tunnel, like gauze stretched across an open wound.

Once inside, the tunnel leads sharply downward and the PCs find, of all things, steps. The stairs are carved into the bare rock. As the team proceeds, they note the walls are covered with petroglyphs and Dr. Carter frequently pauses to take photographs.

Finally, after a kilometre or two, the team emerges into a giant cavern.

Vast, like a sports stadium built into the rock walls of the Grand Canyon. Multiple tiers rise on all sides like a ziggurat. Along each tier are golden idols, trinkets, Kachina dolls, and the ever-present petroglyphs. At the end of the cave, the walls taper, leading toward a central, narrow stairway that culminates in a raised pedestal. There lies the Ark, a plain gold box affixed with two golden angels facing each other, wings flung forward in genuflection. Above that, serving as a kind of apse to hold the Ark, is a pristine piece of curved metal. Only the ends are jagged and black, as if pulled from a wreck. Part of the metal glows, pulsing faintly, illuminating the chamber. Six sarcophagi surround the Ark on the tier immediately below the divine treasure. All around them, a strange repeating petroglyph appears—that of what looks like a stick figure doing a dumbbell squat.

The team has found the legendary Ark of the Covenant. Unfortunately, they have also stumbled into a two-fold trap. The Sons of Belial lay in wait for them. The temple complex is heaped in gold and precious stones. Ornate cups, like offerings, are laid before the Ark. The cool light from the curved metal illuminates the entire cavern. The metal is actually a section of a UFO that crashed in remote antiquity. In point of fact, it was shot down.

It is wreckage from an Anunnaki fighter craft that crashed somewhere in this area near the end of the last Ice Age. The Ark itself is much as described in the Bible, down to the cubit. When the PCs have all filed into the cave, 10 Sons of Belial attack.

A firefight echoes through the auditorium-like chamber, one the PCs hopefully win. With their enemy vanquished, they claim their prize—the one, true Ark!

Inside the Ark is a single tablet, not unlike the one found previously on Mont Saint-Michel. However, when the team opens the Ark, a sickly blue light emits from the broken tablet causing nausea and pain. When the Ark is closed, the irritation subsides. Gold, it seems, functions in relation to this form of energy much as lead does to radiation. Could it be that the adoration of gold in history has its origins here? Is that why golden chalices lay before the Ark as offerings?

Dr. Carter is momentarily dumbstruck. No one has ever encountered anything like this before. She walks in a stupor, marvelling at the walls, the petroglyphs, and the Ark itself. She then begins snapping pictures and taking notes, mumbling aloud: "Must have been an underground glacial river or lake that carved most of this out. Then the natives dressed the stone, but why would they have the Ark?" Impassioned, she strides up to the sarcophagi and demands the PCs help her get inside.

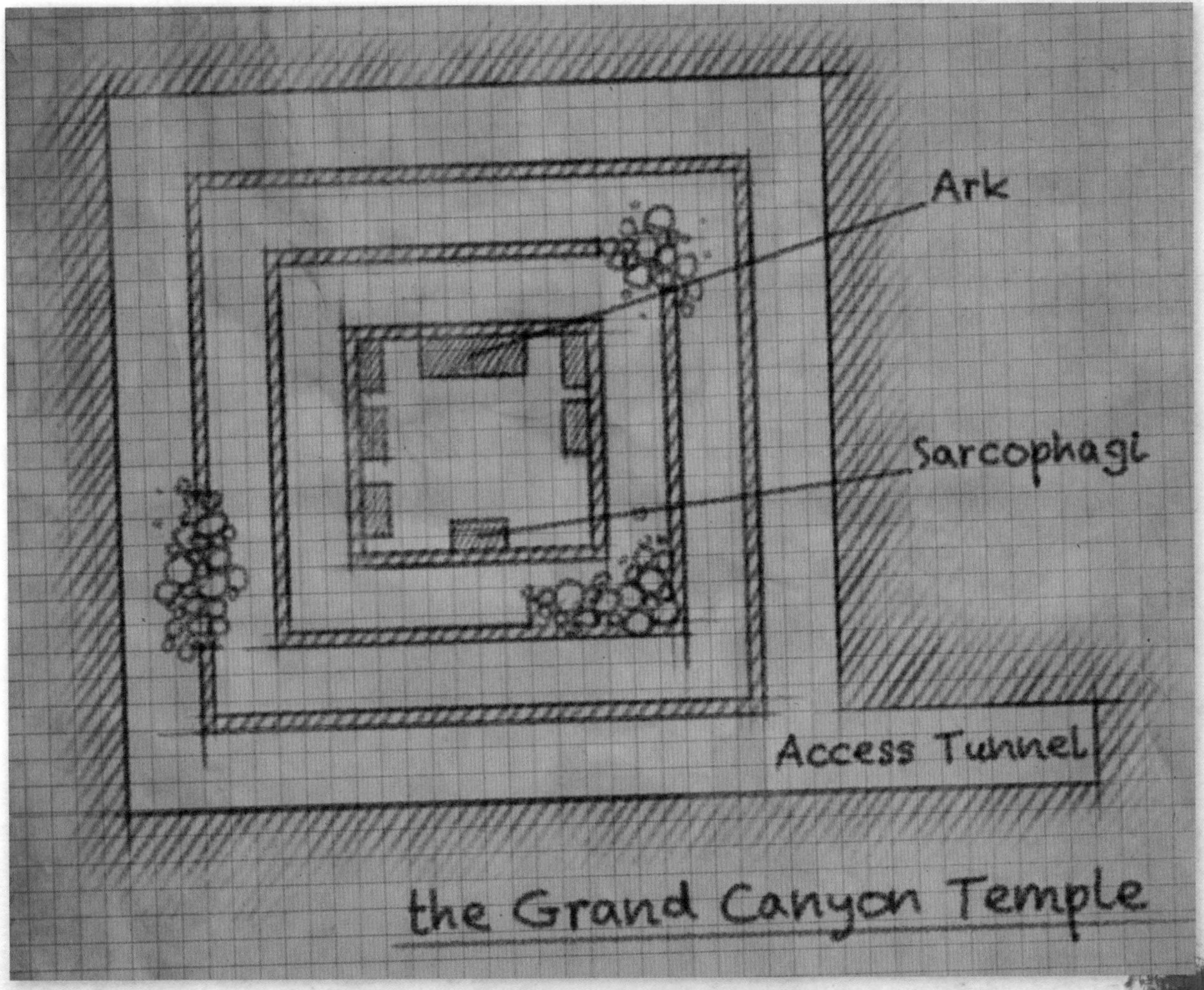

In five of the six, they find desiccated, but remarkably well preserved knights, all dressed in chainmail, and buried with their swords. Each wears the red Templar cross on a white background. The sixth sarcophagus holds an alien being that the team mistakes for a Vrill. It is mummified, but even in its bandages, it is clear this is not human. Dr. Carter takes pictures of the petroglyphs, particularly the strange repeating one. Some show the figures that must be knights, entrusting the natives with a golden box.

All is quiet. The team claims the Ark, but as they do, they set off a very, very old trap.

As the Ark is lifted, the raised platform sinks into the rock. The team hears a great thundering rumble, and the cavern reveals holes inside some of the rounder petroglyphs. These holes begin spewing tremendous amounts of water. The cavern is flooding!

Worse, the water thrums soundly against the back wall, and pieces of the cave begin to break away. There is a great, ancient glacial lake trapped behind that wall. Outside, on top of the canyon, the Allies radio that the same thing appears to be happening around the Grand Canyon at approximately the same height. "Get out of there!" one of the men shouts.

The team now has to decide what to do. The Ark is heavy. Their only real option is to grab the tablet and hope it does not kill them. Do not give them much time to decide. Once they have, describe the following:

The spouts of water erode pieces of rock as they push violently through from whatever vast source they tap. The back wall continues to shudder and then breaks apart. A massive torrent three times the size of Niagara Falls erupts. Water consumes you, plunging you into its depths. Up is down. You have no sense of direction. You have no say in being swept away by the great flood. It carries you rapids-fast through a tunnel, perhaps the one you came through. Then, with the force of a canon, you are shot from the aperture and plunged into an enormous lake below.

The entire canyon is becoming one giant lake. As the PCs manage to surface in the churning water, they see other, similar apertures loosing this ancient water. Everything that was inside the temple is either smashed or sunk. The PCs manage to hold onto the tablet, but probably little else. The sight is magnificent, a wonder of unknown technology and the raw power of nature. The team can only marvel at it.

WRAPPING UP

The team has accomplished their mission. They have recovered the second tablet. Like its cousin, it is very light. In fact, it floats on water. The glow it emits sickens people over time, and the PCs carrying the tablet become ill, as do those around them.

The army hauls the team out of the Grand Canyon—now lake—on to what is now...shore. They return to the Octagon for debriefing and medical treatment.

Several days pass as specialists examine the team. The tablet is taken away to be studied by specialists referred to as "top men." Eventually, Dr. Schliemann briefs the group.

The tablet is indeed identical in size to the first. Glyphs upon it appear to be carved in ancient Aramaic, but they do not propose commandments. Instead, they tell a story similar to that of the Biblical flood. The glyphs are crude, and clearly were carved by hands other than those who dressed the stone.

And they shall be washed clean in water

And all the animals of the Earth will be theirs to preserve.

As the sky rages and burns, the great tides of the Earth sweep all men have done away.

Skies turn dark and ash covers the land.

But light, a first light, pierces that gloom and those who have made the Ark float toward it.

And we are they, and they are us.

From this moment until the ending of the world.

One final time.

To end at last.

Dr. Carter and Schliemann immediately go on about Noah, Utnapishtim, and the Great Deluge. Dr. Carter asks about the Ark. Divers are looking for it, and the curved piece of metal in the lake. Her pictures, miraculously, made it. As developed, she sorts through them. "I have seen that glyph before. I know I have." She refers to the "squatting man" petroglyph.

Schliemann pulls out a series of thick books. He opens several to black and white photos. Each depicts something very similar to the glyph of the squatting man.

"New Mexico, Australia, Namibia, the coast of France," he says, "they have been found all over the world. Some date back to the end of the last Ice Age."

What does it mean? Schliemann and Carter do not yet know. If an archaeologist is among the team, they likely realize that they, too, have seen the glyph before. It appears in hundreds of vanished cultures from all over the world. Their meaning is not revealed in this episode.

Carter and Schliemann want to look to New Mexico next. There, the Zuni people still live. Their oral tradition holds that they were given civilization by space beings. The team is headed there.

Dive teams are still seeking all of the bodies, including that of the alien.

The team is left with many questions, and each of those begs many more. Based on the picture Dr. Carter took of the alien mummy, Schliemann says with great confidence, "That is no Vrill."

So what is it then? What have the characters uncovered?

OPTIONAL MISSION

As mentioned in her report, Dr. Carter was expecting two tablets inside the Ark, as any Sunday school graduate would. Instead, there was only one. Dr. Carter thinks the second tablet might still be found. She arranges to have the team sent to Italy to find that artefact. For this mission, see Chapter 9.

A NOTE ON AXIS NATIONS

Whereas the Allied Bloc has done its best to retain its individuality and the relative independence of each nation outside of the war effort, the Axis bloc has done the exact opposite. It has expanded into a massive single entity breathing loyalty only to the Axis cause. The Axis is ruled overall by a military council, which elects its direct leadership from within and from a body of favoured candidates.

Since the outcome of Operation Valkyrie, the Protector of the Reich, a seat currently filled by Admiral Karl Dönitz, has led the Axis. He oversees the military council, which is made up of many powerful generals and political appointees. Chief among these is the Axis Commander-in-Chief, Field Marshal Erwin Rommel.

However, much of the power of the Axis bloc is actually controlled (or heavily influenced behind the scenes) by the *Blutkreuz Korps*.

Each individual Axis nation clings to its name, borders, and heritage merely as a formal obligation. The true power of all Axis territory is ruled from Berlin. Military units are often kept strictly segregated by nationality as well, with German advisors sent to the head offices of every member nation to ensure proper Axis policy is obeyed and carried out.

Aspects of daily life like trade, entertainment, journalism, commerce, freedom of movement, and law enforcement are fiercely controlled by their appointed ministers from within the Axis bloc. Unlike the Allied nations, the Protector of the Reich, or his appointed officials, eventually oversees all of these aspects.

Each city, state, province, or nation within the Axis bloc is responsible for raising, arming, and training a fighting force. While they may do this in any way they desire (as long as they do it), the preferred method is similar to the American draft. Young men are pressed into service at a local level where officers train them. The best are sent to the next level of military service, where they receive better training, better leadership, and better equipment. This process of being sent up to the next level continues until they are members of the famed Axis Grenadier units. The number of steps it takes to get from local garrison trooper to elite member of the Grenadiers largely depends on where they are initially recruited. A young man from Berlin can find himself a Grenadier in one selection, while a farm boy from Bavaria may take six or more steps.

The Axis is not against conscripting troops from occupied nations and often raises units of French, Dutch, Polish, Romanian, and other nationalities. One of the more unique side effects of the war is the influence it has had on the French Foreign Legion. The Legion has essentially been split in two, with one portion of the Legion still loyal to the Vichy government under Axis control in France, and another portion serving the Free French Forces in North Africa, Asia, and even England.

The only major hold out to the "Axis way" of leadership is Japan. The Empire of the Sun follows much of Berlin's advice and lead, but still manages to remain largely independent. They have their own national identity, goals, and functionality. However, some within Japan still believe they have given too much of their identity to Germany and they are not pleased with the result. If it ever came to it, Japan would no doubt fight Germany for the preservation of its own autonomy.

Much of the work of *Blutkreuz* to control and lead the Axis bloc occurs clandestinely, hidden in ancient fortresses across the globe. The central headquarters out of Schloss Reicher (Reicher Castle) located in the Alps between Germany and Austria and Schloss Hohenfels (Hohenfels Castle) located in Bavaria, Germany are two such locations.

30 Nov 1947

ASOCOM Report/Clio

Operation: Apocalypse

To: Dr. Schliemann and General Granger

Pursuant to your request, I am compiling field reports on Operation: Apocalypse. Frankly, I thought my father was wrong about his theories, but evidence suggests otherwise. As scientists, we must change our opinions whenever the evidence informing them changes. Over the past two weeks, I have seen things I never thought possible. My summary of events follows.

The crew you assigned to me are capable soldiers, but poor excuses for Clio operatives. Only one has a background in academic theology. The others are as useful as I expect a G.I. to be. They tend toward crudeness and often ostracize me as both their intellectual and official superior. I am not fool enough to overrule their opinions in combat situations, however, they are in over their heads when it comes to the history and the science. I regard them as I would any tool in my archaeological kit. I know, General Granger, you do not approve of such an attitude toward these men, but we have no time to spare feelings, if we are to beat the Axis and SSU to the recovery of the remaining Seals.

The mission went thusly:

In London, we encountered Axis resistance as expected. The city was, as you both know, weeks if not days from falling. I sought the copper scroll listing relics taken from Jerusalem by the Babylonians in 586 A.D. At the British Museum, I obtained a rubbing of the scroll. The scroll itself is missing. I suspect the Axis or even the Ahnenerbe obtained it before we got there. In retrieving the scroll, we came upon an uncouth gangster who one of the Rangers seemed to know. I do not like the idea that I am travelling with someone friendly with such people.

The rubbing lists several items not on the other copper scroll found in Qumran. Among these are the treasures of the Temple of Solomon, chiefly, the Ark of the Covenant. That it exists, or did, is astounding. This must thoroughly be studied. The question became clear: why did one scroll list the Ark while the other did not? Recalling old texts, it was my theory that the Babylonians returned the Ark to the Hebrews out of fear, much as the Philistines did before them. The Ark is an artefact of unspeakable power, at least in legend. I deduced that upon its return, the Hebrews would have placed it back in the Temple.

From this premise, it seemed logical that the Knights Templar could have secured the Ark from the ruins of the Temple some 1800 years later. This brought us to Jerusalem and an antiquities dealer with whom my father was familiar. My father's theory posited that the tablets inside the Ark were not the Ten Commandments, but pieces of Vrill technology. This explains the sickness afflicting those who approached the Ark without protection. As with the Seal from Mont Saint-Michel, I assume the rest to also be radioactive. I can only guess the lower radioactivity of the Mont St Michel tablet are intentional. Perhaps it was meant to be read first? Assassins from an unknown cult tried to kill the antiquities dealer, but the Rangers fended them off. At least they prove useful in their single area of competence.

The antiquities dealer turned a map over to me. I did some small amount of research and translation before determining the Templars moved the Ark from Jerusalem to the Cathar outpost of Montsegur. This led us back to France.

The insertion into France was difficult, but we went undetected until we reached Montsegur. There, a Colonel Orbst also sought the Ark. Please arrange a dossier of this man to reach me. He is a foul opponent. Again, at Montsegur, we found the Templars had moved the Ark hundreds of years before our arrival. A coded map found in the chamber once holding the Ark pointed to a North American island off the coast of Nova Scotia called Oak Island.

Dr. Schliemann, those fanciful stories you once told me of buried treasure on Oak Island turned out to be real. Yet, even as we made it back into Allied territory (see my previous report on The Forbidden Zone for details on our escape from France), we found again the Templars — seven hundred years after their dissolution — were still ahead of us. Impossibly, they seemed to have moved the Ark to the Grand Canyon. I cannot begin to tell you, General, how such pre-Columbian contact between Europeans and the New World rewrites history. This must be thoroughly studied.

As your men have no doubt reported, we found the next Seal within a cavernous temple inside the Grand Canyon. A trap sprung by one of your so-called "elite" rangers caused the entire canyon to flood. The Seal floated. The Ark did not. You must recover the Ark. There was only one tablet inside it though. I thought there would be two and I have an idea where we might seek the second.

I cannot fathom what we have begun to unravel here, but I am confident these artefacts, the Seals, were known to other cultures besides those in the Fertile Crescent. The strange petroglyph seen all over the world is what I shall pursue next. That is the next lead I will follow.

I am confident in my abilities to find these Seals, but we are dealing with secrets and forces I cannot yet comprehend. I will submit another report once we have secured the next seal.

-- Dr. Jessa Carter, Captain, ASOCOM, Clio

CHAPTER 3: THE NEW WORLD

THE ROMANCE OF JESSA CARTER
This subplot is optional. A perfectly enjoyable campaign can unfold without any romantic entanglements getting in the way. However, it is in the spirit of both pulp and war genres that a romance serves as an emotional parallel to the action.

Jessa Carter serves that role for one of the PCs. A candlelit dinner in the dining car, drinks, and her hair literally down from the severe bun she normally keeps it in—all these serve to gradually chip away at her icy demeanour. Whomever she likes is free to rebuff her, but it is more fun if the two keep sparring verbally and the inevitable gravity of their feelings pulls them together.

Decide if you want to include this in your campaign.

This entire episode takes place in America, though not all of it in the continental United States. The final sequence is set in the cold, harsh wilds of the Alaska Territory during the SSU's continuing advance there.

Following a lead from the previous episode, the team sets out for New Mexico where they must seek a Zuni elder. Their purpose is to discover the meaning of the "squatting man" petroglyph.

The episode opens with the characters on a train travelling from Kansas to Santa Fe...

ATTEMPTED MURDER ON THE SOUTHWESTERN EXPRESS

The Sons of Belial do not give up easily. They may have lost the tablet inside the Ark, but they are determined that the team not live long enough to enjoy that victory. Aboard the express train they take to New Mexico, Belial Assassins attempt to kill them.

Each of the PCs is berthed in a Pullman Car. These were among the finest rail coaches of their day. The rail line continues to operate for passengers, but there are fewer aboard than there would be outside of wartime. In fact, the train itself also hauls military cargo. Very little in America has not been repurposed for the war effort.

The train's dining service is commendable, a far cry from the C-Rations on which the team usually subsists. They are not used to being served and may fall into a dangerous quietude. When they are split apart, most likely in each of their bunks, assassins come after them.

Two assassins confront each player or NPC. The murderers slip quietly into their cabins to take each person out. Allow the PCs MIND rolls at Difficulty 3 to hear the doors opening.

ASSASSINS OF BELIAL (NO. VARIES)

Use stats for Assassin on p. 146 of ***Dust Adventures.***

Shouting for help quickly alerts the rest of the team, but they have their hands full with their own killers. If one of the PCs can be abducted, the assassins try, but not at the cost of the others getting away. Their orders are to take out the entire team if none can be captured for interrogation.

If the PCs manage to take one of the assassins alive, that assassin tries to swallow a cyanide capsule. If this attempt is thwarted, the team is free to interrogate the individual. What he or she says is little. They work for an organization dedicated to "forces you could not possibly understand." They are fanatics. Having been split off from the Templars long ago, members of this group are prepared for torture. The team sees evidence of such torture on each of the bodies. They give up nothing.

Once the team has dispatched the assassins, the remainder of the trip occurs without incident.

CLOVIS, NEW MEXICO

The team has come to speak with an elder named Sanchez who works as an archaeologist specializing in the rise of humanity in the Americas. They expect an older man, but what they find is a young, vibrant woman. Her first name is Meli, and she is a doctor of archaeology just like Carter. The two immediately take a disliking to each other. Meli resents Carter because she works for the government. The federal authorities have made her expeditions and fieldwork very difficult, of late. Further, as a Native American raised by a traditional father, Meli has suspicion for any government authority. Her people were not treated well. Remember, this is 1947; there are still living Native Americans who remember the United States' war against them.

Meli is about thirty years of age with deep brown eyes and black hair. She is in charge of an expedition digging up what she believes are the first humans in the Americas.

Meli knows the petroglyph called the "squatting man." Her people have a long tradition stretching back to their beginnings. Star beings came from the heavens and took the Zuni out of the underworld. These beings were at war for many hundreds of years. The night sky raged with their fury until, one night, everything changed. A great lightning bolt ripped through the heavens and scarred the sky. An image of a man, trying to hold up the vast weight of the heavens appeared to the Zuni. That image is the squatting man.

Meli considers it an oral tradition. She does not dismiss it as fantasy however. As she speaks with Dr. Carter, Meli begins to notice similarities to someone else. She brings this up. Describing a man in his late fifties who, by the sound of it, looks vaguely like Carter's deceased father. He came here about a month ago, asking after the same petroglyphs. His name was James Caldwell, or so he said.

This is the second hint that Dr. Carter receives regarding the possibility that her father is still alive. She is shaken by this news but eventually brushes it off. The PC who is romantically interested in her can give solace.

That night, the team is invited to the Zuni reservation where Meli's father lives. Her family is poor, very, very poor, and the standard of living is a stark contrast to those in the United States supposedly "going without" for the war. These people were given a raw deal; there are no two ways about it.

That night, the PCs interact with Meli's grandfather (her father died early in the war, part of a team of Rangers much like the PCs). Her grandfather refuses to learn English and speaks only in the Zuni tongue. They call themselves the A'shiwi, or "the flesh." Her grandfather listens to the PCs and relates the history of his people as described previously. He believes in these star beings and a Zuni prophecy that holds that their return augurs the end of this age.

ABDUCTION

The team is invited to stay the night. While they sleep, Meli steps outside to have a cigarette, and Orbst's agents grab her. When the team wakes the next day, she is gone. However, the Germans have left a trail behind them, and many of the people on the reservation are expert trackers. What they do not have is the firepower to take on *Blutkreuz* soldiers.

The PCs, of course, do.

It is up to them whether they attempt a rescue. Dr. Carter is against it at first as she needs to return to Kansas and continue her research. Something must have happened in the skies so long ago. Eventually, she admits the right thing to do is save Meli. Should the PCs agree, proceed with the rest of this scene.

The Germans took Meli to the town of El Paso, Texas. They drove all through the night to get there. The next day, they plan to take her across the border into Mexico.

Things are easier for them there as the Mexican government, while under the banner of the Allies, is not as watchful for spies as the Americans.

However, for this day, they rest at the Lubbock Oasis, a motel along a dusty strip of highway.

Of course, the trail left behind only reveals that the Germans grabbed Meli, forced her into a car, and then drove east. The PCs have to reason out where they took her. They may call on ASOCOM for assistance. On their own, they may deduce that El Paso is the closest and best spot to cross over into Mexico with a prisoner.

El Paso is not very large in 1947, a border town with a dodgy reputation that lies just opposite the notorious city of Juarez, in Mexico. Asking around town, and using the description of white men with a Native American girl, eventually leads the team to the motel where four men are holding Meli.

BLUTKREUZ AGENTS (4)

Use stats for Spy on pp. 145-146 of ***Dust Adventures.***

To: Dr. Jessa Carter

From: Dr. Schliemann, Director, Clio

Squatting man appears to relate to plasma phenomenon. Find Dr. Lance Pereau. USC. Blutkreuz agents present. Burn after reading.

THE CLOVIS CULTURE
The Clovis people are thought to be the ancestors of Native Americans. After the Younger Dryas, a cold snap following a period of warming at the end of the last Ice Age, the Clovis people began to split apart and form separate tribes. So goes the theory. From these, eventually, the Zuni descended.

Named for the stone tools found at various sites in the 1920s and 1930s, the Clovis are thought to be the first people to populate what is now America. The "Clovis First" theory holds that the Clovis were the first people here. It is the predominant hypothesis. However, competing theories, some involving Europeans coming to America during the Ice Age, have since arisen.

The adventure focuses on the Clovis First theory as it simplifies the lineage of people who are already allegedly interacting with alien beings. While there exist thin "theories" about Native Americans and ancient astronauts, they are in no way used here as a substitute for genuine research and the history of these people as told by their own.

If the PCs rescue Meli, they not only do the noble thing, they find some clues. In the motel room is a decoded German radio transmission from Orbst. It leads the PCs to Los Angeles where a well-known actor, Reginald Moore, is apparently serving as an SSU spy. There is no further information as to what the Germans planned to do with this information. If the PCs do not follow this optional side mission, they do not receive this clue.

In either case, their next stop is Los Angeles.

LOS ANGELES

After New Mexico, the team receives a cable from Dr. Schliemann. It is coded, and driven out personally by an NCO from the 509th Airbase located outside Roswell, New Mexico. Local papers spoke of a UFO crash there last summer. Those rumours are still in the air.

Note to the GM: Because the cable went through the 509th, Majestic 12 saw it. This means Howard Hughes now has an idea that Clio is up to something odd. At the end of this episode, the PCs explore one of Hughes' facilities.

Upon arriving in Los Angeles, the team finds a town much more like the 1930s real world version of the city than that of 1947. Remember, this is 1947 with the war still raging. Los Angeles is a boomtown on pause. The great post-war expansion is yet to come. It is still a noir city, though, at least on film. Salacious rags pull down the greatest stars, while military media extols their virtues. "Buy war bonds! Support the troops! Go see a film about the Allied Victory!"

Mixed between the two is the average citizen. Most of the young men are gone. Women have taken over a great many of the jobs those boys used to work. The Depression is over, but rationing is in effect. People still arrive in Los Angeles to pursue dreams of stardom, but the war creates very different stars. Names like Bazooka Joe and Rosie are right up there with John Wayne and Lauren Bacall.

Founded in 1880, USC is the oldest private research university in California. The campus is one place where the PCs do still see young men, though even here, they are fewer than they would be during peacetime. The campus is decorated with propaganda banners. "Join the Fight! Save Your Tin Cans! Nylon is for Parachutes Now, Boys!"

The professor the PCs are looking for is in the science department. Dr. Lance Pereau is a physicist specializing in plasma and plasma fields. He is in his office or the lab during non-classroom hours. The PCs won't have time to look in either of those places because, as they start asking for directions, they spy a man being shoved into the back of a Packard. At least one of the men doing the shoving is a *Blutkreuz* agent they have encountered previously.

The chase is on!

The team either has, or must acquire, a car. Once this is done, by whatever means necessary, they take off after the bad guys. The chase leads across the city and up through Chinatown, among the varied and strange architecture. Chinatown is both a real Chinese neighbourhood and a Disney version of China itself. After the boom in Chinese labour working the rails in the last century, Chinese immigrants learned that their culture was itself a means to take in tourist dollars. So, there is a great Chinese gate demarcating the entrance to the city. Many buildings ape this semi-realistic nod to China's dynastic past.

Pedestrians and food stalls get in the way of the barrelling automobiles. The players need to catch the Packard without killing Dr. Pereau. Any crash causes damage to all persons in the car. This is an age before seat belts.

BLUTKREUZ AGENTS (4)

Use stats for Spy on pp. 145-146 of ***Dust Adventures.***

For running the chase, see the rules on pp. 47-48 of ***Dust Adventures***.

Once the chase is over, the team should have Pereau in their possession. In a safe place, they can ask him questions. If requested, ASOCOM easily provides a safe house, in the form of a little bungalow. Pereau has done research into plasma fields. During the course of his studies, he came across the "squatting man" petroglyph. It resembled, to him, a particular plasma field as would be seen in the skies if something like a solar event occurred.

He is preparing a paper on the phenomena and is surprised ASOCOM even knows about it. ASOCOM is in everybody's business in 1947. Pereau isn't eager to help the PCs. He is actually a communist sympathizer. Even now, the wheels of the Red Scare begin to turn in the United States. In addition to other propaganda, newsreels, papers, and posters are beginning to rally Americans against communism.

Pereau himself is a Marxist, and disagrees with the Soviet approach to communism. He dismisses it as a "perversion of Marx's ideals with a side of totalitarianism." He

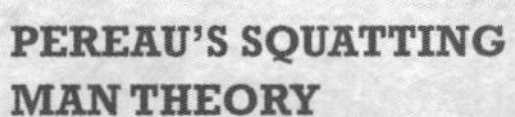

is not a huge fan of the United States government either, believing they have exceeded their mandate under the aegis of national security. There are many nuanced points to be argued. The pre-generated PCs are firmly on the side of Uncle Sam unless a player chose otherwise. They are, after all, in the army during wartime. However, outside characters might have all sorts of differing and conflicting philosophies.

This is a point the team may use to lean on Pereau. He is headed for big trouble as the anti-communist sentiment continues. Eventually, the War Department may out him. He cooperates fully if the team uses this leverage. See sidebar.

Pereau also has another story to tell. Three days ago, he received a strange visitor, Reginald Moore, the famous actor and director. Well, formerly famous. Reginald's stock in Hollywood has been slipping since the war. His *avant-garde* brand of directing has not set well with a wartime audience. His acting choices fall along similar lines. Thus, while John Wayne has rocketed to fame in war movies, Reginald has been left behind.

Moore is bitter about this. He also has a gambling and morphine problem. This led to his being recruited by the SSU as an asset. Moore meets all sorts of famous people in the limelight, and the SSU is always looking for anything that leads back to strong intel or a chance to embarrass and discredit an American war personality such as Bazooka Joe. Stalin's apparatus for propaganda is very proactive.

Moore visited Pereau asking about his squatting man theory at the behest of his handlers. Pereau thought it odd, but Moore passed it off as research for a science fiction picture. Pereau has no idea what Moore really wanted, but the man did mention some vaguely socialistic leanings.

The PCs have another lead to follow up.

THE LIMELIGHT

Reginald Moore is the team's next lead. He lives in the Hollywood Hills and hosts a party that very night. A few cops are present as security but not a major presence. The PCs can request backup from ASOCOM if they feel it necessary. ASOCOM prefers to remain under the radar, but a police raid could be arranged. The Los Angeles department is not the most corruption-free group in 1947. A little money could prompt an immediate raid without having to laboriously go through channels.

Moore is not the celebrity he once was, but his parties enjoy a certain reputation for decadence that Hollywood loves. The PCs may obtain his address via the FBI or by bribing a tabloid reporter. The party is invite-only, but the man at the door is not going to mess with active duty military personnel. The thousand-yard stare goes a long way.

Inside, the entire home is decorated in art deco style popular a decade ago. Booze and, if one looks around, dope are present. The PCs recognize various celebrities.

PEREAU'S SQUATTING MAN THEORY

Pereau's theory centres on the squatting man petroglyph recorded on rocks in hundreds of cultures in antiquity. He believes the appearance of this man in rock art stems from an actual phenomenon witnessed by pre-historic people. According to his research, the event probably took place sometime at the end of the last Ice Age.

The image of the squatting man is nearly identical to that of a plasma event know as a Z-pinch. The event could have been caused by a coronal mass ejection (CME) on the sun. It might also be caused by the detonation of a thermonuclear weapon in Earth's atmosphere. The shape produced looks strikingly like images of the squatting man. Pereau has not considered the possibility that a weapon was to blame, as he dismisses Vrill theories as "military cover for secret projects."

The PCs would need to bring up the possibility of a weapon for him to comment. Pereau also has the controversial idea that the Aurora Borealis may have been caused, or at least affected, by this same phenomenon approximately 12,000 years ago.

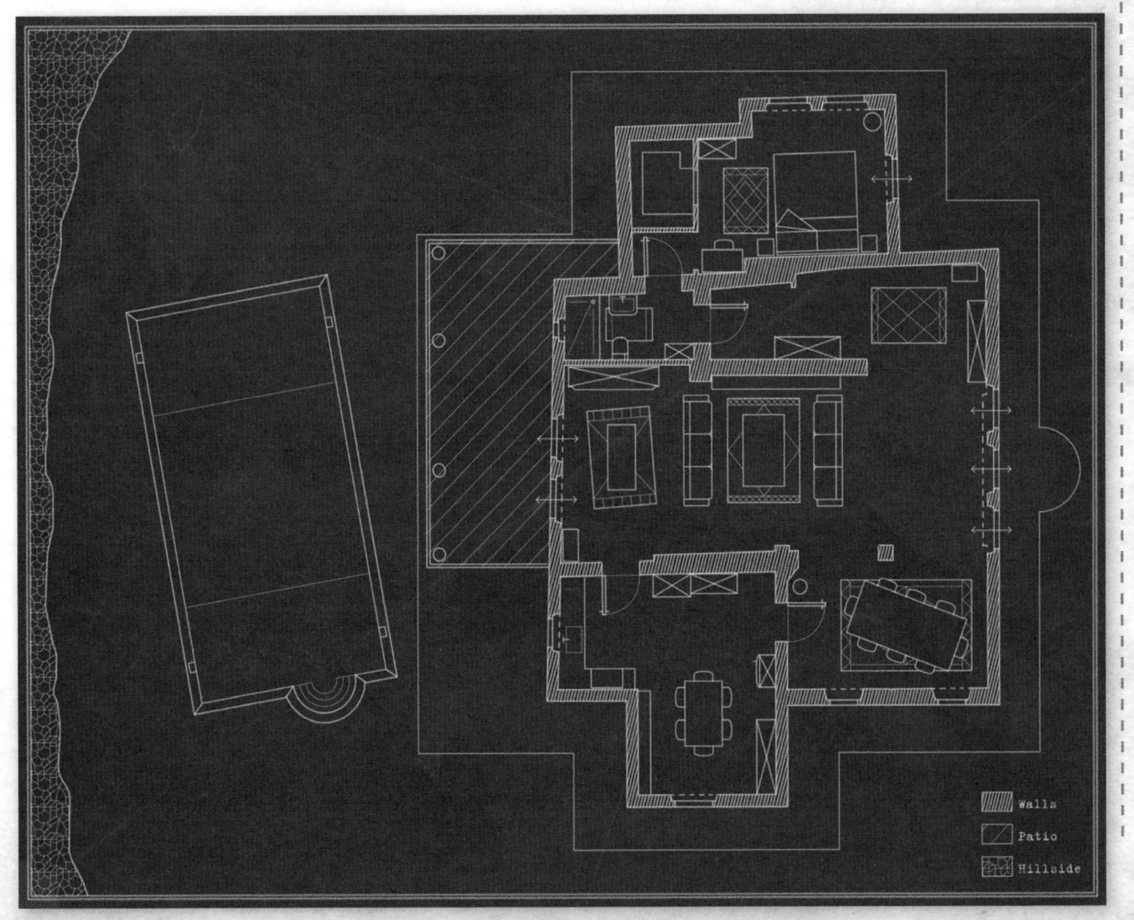

WHAT THE RUSSIANS KNOW
The Russian agents are working for SMERSH. Others, later in the adventure, work directly for Rasputin. These men operate under the direct order of the Kremlin. They know that the squatting man relates to the Vrill and that the Aurora Borealis is connected. They mention another mission involving former SSU officer Natalya Roerich, which also seems to be connected to the Aurora Borealis. This is a red herring. Natalya Roerich's adventure is detailed in the novel ***Dust of Atlantis***.

The main purpose of the Soviets' presence here was to confirm the theory that a plasma discharge, of the kind a powerful weapon would create, is what the squatting man depicts. They were then to proceed to the Alaska Territory to find old Tlingit legends regarding a sacred stone that fell to Earth.

From there, they were to proceed with determining if there was any link to the Secret City. GRU agents with the Red Army were supposed to brief them. The SSU clearly knows about the Seals but, if these Russians are to be believed, they have no idea what the Seals actually do.

When the PCs arrive, if there has not been a raid, they find two large men cornering Moore in a hallway leading to one of the bathrooms. They are Russian SSU agents. One has an accent; the other does not.

SSU AGENTS (2)

Use stats for Spy on pp. 145-146 of ***Dust Adventures.***

If spotted, the two men decide what to do based on how many of the team they have seen. This is up to the GM's discretion. If the Russians saw the whole team, they exit quickly. If they saw only one or two, they hold their ground. Moore looks very much out of his league.

The Russians are not looking for a fight, and following them is the better play here. They do everything they can to leave the party without attracting further attention. If the raid was launched, an asset in the LAPD tipped them off, and they are not present.

Should the PCs follow them, the Russians take a car from Moore's house to an old hotel on Sunset Boulevard. There, they use a pay phone and go inside. They share a single room. The one without the accent does all the talking for the pair at check-in.

If the team wishes to burgle their room, that is possible. The next morning, the agents head to Los Angeles Airport where they get on a plane bound for Seattle, Washington. In their room is a road map of Canada showing a highlighted route into the Alaska Territory. The point at which the Russians intend to cross the border is not marked.

In an ashtray on the desk by the window, the PCs find a partially burned scrap of paper with coordinates scrawled on it. Only a few are still legible. ASOCOM can help extrapolate using Alaska as a starting point. The coordinates lead to an area of the territory currently under fire by the SSU.

Capturing and interrogating one or both of the Russian agents proves difficult but possible. The GM determines how much "encouragement" the Russians require before spilling the beans.

With each of their leads in Los Angeles pursued to its end, the team heads north to Alaska and the Russian offensive there.

ALASKA

NORTH TO THE FUTURE

Alaska is not yet a state in 1947, but it is at war, at least along its west coast. The SSU launched an invasion of the territory that once belonged to Mother Russia herself. Heavy Marine resistance stymied initial gains. The lines fluctuate but, for the winter, have settled.

The PCs have been briefed prior to arrival in the territory. From whatever sources they have from the previous scene, along with Dr. Carter, the team determines the native Tlingit are the likeliest resource for information about the tablet as they hold a long oral history of a stone "which fell from heaven."

Anchorage is their starting point. The team is to meet with a Tlingit native who can guide them to one of the remote communities that still hold the oral traditions close.

They are warned that the Soviets may be present once certain invisible borders, drawn only on military maps, are crossed. There are SSU recon teams inside American held territory.

The Allies still control the vast majority of the Territory of Alaska, and getting in is easy given the PCs are working for ASOCOM and Clio. Their first stop is Anchorage.

ANCHORAGE

The largest town in Alaska is not very large. The entire state has a population smaller than many American cities. The weather is rough, and it is winter when the team arrives. Many of them fought in Zverograd and are used to such conditions. The front is far away from the city, but the citizens walk around armed. There is a tremendous anti-Communist movement in the city. Banners disparage Stalin and his state, while a captured Soviet tank sitting at the heart of a park has been re-painted red, white, and blue. The spirits of the citizens is upbeat, all things considered. The PCs are to meet their contact at a local bar balled The Brick House.

There, a man slightly older than most of the team sits in a booth. He has one leg stiffly held out as if it is arthritic. The Rangers recognize this as a war injury.

Ted Taneidi was in the Big Red One, but took shrapnel to his leg in North Africa. He is a member of the Taneidi Raven clan. He served his country, as he sees it, and has no regrets. He mentions his desire to move to a warmer climate because of the ache in his leg, but believes his grandfather would scalp him if he tried. Ted is fond of playing on movie stereotypes. Ted is something of an interlocutor between the traditional clans that do not wish to integrate with city folk, and those who already have. He takes the group in his 1920s Ford Model TT truck far north to a small outpost. From there, they take dog sleds into the frozen wastes.

He explains all this before they leave. The Tlingit they want to talk to are the elders of another Raven clan that shunned contact with "white aggressors." They are, according to Ted, a superstitious lot who produce something akin to precognition at times. "Told me I'd hurt my knee while in a desert six months before I even went to basic. Gave me a small sacred rock to ward off death. I guess it worked. Saw the Raven when I was laying there bleeding all over the sand we'd just taken back from the Fox." Erwin Rommel was known as The Desert Fox.

TLINGIT VILLAGE

Dominated by large totem poles with contorted faces looking out over the village, the Tlingit live in wooden homes and lodges. Smoke rises from several of the dwellings. Ted speaks to some of the villagers in his native tongue. They all eye you suspiciously.

In the largest lodge, against a massive carving flanked by two more totem poles, are several elders. You know they would have looked exactly the same if you had visited back in 1847. Their way of life has not changed. Their leathery skin, and the way their keen eyes track you, give you reason to think they may have been waiting all that time just for your arrival.

The patterns carved into the wood behind the elders, as well as on the totem poles, depict several anthropomorphic beings. Most prominently featured is the image of a raven. The elders, in their own tongue, speak about the raven and Ted translates.

"In the beginning, there was the sun, and it was good, but the dancing man came and distracted the sun so that the raven could steal it. So he did, taking the orb away and leaving the land in darkness for many years. The great waves crashed over us then, and we fled. It was a raven chick, who felt sorry for the people, that guided us through the darkness and back to the sun, which rested high in mother raven's nest. A warrior climbed the tall mountain to her nest and stole back the sun. When he placed it back in the sky, crops began to grow again, and the vast sheets of ice that covered the land melted away."

The PCs can question the elders through Ted. They know that, at some point in the remote past, the world went dark. A flood occurred which coincided with the appearance of what they call the dancing man in the sky. Their ancestors, prior to the plasma event in the heavens, were entrusted with a stone tablet that fell from the heavens.

Those who later warned them about the flood presented them with the tablet.

The Tlingit buried the stone because it made people sick, and they had lost the box in which they were supposed to contain it. Where they buried it, nothing would grow. No animals would walk near the place. The location of the burial sits below a site now occupied by a mysterious "false city." The elders do not know the purpose of this city. It is the Secret City, built by Majestic 12, of which they speak. See ***Dust Adventures*** pp. 127-128 for more details.

Ted convinces the elders that the PCs must see this city, but the elders are reluctant to allow this. A negotiation takes place to convince them. If the PCs are unable to convince the tribe or, if the GM wishes to play on the tensions between the natives and the American government, the PCs may have to call for military backup. That all depends on the GM's willingness to throw a moral quandary at the PCs.

THE SECRET CITY

A project contracted to Majestic 12, the Secret City was built to mimic Zverograd. The intent was to train the Allies prior to the invasion of that city. The city itself is located between Kurupa Lake and Cascade Lake in the North Slope region of the Alaska Territory. While neither lake is the Caspian Sea (upon which Zverograd sits), the two lakes allow for simulated amphibious assaults.

Also known as Labyrinth City, the Secret City is a twisting maze of tightly packed buildings that suddenly open into huge squares. While every effort was made to duplicate Zverograd itself, intelligence available was limited. Thus, while some sections look like exact copies of Zverograd, others have streets in the wrong places, statues facing the wrong direction, or entire streets flipped from west to east. After the Axis losses at Zverograd reached ASOCOM, it was decided that Allied troops would be better prepared for the fighting there.

An entire subterranean Metro system was dug out of the Alaskan earth to further train soldiers for the bloody fighting underground they would soon encounter. Yet the city itself is now a ghost town. There are no moving cars, though fake and abandoned vehicles are found here and there along the streets and there are no pedestrians or workers. It is as if an entire city has watched its population vanish overnight. A spooky place to be sure.

All of this intel can be obtained from ASOCOM. What they cannot get is the existence of a secret Majestic 12 facility hidden beneath the Metro. Hidden access ways lead inside from the Metro, however. The Tlingit do not know about the secret base as such, but they know massive excavating equipment was used even after the Metro was finished. This key clue should get the players thinking.

The facility beneath the Secret City itself was designed to test the inhuman subjects Majestic captured from the Axis, mostly gorillas and zombies. Both still roam the undercity. Some even come above ground at times. This is another reason the Tlingit no longer come here.

During their excavations for construction of the sub-city, Majestic 12 discovered the tablet the PCs seek. They stored it in the secret facility and began to study it. Unfortunately, the presence of the stone drove both the gorillas and the zombies wild, and the facility was overrun and then abandoned.

Since that time, the SSU has pushed further inland and captured the city. They have had no interest in it until now. They thought it a curiosity and immediately took its purpose to be purely for training. However, now that their agents have uncovered a connection between it and the missing stone, the SSU has dispatched teams to occupy the city. The PCs will need support from the Marines to take the city back.

Remember, most of the city is barren. The SSU only just captured the land surrounding the city. Their real goal is to cut off Allied oil supplies in this part of the territory. Only top-level SSU officers even know that the SSU dispatched a sizable occupation force to this fake Zverograd. The PCs are about to find themselves in a pitched battle for a pretend municipality. Many of them already served in Zverograd and this feels like reliving a nightmare inside some sort of twisted dream.

BATTLES IN THE SECRET CITY

Use the following rules for playing miniature battles in the Secret City using ***Dust Warfare*** or ***Dust Tactics/Dust Battlefield***.

DUST WARFARE

Warfare battles in the Secret City follow rules as normal battles using the Warfare Battle Builder (see Dust Warfare Core Rules, p. 65).

However, the Secret City suffers the following two special rules in Dust Warfare: Despite the deployment rules, the wind and weather play havoc with Air Drop and reserves. When bringing in reserves (from Scout Vehicle, Reserves, Air Drop or any other condition) roll a single die for that unit. On a HIT result, the unit cannot come on board that round and must wait until the next round to try again. If there is a hero in the unit, the die may be rerolled one time.

Regardless of the Condition determined by the battle builder, the scenario may also fall under the conditions of Cold Snap (Campaign Book Icarus, p. 50).

Before the initiative is rolled for the first turn of the battle, the player who placed the first Scenario Point rolls a single die. On a HIT result, the temperature has dropped and the conditions for Cold Snap are in effect for that turn.

In addition, when fighting in the Secret City, replace the Conditions column of the battle builder with the following entries:

CONDITIONS

It is a rare battle that takes place under optimal engagement parameters. Conditions represent some of the unique battlefield elements that can influence a fighting group's effectiveness. Regardless of the condition, all uses of *Wiederbellebungsserum* and similar *Blutkreuz* Zombie abilities are considered to fall under the rules for Second Generation Serum (see ***Dust Warfare Core Rules***, pp. 56 and 120 as well as ***Dust Warfare Icarus***, p. 24).

[0] NIGHT TERRORS

Labyrinth, Alaska is a creepy location. A dead city long ago abandoned by any sane residents or caretakers. Shadows move, lights flicker, and winds rip through the buildings creating an unnatural sound, like the moans and screams of the dead. Soldier units not led by heroes do not remove suppression during the End Phase. While heroes have a calming effect on their squads, when they roll to remove suppression when activated, they do so as if they had no hero in the squad. The Priest's special ability overrides this rule.

[1] WAKE THE DEAD

Units in buildings and forest terrain are not alone. Eyes stare at them from inside shadows and behind rocks. Whispers reach their ears, but as they turn, they see nothing behind them. Fear is in the very wind itself. Units with at least one miniature in a building structure or a forest/wood terrain feature do not remove suppression during the End Phase.

In addition, when a unit in a building structure or a forest/wood terrain feature is activated, roll three dice. Each hit scored results in the unit suffering a 1/1 C attack as mutated experiments from the failed Frankenstein Project assault them. If the unit does not activate in the turn, resolve the Wake the Dead roll during the end phase. This attack is considered to have happened prior to the unit being activated, so any suppression gained from this attack is added to the unit before it rolls to remove suppression. This attack ignores Cover but not armour.

[2] HELL STORM

Rain pours onto the streets as if the heavens were trying to wash the city from the earth. While enemy Soldiers can be seen, they cannot be targeted beyond 20". Vehicles may be targeted at up to 24" and Aircraft at High Altitude only at 16". Aircraft are likewise unable to target Soldier units beyond 16" if the Aircraft is at High Altitude. In addition, fog from the rain distorts reality, and its icy cold delays reactions. All Soldiers units of Armour 1 and Armour 2 are treated as if they have Assault (***Dust Warfare Core Rules***, p. 53). If the unit already has Assault then reactions may not be taken at the start or end of its movement if it Marches.

[3] EERIE CALM

The city is quiet; the weather is fair. While still creepy and cold, everyone is on edge and in awe of the Secret City. A unit may not be given an attack order in the Command Phase until it has been attacked in the Unit Phase. This effect is removed after the End Phase of Turn Three.

DUST TACTICS AND *BATTLEFIELD*

Battlefield and Tactics games are affected in a similar manner. Reserves are blocked on a Shield die roll, and the cold wind and snow has an effect similar to Sand Storms (see ***Dust Tactics Babylon***).

At the start of a battle taking place in the Secret City using Tactics or Battlefield, roll a single die.

[SHIELD] WAKE THE DEAD

Units in buildings and forest terrain are not alone. Eyes stare at them from within shadows and behind rocks. Whispers reach their ears, but as they turn, they see nothing behind. Fear swirls about in the wind. Units with at least one miniature in a building structure or a forest/wood terrain feature roll one less die to remove suppression when activated.

In addition, when a unit in a building structure or a forest/wood terrain feature is activated roll three dice. Each hit scored results in the unit suffering a 1/1 C attack as mutated experiments from the failed Frankenstein Project attack. This assault is considered to have happened prior to the unit being activated so any suppression gained from this attack is added to the unit before it rolls to remove suppression. This attack ignores Cover.

[TARGET] HELL STORM

Rain pours onto the city streets as if the heavens were trying to wash the city from the earth. While enemy Soldiers can be seen, it is hard to react to their movements, as one cannot determine what is really happening. All infantry units roll one less die when rolling for reactive attacks against infantry units.

[FACTION] EERIE CALM

The city is quiet; the weather is fair. While still creepy and cold, everyone is on edge and in awe of the Secret City. All infantry models that do not fly are more cautious and aware of their surroundings. Until the end of turn three, all infantry have their move rates reduced by 1 square (4" or 10cm) to a minimum of 1 square (4" or 10cm).

Axis players with Mindless Zombies also benefit from the unique circumstances of the Secret City. When a Mindless Zombie unit is activated, roll a single die, on a FACTION symbol the unit is treated as if it were within 1 square (4" or 10cm) of the *Blutkreuz* (see ***Dust Tactics***, p. 97).

TERRAIN

The Secret City is massive. Be sure to include many buildings and lots of rubble, statues, cars, and other terrain types that fit a city on the board.

The GM may choose to run this battle using the RPG rules. In that case, abstract the larger conflict in favour of focusing on the PCs.

THE MAJESTIC FACILITY

Once the battle is won, the Allies have control of the city—at least for now. Unfortunately, the SSU already penetrated the sub-city while the battle raged. It is entirely

possible the PCs elected to do the same, in which case the thunder of battle can be heard above. The Majestic facility is sprawling, and encounters with SSU troops, zombies, and gorillas occur.

The facility was clearly well built, but the time since its construction crews fled have left it in a sorry state. Trash and feculence litters the halls, and the continued presence of the stone created mutations among the gorillas and zombies alike. The secret base is a kind of old school dungeon crawling with monsters around every turn. Note, the PCs exposure to the stone is not long enough to cause such mutations. Of course, the GM doesn't have to tell them that.

While the streets above are a replica of Zverograd, the secret facility known as The Labyrinth is modelled on nothing that actually exists. It is not an actual maze, but it might as well be. The twisting corridors loop back on themselves, as it was initially designed to represent the Zverograd sewers and Metro. However, once Hughes got a hold of an Axis gorilla and zombie, he repurposed the tunnels to study them.

Coupled with the power of the Seal, Majestic has

managed to make significant steps in bioengineering here. The fruits of their labours would be their undoing though, and Majestic soon had to abandon the facility. Today, it is a nightmarish ecosystem populated by mutants. The PCs must fight through these to get to the Seal.

Many of the "human" mutants are still wearing military uniforms and lab coats. The apes have been spliced with human DNA to produce something that fits in neither species. Continual exposure to the Seal, as amplified by Hughes' team, has also degraded the mental capacity of these creatures. Once, they possessed intelligence, now they merely survive.

Rather than map out the entirety of the maze, the GM should roll six ***Dust*** dice each turn. Three or more matching faction symbols indicate a success. Three successes get the team to the machine the Seal is powering. Three Axis icons indicate an encounter with four gorillas. Three SSU icons indicate an encounter with five mutant ape-men. Characters with Navigation skills add a die per Rank to the party's dice pool for this test.

SECRET CITY APE-MEN

Characteristics

MB 3 **MD** 1 **PH** 3 **PR** 2

Movement 6 **Capacity** 5 **Initiative** 4

Skills: Athletics 3, Attack: Melee 2, Interaction: Intimidation 1

Special Abilities: None

Special Powers: None

Equipment

Unless otherwise noted, ape-men are armed with a variety of improvised weapons. These weapons are fragile and can break, but they can also be easily replaced. Some ape-men are more evolved and may use a variety of other weapons, including guns.

Weapon	Rng	Dam	Rank	Special
Improvised Weapon	C	2	0	None

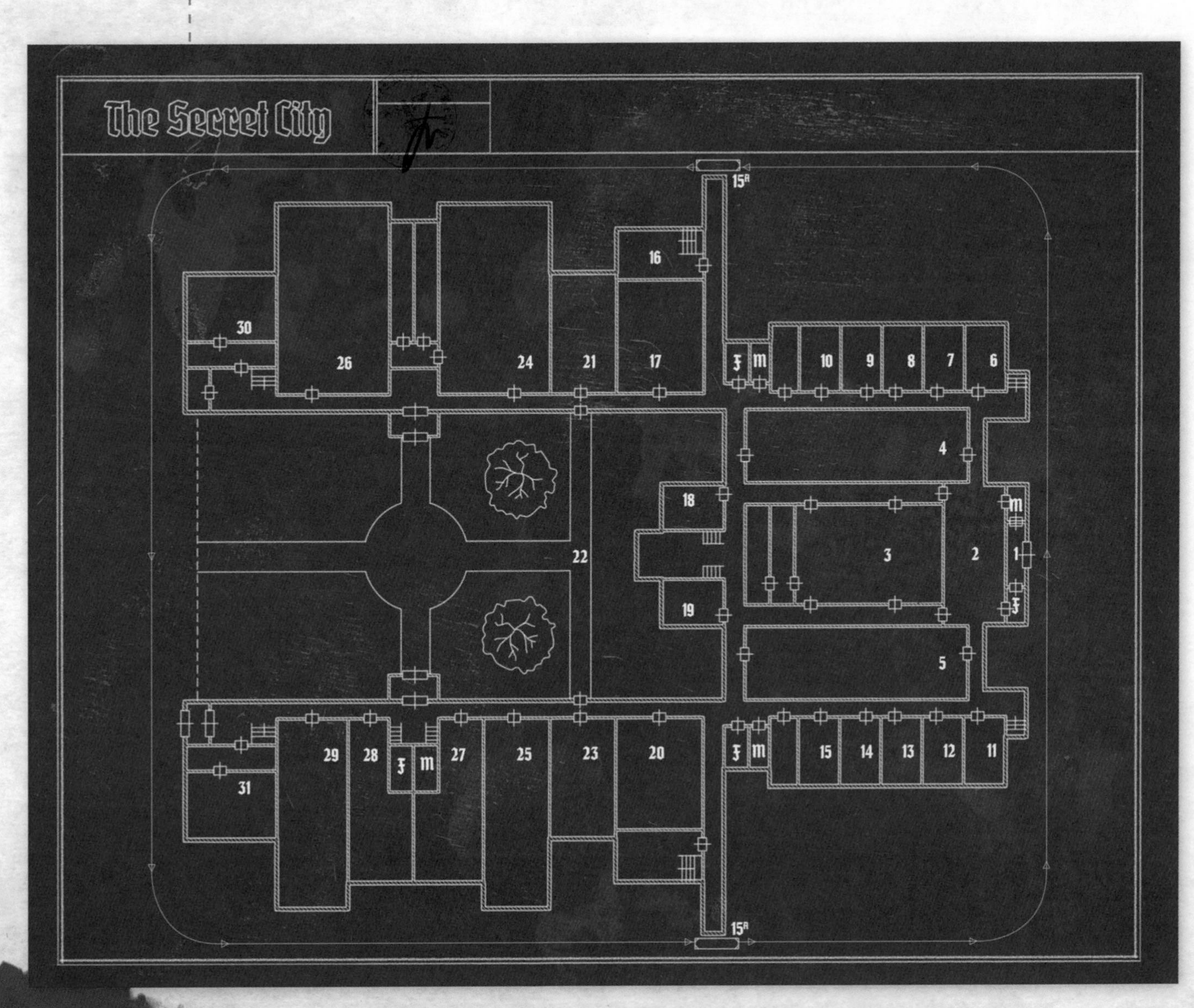

Notes

Ape-men armed with weapons other than improvised have the appropriate Attack skill at 1.

Once through the Labyrinth, the PCs arrive at the Majestic Facility designated SC-1. A map and key follow below.

SC-1 RESEARCH FACILITY

Whether the maze was designed to serve some practical function or it was developed out of the paranoia in Hughes' mind, the central research facility is, if possible, even more bizarre than the rest of the Secret City. The facility is permanently frozen at Christmas time, 1945. As the team makes their way through the facility, it is like exploring the dark corners of Hughes' psyche. People did not only work here; they lived here, and the idea of Hughes' "underground Utopia" is frightening to sane minds.

MAP KEY

1. DECONTAMINATION

The vault-like door on this once hermetically sealed room hangs open. Spatters of dried blood and bloody hand-prints make up a grim finger-painting across the walls. A cold body lies in the center of the floor. Two windows, webbed with cracks, are inset on the east and west walls. Showerheads hang from the ceiling. A very old and rust-coloured trail leads inward.

This was a decontamination chamber as evidenced by the windows and shower spigots. Hughes attempted to make sure none of what he was doing got out, and nothing from the outside got in. His paranoia was, for once, justified. Sadly, the decon airlock did not work. Things got in and things got out. Some of those "things" are still here.

The body is that of a scientist named Rodney Malcolm judging by his ID.

To either side are observation chambers and male and female toilets, respectively. In each toilet is a neatly pressed boiler suit that would have been worn once one went through decon. The scientist wears one under his lab coat.

The blood trail is from a soldier the mutant ape-men hunted and slaughtered for food some time ago.

2. ENTRANCE

You have entered the foyer to a very fine house. An aluminium Christmas tree, surrounded by gaily-wrapped presents, dominates a chessboard-tiled floor. Stairs sweep up, but lead nowhere, suggesting another level to this make-believe house. Instead of tinsel, frozen entrails gruesomely dangle from the tree.

This is Howard Hughes' version of the ideal post-war American home. Blood and other unidentifiable liquids have long-since dried on the walls and floor. A side table even has a set of keys for a non-existent car. Hallways branch left and right. If the PCs turn around and look at the wall they entered from, elaborate murals suggest a pleasant suburban neighbourhood that never was.

A punch key card lies on the floor. This is used to access the labs deeper in the facility.

3. YARD

A barbeque covered in snow, a doghouse with a grey mutt lying inside, his black nose protruding from the opening, and a swing set. This was a yard, or at least it was supposed to be something like one.

Everything here is fake, from the snow to the dog's nose. If the team looks inside the doghouse, they find a man's severed head.

4. LIVING ROOM

An empty fireplace would have once warmed this quaint sitting room. An old radio, nearly four feet tall, stands in a corner. You can imagine kids gathered around listening to Little Orphan Annie and Sky-King. Suddenly, you miss home very much. A window looks out on the frozen diorama vignette pretending to be a yard.

5. KITCHEN

In 1939, one of you had a brother that went to the World's Fair in New York. He brought back a postcard that showed "the kitchen of the future." This room looks a lot like that but, like everything else, nothing here actually functions. A pair of mullioned windows looks out on the cold, dead yard.

As the team takes in the kitchen, three ape-men attack from the south.

APE-MEN (3)

See stats above.

6-15. ROOMS/DORMITORIES

Continuing with the "opulent suburban home" theme, each of these dormitories is designed to look like a room, but all of them are children's rooms. Looking at the baseball gloves still smelling of lanolin, trophies, toy soldiers, dolls, and pink and blue beds, you imagine an idealized childhood Hughes never had.

SECRET CITY INTEL

Among the many files is useful information for the team. Most of the information relates to the "scientific" experiments conducted at this facility. These break down into two groups: documents understandable to a layman, and documents understandable only to an expert. Dr. Carter can decipher some of those, but remember she is an archaeologist.

The files collectively tell the background of the Secret City. Majestic 12 recovered "samples" of Axis Gorillas and Axis Zombies, and brought them here to attempt to modify them further. The results backfired, and the team was overwhelmed by their creations. Of course, all this is interesting but not what the PCs need.

The information vital to their mission also lies within the files. These detail a strange, radiating energy that appeared to be coming from underneath the forest. Whether by coincidence or Hughes' design, the facility was built over where the Tlingit buried the Seal long, long ago. Some scientific speculation suggests the Seal might have corrupted the DNA of the ape-men.

Hughes ordered the area excavated. The Seal was dug up, and was about to be shipped to Area 51, when the ape-men overran the facility. According to these documents, scientists were completing tests in Lab 4 just before the records cease. The

Seal is located there.

The science involved is very complex, but PCs with Knowledge: Science, understand some sort of genetic mixing went on. That mixing was then further polluted from exposure to the Seal.

Aside from these nostalgic bits of detritus, the rooms are unoccupied, though two contain long-dead bodies that were never used as food.

15 A. TRAM

This tram runs round the facility like a cable car would in a modern city. Apparently, Hughes wanted to give the impression of commuting to and from work. Given the size of the facility, it is a practical application of his demented illusion.

The tram still runs, if the PCs wish to try it, but it should break down in an area the PCs should see.

16. DINER

A Depression-era diner with a fresh coat of paint. Things are upbeat here. A jukebox control sits at every table. Clearly, Hughes had a vision for tomorrow. A door leads to the east toward what is presumably the kitchen.

The door swings on a hinge. In the kitchen is the horror of the ape-men's diet. Blood and flesh sit on a butcher's block. An oven and stove still radiate heat. The ape-men were here recently. At the back of the kitchen is a freezer. The players really do not want to look inside there. No, really!

17. CORNER BAR

You might have found this corner bar in your own neighbourhood. It is like so many in America. The stools, however, are all empty and the neon signs have long since gone dark. Somehow, the Christmas lights strung along the bar still wink in red, blue, and green.

As the team enters, they hear glasses breaking. Two of the ape-men, liquored up, are throwing shot glasses at each other in the back. When they see the PCs, they attack.

APE-MEN (2)

See stats above.

18. OFFICE

A secretary with a fashionable hairstyle ought to be sitting at one of the two reception desks in this wood-panelled office. The windows look out on elaborate murals depicting the New York skyline, with the addition of science fiction, ray gun-gothic buildings dwarfing even the Empire State Building. Offices with glass walls and wooden doors line the interior. File cabinets lay at the back.

Unlike other facilities, these offices were actually functional. The team can find intel here in the many files held in cabinets and scattered across the floor. Roll three dice each round the team searches. Three Faction Symbols indicate they find something of value. Three Targets indicate either ape-men stumble by, or the SSU arrives at the entrance. If the PCs left a guard at the airlock, he or she is about to earn their combat pay.

SSU SPETZNAZ (6)

From the bloody battle above, SMERSH dispatched these *Spetznaz* to uncover the secret below before the Americans. The ape-men do not distinguish between SSU and Allies. All are prey to them.

Use stats for *Spetznaz* on p. 153 of ***Dust Adventures.***

The *Spetznaz* are as well trained and hardened as the Rangers. This could be a difficult fight. Should the GM wish, the combat could take place in the "Forest" at 22.

19. CONFERENCE ROOM

A slide projector still functions in the middle of a large conference table. The image on the screen is that of a hulking, simian-looking soldier in an American Army uniform. A slogan fills the bottom: "Go Ape for America!" Cups stained with coffee lie in the positions their drinkers must have left them years ago.

If the players look through the other slides, they see a propaganda campaign designed to introduce Americans to the idea of ape-men hybrid soldiers. Obviously, the project never made it this far. Should the GM wish, another, secret project Majestic 12 was working on could also appear here. That project, and concomitant adventure, is left to the GM's imagination.

20. LIBRARY

Books litter the floor like a child threw a temper tantrum. Shelves are overturned and microfiche is strung from the ceiling like strips of meat left out to dry. No doubt there is a great deal of knowledge in this library, if anyone could now find a way to organize it.

Roll three dice. If two or more Targets appear, there are four ape-men here. If not, the PCs may explore the room. It is up to the GM if they find anything worthwhile. If the team is behind on the plot, this is a good device to deliver clues to steer them back on course. As in room 19, this is also a good place to drop clues for future adventures.

21. TERRACE

You have just stepped out into desert dusk, the sun slung low in the sky, cut in half by the horizon. The sounds of wind fill your ears, as do the noises of insects. However, there is no wind, no insects, nor even a sky. It's all looped audio recordings and a high-resolution projection against a wall opposite. Still, if you had to work down here for months at a time, this might be a welcome environment, if not a bit surreal and creepy.

After they take in the scene, a shadow blots out the sun like a solar eclipse. This shadow is no satellite, but an ape-man who was brachiating above. He attacks the people who disturbed his safe area.

APE-MAN (1)

See stats above.

22. THE PARK

It could have been cut by a giant razor right out of the picturesque center of any small town in America. This is a park. A central fountain is dusted with snow, trees have shed their leaves but are strung with Christmas lights, and a small pond is scarred with a matrix showing skater's paths along the ice. The room itself is huge, the sky fitted with bulbs representing stars. Bing Crosby's White Christmas plays quietly from unseen speakers. It would be a peaceful scene, if only those hulking shadows in the crepuscular light weren't rapidly moving toward you.

There are two ape-men for every player present. Half of those are armed with Thompson sub-machine guns. The other half wields rebar and other scavenged items as clubs.

Benches, trees, and the like provide some cover. The ape-men do not attack with any discipline. The PCs have to capitalize on that advantage.

APE-MEN (2 PER PC)

See stats above.

23. EVAC ROOM

A room with a round shaft leading up to the vanishing point above you. Scaffolding around the aperture suggests a vehicle was once mounted within. A control panel, now smashed, is in the corner. At one point, this must have been a quick route to the surface.

This was an evacuation room. The door coming in said so, but it is no longer readable. However, the shattered console is labelled. Whatever vehicle rocketed out of here left blast and scorch marks on the concrete floor. At least someone got out. There are rails in the shaft, which would have guided the escape vessel. They can be used along with rope, to climb back out. Alternatively, enemies from above, such as the *Spetznaz*, could infiltrate the facility from here.

24. GYM

A full gymnasium featuring rowing machines, free weights, and a half basketball court. The lights flicker on and off, casting the shadows of workout machines along the walls. Jump ropes and medicine balls are scattered about. You see no activity.

This room is otherwise empty.

25. LAB 1

NOTE: An access card is required for entry into this room.

Splayed open like a high school biology frog is an ape-man on an operating table. The room is ice cold and the body well preserved. Various medical devices are scattered across the floor.

The ape-man is dead, and the other ape-men fear this room.

26. POOL

The pool is a miniature vignette of an arctic sea—small chunks of ice float like bergs in the freezing water. Somewhere at the bottom appears to be a corpse.

The body is that of a scientist. He has a card for the labs. Getting to him is difficult. Anyone diving in must make a Physique test against a Difficulty of 3 or suffer 1 damage from hypothermia.

27. LAB 2

NOTE: An access card is required for entry into this room.

Complex vats nearly eight feet tall line the walls. Each is filled with a bright green liquid. Two contain what appear to be ape-men in some sort of suspended animation. Two others contain human beings. Tubes on top of each vat spider their way downwards toward a central hub. Attached to that hub is a control panel.

The humans are, upon close examination, zombies, but in well-preserved states. The ape-men are the last generation

created here. Waking any of them, and thus opening the vats, is a Knowledge: Science check at a Difficulty 2. Any so woken are drowsy and disoriented. Sedatives are found in a medicine cabinet pulled from the wall and left on the floor.

28. LAB 3

NOTE: An access card is required for entry into this room.

Petri dishes, and Erlenmeyer flasks, and beakers, oh my! This room is a mad scientist's playground, perhaps literally. A skein of tubes and the aforementioned containers wrap around the walls on sturdy tables. A large, stainless steel cooler lies at the end of the room. A chalkboard sits in the center of the room but has been erased of all equations. Instead, it merely says: "Help us."

This is where genetic samples were mixed and matched to create the ape-men, which now plague the site. ASOCOM would love to get their hands on some of these samples.

29. LAB 4

On a stainless steel table, under a still functioning halogen light, is the Seal. It is translucent, with a web work of tiny, gold wire veins inside. It is right there; nothing stopping you from taking it.

The above description serves to make players think there is some sort of trap. There is not. They may take the Seal and leave. Of course, any *Spetznaz* still in the facility take issue with this. More could arrive down the shaft in the Evac room if the GM wants to throw another encounter at the team. Like the other Seals, glyphs are laser etched on the surface. These are not readily translatable. The GM may select something suitably foreboding for a later translation.

30. TUNNEL X

Black and yellow danger stripes warn against entry to this area. Stencilled letters one foot high read, "Tunnel X." A rail, like that of a tram, is set into the concrete floor. The tunnel disappears into darkness far, far ahead.

If the players wondered where all the ape-men went, this is the answer. Far down the tunnel (over a kilometre) is a living facility that once housed the apes. If the PCs decide to explore the tunnel, they hear the whooping and shouts of ape-men the further they go. If they continue, do with them as you wish. The facility is not detailed here. It would require some heavy troops to get in and out of the ape-men's lair alive.

31. TUNNEL Y

Black and yellow danger stripes warn against entry to this area. Stencilled letters one foot high read, "Tunnel Y." A rail, like that of a tram, is set into the concrete floor. The tunnel disappears into darkness far, far ahead.

This tunnel is identical to Tunnel X except that it eventually leads to where the zombies "lived." If the PCs travel down this tunnel, they come to a severed arm gnawed to the bone—clear evidence of zombies. If they keep going, throw a small horde at them.

If they persist, they may wind up dead themselves.

WRAPPING UP THE SECRET CITY

Hopefully the PCs have the Seal in their possession. The SSU now knows of their involvement, if they did not previously. The GM may wish to drop Novikova's name to build up to her later introduction.

The Seal begins to sicken those around it as the other six do. Obtaining the Seal successfully concludes the objective for this episode.

GETTING OUT

The PCs may have marked their way through the Labyrinth as they went, but if they got lost at any point, such markings might prove more harmful than useful. Repeat the same dicing process to get out of the mazes but add a die for having left marks if the GM desires. Once outside, the team must contend with any remnants of the enemy not previously dealt with. Getting back to friendly lines ends the episode.

WRAPPING UP

The team has won the next tablet. It is larger than the others previously found. It also appears to be powered within by some sort of crystal that is not VK. No one has any idea what this is. The stone is taken back to the Octagon for study. While the PCs were exploring the Labyrinth below the Secret City, Marines captured many SSU troops. One of them talked.

It seems that this officer was unhappy about his command being overridden by SMERSH. His troops were ordered to this "worthless fakery of Zverograd." He knows that it relates to an operation in Brazil. He gives up a single name, Colonel Ursula Novikova. ASOCOM confirms that SSU agents are fomenting rebellion in Rio de Janeiro. An intercepted communication from SSU agents there indicates another Seal may be located somewhere on that continent.

The PCs' next stop is South America.

I began with Clio not long after my country entered the war in 1941. My father's reputation, as well as my budding own, garnered me influence and Above Top Secret clearance. I expected many things would reveal themselves to me. I suspected battle plans and secret weapons. Instead, I learned that we are not alone in the universe. The Vrill, they almost seem common to me now, six short years later. Father, dad, I wish you were still here to read this, to advise me.

Following the discovery of the "squatting man" petroglyph in the Grand Canyon, the Rangers and I took a train to Clovis, New Mexico. Dr. Schliemann, your old mentor, found the same petroglyph at a site in Clovis. I was excited. I could feel the wellspring of history waiting to open before me. Oh, dad, it was exhilarating. Then the assassins showed up.

I cannot believe I typed that sentence. Never could I have imagined my life taking such turns. One of the Rangers saved my life. I believe he fancies me. I suppose if I were a typical, obsequious woman, I would be flattered. Perhaps, I am at that. Just between you and me, dad, all right? I keep up the cold fa□ade you taught me I'd need as a woman in the academic world, but tonight I cried when I was alone. I cannot honestly say I am cut out for this.

An archaeologist in Clovis told me she saw someone who, upon her description, reminded me of you. He, too, was seeking the squatting man glyphs and, for a moment, I imagined you might still be alive. It was a nice moment. She is Zuni, and her people have an oral tradition of "sky beings" who bestowed the ways of civilization upon her people. These same sky beings warred with another race from the heavens. The squatting man, she says, is a recording of that war.

A nice story, but according to ASOCOM scientists, it matches a certain kind of plasma wave. The Rangers and I next headed to Los Angeles, where a scientist first put forth this theory. Blutkreuz tried to grab him before us. Again, I grudgingly admit, the soldiers came in handy. The scientist thinks a powerful weapon might cause the plasma field, which would have been visible in many parts of the world. Maybe the Zuni people's mythology is more than just a story?

From Los Angeles, and a movie actor turned SSU spy, we went north to Alaska. The Native Tlingit have an oral tradition about a stone that fell from heaven. The location, they said, was under a secret base – a base built by Majestic 12. Horrible experiments took place there. I never thought we, I mean the Allies, the good guys, right? I never thought we'd experiment on our own soldiers. It was horrible dad, but we retrieved the next seal. I feel so small in the face of this wall of history. I thought it was a wellspring, but it may turn out to be an abyss.

CHAPTER 4: REVOLUTION

HOWARD HASKEL
Born in Michigan in 1911, Howard Haskel has been with the OSS/ASOCOM since the beginning of the war. Prior to that, he was a "diplomat." His specialty is Brazil and, more broadly, South America. Prior to the war, he was working with other Allies for the U.S. Now, he spends a lot of his time tangling with the SSU and tracking Nazis gone missing under Odessa. Most of these, he confides, find their way to Argentina. The PCs are going to meet some down the line.

Haskel is gregarious and carefree. This attitude probably keeps him sane in a country that is rapidly falling apart.

Following the clues found in the previous episode, the Rangers find themselves en route to Brazil. The heat and crowded streets of Rio serve as stark contrast to the cold wilds of Alaska.

BRAZIL

The history of Brazil stretches back some 11,000 years to the oldest human remains found in the Americas. Since that time, it has gone from a series of indigenous tribes, to a Portuguese colony, to an independent state. Getúlio Vargas has been Brazil's leader since the 1930s. Currently, he rules an authoritarian regime that is unpopular with many.

This unpopularity gave the SSU cause to believe a revolution in the cities might lead to a communist conversion. That would be quite the coup for the SSU. Agent provocateurs, propaganda experts, and soldiers are backing a pro-communist revolt against Vargas. The

situation the PCs find when they land in Rio de Janeiro is calamitous. Riots explode on the streets, neighbourhoods burn, and Allied walkers, modified for police duty, attempt to control the crowds.

The Allies who, in one of many "deals with the devil," supported this brutal, oppressive regime out of expediency, back Vargas. While ASOCOM has advisors, spies, and even a limited number of troops stationed here, the loss of continental Europe, and now much of England, is the Allies' chief priority. Things have gotten out of hand very quickly in Brazil since the eyes of ASOCOM have been elsewhere.

SAFE HOUSE

The PCs land with their plane under fire from SSU-backed rebels in the tree line.

Mortars tear chunks out of the tarmac as the chatter of SSU machine gun fire sweeps down from the tree line. You run to the waiting jeep and pile in. Your driver, wearing a jungle print shirt over fatigue pants, is less than phased. "Commies, what can you do, right?" He smiles, shifting a cigarette between his teeth.

Once away from the airport, the PCs catch their breath. The man driving, Howard Haskel, wears no rank insignia. The PCs may assume he is an ASOCOM agent. He shares the current state of the country, as described above, with the team as he drives them into town. The safe house is located downtown, or what is known as the *Zona Central*. Haskel takes a circuitous route because burning cars and other improvised barriers block several roads.

They stop at a high-rise hotel just blocks away from the American Embassy, now under siege. The PCs can intervene if they wish, but their mission does not involve the embassy.

Once in the safe house, the PCs can get the scoop on Colonel Ursula Novikova. Haskel tells them she is a Colonel in the Soviet Army who transferred to SMERSH two years ago. She has spying and combat experience. According to what Haskel knows, her loyalty is to Rasputin not Stalin.

One of Haskel's assets photographed her in the *favelas* less than 48 hours ago. She is blonde, tall, and striking. "Something to write home about, huh, boys?"

What she was doing in the *favelas* is beyond him. She is not, to the best of his knowledge, involved in the revolution but is here on business for Rasputin. Haskel intercepted a message sent to her at a local telegram office and decoded it.

"Find the Sun Disc. Proceed to El Dorado. Retrieve the Seal." Haskel has no idea what it means other than the legend of El Dorado.

An offer to take the PCs to the poor *favelas* is interrupted by one of Haskel's local assets shouting from the window.

Looking out, one sees a mass of people about to storm the "safe house." It seems the crowd has been informed of the Allied presence here. Since the Allies support Vargas, the crowd is angry. The PCs need to get out quickly. Unfortunately, the crowd below prevents them from exiting at street level. The roof is their only way out.

Haskel and his associates set fire to all the documents in the apartment and follow the PCs out afterward.

ON THE ROOF

From this vantage point, the characters spot a telegraph wire they can use as a zip line to a roof across the street. From there, they can make their way down to street level and run. However, there is a chance the crowd could spot them, and they have no transportation if they do.

Stealth checks at Difficulty 2 get them to the ground safely. The GM should decide if the crowd notices people three stories above or not. Most people are focused on storming the safe house after all.

If anyone is spotted, best make it Haskel and his men. This isn't a glorious way for a spy to go out, but glory and war are only partners in propaganda, not on the field. The PCs can do little to help Haskel as the crowd swarms around him and beats him to death. The same goes for anyone with him.

ALONE IN RIO

The PCs are once again on their own. Dr. Carter is winded from the run and clearly afraid. The city is bubbling over, and it's hard to say where friendlies might be located. As the team thinks about what to do, keep them moving using the rioting crowds and firefighters between Vargas' men and the SSU backed guerrillas.

Eventually, they are going to either try to find friendly lines or make for the *favelas*. Friendly lines are at the embassy, but that is being overrun. Where other Allied advisors are inside the city is unknown. If the PCs have no idea how to proceed, Dr. Carter has a colleague who lives in the city. She remembers his address, as she has a photographic memory.

The PCs can make their way there.

FUNES

Ireneo Funes is an archaeologist from Argentina currently living in Brazil and working for a government museum. He is a friend of Dr. Carter's and, quite possibly, the PCs saviour in this scene. With the city in tumult, and nowhere to go, Funes home is a welcome redoubt.

He lives in a modest residential neighbourhood in *Zona Norte*.

EL DORADO

Sometimes dismissed as a mistranslation, El Dorado technically means "the golden man." Kings of the Muisca of Columbia used to dip themselves in gold and ritually bathe in a sacred lake. Over the years, this idea became conflated with a city of gold.

Whether one calls it El Dorado or something else, lost cities have populated the imaginations of Westerners since the conquistadors first arrived in the Americas. Francisco de Orellana and Gonzalo Pizzaro (the younger brother of him who destroyed the Incas) sought the legendary city. Records state they did not find it. In any case, a series of fortune hunters has likewise sought the lost city and its riches. To date, no one has found it.

The El Dorado referred to in the telegram addressed to Novikova is, in fact, a city with much gold. While the buildings are not gold, the temple at the centre is. This is because it is powered by one of the Seven Seals. The gold keeps the radiation inside and crystals focus the energy. At one time, it powered a great machine, though it has long since ceased to function.

The El Dorado the PCs seek is located in the Amazonian jungles of Bolivia.

FAVELAS
Some 1,000 shantytowns, or *favelas*, exist in Rio. They are crowded, poorly built and semi-lawless. The largest among them cling to the hills flanking the city. Poverty, as Americans know it, is different than *favela* living. PCs will note these places have more in common with Hoovervilles than any ghettos found in American cities.

Funes is a man in his mid 60s. He is trim, prone to wearing a Panama hat and a tie. He knew Dr. Carter's father and expresses his condolences. "You have become your own woman since I last saw you, Jessa." He always calls her by her first name.

Funes is a more typical academic than Carter or her father. He does not believe in the nonsense that Clio is on about. History, for Funes, is very much written. There are only small pieces yet to be worked out.

He discourages Carter and the team from pursuing Novikova or El Dorado any further. The jungles are dangerous and the SSU is not fooling around.

Among the rumours he does know to be true, is the Nazi presence in his homeland of Argentina. "Dreadful people, and not uncommon to see them walking around." He dislikes them, but does not have the hate for them that their enemies have earned. He is more interested in making sure they do not seize control of his homeland.

Funes agrees to take the team to the *bruja* woman in the Rochina *favela*. He is not happy about it but, like her father, he knows better than to try stopping a Carter when their mind is made up.

ROCHINA

Corrugated iron roofs top makeshift dwellings steeped in a wave against the blue sky behind them. This hill favela boggles the eye, more like a growth than anything planned by men. Some 50,000 live here in abject poverty. The sweat, cooking oils, and stench of garbage overpower you as you approach.

This is not a place to wander aimlessly. The tension is palpable in the air. Many of the poor feel slighted or even oppressed by Vargas. Soviet flags hang outside many residences, but the police are on patrol. Big, blue riot-walkers stomp down the narrow streets. The *favela* is not in riot, at least not yet, but the authorities are prepared.

This is not an area where the team wants to openly wear their armour and uniforms. They stand out as Americans, but not unduly so. Carrying around assault rifles and the like will get them in trouble with both the locals and the police.

The *bruja* lives in one of the squalid shanties that make up the complex labyrinth of Rochina. Inside, she lives alone, a mangy cat her only companion. The small one room home smells of spices and incense. When Funes speaks with her, he does so in a language older than the Portuguese colonization.

They reach some sort of arrangement and Funes asks Carter for money. Once she hands this over, the *bruja* slips it under a sugar skull on a nightstand. She then takes a bottle of rum and several grass reeds. She swigs the rum but does not swallow it. Instead, she spits it in a mist over each of the team member's faces. She then whacks each with a fistful of the reeds and says a prayer in her native dialect.

As she does this, her bare, brown feet slap the cold tile floor. A kind of dance begins, and she forms the team into a circle then dances round them three times. She addresses the team in her own language. Funes translates.

"She says you have bad spirits bound to you. Blood is on your hands. Much more blood will find you before your quest is over. You seek El Dorado, or you think you do. Soon, you will understand its secrets but at great cost. Go then. I will give you a stone that shows you the way to what you seek. Take it and be gone."

With that, she hands them a small crystal tucked in a gold plated box. The rock is hewn with a few indecipherable sigils upon it. As the PCs hold it, they gradually feel nauseous. The stone glows very faintly when pointed toward Peru.

The PCs can ask whatever else they want, but the woman refuses to answer anything more. The money she demanded appears to be just enough to cover the box. If the team asks Funes why she helped, he shrugs. *"She has her own ways. There are things that are supposed to be in her world, and she facilitates those things."*

AMBUSH

Once the PCs leave the *bruja's* home, Novikova and her men tail them. The group moves in a practiced way, employing locals to help follow the team and alternating between these locals. The routine is protocol. It is now night, for the *bruja* only performs that ceremony near midnight. The PCs witness a flurry of activity in the *favela*.

Men and women alike come out of their homes. They are armed with sticks, rocks, pipes, and simple firearms. The crowd flows toward Rio, more and more joining like a flood intent on deluging the city. The crowd is organized, and leaders appear here and there, barking orders. Among the crowd, the PCs see a couple of houses explode from the inside as SSU walkers rise up ready for battle. Some of the citizens, now that the team looks, are clearly Russian, *Spetznaz* out of uniform.

As all this happens, Novikova springs her trap. When the PCs are making their way through one of the narrow alleys the *favela* calls streets, they find themselves cut off. SSU agents are covering each exit. They want the stone. Novikova suspected the old woman was lying regarding El Dorado. However, she could not force the woman to talk given her standing in the community.

SSU SPETZNAZ (6)

Use stats for *Spetznaz* on p. 153 of ***Dust Adventures.***

The fight is designed to go against the players. This should spur them to run. Their only option is to take to the roofs. Thus begins a foot chase over the uneven, and sometimes fragile, roofs of Rochina.

Every round, each player rolls four ***Dust*** dice. If the result shows three Faction symbols, the PC steps onto a weak spot on a roof and falls through. It takes another round to recover. Use the normal chase rules found in ***Dust Adventures.***

If Novikova recovers the stone, the PCs need to find another way to El Dorado. In this case, Funes is able to help them. After all, if the PCs cannot reach El Dorado, this episode ends rather anti-climatically.

If Novikova fails to get the stone, Funes turns traitor. He puts a tracking device in one of the PCs rucksacks or otherwise hides it on their belongings. Only if the team looks for such an item is it found. In this case, Funes has been bought by the Russians not through money, but through an assurance that they very much want to eradicate the Nazis in Argentina. With Funes' help, they promise to do so. The Russians are not lying. Stalin has not forgotten Hitler's betrayal, and the Russian people have not forgotten what the Nazis did to them. They want revenge.

Once the chase is concluded, the team witnesses a battle mounting between Vargas' forces and the mob. The mob is backed with Soviet walkers and *Spetznaz* troops. As the two sides tangle, Soviet paratroopers dive out of planes and glide to the hills surrounding the city. The Soviets have been planning this for some time.

Back at Funes' place, he has either already put a tracking device on the PCs or does so now.

He wishes them well. In his deal with Novikova, it is specified that Dr. Carter not be injured and be given safe passage out of Brazil. They do not harm her, but they do not let her leave on her own either.

The team needs to make haste getting out of the city, as SSU troops quickly block off the roads. That is one of the paratrooper's objectives. Once free of the city, they can make their way to Peru, where the stone leads them to the *bruja's* granddaughter, Louisa. It is up to the GM whether SSU troops are encountered along the road to Cuzco. They are not expecting trouble, but an authoritarian regime does like to control its roads.

Once inside Cuzco, the team sticks out to some degree. While there are other Americans and Europeans here, all carry special identification papers issued by the SSU. Thus far, only those deemed "dangerous" have been rounded up.

GETTING TO PERU

Peru is currently part of the SSU following a revolution and the arrival of SSU troops. As Americans, the PCs cannot simply fly into Cuzco, where they are headed first. ASOCOM can provide fake passports, but the team is not liable to hold up to scrutiny. The best option is to cross over via the jungles on the Brazil/Peru border. ASOCOM has assets that can smuggle them across this way.

From there, they make their way to Cuzco.

CUZCO

Cuzco was the Incan capital city before the arrival of Francisco Pizzaro in 1532. Pizarro and his men witnessed the ritual of Incan Kings covered in gold dust riding a barge to the centre of Lake Titicaca. They were well aware of the vast wealth the Inca had. A meeting was arranged in a central plaza inside Cuzco. There, the Spaniards ambushed the Inca and killed them. They captured the leader, Atahualpa, who rode into the plaza on a golden litter.

Pizarro ransomed Atahualpa for gold. From every corner of the empire, gold poured in, but it was not enough for Pizarro. He strangled Atahualpa rather than releasing him. The Incans knew the Spaniards wanted all of their gold and hid much of it in the city called Paititi, or El Dorado.

El Dorado translates as the "golden man," not a city of gold. However, a city of gold called Paititi has long been thought to exist somewhere in the Purina Amazon. In this adventure, the city is real.

Right now, the PCs need to find the location of the city. Inside the Quirikancha—the courtyard of The Temple of the Sun—the PCs meet the *bruja's* granddaughter. Once they display the fragment of the strange crystal, Louisa recognizes them. The stone glows brightly when they approach her as she wears a similar stone around her neck. It also glows. Of course, she is not the only one waiting for them.

The *Ahnenerbe* is here as well.

IRENEO FUNES

An Argentinean, Funes moved to Rio over a decade ago when he was brought aboard the national museum. He is knowledgeable about pre-Columbian civilizations and steeped in the legends of El Dorado. He does not buy into these legends, however.

Funes has actually met Colonel Novikova. She visited him not long ago—a few days—asking about El Dorado. He disappointed her by giving her his honest opinion that the city is but a legend. She insisted it was not, and produced several intriguing pieces he could not identify as belonging to any known pre-Columbian culture.

Funes advised her to seek a woman in the Rochina *favela*, a shaman, or *bruja*, who might know of such things.

Funes may betray the party later, for what he sees as the greater good.

THE *AHNENERBE*

Since the fall of the Nazi regime and the death of Adolph Hitler, the *Ahnenerbe* has sought a way back to power. Among their unique acquisitions is the original interview recording with the alien, Kvasir. From him, the Nazis learned of the Seven Seals. In fact, they were the first to learn of them, but they lost power before any could be recovered.

Operation Odessa moved many loyal Nazis to South America, particularly Argentina. There, they have continued research and experiments, but have been hampered by a lack of VK. Part of the VK they do have is used to create the *Ubermensch*, a fearsome Teutonic warrior dreamt of early on even before the war. He is the Aryan ideal. The *Ahnenerbe* has a limited supply of them. The *Ubermensch* they possess reminds the PCs of the monstrosity they found in Angers Castle in France.

The *Ahnenerbe* have two of these warriors with them.

Because the Nazis have been in South America for some time, they are well positioned to intercept the PCs once they learn that ASOCOM believes El Dorado is real. How they discovered this is unknown, but a mole may be involved. Not every Nazi who fled the Axis came to South America. Some were recruited by the United States and work for ASOCOM as part of a project known as Operation: Paperclip.

Colonel Heinz Lohse, a thoroughly despicable creature, leads the *Ahnenerbe* in this mission. Colonel Lohse is an ideologue. He believes in the Aryan race, World Ice Theory, Atlantis and Ultima Thule. He is convinced the German peoples' destiny is to unite the Earth and fight off the Vrill when they return. To do so, he believes the Nazis must seek the help of the Anunnaki.

LOUISA

Louisa traces her ancestry back to the Incans. The *bruja* is her grandmother who taught her some of the *bruja* ways. When she sees the crystal, she recognizes it from her grandmother's things. Her grandmother came to her in a dream—so she claims—and told her to come to Qurikancha to meet these white men who might redress what previous white men had done before them centuries before. *"The white man will defeat the white man, and all of them will die. Then we will inherit our homes again and rise as the empires we once knew."* Her grandmother made her memorize this.

Louisa is less impassioned about this than her grandmother, for she has less faith in the old ways than the *bruja* does. While Louisa has a very vague and limited clairvoyance, she believes her people are slated to become victims of the European's war. Already, communists have seized power in Peru.

Louisa consults at the Cuzco museum. She is an expert in Incan history, and has therefore encountered the SSU agents in Cuzco and knows they have already mounted an expedition to find Paititi. If the PCs want a chance to stop them, they need to move fast.

Louisa explains that the walls of this building used to be sheathed in gold plate. Pizarro took it all along with much more. Louisa also answers any questions the PCs have, if she is able. She believes in Paititi, but does not believe in aliens should that come up.

While she explains the gold plated walls and the capture of Atahualpa, the *Ahnenerbe* observe. The building is mostly full of tourists, but they are beginning to clear out. The PCs therefore have a decent chance of spotting their watchers. A bonus die to any relevant checks is granted once the building begins to empty.

If they are seen, the *Ahnenerbe* may realize their cover is blown. If they are not spotted, they wait for the meeting to end and follow Louisa and the players back to her apartment. There, she says she will show them the way to Paititi as recounted by a Spanish monk in the 16th century. She has surreptitiously taken the manuscript from the dusty files of the museum. A European archaeologist, studying it prior to the war, brought it to light when he found a similar account in the Vatican archives.

LOUISA'S APARTMENT

Louisa invites the team back to her place to show them the document. On the way there, they have a chance of noticing the *Ahnenerbe* following them. If so, they can try to lose them, but the *Ahnenerbe* has sent former Gestapo. They are very adept at tailing someone and work in singles and pairs. The Difficulty is therefore 3.

If it becomes clear to the Nazis that the team has made them on the streets, they make their move in the most secluded place possible, likely an alley. If the Nazis are not spotted, the team makes it back to the apartment unassailed.

There, Louisa pulls the fragile leather-bound book down from a shelf. She has kept it here, casually, as if the great powers of the world are not after its contents. She opens the book and reads in Spanish that she then begins to translate (see opposite).

AHENENRBE (3)

Use stats for Axis Grenadiers on p. 144 of ***Dust Adventures.***

UBERMENSCH (2)

Use stats on p. 194 of ***Dust Adventures.***

The Nazis' goal is to grab Louisa or the book. They are not interested in the characters themselves, though they will dispatch them if they get in the way. Because this is SSU territory, the Nazis have less intel than they would in Argentina. They only know about the meeting between the characters and someone important, because they have assets in *Blutkreuz*. *Blutkreuz* itself has already found a way to Paititi.

The Nazis do not want to be captured by the SSU. If a firefight breaks out in the apartment, local authorities arrive within five turns. The Nazis escape before that with or without the book or Louisa. They already have an ace in the hole, which is not revealed until the endgame plays out.

Once the *Ahnenerbe* threat has been dealt with, Louisa and the PCs should also leave the area. Police involvement inevitably brings the SSU. Louisa shows the PCs the diary and the map. She believes, based on elements of the monk's account, that she knows the location of Paititi.

Their next trek leads them deep into the jungles of Peru.

THE PERUVIAN JUNGLES

The jungles of Peru are part of the Amazon Rainforest. They are deep, largely unexplored, and dangerous. Venomous snakes and unfriendly native tribes both lurk within. Navigation is extremely difficult but, as Rangers, the team has been trained in jungle warfare.

Prior to their excursion, Dr. Carter consulted some maps and drew a map of her own to the city based on those.

Day upon relenting day cause you to shed sweat by the pint. The jungle is hot. Insects and birds call out between the trees and deadly snakes hang from thick branches. You've seen no other human or even evidence of human passage. Your armour is heavy, even carrying it on your back does little to help against the heat. You are fatigued beyond words. Only the songs you learned in training buoy your spirits. Rangers lead the way, but maybe that's the way to hell.

Sticky, hot, and swarming with mosquitoes, these jungles are as bad as any encountered on Pacific Islands. Dr. Carter keeps up, but she is not as used to marching in these conditions as the team is.

A native tribe, long-descended from the Incans who originally protected Paititi, picks up the characters' trail. They are very stealthy, and the GM should allude to the feeling of eyes on the party, but when they go to check, they find nothing. Not a footprint, nor a broken stalk of grass. It is spooky. Difficulty 4 to spot these natives.

The tribe does not interfere with the team at this point. They have already tried to prevent the SSU from taking Paititi, and were slaughtered by the SSU's superior firepower. This time, the tribe is watching closely. They are not fools. While they are isolated, a few of them do travel to the cities and know of the war. Those members know the Allies are the least of the three evils. The leader of this group is such a man. He may decide to approach the team before they reach Paititi.

APRIL 1, 1533
We are deep into the jungle. Surely, Eden itself could not be so hot, and yet I hear tales of a tree of life and twins who survived a flood. I am reminded of Noah, and the stories of our own Christian Bible. These people have no written language. They pass their stories down one from another, generation to the next.

Pizarro thinks them barbarians, but I see they are more than that. There is a deep wisdom in their eyes. They are heathens, certainly, but has not God fashioned them as such?

APRIL 2, 1533
I have come to know these men. They wear such strange plumage. They say things no European has heard before. Our translator is weak and sickly. He has taken on the illness that we have brought with us from Spain. These people are vulnerable to it. If Pizarro does not wipe them out with his cannons, God will see that our diseases do. This is the way of the Lord. Christ died on the cross for our sins. Whose sins do these people die for?

Tonight around the fire they spoke of something. I do not know what. Gestures and rough-hewn attempts at communication indicate they will show me something. I hear the words "Paititi" and "El Dorado." This is what Pizarro is after, and they are leading me to it. Perhaps they are barbarians after all.

APRIL 6, 1533
There are no words for this day. These folk did not build this place. This place... I have not even mentioned it. Today we came upon a miracle. We came upon such a thing as has not been seen since miracles walked the world routinely. This is more than the Tower of Babel; this is more than Eden itself. This is a city made of gold. Each building is plated in glistening gold. The sun skips off these priceless walls and drips to the streets below.

They brought me inside the central pyramid. It is aligned to the stars in Orion's Belt, if I am able to understand my host's meaning. The interior is like nothing I have ever seen. It is a machine, but no machine built by men. I cannot begin to understand its meaning or what it does. I do not believe the natives remember either.

The place frightens me. There is no presence of God here. I cannot feel the Lord. I am alone.

I must never tell Pizarro about this place. Something unnatural lurks here.

THE WIDE SWATH

As the PCs trek through the jungle, they come upon what, at first, looks like a clearing.

CATEQUIL

Catequil is the current leader of his tribe. Their purpose, since the invasion of the Spanish in 1532, has been to keep Paititi hidden from outsiders. As the SSU came to Peru, Catequil's elders knew it was only a matter of time before the city was discovered. Catequil suggested enlisting the help of the Americans, but the elders refused. They knew all too well what Europeans have done with Incan treasures.

Now, those elders are dead, futilely trying to defend their city from the SSU and the Axis. Catequil and his small village are all that remain. As the last "elder"—he is only 30—Catequil decided to approach the PCs. He knows the secret will not be kept, but he believes the Allies offer the best chance of keeping the secrets of Paititi out of even worse hands.

Catequil describes a golden pyramid they call the Temple of the Sun. There, the SSU began excavations, but the Germans are there now as well, though he only knows of one faction. The *Ahnenerbe* is there too. Catequil describes the "walking beasts" that tore through the jungle. He can affirm they were Axis, and that the SSU and Axis are fighting over the city now.

Without warning, the jungle opens up before you. At first, you think you have stumbled upon a natural clearing but soon realize it is manmade. Someone, or rather something, has cut a swath through the jungle. Trees felled like matchsticks. The rough loam of the jungle has been ripped from the ground as if by a great hand. The trail left is symmetrical, like a canyon cut through the canopy of the Amazon. What could have done this?

The PCs do not know, but modified Axis walkers cleared the area. With huge, rotating blades instead of regular weaponry, these Luthers cut right through the jungle like a lawn mower. The PCs encounter these modified walkers once they reach Paititi.

FER-DE-LANCE

This encounter provides both danger and opportunity. The fer-de-lance (known locally as "jergón sacha") is one of the most dangerous snakes in South America. Their bite may cause necrosis (requiring amputation) or even death. Should the GM wish it, one of these serpents attacks a PC. They are quick and well-concealed. The unfortunate hero sees their leg swell and begins feeling very ill—headache, nausea, and light-headedness.

There is little the team's medic can do for a snakebite unless they came into the jungle specially prepared. However, the native tribe that has been tracking them may now intercede. They have remedies of their own and treat the injured PC at a nearby village. Their leader, Catequil, is familiar with modern culture, though not overly so. He is one of the Incan descendants of this tribe who occasionally ventures into the cities.

Once the injured party member has been taken care of, Catequil offers to help the PCs reach Paititi.

The PCs best bet is to allow Catequil to lead them into Paititi. They could simply follow the well-travelled rut the Axis made in the jungle, but Catequil can sneak them in closer to the Temple of the Sun.

PAITITI

There, among the tangle of vines and other growth, beneath the great biomass of the Amazon, peeks a stepped pyramid made of gold. All around you, mounds in the vague shape of pyramids suggest the layout of a city, but one overgrown centuries ago. Even still, hints of gold catch the delicate rays of sun that make it through the canopy above. The Temple of the Sun, standing before you, is over two hundred feet high and, if your eyes do not deceive you, coated base to tip in solid gold.

Paititi does not look like Machu Picchu or any other Incan ruins we are now familiar with. It is only now being excavated. As the PCs approach, they hear the faint popping of small arms.

Small arms echo in the jungle dark. The vegetation is so thick you can only see ten or twenty feet ahead of you. A roaring begins, something like a jaguar fused with a Harley motor. It is terrible. A headless body is suddenly thrown from the jungle in front of you. No, not merely headless. Most of the upper torso has been torn away. The next second, ripping through the trees, emerges a giant Luther with two arms wielding circular blades. They have made quick work of the SSU solider that now lies dead at your feet.

This is their introduction to the battle that rages for Paititi. The SSU are going toe-to-toe against the Axis. The Axis is using walkers armed with circular blades as well as traditional Luthers. The SSU have standard walkers but more men.

The battle converges on the Temple of the Sun—right where the player characters happen to be.

The team has two options. Join the fight, or attempt to gain access to the temple while the battle rages outside. The second choice is the better option right now, but they will have to deal with the victors later.

This is an abstract battle. The PCs encounter only those forces the GM wishes. Use *Spetznaz* for the SSU and Grenadier stats for the Axis. The battle is a great distraction allowing the team to reach the pyramid relatively unchallenged.

THE TEMPLE OF THE SUN

Catequil tells the PCs that the way inside is through the top. There is no entrance below. The PCs therefore need to climb up the small mountain the pyramid has become. There is a 1 in 3 chance the team is spotted climbing the pyramid by one of the blocs below. The GM decides which bloc. Roll once for every 50 feet. A Faction Symbol result indicates they have been spotted. Successful Stealth checks obviate the need to roll. The blocs do not spot the characters in this case.

If they are spotted, the bloc sends men to shoot them off the pyramid. Given the conditions on the ground, they cannot spare too many.

Once atop the pyramid, Catequil clears away some brush that was obviously arranged to camouflage the entrance. He presses his hand onto a gold plate, and the noise of gears precedes the opening of an entrance with a stairwell leading down. Catequil closes it immediately behind him.

It takes any other bloc at least ten rounds to figure out how to enter the Temple of the Sun.

The "temple" is actually a giant machine found by the Incans. They did not build it. Those who preceded them did not build it. This machine was built in remote antiquity just after the Flood. It was erected by the Anunnaki. No one alive knows how to work the machine. Indeed, after millennia of disuse, it may not even function. At some point, it was a power plant. One that utilized the ley lines of Earth's magnetic field to transfer energy over a network used by the Anunnaki. The Great Pyramids,

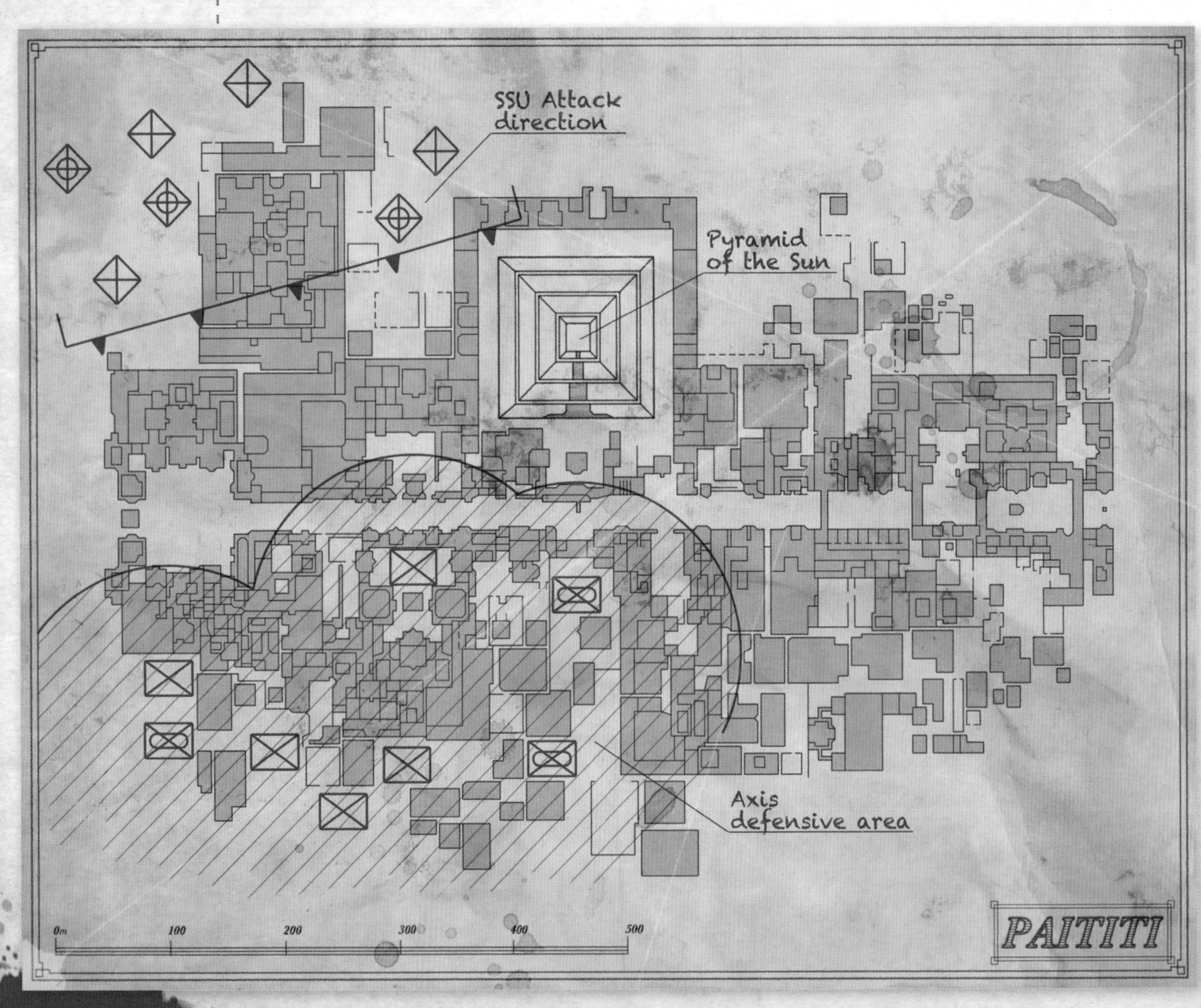

too, are based on such a design though built as a copy of the original transformer in pre-*pharaonic* Egypt.

Gears carved of stone populate the interior. The stairway leading deeper into the pyramid is utilitarian, not ceremonial. However, there are symbols painted over the underlying structure that were put there by the ancestors of the Inca long, long ago. As the characters descend, they duck and weave among the various machinery—some stone and some metal.

After a 50 metre journey, they come to what was once an operations room. There are stone seats (actually another, living material which has since petrified) positioned before consoles. These consoles look like obsidian balls and no longer function. Each seat has been turned toward the centre of the room. A web-shrouded skeleton sits on each.

In the centre of the chairs is a casket made of gold. It looks pod-shaped, not at all Incan. Inside is a human skeleton, that of a great king. He sits inside a suit made of gold. The suit itself looks a bit like the armour worn by Winter Child. In fact, it has the same purpose, to contain the power of the being within. The suit does not fit the skeleton. It was made for an Anunnaki.

Inside the "casket" are jade carvings, gold coins, and other items of value. One is the Seal the PCs are looking for. That sits at the head of the remains. An aperture shaped like the Seal lies on the wall. If placed within, the pyramid begins to power up, and gears rotate, but the old machinery fails and nothing happens.

Catequil says that all their culture comes from this tablet. That is legend and not strictly true. In fact, their culture comes down through the survivors of the Anunnaki-led human civilization wiped out during the Flood. Catequil only knows the distorted version of that—a brother and sister brought civilization, agriculture, and the like to the Inca after a great flood.

The king in the casket is an early king of Pre-Incan people. He is, literally, the "Gold Man" or El Dorado. The Inca, when the Spanish first encountered them, would cover their king in gold dust and take him by barge to the centre of Lake Titicaca where he would deposit gold objects as offerings. This, too, is a distortion of why the gold suit exists. It is, in fact, akin to a radiation suit. Once, this pyramid ran on Anunnaki energy—that selfsame energy hidden in the Middle East. That has since run out. The people who survived the Flood gradually lost their knowledge. Their decedents mythologized the original historical uses of gold and the story of the Flood.

The PCs may take whatever it is they like, but the Seal is all that matters for the adventure. The suit is incredibly heavy, being plated in gold, and was once powered to assist movement.

By the time the PCs have made it down to the casket, the bloc that won, or pursued them outside the pyramid, gains entrance. Alternatively, the team might get out just as the battle draws to a close.

AFTERMATH OF THE BATTLE

The SSU likely win. They have more resources in the area to draw on and they can call in air support. Even now, helicopters are headed to Paititi to reinforce the SSU's position. The team has a small window to take on the remaining SSU soldiers and escape. One of the best ways to do this involves using the Axis walkers to tear into the remaining SSU troops. This ought to be a cinematic encounter, with a firefight between the team and the SSU made epic by the use of walkers fighting each other, one or two equipped with spinning saw blades.

It is a rumble in the jungle and the PCs have to win to get the Seal out.

The GM should decide how many troops are left. It is possible some of the Axis were captured as well. A sample force of surviving SSU is provided below, but GMs should modify this based on the current capabilities of the team. Once this second, smaller battle is over, the team is to take the Seal of out of Peru.

SSU FORCE

10 or more *Spetznaz*

1 or 2 medium walkers

Scale the encounter based on the PC's current strength. They've got the Seal. You want this to seem more dangerous than it is. At the end, indicate the helicopters are arriving. That should get the team hauling tail out of the area.

NOT OUT OF THE WOODS YET

The team may have made prior arrangements to get out of Peru. The Allies could provide a submarine exfiltration, but the team will have to hump it to the Amazon and take that further into the jungle to rendezvous with the sub. Other plans may involve getting back to Brazil where the Allies, presumably, still have control.

Whatever route they take, the team has one last adversary to deal with—the *Ahnenerbe*. They did not have the manpower to engage in a direct confrontation with either the Axis or SSU and thus decided to wait until a victor emerged. This they have done. How they found the location of Paititi is left as an unanswered question. It may be they interrogated Louisa after the characters left. They may have also used spies in SMERSH. Possibly, they even used clairvoyant powers. Who can say what occult resources they have in Argentina?

The Nazis ambush the team when they are at their weakest. The Germans are not as stealthy as Catequil and his men, and the team has a much better chance to spot them (Difficulty 2). If spotted, the team is not surprised.

The GM needs to decide how and when the ambush takes place. Any surviving *Ubermensch* are with the *Ahnenerbe*. They have at least five former SS troopers with them.

AHNENERBE (5)

See stats in ***Dust Adventures*** p. 194.

UBERMENSCH (VARIES)

See stats in ***Dust Adventures*** pp. 148-149.

WRAPPING UP

Hopefully, the PCs have the Seal in their possession. If not, one of the other factions does. (See **Seals Lost** in **Chapter 10** for what to do if the PCs fail to capture each Seal). The ending of the adventure does not depend on the PCs having all Seven Seals. It is probable the team returns to ASOCOM for a debriefing. There, Dr. Schliemann informs them that their next target is the Chintamani Stone.

Dr. Carter and he explain the nature of this Seal in the next chapter. If the team does not have time to return to The Octagon, a coded cable can relay the information from Dr. Schliemann.

Their next destination lies to the east, in the strange, debauched city of Vladivostok....

We came into Rio under fire. The airfield was full of craters. The SSU was trying to foment a revolution there like they have done with most of South America. The Ranger I told you about, he gave me a wink on the plane ride over. I don't know. I don't need a man in my life. You taught me that. I'm digressing. Focus, Jessa.

We barely made it out of the "safe house" only to arrive in the poorest neighbourhood I've ever seen. The conditions those people live in turned my stomach. Of all the legends you told me as a kid, El Dorado was one I was certain had to be made up by greedy men. Turns out it wasn't. A witch woman in Rio put us on the trail of the lost city. Unfortunately, the SSU weren't our only opponents. Nazis, dad. They're still out there, living in Argentina. They didn't get the Seal, but they very well might have.

The city, which the natives call Paititi, really is made of gold. I could not fathom it if I hadn't seen it for myself. SSU walkers and Axis walkers fought each other for control of the temple in the city centre. We snuck in and grabbed the Seal. Dad, that was no temple. That building was some sort of machine. I think the Anunnaki made it. There's... I can't believe I'm saying this... there's a whole missing part of our history we've been kept in the dark about. That temple was older than the pyramids. I think they are linked. Possibly, the pyramids are some sort of power plants. The mind staggers.

I'm scared, dad. I'm scared for my life but even more afraid of what I'll find at the end of all this. God, if only I could talk to you. You'd know just what to say to me.

-- Jessa

CHAPTER 5: THE CHINTAMANI STONE

RASPUTIN'S GOALS
A mystic, a seer, and a psychic, Rasputin is far more open to the supernatural than Stalin. While Stalin wants to mine alien technology only for its practical application in theatres of war, Rasputin is convinced other powers, perhaps more consequential, can be drawn from this alien technology.

Rasputin knows a good deal more about the Seven Seals than the rest of SMERSH. He chooses to keep this knowledge secret. In addition, he has men loyal to him bent on the recovery of the Seals. Rasputin has some idea that the Seals must be collected to open an ancient doorway. He is not yet sure where or how this comes to be.

He and Stalin remain friendly in public, but are rivals in private. The search for the Seals may give one side or another an advantage in their inevitable struggle for power.

The fourth Seal sought by the PCs is known as the Chintamani Stone. A Buddhist legend, the stone allegedly fell from the heavens and is considered sacred. Like the other Seals, a similar origin/discovery story predominates. The Chintamani Stone is said to have been found in a chest that fell from the sky. Four other relics were also contained within this same chest. Variously reported to be a jewel or a stone, the Chintamani supposedly possesses wish-fulfilling power. To date, no one has found the stone, but one Nikolai Roerich spent some time in search of it during the 1920s.

The PCs have little to go on. An intelligence agent code-named Kestrel sent a coded transmission to ASOCOM before disappearing in Vladivostok. Kestrel was found murdered the next day. His message related the discovery of an Axis project to find Shambhala, the lost Buddhist paradise. In his message, he said the SSU was on to the lead as well. The Chintamani Stone is referenced, though Kestrel clearly had no idea what it meant.

Dr. Carter and Dr. Schliemann make the connection between the lost city of Shambhala and the Chintamani Stone. The PCs are sent to Vladivostok to pick up the trail Kestrel was following. Dr. Carter speaks excellent Russian, though it may prove helpful if at least one of the PCs does as well.

VLADIVOSTOK

This coastal city is home to the Soviet Pacific Fleet. Of course, most of the fleet is currently deployed elsewhere. Far away from Moscow, Vladivostok has served as a "pressure valve" for SSU men and women on leave. Stalin has overlooked the presence of the *Vorovskoy Mir* in the city, because even he recognizes the need for an area where soldiers can engage in illicit activities. Once the war is won, he plans to crush the *Vorovskoy Mir* and bring the city completely under his control.

For now, the city is a relatively lawless place. The authorities look the other way as contraband flows through Vladivostok. The black market is one of the chief means by which the average SSU citizen supplements their rations. It is a necessary evil for now. As a den of iniquity, Vladivostok has quite the reputation. When the Japanese seized Shanghai, much of the "Whore of the Orient's" duties fell to Vladivostok. Stalin is not happy with the compromise, but his priority remains the war.

Vladivostok looks less like a Soviet city right now and more like old Shanghai. Neon glows in the cold nights and prostitutes lure soldiers into dark clubs where American swing music can be heard. Sailors on leave, along with members of the other SSU forces, are the predominate clientele. Westerners exist here openly, though they all fall under the watchful eyes of SMERSH. Stalin has gained intelligence from such westerners operating as spies within the city, and he is content to allow them to continue to do so as long as his intelligence apparatus has control over what actually plays out. Having a Petri dish of foreign spies on his territory is of great benefit to him right now.

Under Stalin's watchful eyes, another player has emerged—General Rasputin. As he is the Director of Intelligence, all information passes through men loyal to him. Most of this reaches Stalin. That which Rasputin wishes to remain secret does not. See sidebar for more information on Rasputin's involvement. See p. 144 of ***Dust Adventures*** for more information on Rasputin.

Vladivostok is also infested with Axis intelligence agents. In fact, Orbst himself has a team working on his behalf to find the Chintamani Stone. All of this intrigue revolves around the murder of the ASOCOM agent known as Kestrel. The first part of this episode involves the PCs navigating the dicey, espionage-laden streets of Vladivostok while trying to find out what else Kestrel might have known and why he was murdered.

The first scene opens with the PCs arrival by merchant ship, to Vladivostok.

Her buildings are not so different from any other Russian city marked with the might of the Soviet Empire, but there is an Asian inflection to the designs as well. This influence from the East cannot prepare one for the sheer vitality this city enjoys. It is unlike any Soviet city you have been to before. Vladivostok remains unscarred by the war and serves now as a kind of free zone of illicit activity inside the SSU itself. Rumours abound as to why Stalin allows this, but most agree Vladivostok will not continue as it is once the war is over.

Multicoloured neon bathes gritty snow that falls in heaps along the narrow streets. The Pacific is cold up here, and the wind chills the coastal city to degrees not experienced in civilized climes.

A Note to GMs

This episode differs from previous episodes in that the PCs have more freedom to pursue scenes as they see fit, or as the course of their decisions leads them. Vladivostok in particular is designed less as an encounter and more as a mini-setting. The forces at work in the city all have their own agendas, and how the PCs interact with each determines the final outcome.

The GM needs to use their imagination to fill in the inevitable blanks between what he or she expects the players to do, and what they actually wind up doing. There is a freeform element to much of the episode. Be forewarned, PCs often do the strangest things when no single path is clear. Heck, they do the strangest things when the path is completely clear!

The PCs debark from the merchant trawler. They have been provided with false papers. SMERSH, running a check on them, see they've been involved in smuggling and the like in the South China Sea and elsewhere. This cover has the advantage of being believable but the disadvantage of exposing the team to arrest. Mostly, the authorities expect this sort of rabble to wash up in the port city.

The pier is full of young touts and porters eager to serve as guides for the PCs. Most of these are orphaned Russian kids trying to eke out an existence in wartime Vladivostok. The older kids are rounded up and conscripted into the Red Army.

The first order of business is following up on the death of Kestrel.

The PCs have several options to pursue as noted below. Kestrel's murder is the catalyst that set in motion a whole series of events going on behind the scenes in Vladivostok. The team may encounter some or all of the possible events. Their decisions, and the GM's wishes, determine how things unfold.

CHARLES LAUTNER III
CODENAME: "KESTREL"

Lautner was approximately 50 years old. He served with distinction during the First World War. A minor Baron by birth, his family's wealth was all but wiped out during the Great Depression. Lautner developed a drinking and gambling habit and soon became the black sheep of the family. He drifted for a while, until he found himself in Shanghai where a man like him could get lost. In the mid 1930s, the Foreign Service recruited him for espionage work. Kestrel was central to revealing some of the Japanese Empire's earliest plans.

While he was not the most stable of intelligence agents, his natural charm and aristocratic breeding gained him access to the upper tiers of society. Conversely, his troubled past allowed him to win friends on the lowest levels of society.

With the fall of Shanghai, Lautner did some work in China before being moved to Vladivostok. There, he passed on valuable intelligence while making a name for himself in the black market. ASOCOM helped in this regard, as it bolstered his cover. Kestrel was murdered a week before the arrival of the PCs.

THE MAJOR PLAYERS IN VLADIVOSTOK

The following section outlines the who's who of the city. Each person is tagged to a specific location, but the GM need not restrict him or her to that place alone. Use their motives and their knowledge to determine their actions. At the end of the section, you are presented with a scenario for Kestrel's murder. As GM, you may use this or toss it aside in favour of another route. The only necessary discoveries involve things that the PCs need in order to proceed. If they fail to find any of this intel, the GM must find another way for it to fall into their hands.

ARKADY THE PIMP

A nasty piece of business, Arkady is a member of the *Vorovskoy Mir*. Many also consider him a traitor to that organization because he fought for the Soviets earlier in the war. Called "the pimp" because that's how he made his start prior to landing in prison, Arkady has since branched out. He deals in black market food and drugs, as well as prostitutes. His connection to Chinese gangsters gives him a supply of "Oriental" girls for men on leave to sample.

Without morals, Arkady only lived by the *Vorovskoy* code. Sadly, he is known as a "suka," having sided with the Soviets in the war. Those who consider themselves true *Vorovskoys* would see him dead.

He operates out of an old, Tsar-era hotel near the ocean, taking up the entire penthouse level. The hotel was constructed during an ill-planned attempt to turn Vladivostok into something akin to the Paris of the East. It never materialized. Stalin has similar post-war plans.

Kestrel owed a significant amount of money to Arkady. This is one possible motive for his murder.

REINER WULF

Wulf was a merchant marine and U-Boat officer during the First World War. At least that's his cover story. He was, in fact, driven to leave Germany with the rise of the Nazis, as he was loyal to the Weimar. After the Nazis were exiled and hanged, Wulf felt he needed to serve the Fatherland again. He thus became a spy for *Blutkreuz* or, rather, an asset. He is not actually a member of *Blutkreuz*, but Orbst has gotten valuable intel from him in the past.

Wulf does not trust Orbst, believing he has his own agenda beyond that of the Fatherland. As such, he has been recruited directly by Sigrid von Thaler to keep tabs on what Orbst asks about in the city.

In theory, Wulf is now a triple agent. He is a true patriot loyal to von Thaler and the Fatherland.

Wulf has little personal reason to have killed Kestrel, but may have done so on von Thaler's orders.

He spends most of his time in flophouses or in one of the brothels, where he is fond of one woman in particular.

VASSILY KAMINSKI

Vassily is a member of SMERSH in Vladivostok, but he actually works directly for Rasputin. His loyalty to the General of Intelligence is unwavering. Kaminski believes that Stalin's ego, much as Hitler's ego before him, will eventually lead to ruin for the SSU. He has therefore thrown his support behind Rasputin.

However, Kaminski has spent too long in Vladivostok, and has become corrupted by the city's many vices. He is addicted to morphine accessed through illegal shipments making their way through port. The addiction caused him to make some recent missteps, and he has been trying to keep these from Rasputin. Kestrel was on to one of Kaminski's blunders thus giving Kaminski good reason to take him out.

Kaminski lives in a nice flat in a residential area of the city.

ALEXANDRA KOROKOVA

This former Russian aristocrat now makes her living as a "taxi dancer," not quite a brothel prostitute, but certainly in the same business, at least in Vladivostok. As a taxi dancer, she is paid for dancing with men at clubs. Each dance is paid for separately. Negotiations for more intimate services are made afterward with a percentage going to the host club.

After the Bolshevik Revolution, many "White Russians" (those loyal to the Tsar) were forced to flee. Some wound up in other countries, and many went to the Russian Ghetto of Shanghai. Alexandra lived there until the Japanese occupied the city. Things became tougher for the Russians there, and she came to Vladivostok to help take care of her family. A circuitous route of other White Russians enables goods to be sent to Shanghai via smuggling channels.

Alexandra is out for her family and herself. In the course of her work, she comes across useful bits of information. Among these is the knowledge of half a map supposedly showing the location of Shambhala. One of the SMERSH agents had it in his possession. She copied it while he slept.

Kestrel might have tried to take it from her, resulting in his murder.

A SCENARIO FOR MURDER

This is a sample scenario describing what might have gone down and why. The GM is free to use this as he or she sees fit or leave it out altogether. In the last few weeks, Vassily Kaminski received a message regarding the Chintamani Stone. The agent had obtained half a map from a White Russian refugee coming back to Vladivostok from Shanghai. The man was old, a bit crazed, and offered the map as passage. The map made its way to Vassily Kaminski.

When the message came in about the Chintamani Stone and Shambhala, Vassily knew he had valuable information.

He did not know that the taxi dancer, Alexandra, copied the map.

Kestrel found out that Kaminski had the map and burgled his flat before he could turn it over to Rasputin. Kaminski was in a morphine haze when this occurred, and has no idea where the map went. Kestrel, for his part, contacted Alexandra about the map, knowing that Kaminski was a client of hers. The two have an on-again, off-again relationship. Vassily is not the only agent after Alexandra's affections.

Wulf is in love with Alexandra and when he saw Kestrel and her together for the second time, he murdered Kestrel in an alleyway. He robbed him to make it look random. In the process, Wulf acquired the original map.

There are now two maps, one original and one copy. Alexandra is a very talented artist, and her copy is identical.

The PCs have two sources from which to obtain the map. Unfortunately, Wulf has already told Orbst and von Thaler about his copy. Likewise, Kaminski got a message through to Rasputin about the map that was then intercepted by Stalin loyalists in SMERSH. In other words, everyone knows there is at least one copy of a partial map showing the location of Shambhala. That map has just become the hottest piece of property in Vladivostok.

HOW THINGS MAY FALL TOGETHER

The following is one way the Vladivostok episode may play out. The GM has enough information on the parties involved to arrange another outcome altogether. What is most important is for the PCs to get one of the maps, or at least a copy.

The PCs arrive in Vladivostok and begin looking for information related to Kestrel's murder. Searching his flat is a good option. While there, the team finds that Orbst has also sent *Blutkreuz* agents to search the flat. The two teams tangle. A picture of the taxi dancer, Alexandra, is found, along with a matchbook from the club she works at—*Xaoc* ("Chaos").

If the PCs drive the Germans off, they get the clues.

BLUTKREUZ AGENTS (3)

Use stats for Spy on pp. 148-149 of ***Dust Adventures***.

Assuming they now have this lead to follow, the team proceeds to Club Xaoc, modelled after American nightclubs of the day. An expatriate French band plays popular music from both Russia and America. Wulf is hanging out at the bar when the PCs arrive, and takes note of their asking for Alexandra. He tries to eavesdrop on their conversation.

Alexandra doesn't have much use for the map itself, but she now knows the Allies want it as well. That makes it valuable. With enough money, she could leave Vladivostok and get her family out of Shanghai. She demands $5,000 American or the equivalent in gold for the map. She claims not to have it on her person which is true. She gave the map to a friend for safekeeping. This "friend" is a Chinese sailor who is in port for a few days. If she does not come to retrieve the map before his ship departs, he is to take it to relatives of hers in Chinese territory. Of all the people encountered in this scene, the Chinese sailor is perhaps the only one who intends to do what he says.

The sailor is staying in nice hotel along the port. If the PCs get the money they return to Xaoc to give it to Alexandra only to discover that a "gruff German customer" who fancies her has abducted her. Wulf, consumed by jealousy, took her against her will. He holds her at his flophouse.

Orbst is on his way to collect the map from Alexandra when the PCs find out she has been taken. The two groups tangle inside Xaoc. Arkady the Pimp owns Xaoc and is very intrigued at this turn of events. Meanwhile, word has passed to Vassily Kaminski, through one of the other taxi dancers, that Alexandra told some Americans she had a copy of the map.

For all parties involved in any firefight at Xaoc, use stats for Spy on pp. 148-149 of ***Dust Adventures***. There are three members of any given faction.

It is now a race to Wulf's flat to get Alexandra before anyone else does. The GM may decide the team gets there first, or arrives just after another faction. Between Arkady's gangsters, Orbst's men and Vassily's SMERSH agents, they have their hands full. Once they get a hold of the map, they have to escape from Vladivostok.

The map shows an area without names. It could be anywhere. The PCs need the second half of the map. A note on the back of the map they have (copy or not) lists a Russian family name. Alexandra knows of the family. They were close blood relatives of the Romanov's. Those who survived the Bolsheviks currently live in Japanese-occupied Shanghai. The trail now leads to China.

THE WAR IN CHINA

At the beginning of the war, before Germany set their eyes on the rest of Europe, the Japanese were already expanding their Empire into China. That was in 1937, and the war in China has gone on for ten years. This unrelenting invasion ravaged China. After Pearl Harbor, the United States backed the Chinese Nationalists under Chiang Kai-shek as they fought against the Japanese. When Chinese communists formally joined the SSU, they too became the enemy of America.

In the years since, the Chinese nationalists, bolstered by Allied support, have pushed back against Axis expansion. They now have a narrow corridor leading to Shanghai though which they are launching an attempt to retake the city and its valuable port, and ASOCOM is helping.

The PCs link up with ASOCOM units in China, flown in over "The Hump"—a dangerous route of resupply

SHANGHAI

Shanghai was a hotbed of espionage activity prior to the onset of the Second World War. Nations saw the inevitable conflict coming and Shanghai, at this point ruled by the West, became a major source of intelligence and counter-intelligence operations. When the Japanese took control of Shanghai during the war, much of this activity ceased as westerners were put in internment camps. The city, once known as The Whore of the Orient, went dark. Her taxi dancers serve only the Japanese soldiers now, and the multilingual buzz that once filled the streets, is now gone.

This has been the condition of Shanghai until the invasion. Historically, no such invasion took place, though the city was liberated. Ultimately, the nationalists lost the civil war that followed, and Chiang Kai-shek wound up in Taipei.

Much of the spirit of the city has been borrowed for Vladivostok though, as history went, nothing like that occurred. Liberties are taken where necessary to fit the themes and events of the ***Dust Universe***.

the Allies make from Assam, India to Kumming, China. Once in Kumming, the team proceeds northeast to Shanghai. The journey to Shanghai takes 30 hours. Again, this is a spot where the GM can simply indicate the journey in the fashion of an Indiana Jones film.

Once outside of Shanghai, the PCs link up with another wave of troops entering the city. The Battle for Shanghai is destined to go down as among the bloodiest urban combats of 1947.

THE BATTLE OF SHANGHAI

The Battle of Shanghai is in its second day when the PCs arrive. Using a narrow corridor carved out via great losses, the Nationalist Chinese, assisted by the Allies, have launched an invasion of the city. The Allies dropped walkers for use in the attack, but their numbers do not match those of the Steel Samurai the Japanese have at their disposal.

The Japanese were not expecting the attack, and a great many of their resources are occupied defending their islands from American Marines. There is a chance the Allies can retake the city and then fortify it. While the port is very important, the symbolic victory of recapturing Shanghai would recruit more Chinese to the cause of fighting the SSU.

Allied aircraft carriers hit the Japanese naval defences around the city hard, and continue to drop bombs over Shanghai even as they are engaged in dogfights with the Japanese. The citizens are rather accustomed to the bombing, and are seeking out safe redoubts with a calm sense of urgency.

Japanese troops engage with Chinese on the streets. The PCs need to reach the Russian ghetto where the family Alexandra knows, the Dhukovs, live. The team must navigate the urban war going on around them and reach the Dhukovs. Of course, the Axis already has Japanese units headed to the ghetto for the same reason. Orbst radioed ahead to ensure the Allies did not get to the Dhukovs first.

Along with the invasion, ASOCOM Rangers (not the team) attempt to liberate the Japanese internment camps. If the city isn't captured, the Allies want to get their citizens out.

ENCOUNTERS IN SHANGHAI

The PCs arrive in the midst of the Battle of Shanghai. Making their way to the Russian ghetto brings them into contact with parts of the city under siege. The path also brings them into contact with a moral quandary, one of many found during wartime. Below are a few examples of encounters the GM can use. They are by no means exhaustive, and the GM is encouraged to supplement as they wish.

BURNING ORPHANAGE

The PCs stumble upon an orphanage that has taken a direct hit. The resulting fire leaves children screaming from the windows. One of their caretakers, bleeding from the blast, begs the PCs for help. It has nothing to do with their mission, but the PCs are the kids' only hope. There's enough wreckage they can use to create a makeshift ladder to get the kids down. Do they want to spend the time doing so? They must weigh the costs carefully.

STEEL SAMURAI

The PCs round a corner in the former French Concession of Shanghai, and run into a Japanese walker and an infantry unit. The PCs may try stealth to avoid the walker, or they may have requisitioned their own walker to combat it. These walkers were built using help from the Germans and their expertise with Vrill technology.

Steel Samurai	
Type	Vehicle-Walker (Medium) [Cost:2]
Handling	0 [Cost:0]
Speed	9 (25km/h / 15mph) [Cost:4.5]
Range	300km
Weight	7 tonnes
Length	5m
Height	4m
Capacity	10 [Cost: 5]
Armour	4 [Cost:3]
Crew	1 (pilot) [Cost:0]
Weapons	Giant Sword, Chainsaw, 40mm Autocannon [Total Cost: 13.5]
Sensors	Standard [Cost:0]
Other	Smoke Launchers [Cost:1]
Flaws	Bulky 4, High Maintenance 1, Skill Based 2 (Pilot, Attack) [Total Flaws: 7]

Weapon	Rng	Dam	Rank	Special
Giant Sword	C	3/3	1	None
Chainsaw	C	2/4	1	Cutting 2
40mm Autocannon	A (15)	3/2	1	None

Gizmo Points: 22

Gizmoteer Rank: 5

JAPANESE SOLDIERS (10)

IMPERAL JAPANESE SOLDIER

Characteristics

MB 2	**MD** 1	**PH** 1	**PR** 2
Movement 3	**Capacity** 3	**Initiative** 3	

Skills: Athletics 2, Attack: Melee 2, Attack: Firearms 1, Attack: Heavy 1, Awareness 1, Interaction 1, Repair 1.

Officers and NCOs: Add Attack: Melee (Katana 1), Willpower 2

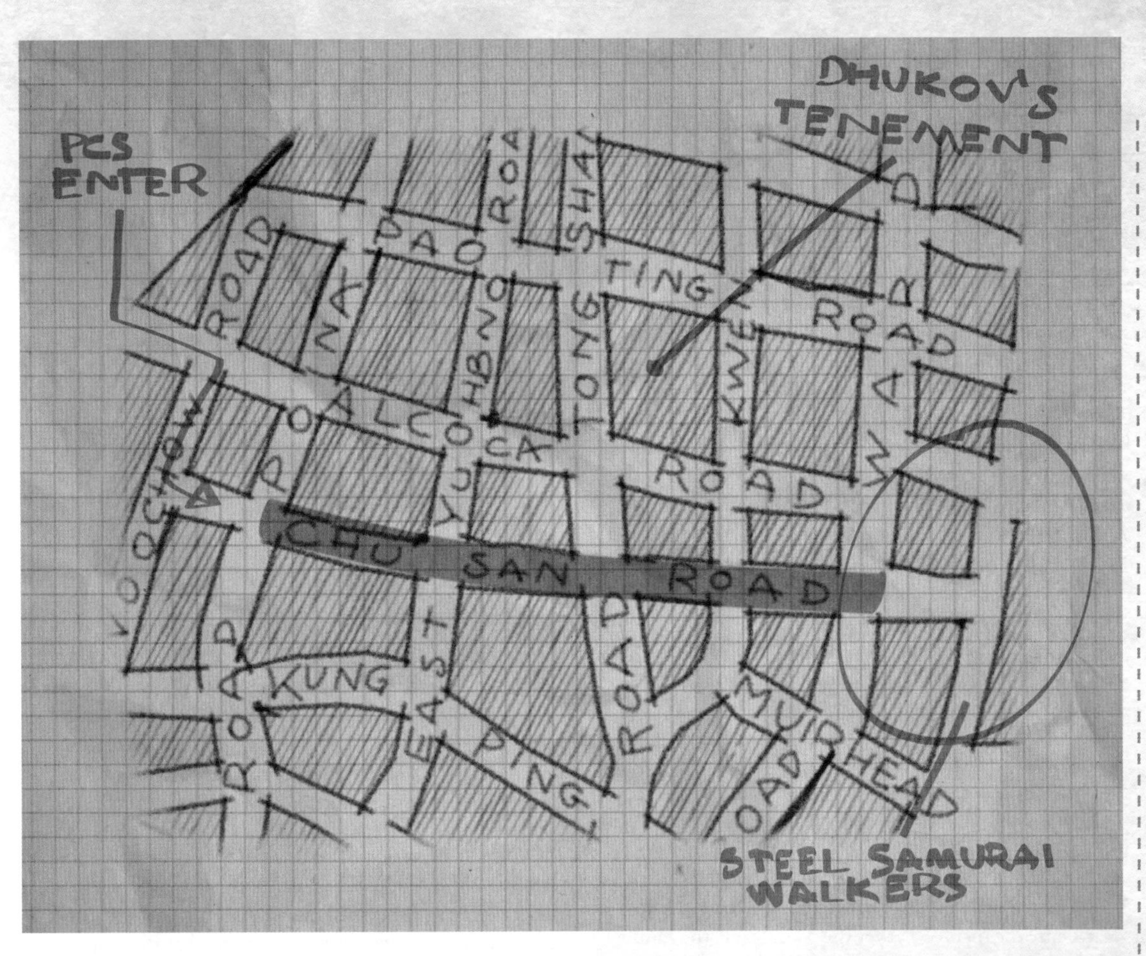

Special Abilities: None

Special Powers: None

Equipment				
Weapon	**Rng**	**Dam**	**Rank**	**Special**
Type 100 SMG	10	3	0	Ammo, 4, Rapid Fire, Reload 1
Type 92 MG15	15	2/ 1/2	0	Ammo 6, Autofire, Rapid Fire
Bayonet Knife	C	1	0	None
Katana	C	2	0	None
Type 94 Nambu Pistol	5	2	0	Ammo 4
Howa Type 47 AR	15	2/1	0	Ammo 5, Rapid Fire

THE WHITE RUSSIAN GHETTO

The Russian Ghetto houses the bulk of the Russian community in Shanghai. Because these refugees fled the Bolsheviks, they are not considered communists. Therefore, the Japanese have largely left them alone. It is only because of Orbst's message that the Japanese have come to find the Dhukovs. Orbst had no idea the message would arrive during an invasion, and expected his Japanese allies to round up the family with little difficulty.

Instead, they are driving into the ghetto with three walkers and 30 men. The PCs must get to the family first, or rescue them from their captives. This is no easy feat. A map of the ghetto appears below.

THE DHUKOVS

This royal family traces a very close relationship to the deposed Tsar and his family. Rasputin has an interest in them, as he was fond of certain members of the Romanovs. He has lost track of them over the years, but the family may ally with him later. Such an alliance is outside the scope of this campaign, but it gives the GM some loose ends to pursue later.

The Dhukov family was among the patrons of Nikolai Roerich in the 1920s. He left them a map he claims he made when he found the lost city of Shambhala. At least that is how the story goes. The family does have the other half of the map. They divided it in two so they would have something to bargain with if they ever had need. The other half is already in the PCs possession, or at least a copy of it is.

An aging, senile member of the family decided he could no longer tolerate exile. He would return to Russia and offer his half of the map for forgiveness. An ill-conceived play to be sure.

The Dhukovs themselves have yet to plan any expedition to the lost city. According to the map, when fitted with the other half, the city lies in the Gobi desert. That is a far cry from where it is commonly located somewhere in the Himalayas.

THE GOBI DESERT
A 500,000 square mile area of desert, the Gobi is a place inhospitable to human habitation. In the 1920s, an American archaeologist set out to find the missing link somewhere in the Gobi but instead found the first dinosaur eggs. Conditions are harsh, with temperatures reaching extremes. The Gobi is a cold desert, and ice and snow cap some of the taller dunes. The sheer size allows for various types of terrain. Among those are steppe and scrubland as well as the dreamlike Taklamakan Desert.

The PC's destination lies within the Eastern Gobi desert steppe. Both the SSU and the Axis currently clash in this area. Veterans of North Africa find the war here familiar.

Water is not as impossible to find here, as it is in other areas of the desert. However, fatigue overcomes those travelling and the trucks sent with the team are prone to breaking down in the extreme conditions. The GM does not have to play through these events, but can describe them as part of the experience of getting there.

Alexandra's family, the Korokovas, is in the ghetto as well. The PCs are unlikely to know any of them unless Alexandra asked them to help her family. Since she did not know about the siege, she probably assumed she could get them out with the money the PCs gave her. In that case, she might provide an excellent means for getting out of the city as she has hired an outdated U-Boat, run by a mercenary crew, to smuggle her family from Shanghai. The U-Boat is sitting under the Whangpoo River between Shanghai proper and Pudong.

Once the PCs get the Dhukov family, they run into a problem. The family does not want to give them the map unless the team helps them out of the city. At this point, a couple of the mercenaries, along with Alexandra, arrive in the ghetto. This odd reunion causes another point of dispute—there is not enough room on the U-Boat to get both families out.

Alexandra is not going to give up the fact that she has the U-Boat, but the PCs may suspect she has a way out if she had a way in. What they do next is up to them. Several scenarios may result:

- The team gets the Dhukovs out of Shanghai separately. Once they do so, through whatever means, the Dhukovs hand over the map.
- The PCs forcibly take the map from the Dhukovs. It is not terribly difficult for armed soldiers to search and procure the map. Whether the team leaves the family to its fate or not is up to them.
- The PCs learn that Alexandra hired a mercenary submarine. They persuade or force her to take them, and possibly the Dhukovs, out of the city.
- Simply by retracing their steps, the PCs can fight their way back to friendly lines and link back up with the Nationalists. Of course, this offers no small amount of danger as the way they came into the ghetto has since shifted between the two sides. The team has to engage with, or avoid, Japanese forces including Steel Samurai walkers.
- However they make it out of the city, the team should now have both pieces of the map. Consulting a map of East Asia reveals the position of Shambhala somewhere in the Gobi Desert. With navigational skills or help from ASOCOM, they can locate the precise location.

Dr. Carter remarks on the dangers of the Gobi and how even the great Genghis Khan respected its reputation as a killer of men.

TO THE GOBI

The section of the Gobi the PCs must reach lies inside the Japanese puppet state of Manchukuo. While the team thinks they are looking for the Lost City of Shambhala that is not what they find. Shambhala itself lies further along their path.

What the PCs find is actually the lost tomb of Genghis Khan. Once sought by historians and fortune hunters alike, the tomb is one of the great lost treasures of the world. Filled with death traps, the tomb houses a deadly array of protections. Combine this with both a Japanese unit led by Orbst and SSU troops under the direction of Rasputin, and the PCs are about to put themselves into the middle of a very deadly mystery that has gone unsolved for 700 years.

The PCs have to make a perilous trek across open desert, for flying across the Gobi invites both the SSU and the Axis to shoot them down. The PCs make their way from a starting point in southwestern Mongolia. Once they reach their goal, they find the Great Khan did not possess a Seal, but his tomb holds keys to the location of Shambhala.

MONGOLIA

Most of Mongolia currently falls under the Japanese Manchukuo puppet state. The Allies took back a portion of the southwestern area of the country. It is from this safe area, surrounded on all sides by the SSU and the Axis, from which the team departs. They must venture far into the Gobi Desert by convoy in order to reach the location of Shambhala. When they arrive, they find the tomb instead.

In a small base inside Allied territory, the PCs can cable ASOCOM by code. Schliemann insists that Shambhala has never been located in the Gobi in any known account. Dr. Carter agrees with him, but insists that the map points there. Of course, this map, yet again, simply points to another map. Such is the life of treasure hunters.

The PCs must make the long journey to the point indicated on the map while combating both harsh desert conditions and the enemy.

ENCOUNTERS IN THE GOBI

The PCs are most likely to encounter units from the SSU or the Axis. Neither is something they wish to run into. If encountered, assume a small unit has been separated from its main body. They each have one light walker and perhaps 20 infantry total.

The GM should adjust the encounter to the team's current strength, if necessary. Use the appropriate stats from ***Dust Adventures.***

THE GREAT KHAN'S TOMB

Buried for over 700 years, the secret location of the tomb died with those who built it, but secrecy is not its only protection. Deathtraps await those foolish enough to loot the emperor's tomb.

The PCs may either arrive first, second, or third. They are in race against the SSU and the Axis. The map and key assume the PCs arrived after the SSU but before the Axis. It is not until they see the SSU soldiers left outside as guards that they spot the location of a hole into the earth.

The Tomb of Genghis Khan

Genghis Khan controlled the largest contiguous land empire ever known to man. It stretched from the Sea of Japan all the way to Central Europe in the 13th and 14th centuries. The Great Genghis Khan died in 1227 B.C. His body was buried in secret, with those who buried him killed so that they could never reveal the location of the tomb. As the commander of arguably the greatest empire in history, riches were no doubt heaped upon his tomb. Among these was a curious tablet, though not a Seal. The tablet is a map, though it doesn't at first appear as such. It lies within the Khan's tomb, guiding his way to Paradise.

Since the time of his death, man has searched for the Genghis' treasure. None have yet found it, even today in the 21st century.

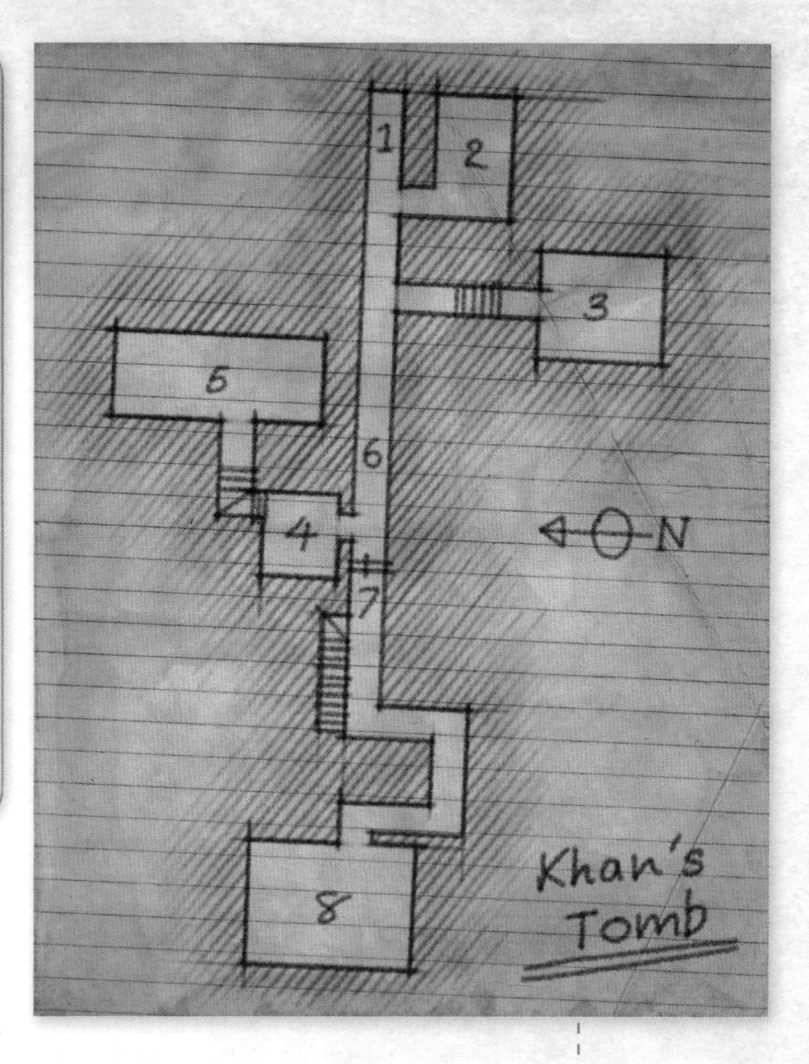

Once inside the tomb, Dr. Carter quickly determines that this is no lost city but the lost tomb of Genghis Khan himself. Remember, everyone thinks they've found Shambhala.

Below is the map of the Khan's Tomb as well as the map key.

GUARDS (8)

Use stats for *Spetznaz* on p. 153 of ***Dust Adventures***.

1. ENTRANCE

The desert has preserved the tomb. The still air has not been ruffled by human breath in nearly eight centuries. Cobwebs, like the finest silk screens, hang in front of you. The light from your torches penetrate the gossamer threads revealing shapes beyond.

The shapes are actually bodies, desiccated in the desert air. They could almost pass for sleeping men. These corpses are piled like cordwood, without ceremony. Dr. Carter notes that they must have been the workers who dug this tomb, their secret sealed with their deaths.

2. TREASURE ROOM

Also a trap room, the team trips said trap as soon as they set foot on the stairs. The stairs become a chute that deposits the characters into a treasure room. Gold and silver objects, taken from the far corners of the world, are twined together with webs and chests of more valuables.

When the slide ends, the door shuts behind the team, apparently sealed. A noxious and deadly gas slowly fills the room. As the first to spring the trap, the team finds no human remains here. They are to be the first of the Khan's victims in a very long time. Physique checks are made at Difficulty 2 every round inside the swirling vapours. 1 Damage results for each failed test.

The trap itself is designed to keep the victims in the room. High up on the ceiling from various vents, the gas pours in. Of course, this trap was designed prior to the invention of portable explosives and firearms, so the PCs should be able to blast their way to safety. If they wish to loot the chamber, that is their affair. Make up what treasure you like.

3. ADVISOR'S CHAMBER

In a single stone casket lies the Khan's advisor who committed suicide upon his master's death that he might serve him in the afterlife. He wears accoutrements of jade, silver, and gold.

4. CHAMBER OF THE WIVES

The Great Khan's wives, too, gave their own lives and were interred with their lord to please him in the next world. Twenty caskets stand upright along the wall.

THE DISSIDENTS AND LANGUAGE

The original survivors of the Great Flood had but one language among them. This inspired the stories of the Tower of Babel and the breaking of the first language into many. These monks speak that first language, or at least an iteration of it. They have preserved this language, and their culture, from those they consider impure human stock. Only those of blood untainted since the scattering of languages are true humans to these people. In their way, though peaceful, their ideology is not all that far removed from that of the Nazis.

5. FALSE DOOR

This door is set in the stone surrounding it with nary a visible way to open it. If the PCs still have enemies afoot, this dead end is a great spot for them to show up. The door cannot be opened because it isn't an actual door.

6. HALL OF BLADES

Stepping on trip-panels in this hall causes a series of pendulum-like blades to arc down at the team. Athletic checks at Difficulty 2 allow the PCs to avoid the pendulums. Otherwise, they take 2 Damage. If the character does not have Athletics, they may make a Mobility check at Difficulty 3 instead.

7. DEAD END/SECRET DOOR

This is the apparent end of the tomb, left purposefully incomplete. A couple skeletons lie amid what looks to have been a cave-in. This is all a ruse. The tomb was completed, and a secret door lies on the southern wall which may be discovered with a Difficulty 3 Awareness check. This door leads to the hall, which opens into the Khan's tomb itself.

8. THE KHAN'S BURIAL CHAMBER

Your lights play over a stone sarcophagus in the centre of the room. Limp cobwebs hammock between treasures opulent and rare, but the most curious of all is the tablet sitting in the hands of a giant, bronze Buddha.

Curiously, as noted by Dr. Carter, the Khan was not buried in the Mongol fashion. The tablet is designed to slide in and out of the statue. Inside the sarcophagus, the team finds the Khan's body, a host of treasures and the bare skull of what they presume is an alien. The skull lies just above the Khan's head, an object of obvious reverence.

The team may have to fight their way back out of the tomb, depending on who remains inside or waits above. Once they defeat those remaining troops (or evade them), they make a run for a rendezvous with an ASOCOM plane, its fuselage scarred by flak damage. Dr. Carter frantically decodes the recovered tablet. She believes it is a star chart, but she cannot make the necessary calculations. She sends the information by radio to ASOCOM. The team must now hole up and wait for a response.

This takes them to India, where they land on an Allied airfield in New Delhi for some much-needed downtime. The team is free to wander about town. If the GM wants to have enemy operatives in the city, they could spot the group, but this isn't part of the mission as written.

If they have a scientist among them, he or she could help decode the star chart, but it really requires not just an expert but also a computation machine. The data is fed into Prometheus (Alan Turing's machine) and spits out a location and a date. The stellar configuration on the plate dates to around 10,000 B.C. as seen from a remote location in Tibet. After Dr. Carter receives this information, she consults a modern map and locates Shambhala among the Himalayas in Tibet. Of course, the Axis went to some lengths to invade Tibet, so they are probably on the same trail. The team needs to jump over treacherous mountain terrain and get to the city before the Axis.

Of course, nothing ever goes according to plan.

SHAMBHALA

Shambhala, the legendary paradise of Buddhist philosophy, is in fact a real place located in Tibet (at least for the purposes of ***Dust***).

Allied photographs of the area reveal nothing. There's no city evident and, fortunately, no Axis. That's what the aerial photos and local intel says, but the reality is quite different.

SECRETS OF SHAMBHALA

Shambhala ***is*** a paradise, but not a natural one. What we call terraforming happened in a lost valley in the Himalayas. The Vrill, long ago, built various locations around the globe while securing VK. Vrill can breathe in Earth's atmosphere, but the conditions aren't ideal. They therefore "Vrillformed" certain areas and this is one of those, now long since abandoned.

As the Flood washed over a great part of the world, and the survivors escaped by various means, some wound up in this valley. Upon arriving, they found what seemed an impossible paradise. Cool, sub-tropical conditions reign in the valley, the product of Vrill machinery. The air, too, is different. The PCs find breathing harder. Add a Difficulty 1 penalty to any strenuous activity checks while in the valley.

Exposure to the field has, over time, vastly increased the lifespan of those living there. The residents of the valley have been known to live for up to two hundred years. They believe themselves the font of all Earthly wisdom. It could be construed, were one willing to do so, that they are the founders of Buddhism. Certainly, their philosophy is similar. The residents remember the Anunnaki through ancient records kept within their city. More importantly, they have learned partial control over the remaining Vrill technology. The valley appears on no maps because none can find it. It is essentially "cloaked" from the eyes of the rest of the world.

Many hundreds of years ago, a schism occurred within the city. One faction felt that life had lost meaning and that they had travelled off the true Wheel of Time and Rebirth. Living so long prevented proper reincarnation rather than assisting it. These dissidents left, possibly founding Tibetan Buddhism. The team runs into these dissidents living in a remote monastery.

A RAPIDLY CHANGING COURSE OF EVENTS

Plane travel is really not going well for the PCs on this mission. After crossing into Tibetan airspace, two advanced Axis jets intercept and shoot them down. The team has only

A Theory on Psychic Powers

This is one possible explanation for psychic powers found in the *Dust Universe.* The world is based in super-science, sometimes pseudoscience, rather than magic and the outright paranormal. This theory cleaves to that model.

Psychic powers are not, of themselves, actual powers but the effects of advanced alien technology. As Arthur C. Clarke once famously noted, "Any sufficiently advanced technology is indistinguishable from magic." That phrase applies here. The ley lines that wrap around the Earth are geomagnetic power lines that either the Vrill discovered or exploited for their own purposes. The network of ley lines formed a grid, or matrix, not unlike today's internet. Information, energy, and other things man cannot know passed from one nexus to another. The Vrill used this to power their bases, communicate with one another, and more. It allowed them to use their telekinetic abilities and other psychic phenomena.

In reality, they were just tapping into vast stores of energy and using their minds as a remote control. In time, the Vrill left, and humanity spread to the corners of the globe. They, too, found they could use some of the same techniques as the Vrill in certain locations (Stonehenge and the Giza Plateau for example). These became holy sites and megalithic structures, followed by temples and churches.

The valley is such a place, as are many other legendary locations around the world. The monks are able to use this energy much better than any known people today, because they have an unbroken history stretching all the way back to the Anunnaki and Vrill visitations. Possibly, they are genetically related to the aliens. Maybe all humans are.

The powers Sigrid von Thaler and Rasputin display, according to this theory, tap into these same reserves. Clairvoyance is remote viewing using the ley lines. Mind reading and past life reading simply tap into the vast data storage centres left behind. Everyone who ever was, or ever will be, leaves their psychic trace along ley lines, and Vrill "computers" remain buried in the ground to record it all. Predicting the future is akin to Googling these vast servers for a projection based on thousands of years of data.

At least that's what some fringe theorists say. Is it real? That's up to the GM and the players.

enough time to bail out. For a detailed method of running this scene, see the adventure (also called ***Operation: Apocalypse***) in the core book. The PCs are shot down there too. The team bails out but, much like an Indiana Jones film, a solution for one problem just leads to an even worse problem. In this case, they land in the mountains of Tibet where Orbst and his men are looking for Shambhala. They have not found it because of the aforementioned cloaking system. Sadly, the PCs have no such camouflage.

Blutkreuz is all over the target area, but the Vrill tech prevents not only them seeing the valley, but actively steers their minds around the valley. Assume that whichever group of *Blutkreuz* finds the team first has a light walker as well. This walker is adapted for mountainous terrain and cold weather.

SAMPLE BLUTKREUZ UNIT

(Use the relevant stats found in ***Dust Adventures.***)

5-10 Soldiers and 1 light walker. (The GM should determine how hard the PCs get hit with this one).

A fight erupts in the mountainous terrain unless the PCs avoid detection. Within rounds, the fight brings more Axis forces to the fray. The PCs are outnumbered and outgunned. Really slam them as the rounds go by. This is one encounter they don't have to "live" through.

The Axis defeats the team unless the GM wants to let them escape. If they all fall, make it seem like it's a Total Party Kill. Make them sweat, but when the Axis comes to capture survivors or finish them off, they cannot find them. They shout at each other in German, asking how these wounded men could have crawled away.

Meanwhile, the team can see the Axis plain as day. Just what is going on?

The dissident outcasts of paradise are to blame. They, too, know how to use the Vrill technology in the area. It can "cloud men's minds." The dissidents saw the plane shot down and have come to investigate. Unlike their counterparts inside the Vrill field, these men and women know of the outside world and its war. They do not want the Axis to gain the technology inside the valley, but they are people of peace. They will not raise their hands against their brothers. However, the PCs have made no such oath. The dissidents want the technological field to collapse, to end the perverted reign of their former brothers.

They know the PCs' mission. How they know this is not made explicit, it is one of many pulp mysteries. However,

SHAMBHALA
In Tibetan Buddhism, there are three Shambhalas—the Earthly city, the inner city inside us all, and the heavenly kingdom where deities reside. The Shambhala in this adventure represents all three. Once upon a time, this was a Vrill outpost. The Vrill, in legend, became Gods. The people who settled here have a rudimentary understanding of Vrill technology, but still see it as mystical.

There are doorways that open automatically for citizens, but not for PCs without a Mind roll at Difficulty 2. This reflects the "inner Shambhala" that is actually a psionic grid running through the city. Not unlike the modern Internet, the same field that cloaks the city encompasses it in a network individuals may tap into. None of the PCs likely have this talent, but Ilsa does to some degree.

Like our own Internet, Shambhala's grid has various levels. There's a public psionic field where the Shambhalans can access doors and fountains and the like. Under that, more specifically inside the stepped pyramid dominating the city, is a deeper grid where the memories of the Vrill and ancient humans are stored.

The overall effect appears magical on the surface but, like many things in the ***Dust Universe***, is actually backed up by fantastical pseudoscience. The GM can play this however he wishes. The PCs may it is reasonable that the Vrill tech can catch encoded radio waves. The dissidents might have acquired details that way. In any event, they want the PCs to succeed in their mission because the Seal is the key that makes the Vrill field function. If the PCs remove the Seal, the field drops and "paradise" falls.

The dissident monks bring the PCs back to their monastery. It is old, very old, a building out of both time and place here on this remote mountain. There, the PCs recover almost immediately despite the nature of their wounds. As they heal inside the monastery, a lovely woman joins them. She is blonde-haired and blue-eyed, an Aryan ideal. In fact, she was a Nazi, part of an *Ahnenerbe* expedition that first came to Tibet in 1938. She, too, was injured and found by the monks. While staying here, she gave up her old ways and became enlightened, or at least began her way along that path. Her name is Ilsa, and she explains what it is the monks want her to do.

Ilsa speaks English and German. She wears robes like the other monks. These monks, both men and women, are not the ascetics Westerners think of when they think of remote mountain religious orders. These people laugh and play. There are children here. They embrace life.

Of course, what they want the PCs to do is not at all peaceful. Therein lies the dichotomy of all men—even peaceful ideologies bend in the winds of war. The monks rationalize this by considering they work for the greater good. Perhaps they do.

THE ROAD TO SHAMBHALA

The PCs are brought before a meeting of monks in a room with an enormous mandala of pure gold on the floor. There, the elders (men and women both) speak through Ilsa. A few have learned a smattering of English and German, but consider such "new" languages beneath them.

The proposition offered is simple. The monks guide the PCs to Shambhala. Once there, they must sneak or shoot their way inside and retrieve the Seal. While the monks in the valley have Vrill technology powering their field, they have never developed sophisticated weaponry—the PCs with their modern firearms should have little trouble dispatching the enemy. Of course, the same energy that grants them longevity also makes them very hard to kill.

The monks are leaving out the part where they themselves claim the Seal. They cannot leave it in the hands of lesser people. While they embrace life, they do not embrace the lives of these subhumans. Dispatching the characters fits within their strange moral boundaries.

Ilsa does not know this part of the plan. She accompanies the team to the valley. Any supplies the team needs are provided, though the monks have little in the way of modern goods or equipment.

THE VALLEY

When the PCs first approach the valley, they see only more mountain and snow. The monks with them then use their "powers" to uncloud the PCs' minds. When this happens, the characters see a lush valley that should not be there. Among the green flora are homes, walkways, beautiful gardens, and ponds. The homes are simple wooden shelters. Here and there the team spots tall obelisks. Each of these appears made out of VK crystal. These "devices" maintain the field.

When the PCs cross the threshold of the field, their breathing gets more difficult. Ilsa can explain. While everything looks tranquil on the surface, the monks here are trained in the very oldest of martial arts. They have fine swords and spears. True, the PCs guns give them an edge, but the monks are resilient to damage.

A map of the Valley appears below.

The Seal is located atop the central pyramid. See below.

SHAMBHALA MAP KEY

LAKE OF NAGAS

This peaceful, tranquil lake exists at the heart of a valley that should not be. Cool, blue water reflects white clouds. In the centre of the lake lies an island on which the city of Shambhala sits. Her stupas collect around a central stepped pyramid. There are four gates leading inside Shambhala. Small boats skim across the glassy lake toward the city.

Surrounding the lake is a slender beach. Forest runs up close enough for the team to stay in cover. The denizens of the city expect no visitors, as their cloaking field is rarely penetrated. Simply put, most people never see this place. Stealth is their defence, and they have otherwise become lax.

That said, the island offers no causeways. Getting there means either swimming or taking one of the boats. This is where the PCs need to start making some tough choices. The monks are not equipped to stand up to modern firepower. However, they will not give up their city or its prize. The team has the option of either fighting them in melee (and hopefully not killing them), or shooting their way into the central stepped pyramid.

They can take boatmen out using stealth, but the pyramid itself is busy with people.

THE FOUR GATES OF SHAMBHALA

Entrance to Shambhala is possible through four guarded gates, each of which is open during the day. The PCs can attempt disguise, but at Difficulty 3.

understand that nothing here is magical but rather mental, or they may chalk it all up to Vrill tech they cannot understand.

Part of how that plays out depends on the sort of campaign the GM wishes to run. If it is one fuelled by the occult, then the PCs might begin to understand the psionic grid. If not, then these things are just left over Vrill tech, which never need explanation. In either case, they are neither magical nor supernatural.

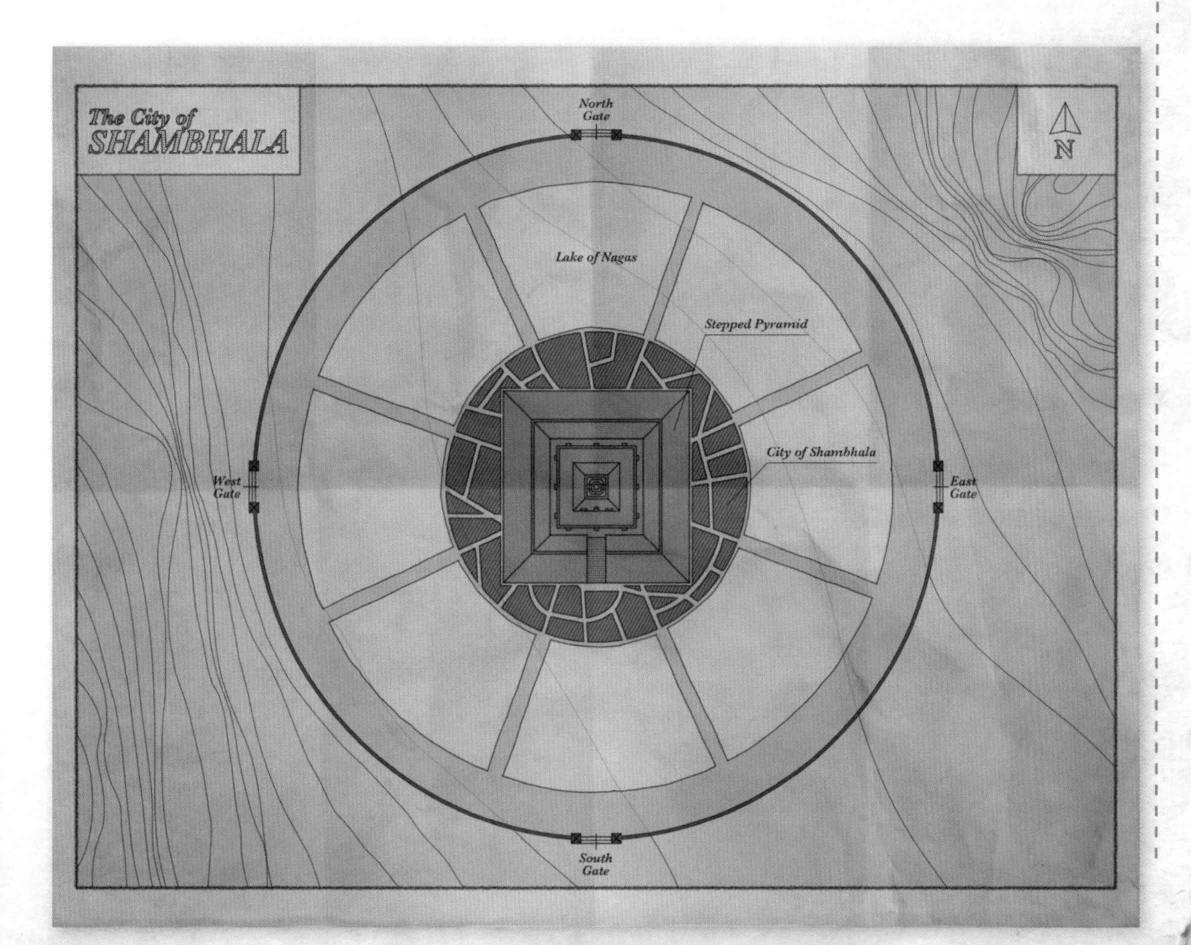

OVERVIEW OF THE CITY

Shambhala is broken into eight sections representing the eight aspects of consciousness. These are the five senses, the self, thought, and the stores of past impressions or incarnations. The latter are explained in the sidebar. The shape of the city resembles that of a lotus flower. Eights roads lead to the central stepped pyramid. Everything is made of stone cut with laser precision.

The stonework is ancient, but human by design. The Vrill themselves used other construction materials, but their base is beneath the city and only a few of the monks, called Bodhisattvas, know of its existence. The Seal is at the top of the pyramid. The underground base is likely the reason the Axis used the Hollow Earth tunnels to invade Tibet. The cloaking field is why they haven't found it yet, but, as often happens in dramatic pulp adventures, the Axis does find the valley—just after the characters do!

Much of the city appears empty. The citizens have a small genetic pool that withered over the years. The city clearly was designed for a larger population, but that time has long since passed. This is a city in decline. It looks pristine from the outside but, once beyond the walls, the team finds crumbling buildings, roads in need of repair and the like. It is by no means a ruin, but it is clear the city saw its heyday some time ago.

This helps the team make their way toward the stepped pyramid. If they don't think to head there, Ilsa can "tune in" to the frequency of the Seal. She correctly believes it comes from the top of the pyramid. The GM likely doesn't want to spend hours exploring the city, and such a "dungeon crawl" is not planned for here. However, the city could certainly be detailed by an industrious GM who wishes to make this into a mini-adventure all its own.

As this is pulp, exploration comes second to plot and action. Have the team make a few Stealth roles once past the gate. Once they get to the pyramid, it becomes more difficult. The Seal is at the apex of the pyramid, fitted in a stone recess.

Exactly who the team encounters along the way, if anyone, is up to the GM. Again, as mentioned above, the monks and citizens are armed with swords, spears, and martial arts knowledge, but nothing that would stop a modern Ranger. If the PCs are made, the citizens easily alert each other using the psionic grid. Said grid also conveniently locates the PCs based on whoever triggered it. Thus, if the PCs fail to take out some sentries in a round or two, the guards access the grid and the whole city knows exactly where the "call" came from.

This quickly escalates the situation. The PCs may be swarmed by monks and need to decide how to deal with that. One way is fisticuffs. The other way is a slaughter by automatic gunfire. This is a call the team needs to make. The monks are not their friends, but they are not exactly combatants either. Do the PCs gun them down to reach their prize?

That is a moral quandary the GM should encourage the PCs to play out. Dr. Jessa Carter and Ilsa are both unwilling to slaughter these people. For one, Dr. Carter values the information they could give the world. More than that, neither NPC wants to be a partner to murder.

If the team is overwhelmed, they may be captured. If the GM wants to give them an "out," have the Axis arrive. They come with two medium walkers and fifty troops. They have no qualms about gunning down the city's residents. This slaughter gives the team time to get to the pyramid without having to kill masses of noncombatants.

Should the team come up with an alternate method of evading the monks—such as accessing the grid—the GM may allow it.

CITIZENS OF SHAMBHALA

CITIZEN OF SHAMBHALA

Characteristics

MB 3 **MD** 4 **PH** 3 **PR** 2

Movement 3 **Capacity** 3 **Initiative** 5

Skills: Attack: Melee 3, Awareness 2, Interaction 2, Knowledge: Occult 3, Knowledge: Anunnaki 2.

Special Abilities: None

Special Powers: Damage Resilience (2)

Equipment

Weapon	Rng	Dam	Rank	Special
Knife	C	1	0	None
Sword	C	1	0	Penetrating 1

DESCRIPTION

The citizens of the city of Shambhala all share a small genetic stock. They are a people dying out, though their arrogance causes them to ignore this impending reality.

STEPPED PYRAMID

This four-sided pyramid dominates the city. It is the tallest edifice on the island. Carvings in a vaguely Mesoamerican/Egyptian fusion cover portions of the edifice. This mishmash of cultures is evident elsewhere in the city, because the founders of this place were among the first civilized humans on Earth. Of course, much of this has been lost to time.

However, the pyramid itself is also a massive storage device. Like a huge server, it has a "hard drive" where the memories of previous inhabitants exist as information. The psionic grid can access this. However, the grid was originally designed for the Vrill. Only the very first people here had perfect working knowledge of the grid. The monks can access it, but not in a way which is orderly. Searching for specific memories is haphazard.

In adventure terms, the storage of memories allows a great plot device. The PCs may very well be missing information the GM feels they ought to have by this point in the story. A great way to "info dump" is to allow the PCs strange, dreamlike flashes of the past that fill in missing details. See Jessa Carter's diary entry at the end of the chapter for an example of how such a scene might play out.

Essentially, the PCs access the grid and, in so doing, open their mind to a flood of memories. So many memories wash over them, that they must make a Difficulty 2 Mind check or be overcome for three rounds per attempt.

In practical terms, this "accidental" retrieval of information can lead the PCs to the next Seal. Flashes of memories give them cryptic clues leading to the next episode. While specific locations for the Seals are not attainable, the GM can lean on this plot device to keep the characters on the right path.

Clues to the other Seals, or future adventures of the GM's design, can also feature in these dreamlike "downloads."

THE AXIS

As the team reaches the pyramid, the Axis storms the island. Sigrid von Thaler has had *Blutkreuz* psychics searching for any sign of the city. When the PCs broke the barrier between the Himalayas and the valley, that set off a psychic ping onto which her psychics locked.

Since the Axis was combing the area for the city, some troops were close enough to arrive not long after the ping. This provides a climactic end to the episode and a foe more worthy of lighting up with machine guns and heavy weapons.

AXIS GRENADIERS (50)

See stats in ***Dust Adventures*** on pp. 148-149.

LUTHER WALKERS (4)

See stats in ***Dust Adventures*** on p. 85.

WHAT THE TEAM NEEDS TO DO

The team's goal during the Axis assault is to get to the top of the pyramid and retrieve the Seal. The Seal is inside a pagoda-like structure that tops the pyramid. It sits in a stone recess and glows faintly. While it is in the vicinity of the psionic grid, the Seal is NOT compatible technology. The grid recognizes the Seal, but cannot run it. This is due to it being made by the Anunnaki rather than the Vrill. It turns the pyramid on, but it cannot "speak" with it.

The Seal was brought here to hide it, not to use it.

Two monks guard the Seal at all times. Lifting it out of the recess is no issue. Getting it out of the city during the Axis assault is. Note: once removed from its recess, the Seal

effectively "turns off" both the Vrill psychic grid and the field preserving and hiding the valley.

The GM should decide how difficult the team's objective is. The Axis did not come prepared to get across a lake, so they have to use the boats the same way the players did. The two walkers are not able to cross the deep lake, unless the GM wants to make things more interesting. In that case, the lake is shallow.

The Axis sends ten teams of five men each to surround the small island and to look out for escapees. One of these teams may spot the team. Alternatively, the team may successfully slip out of the city with the Seal undetected.

If the party is seen by the Axis, ten are able to get to the position on shore where the team is headed. One walker arrives a round later. The longer the battle goes on, the more troops join the fray against the PCs.

Once the PCs are out of the valley, they are effectively home free. The GM may want to make it seem as if they aren't but, if they've come this far, they earned an escape.

WRAPPING UP

The PCs have (hopefully) secured the Seal from Shambhala. While there, ancient memories mingle with their own to point them toward the next Seal. The specific nature of this information is left to the GM, but an example follows in Dr. Carter's journal.

The team needs to get out of Tibet. This is occupied territory. India is the nearest friendly line, and they are smart to head there. Back in Delhi, the team contacts ASOCOM with an update. Dr. Schliemann takes the information gained in Shambhala and, after some research, comes back with a solid starting point for the next episode. This research takes a few days. During the downtime, the team and Dr. Carter can trade theories, while the romantic interest between her and one of the PCs builds. At this point, Dr. Carter and the team have been through quite a lot, and her intellectual defences are beginning to erode—she trusts the team even if she is arrogant in her relationship with them.

While in Delhi, one or more of the other factions after the Seals may attempt to capture one of the team. Which faction makes an attempt is up to the GM. Remember, if the PCs failed to claim one of the Seals up to this point, downtime segments at the end of episodes are a good time to reveal clues as to where that Seal may be. See the Seals Lost chapter for information on who and where this Seal may be. The PCs are about to embark on one of the longer episodes in their quest. Let them gear up and prepare, as they need.

We recovered the Chintamani Stone, but I cannot fathom the circuitous path we took to achieve our goal. I shouldn't even be keeping this journal. It's against protocol. If it slipped into the enemy's hands, who knows what damage it might cause? But I have to write this down. I have to air it somewhere. My intel reports back to ASOCOM cannot contain the way I feel. Feel, dad, you would scold me for allowing feelings to get in the way of science, but this is science like you and I only dreamed of. I'll start from the beginning, or try. I hope, somehow, against all my rational thoughts, you somehow know I'm writing to you.

Intel led us to Vladivostok. We arrived with forged documents. The city is how I imagine the Wild West might have been. Where everywhere else in Russia is under the totalitarian thumb of Stalin, Vladivostok is lawless and largely run by criminals against Stalin. ASOCOM briefed us that Stalin and Rasputin are using the city as a vent for their army's frustrations as well as a place to catch intel from the other blocs. The city is certainly alive with rumours and information.

While there, we found the dead ASOCOM operative. Our investigation into the killing eventually led us to a White Russian whose family had been exiled by Stalin. The convoluted interplay of larcenous characters and shady espionage assets is something I'll spare you, dad. Suffice it to say, I am beginning to trust the Rangers I'm with. I would have had no hope of navigating this intelligence labyrinth without them. The one Ranger who I've told you about, I'm getting closer to him, dad. I haven't had... no that isn't right... I haven't allowed myself room for matters of the heart since mom died. I put everything, all of me, into archaeology and then Clio. But with each new turn this mission takes, I feel death's cold breath against my neck. If I am to love, why not now? What if the war never ends? What if this is my only chance?

I'm laughing at myself now, imagining you shaking your head at the above words. I'll move on. "Back to the task at hand, honey." That's what you always said. And so, back to that task. We followed the White Russian's family, and a map, to Shanghai. The Chinese Nationals are trying to take the city back. I am almost getting

used to being in the middle of combat. I could never have imagined myself like this.

In Shanghai, we found information that led us to what I thought was our goal—the city of Shambhala. Yes, dad, the one you said was a myth. It seemed like it was in the middle of the Gobi Desert. But, dad, oh my God, we found the Tomb of Genghis Khan himself! I cannot tell you how exciting that was. Well, you'd know, as an archaeologist.

I want...I wanted the war to be over. That discovery alone could be a lifetime's work. But we were again under fire. The Seal was not there. Shambhala was located in the Himalayas where Dr. Roerich said it was before his exile from Russia. You and he were friends for a time, weren't you?

Anyway, dad, we went there, to Tibet. We found a valley, which simply should not exist. A tropic-like spot of warmth in those frigid climes. Vrill technology seemed to have created both a field to preserve the city in a radically different climate as well as a way to hide the city. No wonder no one found it. Our guide turned out to be a former Nazi, but one who... how do I say it? Through enlightenment, she somehow abandoned the crazed ideas of those awful people.

She did something with her mind and the valley was suddenly there. Right there, dad, where before we saw only snow and the white peaks of the mountains. The city was in disrepair. The people there, they are old, I think, long lived, but they... Oh, dad, I saw history alive before me. No, that isn't right, I became history! I was there. Oh, how to explain? It was like a dream. The Vrill had some way of storing information, memories, the actual past. We accidentally accessed this vast warehouse of memory and, suddenly, I was there when the Ark was built. I felt the hard acacia wood in my hands. I was there when the Seals were placed inside. Aramaic was spoken around me, but I understood it as if I would my native tongue. Then I was on a ship, some thousands of years later, taking the Ark across the vastness of the Atlantic to the New World. I kept skipping around like that, living in moments of memory that were not my own. I saw Shambhala, if only for a moment, in its glory and watched my own hand — a man's hand—draw a map. My memories mixed with these foreign recollections, but I was able to preserve enough information that Dr. Schliemann used it to lead us to our next Seal.

I have been those dead people, dad, if only for the briefest of moments. I feel as if they live inside me even now. On the periphery, like dark shapes I cannot quite make out, are forces I cannot comprehend. Alien minds, dad. Minds we cannot understand, minds that, if they were to somehow interface with ours would drive us mad.

The knowledge they have, it was so tantalizingly close. Only archaeologists like us could understand what I am about to say. I'd risk going mad, dad. I would. If only for the chance to know what those aliens' minds know — the entire history of our race.

I have to go. We're prepping for our next Op. Ha! Listen to me. I sound like one of the troopers.

I miss you, dad. Always. If only one of those dead memories could have been of you and me.

-- Jessa

CHAPTER 6: RONGORONGO

LIEUTENANT LOUIS LACHANCE

Lachance has served in the French Colonial army for several years. A young man, his thick moustache is forever covered in beads of sweat from the constant heat. Even in monsoon season, the air is thick and hot. Lachance was recruited by ASOCOM not long after that organization was formed. He serves as an intelligence officer under Charles de Gaulle.

Lachance knows that the SSU is backing the Viet Minh. They want to do in Southeast Asia what they have already done in South America—foment revolution. This tactic would offer them ample resources and troops to add to the Red Tide. Rather than simply invade and occupy nations, the SSU decided to convert them, flipping each over to the crimson colour they hope will dominate the globe.

Following a lead found in Shambhala, the team is on the trail of the next Seal. Pursuing clues in the Free French capital of Saigon, they come across a young revolutionary named Ho Chi Minh and set off into the jungles of Cambodia and the mysterious complex known as Angkor Wat.

There, Dr. Carter recognizes the layout of the temples as identical to the pyramids on the Giza Plateau in Egypt. A clue leads them to the strange, megalith-riddled island of Nan Madol. The treasure they seek there has already been captured by the Japanese and hidden elsewhere in the Philippines. Into combat they venture once again to uncover the secret of Yamashita's Gold. Among the plundered treasures they find proof of the Seal's location—on the famous Easter Island.

SAIGON

One of the two hearts of the Free French Empire (the other being Dakar), Saigon is currently the capitol of Free France. Charles de Gaulle visits the city frequently and is there now. In 1947, America's involvement in Vietnam is nearly two decades away. The French have controlled Vietnam as a colony for some time. Early on in the war, the Japanese tried to capture Vietnam but failed.

A resistance force called the Viet Minh fight against French occupation. With mainland France occupied, the Viet Minh have been making great strides. The leader of the Viet Minh independence movement is Ho Chi Minh. In the real timeline of events, Ho Chi Minh becomes leader of communist North Vietnam and America's opponent in the Vietnam War. In 1947 of the ***Dust*** timeline, the Americans are only on his mind insofar as they are allied with France.

Saigon itself is an old city bordering on becoming cosmopolitan. The Viet Minh actively conduct a terrorist campaign against French rule but, compared to cities under siege, Saigon is very, very relaxed. The players are welcomed by French officials and set up in luxurious accommodations. Fresh sheets, clean water, and daily baths are not something the G.I.s are used to.

Of course, given the course of the war, the SSU is already backing the Viet Minh. That means agents of SMERSH are present, including the team's previous nemesis, Colonel Ursula Novikova. She continues to serve the aims of Rasputin and is searching for the next Seal.

Viet Minh, operating partially out of Cambodia, found artefacts dating to the Khmer rulers. Some of these were brought back to the capitol. No one thought much of them until word reached an SSU advisor who reported it to SMERSH. Word then reached Rasputin who, for reasons he did not disclose, was convinced the pieces related to a forgotten expedition made by Alexander the Great to Angkor, the city of lost temples.

Of course, the PCs only have access to intel related to the artefacts. They do not yet know they come from Angkor or that they relate to Alexander the Great. They also lack access to the Viet Minh. They therefore need to work out a way to establish contact and gather intel about the artefacts.

Upon arrival, Lieutenant Louis Lachance, a member of ASOCOM, greets the team. He shares everything he knows with the PCs (see sidebar).

Lachance needs to be dealt with diplomatically. The team is far away from their traditional ASOCOM handlers. They are given respect because they are soldiers, but no more. Lachance is not going to help them until he is persuaded. Persuading him is going to be extremely difficult. Interaction tests are at Difficulty 3.

The PCs could try telling him the truth, which might actually work. They might also try to dig up dirt on Lachance and blackmail him. Finally, they could try to contact ASOCOM directly and have them put pressure on de Gaulle and Lachance. The problem is, here in Vietnam, ASOCOM's threats seem pretty far away.

The GM must decide which techniques work on Lachance. This is a roleplaying encounter not a combat one. Their skills with firearms are not going to get them past this. They have to find a way to get Lachance's assistance.

Only he knows who among the Viet Minh is a double agent. He is very hesitant to share this information. Once the PCs do convince him, they need to visit the Viet Minh agent's house. She lives on Rue Pasteur. On the way to his place, a bar frequented by the French explodes—a target of Viet Minh terrorism.

The Viet Minh agent, Kim Ly, lives above a pho noodle house. Her place is small and shared with her younger brother. The PCs may decide to follow her or gain access to her apartment after she leaves. They may also interrogate her, but she keeps insisting she is nothing but a barmaid. She is a barmaid, but she is also much more. As a double agent, she fears being exposed by either side. Kim Ly does not like the French, but she likes the communists even less. The Viet Minh are in league with the SSU and she does not believe that is any way to independence.

WHAT KIM LY KNOWS

Kim Ly did not get the artefacts herself. She acquired them from another Viet Minh who was sweet on her. She was going to take them to Lachance, but an SSU advisor, Han Chen, intervened. He took the artefacts. She was able to use her network to determine that Novikova took them and believes they come from Angkor, deep in the Cambodian jungle.

Kim Ly saw the artefacts and can verify that a few of them looked like "old Western coins." She is not qualified to say how old. They are actually Persian coins Alexander brought with him after defeating Darius II.

It is left to the GM's discretion as to whether Novikova receives word of their arrival or investigation. If she does, she may send people to keep tabs on the team or kill them outright. Use the Spy stats on pp. 148-149 of ***Dust Adventures*** for any of her men.

SIAM

In the world of ***Dust***, Cambodia is part of what is known as Siam. As an independent country (a member of the Neutral Nations Organization), Siam is careful with foreigners. While there is little they can do to keep them out, they do officially ban foreign soldiers. ASOCOM provides the team with false IDs.

Their first destination is the town of Siem Reap, not far from Angkor. Siem Reap was a small village until the early 1900s when Angkor was rediscovered by Europeans. Soon, the village became a tourist destination, though the war has since drawn that down to a trickle. Angkor is a well-known city, the largest in the world at the time (circa 1300 A.D.). It eclipsed the size of Rome, Paris, and London. Some 1,000,000 inhabitants lived there under the Khmer kings. Decocted to Buddhism, the "wats" or temples of the city are legendary.

Lachance is primarily concerned with that, and it is only by ASOCOM directive that he is tending to the PCs concerns. Talking with him, one gets the impression that he'd much rather be engaged with more pressing business. Further, it is clear de Gaulle assigned him this task to keep the team out of the way. De Gaulle is not about to lose the new French capitol, ASOCOM's plans be damned.

Thus, the team encounters tension from the outset, and Lachance tosses as much bureaucratic red tape their way as he can. He simply wants to be rid of them. No matter how much they profess their mission is of utmost importance, Lachance sides with his own.

He knows about the artefacts. They were given to a Chinese SSU advisor. A few days after, Colonel Novikova arrived. He knows she works directly for Rasputin, and has dismissed her involvement with the Viet Minh. She is after the artefacts, or possibly the location where they were found. Personally, Lachance cares about neither.

The team can easily hook up with one of the tours headed to Angkor. Depending on how they crossed the border into Cambodia, they may be relatively unarmed. Siam does not allow foreigners to bring weapons across the border.

The tour is a bit of a surreal affair. In a world ravaged by war, the normality of historical tours is something to behold. Mostly flooded with Europeans who have decided to wait out the war in a neutral country, Siem Reap still makes most of its money from these expatriates. Most are dilettantes, dandies, and those with money who can afford to live this way. One of them is not at all like that.

Raymond Dukowski is an American Marine. He went AWOL after seeing action throughout the Pacific Theatre of Operations. Private Dukowski decided he was done after the Battle of Peleliu. When leave came up, he headed for the hills. Since early 1945 he has been travelling around Southeast Asia in a state of shell shock. His thousand-yard stare is spooky, even to other combat vets.

When he sees the PCs, he begins to act sketchy. He can tell another soldier when he sees one and he is afraid the team is there to bring him in. A bus takes the group to Angkor. Once there, Dukowski tries to disappear. He has no plan. He simply reacts to what he perceives as a danger.

In attempting to slip away, he no doubt gains the attention of the PCs. If they pursue him, they must venture deeper into the city of Angkor. The tour guide yells at them but does little else. Dukowski happens to stumble upon Novikova and her men digging out a collapsed entrance to one of the wats.

If the PCs wander off, but do not follow Dukowski, they hear the sound of picks and shovels before very long.

When they spot Novikova, she is reading a diary and appears to be matching its contents to the temple she now stands before.

COLONEL URSULA NOVIKOVA

See pp. 127-128 of the NPCs Appendix.

SPETZNAZ (12)

See p. 153 of ***Dust Adventures***.

Novikova has a Russian GAZ-47 amphibious vehicle. She and her men have almost made it into the tunnel. Novikova sent one of her men inside. The others provide cover for that man. Novikova retreats rather than risking capture. The scene assumes she escapes, but the PCs might pursue and capture her if the GM allows. Assuming the PCs win the battle, read the following:

Through two broken Bodhisattvas leaning against each other, you crawl into the hole dug by Novikova's men. Past several feet of darkness, you emerge into a vast chamber. Vishnu, some of her many arms broken, towers above you, a beam of light falling through a crack in the ceiling lands on her stone eyes. The Russian who crawled in ahead of you groans under the piece of the ceiling that just collapsed on top of him.

The man, Sergei, is in tremendous pain. Novikova has also abandoned him. The PCs are in a good position to get what information they need from him. He came in under Novikova's orders to find a diamond supposed to be located in the third eye of Vishnu. Now that the PCs know what they are looking for, they can climb up the statue where they find a diamond in the centre of Vishnu's forehead. The facets are nearly perfect, but it isn't actually a diamond. It is a gem vaguely reminiscent of VK.

Elsewhere in the room, also the victim of a death trap, is a very old skeleton. It wears Macedonian armour—which Dr. Carter can identify—and has a pouch containing a few coins. "This is one of Alexander's men..." Dr. Carter says quietly. She is clearly astonished. Alexander made no recorded campaign to Siam. She explains as much.

Suddenly impassioned, Dr. Carter grabs the wounded man by the collar. "What does the diamond do? Why was Alexander here?" If the PCs allow her, she keeps shaking him. Obviously, they could leave him here to die or be taken by Siamese authorities.

Sergei gives up what he knows. Novikova answers to Rasputin. She reports to SMERSH, but her reports are often incomplete. The man reveals Novikova possesses a diary belonging to a Moslem explorer from the 15th century. In it, a history of Alexander's conquest is recorded along with drawings of temples and the like. He never had a chance to see the diary for very long. If the PCs want answers, Sergei says they need the diary. To get that, they have to catch up with Novikova. He knows they were leaving Cambodia for Sumatra. He even knows the hotel SMERSH uses there.

The PCs have the crystal, but they have no idea what to do with it. They must go into the lion's den, in SSU occupied Sumatra, and get that diary.

SUMATRA

Sumatra was conquered by the SSU, mostly the Chinese. The SSU flag flies over all hotels and government buildings in Medan, the capital of the North Sumatra province and the largest city on the sizable island. The airport there has been requisitioned by the SSU. Colonel Novikova intends to fly out from there. Her destination: Micronesia, specifically the island of Nan Madol.

Sumatra is not as well defended as most SSU territory. It sits on its own, away from the better part of their conquests. Troops there are often pulled away to more important locations. Sumatra is a waiting game for the SSU. They planned to use it as a launching point to stage an assault on either the rest of Indonesia or Southeast Asia. To date, neither has happened.

ASOCOM can provide only limited resources. An older plane is provided to fly over the island, where the PCs must parachute outside of Medan. From there, they must make their way to the hotel where Novikova is staying. In so doing, the team finds themselves aboard a Tupolev chartered by Novikova.

The situation in Indonesia is perilous. The Allies try to make headway, but the Pacific Theatre of Operations against the Japanese is more pressing. They have lost many islands to the Axis and are attempting to win them back. This leaves the PCs without a lot of support. It is up to them to get into the city and obtain the diary.

The PCs may think of a different plan. One such course of action may be having the plane drop them directly over the hotel. The hotel is one of the larger buildings in Medan, and skilled jumpers can guide their chutes in using new technology. Air Cavalry (Parachute) rolls are made with a Difficulty of 3 for the PCs to glide onto the roof. Catastrophic failure finds them hung up on another building or possibly falling to their doom.

Imagine the scene: in the dark of night, the troop plane comes in just under the clouds. The PCs make the jump—Dr. Carter doing a tandem jump with one of the Rangers—and pull their chutes under the moonlight. They guide themselves toward the top of the hotel, landing with barely an inch to spare.

Next, they rappel down the side of the hotel to one of the balconies, Gaining access to that room, they use it to enter the hallway and pick the lock on Novikova's door. There are two men in the room. Novikova is nowhere to be seen. Neither is her diary.

Depending on how stealthy the team was on entering, the men may not wake at all. The PCs recognize them as men wounded in a previous encounter (if any survived). The PCs no doubt want to interrogate the men. Once they do, they find out Novikova is boarding a Tupolev at Medan Airport as they speak. It is now a mad dash to the airport to catch that plane.

MEDAN AIRPORT

The airport is closed to non-SSU personnel. The entrances are guarded, but the PCs can cut through the wire and slip in, hopefully, undetected. The Tupolev is a big plane and stands out. Other fighters and a helicopter are also present. Most of the planes are actually civilian aircraft. The SSU is not quite ready to make the push further into Indonesia.

Two men stand outside the plane's open ramp. One puts a cigarette out on the ground, says "Time to go," in Russian, and the two board. If the team wants to get on, now is the time to do so.

If they wait, they need to find a fast vehicle to catch up with the plane then try to board via the landing gear. This option is far more difficult but also more cinematic.

The two men are part of the crew of the Tupolev. They chat about the dangerous nature of this mission. The plane is flying into a potential battle zone between the Allied Navy and the Japanese Fleet. The Rangers need to take the two men out quickly and quietly. Any chance for one to scream alerts Novikova and her team in one of the forward compartments.

If the team takes the two men out silently, they surprise Novikova and her men. That does not mean Novikova and her men give up.

Aboard the plane, a firefight is about to take place. If Novikova can push the team back into the cargo bay, she activates the tail door. Large crates begin shifting and sliding toward the PCs. They must dodge these while preventing themselves from being sucked out the back of the plane. (Athletic rolls at Difficulty 2 or Mobility rolls at Difficulty 3). This goes on for some time. If the team is losing, spring the next event more quickly. If they are winning, wait until the combat is over.

PIRATES!

The plane does not go unnoticed by those below. During the flight, anti-aircraft fire rakes the fuselage and the plane spins out into the sea. The PCs survive, though the GM may impose wounds. The bulk of the plane remains intact, but quickly sinks. The surviving SSU operatives equal the player count. So, if there are four PCs, then there are four Russians. Novikova does not count toward this total. Who shot them down is unclear. It could have been either the Americans or the Japanese.

The PCs find themselves in a rapidly sinking fuselage. There are inflatable rafts aboard. Swim checks are Difficulty 2. When everything sorts itself out, the Russians are in one raft, the PCs in another. Oh, yeah, they are also in shark-infested waters. Things never really seem to improve for the PCs, do they?

Fins circle the two rafts, and dark shapes are evident below the surface. The PCs and the Russians both have rather flimsy boats intended for less people. At a certain point left to the GM's discretion, the rafts list because there are too many passengers. Both Novikova and the PCs are in, metaphorically, the same boat.

Novikova is careful not to deploy the emergency flares included in the raft. She knows that any bloc might respond, and she has no intention of being captured. The PCs also have flares in their raft. They may decide to use these if they like.

If neither party uses a flare, they float in the sea for two days. Fresh water quickly runs out, and everyone is hungry. The old sailor's code of drawing lots begins to look like the sane choice. Then, on day three, parched, their skin blistered by the sun, a ship arrives. It flies no flag, but appears to be a merchant vessel armed with twin .50 Cal Victory Machine guns in front. It is a pirate vessel.

MALACCA STRAITS PIRATES

The war has endangered the fishing industry many native Indonesians rely on. Coupled with the inability to reliably acquire necessary goods, many have turned to piracy. This tradition began long before the war, but the war has made it all the more attractive. Many ships travel in convoys, and the Malacca pirates are forced to work in groups or become privateers. The particular pirate vessel that finds the PCs and Russians is the *Indra*. She is a merchant ship modified for a gun emplacement on the bow. She is a quick ship, slipping along her enemy and taking them unaware. The survivors they find from the Tupolev are essentially sitting ducks. The twin .50 Cals can chew through both groups in an instant. Barring any unforeseen brilliant moves by the PCs, the two groups are captured.

A merchant ship, her name in Vietnamese script, towers above you. Her shadow falls across your comparatively tiny raft. A man with missing teeth, all of 20, smiles widely as he points a pair of twin .50 Cal machine guns at you. At least the weapon is American, and maybe these pirates are better than the sharks.

There is little the PCs can do to negotiate or shoot their way out of this situation. Certainly, they have the option to try either, but it is not likely to end well. The pirates order them to place their weapons on the floors of the rafts—they want to salvage these—and prepare to climb aboard. A rope ladder is tossed down and the characters are ordered to ascend one by one.

Once aboard the *Indra*, the PCs and the Russians are thrown into a makeshift brig. A former freezer, the brig is little more than a room with thick walls and an outside lock. It is not currently frozen, fortunately.

Allow the PCs time to acclimate to their capture. Novikova is clearly in charge of her remaining men but begins as unwilling to cooperate with the PCs. After some time in the brig, she considers a temporary alliance.

The pirates are mostly fishermen, but a few professionals exist among them. One is an AWOL member of the Chinese army under Mao. He is a Nationalist sympathizer and struck out on his own when he was able. The captain is a 40 year-old male. His name is Prank, and he hails from a tiny island that does not appear on most maps.

Prank comes by late that night with three guards. He wishes to learn the identity of his captives. Prank is less concerned with individual identities than with nationality. His captives have value according to how much a bloc will pay ransom for them. Prank is intelligent, and understands those of higher rank may possess more intel and thus be more valuable.

His questions come in broken English. If the PCs make a Mind roll at Difficulty 2, they note that Prank seems unable to distinguish Russian accents from American. This could give them some leverage.

After Prank interviews the survivors, he leaves them in the brig. They have already been searched and, unless a PC hid something very carefully (or uncomfortably), the pirates took everything they had. They have no money, no weapons, and nothing to bargain with but their memories.

While sitting in the brig for the better part of the night, there is little doubt the subject of escape will come up. Novikova has nothing to offer the pirates, though she says she does. The SSU, she says, have patrol boats that would be willing to overlook the *Indra's* activities. The PCs may fashion a similar story. In that case, an Interaction (Social) roll is required.

Even a success does not guarantee the PCs negotiate a favourable position. The GM needs to take this on a case-by-case basis.

The most obvious, and possibly best, option lies in teaming up. The Russians and the Americans both possess superior combat and tactical skills. When food is served, the door must be opened. Four pirates armed with assault rifles are present during this time. The PCs and the Russians need to gain the element of surprise and take them out quickly, if they hope to avoid detection.

In total, there are only 20 pirates aboard. They rely on speed, stealth, and a small arsenal of Axis Double Barrelled *Panzerschreks* to take on their prey. Unlike privateers, the *Indra* remains an independent, and illegal, pirate vessel.

PIRATES (20)

Use stats for Hired Thugs on p. 154 of ***Dust Adventures***. Add assault rifles of choice to their equipment.

STORMING THE INDRA

The PCs and Russians may concoct any plan they like. Since a myriad of routes are available, the GM must necessarily evaluate the merits of each plan. If the PCs have come up with something very clever, give them bonuses as you see fit. If not, they might face all 20 men along the deck, the bridge, or the cargo bay.

The pirates have the weapons to begin with, and they have more men (add a pirate per PC if the GM deems it necessary). Overtaking the pirates requires some element of surprise. Remember, the pirates have automatic weapons. How this plays out is not something we can cover here. As noted, the PCs have many options, and the GM should use their best judgment.

A full-on assault is liable to end with a lot of dead PCs. Charging automatic weapons rarely works out well.

TAKING CONTROL OF THE INDRA

Beating the pirates is just one part of the equation. Once the PCs and SSU have the ship under their control, two elements become apparent:

One, no one knows how to pilot a ship (unless a non-pregenerated character has that ability). The Russians certainly do not. That means at least one of the upper-level crew needs to be pressed into service. Doing so is not difficult, as none of the pirates wish to die.

The second problem lies with the truce between the PCs and the SSU. Both have similar objectives, but neither wants the other to reach theirs first. Novikova is very shrewd and waits to make a move. The PCs may make their move whenever they wish.

If the two parties speak openly, they realize that the Axis and the Sons of Belial are the greater threat right now. An extended truce might be had depending on what the PCs are willing to share. Also the pirates took the diamond/crystal. Who has it now depends on how quickly the PCs reacted. Remember, while Novikova knows the PCs beat her in Angkor, she is not certain they recovered the diamond.

Should the PCs fail to get the diamond with due haste, the SSU does. They then hold all the cards. The PCs must offer something especially attractive to negotiate on level ground. Of course, if the battle with the pirates killed more of the SSU, the PCs may have an advantage in numbers.

All of the equipment and weapons each group carried is found in the galley. The pirates prepare only for short trips, attacking a single ship then retreating to the safety of atolls and the like. Provisions for a few days at sea are aboard.

WHAT THE SSU KNOWS AND WANTS

Colonel Novikova needs the diamond to find the next object in her quest—a cave under Nan Madol. Once she finds the cave using the diamond—much as the PCs used the stone in episode three to find the lost city—she plans to dive and enter the cave.

Nan Madol is Novikova's goal, but the PCs do not necessarily know this. In the best of circumstances, they have the diamond and, probably, Novikova has the diary. One without the other is like having only half a map (and the PCs have experienced this once before). In the diary of the Moslem explorer are instructions on how to use the diamond as a kind of Viking sunstone. It should be noted the diamond is not of Viking origin, but the utility of the gem is similar to those used by Norse navigators.

Essentially, the facets of the gem serve as demarcations between latitudinal lines. By aligning these with the sun, one can uncover the secret cave located under Nan Madol. The people who founded Nan Madol were refugees of the Great Deluge. These people possessed superior navigational skills and technical prowess. Unfortunately, the Flood ravaged their culture, and the survivors took what knowledge and artefacts they could. Upon Nan Madol, according to the diary, lies an object sacred to this lost civilization. The diary affords these forgotten people no name.

Novikova must be convinced to share the diary. The PCs need to use every negotiation tactic at their disposal; else the parlay degenerates into combat. If this is the case, and the SSU is losing, Novikova dives over the side. She leaves the diary behind in her haste.

If the two parties work together, they may make a straight shot for Nan Madol. While the path there is laced with Japanese and American warships, the *Indra* remains undetected. As a small ship, it presents little threat. The GM may decide a few reconnaissance missions do flybys to keep the team on their toes.

THE DIARY OF MUSEF IBN-AL RASHID AL KAFNA

Praise be to Allah, my journey continues. Again, I follow the trail of he who is called the Great One, Alexander of Macedon. On this trail I feel some otherworldly connection to him, as if he and I were not separated by 1700 years. The stories of Delphi appear true: Alexander was seeking more than conquest.

I cannot say when or where the obsession took hold of him, but I can say it began for me in Riyadh. I had slim hopes for a promising academic career as the Christians, once again, swept southward in a campaign of expansion. They brought with them more than the sword and cross. They brought legends. I have traced some of these to our own libraries in Timbuktu. I believe the northern Christians bring sagas perverted by the ages but based in truth. Such is the fate of people who do not write down all their histories. Allah be praised, we are not so uncouth.

Before our great empire, blessed under the name of Allah, there existed a civilization the likes of which our age may only dream. Shining cities lay spread under the mantle of stars at night, jewels in an earthly crown we have long since forgotten. Then, a great catastrophe befell those people. They were wiped out by the fury of the skies and the sea. Great and impossible achievements were as common to them as spices are to us.

All of this, in the cataclysm, was lost. Yet survivors, ordered by their gods to keep the one and secret history, fled to the many corners of the map. Each of them brought a part of the story. I believe their gods intended this, or that Allah, blessed is his name, manifested under the masks of their gods.

Alexander found the trail of this lost world. What secrets might it unearth? What deep, and possibly fathomless mysteries, are we not privy to? I have a compass and a telescope. I have running water and the pleasure of indentured women. I am a civilized man, and yet when I read the fragments that remain of this story, I feel as those northern barbarians must feel when seated beside a Baghdadi prince. We have forgotten too much. May Allah will it: we shall regain this lost memory again.

NAN MADOL

Like a fort constructed by giants, Nan Modal features tier after tier of massive basalt pillars. Each lays across one another in a pattern that reinforces the entire structure. It looks, to your untrained eyes, like shelters soldiers such as yourself might build against an incoming air attack—primitive, yet displaying a vast technical knowledge.

Novikova brought enough dive gear for her and two of her men. The pirates confiscated this. There are sets of apparatus for three people. The two parties must decide who goes under. Novikova insists she and one of her men dive with one PC unless she is convinced otherwise. Again, this is at the GM's discretion.

Once the composition of the dive team is settled either the PCs or Novikova use the diamond to plot the exact location of the cave they seek. The cave lies some 50

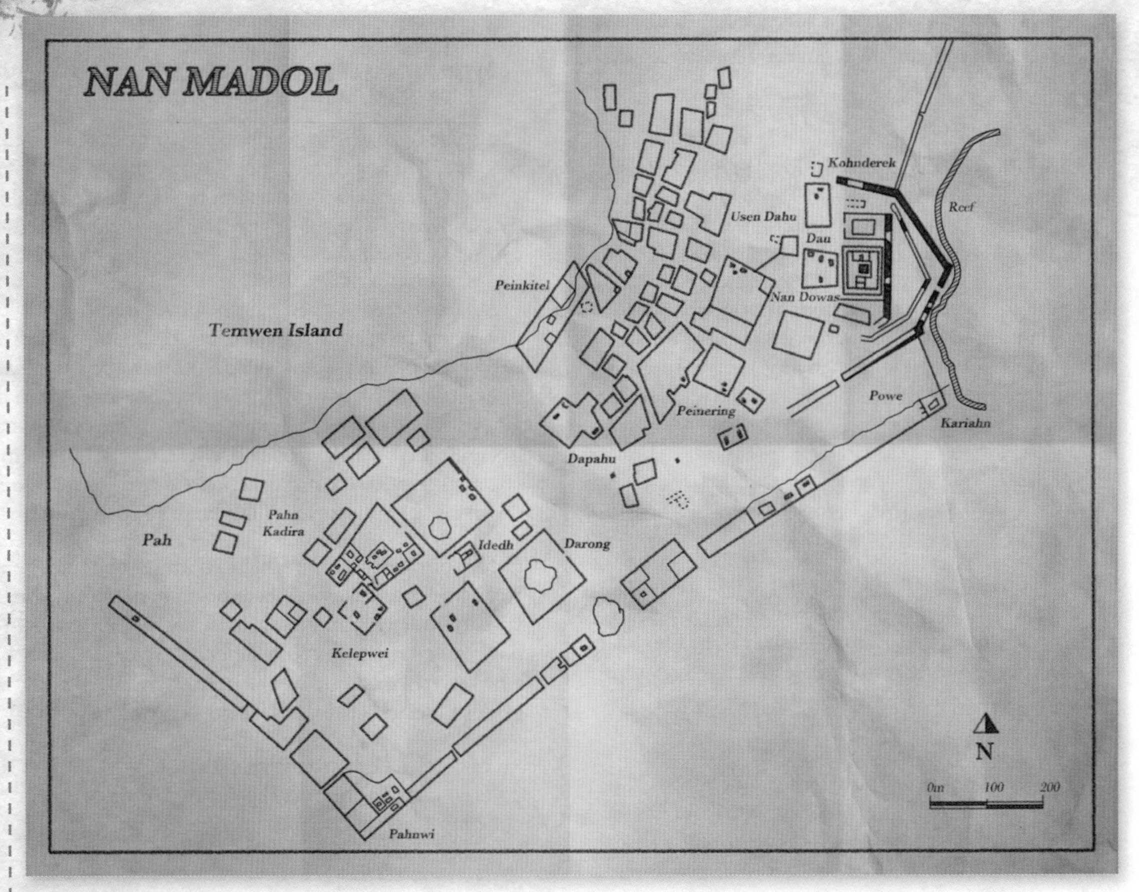

NAN MADOL
A mystery off the coast of Pohnpei in Micronesia, Nan Madol is an artificial island created by giant basalt monoliths. Moving these massive rocks and lowering them into place would have been a near impossible feat during the time conventional academics date the site (600 A.D.). If the stones were moved before the area was submerged, it would have been easier (though still extremely difficult given academia's picture of Stone Age man) to create the artificial island. If the stones were moved before much of the area was submerged by glaciation, that means it is around 12,000 years old.

No one at that time should have been able to build such a site as Nan Madol. The island Novikova seeks is one of a number of such artificial islands constructed with vast basalt pillars piled in a pattern similar to Lincoln Logs. Whoever created this site has been forgotten, and modern archaeology has swept the anomaly to their dustbins.

metres beneath the surface but is not readily spotted. Mind checks are necessary to spot the entrance.

Once this is done, the characters that find the entrance swim through several metres of dressed stone overgrown in coral. Once past the tunnel, the divers emerge into an air pocket.

The cave is natural, but hewn to a refined shape by hands long since dead. This part of Nan Madol was built atop a small hill. The builders understood the Great Flood had not ended and decided to secret away their prize in this cave. Once the divers emerge, they discover stagnant, but breathable air. The chamber has a ledge running alongside around its circumference. A recession on one wall appears to contain a rough stone sarcophagus.

Beside the sarcophagus, heaped against its base are stone bowls filled with precious jewels and gold. The sarcophagus lid is ajar. Judging by the amount of dust accumulated on the part which is open, and that which has not been moved, a year at most has passed. Dr. Carter notices this if the PCs do not. Lifting the lid is a Physique check if attempted alone. Once done, the interior reveals a mummy similar to, but not identical, the alien remains found in the Grand Canyon.

The creature is approximately seven feet tall. The head, as wrapped in the mummification cloth, has features that are distinctly non-human. Beside the figure lies a wand-like piece of metal the PCs recognize as being very similar to the metal UFO fragment found in the Grand Canyon.

Dr. Carter immediately identifies the burial as that afforded a king or religious leader. Examining the body, she avers that it is not a Vrill. Novikova pulls her back as she examines, cautioning, "This is not yours alone." Rough glyphs are hewn into the stone sarcophagus similar to those found on the Seals.

Among the glyphs on the sarcophagi, one is notable for having been defaced. Someone attempted to erase an entire line of these glyphs, but the underlying patterns are still more or less readable and can be copied and clarified with a simple rubbing.

The glyphs describe a treasure contained within the "casket of our God." That treasure is not the slim stick found. PCs looking closely note a broken chain of gold lies around the corpse's neck. Someone recently removed the item that was attached to that necklace.

Novikova seems to know what is missing. Pressed, she admits that she removed the pages of the diary. She is not, in fact, working merely for SMERSH but for Rasputin. Those pages were sent to him at The Kremlin.

In order for the PCs to find out what is on them, she proposes a deal. She needs to gain access to the Allied side of the Philippines. The Japanese have, for years, been amassing treasure in the area and burying it all over the islands. This is part of what she calls Project Golden Lily. Since the item here, which she says is a medallion, is missing, they must pursue another treasure—one in the possession of the Japanese. Novikova hoped to avoid this more difficult acquisition, but she now has no choice.

She does not reveal what they are looking for in the treasure, as she does not trust the team anymore than they trust her. The deal is she will lead them to a double agent working for Japanese intelligence and then, together, they will recover the treasure.

Assuming they accept the offer, the adventure proceeds to the Philippines.

THE PHILIPPINES

The islands have been inhabited for 22,000 years. Long, long ago, in times forgotten by men, survivors from the great civilization spoken of in Musef's diary brought relics from their culture to the Philippines. Unfortunately, the Philippines were merely a stopover on their way to Easter Island. Neither Novikova nor the PCs know this yet.

In 1521, Ferdinand Magellan arrived. The Spaniard brought conquest to the Philippines as well as a lust for gold. He sought out ancient legends of a treasure buried on the islands and, in time, recovered some of that gold. Magellan moved much of the gold back to Spain but kept some for himself on the island of El Nido. The Japanese have discovered this trove and added to it. The treasure currently lies in the caves located along the single mountain on El Nido.

Unfortunately, the island is now under siege. Allied Marines landed earlier in the month as part of MacArthur's promise to take back the islands. The Japanese are incredibly hard to dislodge, and the fighting is brutal. As the PCs approach the island, they are spotted by an Allied plane. They need to immediately identify themselves or be bombed to the bottom of the sea by their own side.

The lieutenant they reach on the other end of the radio tells them a USN PT Boat is en route. It quickly pulls alongside the vessel. Destroyers in the distance shell El Nido. The navy comes aboard, searches the ship and likely finds some of the pirates' contraband. Everyone is taken into custody and brought to the battleship USS Colorado.

Aboard the Colorado, the PCs speak with the captain and, through radio, to ASOCOM. ASOCOM confirms the importance of their mission. The captain does not like having Novikova aboard and wishes to put her in the brig. The PCs have the final say once they speak with ASOCOM.

The treasure cave is currently part of a Japanese network of tunnels dug for defence. The PCs have to fight their way inside with the assistance of the USMC who are pushing further inland. The captain shows them on a map where the mountain is found, but he does not know the location of the cave. Novikova brings up her contact. The captain

says the marines on the island may have captured him. He suspects this because, unlike almost all of the other defeated Japanese, he did not commit *sepukku*.

The PT boat takes them in close enough for the team to wade ashore.

Dusk, lit with the cacophonous array of artillery exploding in photo negatives deep within the jungle. The beach crawls with resupplies, as Marines have established a beachhead. Wounded men lay under mosquito nets moaning in the darkness.

Somewhere, a wind comes from inland bringing with it the smell of gasoline and burning flesh—napalm.

As if to punctuate this scent, a fireball erupts along the tree line, consuming the forest in heat, lighting the darkening sky as if it were momentarily day.

The prisoner has yet to be moved to the beachhead. The PCs must hump it into the jungle and link up with a marine platoon holding the prisoner there. The trek through the jungle is unpleasant, and their guide gives them malaria pills. After an hour of hacking through dense foliage, the team arrives at the platoon's camp.

The platoon's lieutenant has been briefed via radio and allows the team and Novikova to speak with the prisoner. Unless a member of the team speaks Japanese—Dr. Carter does not—only Novikova is able to converse with him. The conversation is clearly strained. The man, Shiguero, was promised a portion of the gold in return for his information. Novikova is no longer able to keep this promise as the Allies invaded before the SSU could get to the island. A new deal must be struck. Alternatively, the prisoner can be persuaded by other means. This is, after all, a war. What moral boundaries the PCs are willing to cross is their decision alone. One of the less pulp aspects of ***Dust Adventures*** is confronting the harsh realities of a world at war.

Via one method or another, the PCs persuade Shiguero to draw a map of the cave system. He marks on this map where the treasure cave is located. The entire area is still under Japanese control and, even as they speak, the Imperial Japanese Navy is coming to engage the Allies. This is ***not*** the World War II we remember. The IJN (Imperial Japanese Navy) is by no means out of the fight. They are vital, bold, and quite capable of retaking the island from the marines.

THE PLATOON

Lieutenant Hardy has been directed to assist the PCs, though he thinks it is a suicide mission. The marines have two walkers and thirty men capable of fighting. They are going to attack a fortified position. The attack can be

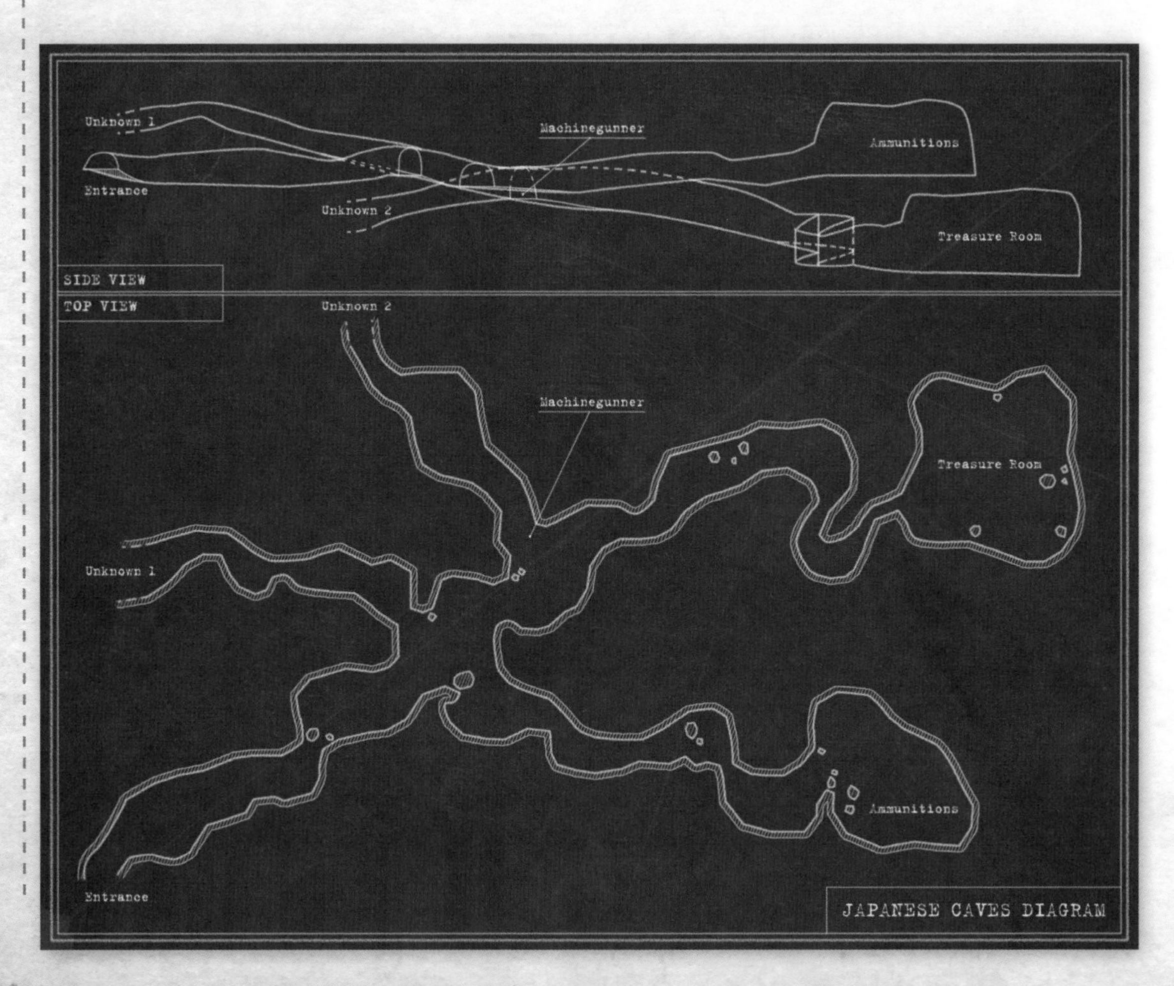

presaged by an airstrike from a carrier. That evens things up a bit, but the Japanese are dug in.

Once the airstrike is over, the PCs decide how to approach the situation. Of course, they may forego the airstrike and elect a stealthy option for accessing the Japanese caves. This is very dangerous, as they need to go in alone. They cannot sneak an entire marine platoon and two walkers past Japanese patrols.

Four successful Stealth rolls in a row are needed to penetrate Japanese lines. The character with the highest score may roll. If successful, the team arrives outside one of the caves. If not, they are spotted by a Japanese patrol. A firefight ensues. The Japanese also have Steel Samurai in the area. Only one battle ensues regardless of multiple failures.

JAPANESE PATROL (6 MEN)

See p. 83 for Imperial Japanese Soldier stats.

The firefight draws the attention of another patrol, this one with a functioning radio. In 1-4 rounds, reinforcements arrive. If the PCs do not bug out, they are likely killed or captured. The GM may conduct the capture (and hopefully the escape) as they wish. The team is brought into the cave system if captured.

Assuming they either sneak in or defeat the initial patrol quickly, the PCs likewise arrive at the mouth of a cave marked on Shigeru's map. The PCs take a route directly to the treasure cave, but encounter a group of Japanese soldiers resupplying a machinegun along the way.

JAPANESE SOLDIERS (3)

See p. 83 for Imperial Japanese Soldier stats.

Getting in is relatively easy. It is getting out that becomes a problem, but first the PCs discover the treasure cave. Gold and silver treasures are heaped in wooden crates emblazoned with Japanese Rising Suns. Opening one or another reveals a trove of priceless antiquities. Novikova knows exactly what she is looking for. She proceeds directly to a box marked with the Kanji character for "death." Quickly prying off the lid, she begins to root through the crate.

In frustration, she swears in Russian. Dr. Carter translates. "She says it isn't here."

Novikova kicks the crate. "No! No, it is not here! Just a gold plate! A goddamned plate!"

When asked, Novikova admits she was looking for one of the Seals. Unfortunately it is not here. Instead, there is only a disk.

Dr. Carter grabs the disc. It looks like a phonograph record, but carved in gold with a spiral beginning at the centre and winding round the entire surface on one side. As she examines the disc, a bombardment shakes the cave. This time, though, the bombardment is not coming from the Allies. The Imperial Japanese Navy has arrived.

FIGHTING THEIR WAY BACK OUT

The team now needs to get out of the tunnels and back to friendly lines. However these lines are no longer where they remember them. While the team has been in the tunnels, Japanese reinforcements have reached the island. The bombardment has driven the marines back. It is night when they emerge. Fighting rages all around them, tracers zipping like angry hornets in the dark. Explosions rock the jungle and the PCs have a very real chance of being struck by shrapnel. Roll four Dust dice every six rounds. Three Targets indicate someone is hit for shrapnel damage. Treat as a grenade rather than a mortar for purposes of this damage.

The team knows where Allied lines were, but they do not know how far they need to travel to get there now. In fact, they only need to move a couple kilometres, but these klicks are hard going.

Along the way, the team encounters a Japanese unit engaged with the marines. The Japanese have two walkers in the battle. The marines only have one. From here, when a lull in combat occurs, one can hear the waves of the Pacific rushing against the shore. Lights out on the water flash as the two navies exchange fire.

Bursting forth through a clearing in the jungle, you come face-to-face with a Japanese walker. The unfamiliar design kicks on its legs as a shell rockets toward a marine position. Tracers zip through the sky. You've wandered right into the middle of a firefight.

The marines are in trouble. Without the PCs help, they are killed to a man. There are five marines and one Mickey versus 10 Japanese and two Japanese Steel Samurai.

JAPANESE SOLDIERS (10)

See pp. 60-61 for Imperial Japanese Soldier stats.

STEEL SAMURAI (2)

See p. 60 for Steel Samurai stats.

MARINES (5)

See p. 147 of ***Dust Adventures*** for stats.

MICKEY WALKER (1)

See p. 79 of ***Dust Adventures*** for stats.

Once the firefight is over, the PCs can bug out for American lines with wounded marines in tow. If the GM wants to throw more Japanese troops at the heroes, that is up to them.

BACK ABOARD THE USS COLORADO

Dr. Carter has been fixated on the golden disc since they recovered it from the Japanese tunnels. She has turned it over and over again in her mind. If the team does not come up with an idea about the spiral grooves, she does. "It's a phonograph record!" she says with astonishment. She then shows the team how the grooves are like the grooves of a record. "Someone get me a record player!"

The navy men throw odd looks in her direction, but the captain has a phonograph in his cabin. He escorts the team there. Nervously, and with reverence, she places the disc upon the turntable.

At first, there is nothing but static. Then the needle finds whatever code lies inside the golden disc and a sibilant sound, like bird song, but somehow human, begins to emit from the player. It is like nothing you have ever heard before. Something from the depths of ages and pulled from the deep gulfs of history. These are human beings speaking, or almost singing, in a language that likely has not been heard for many thousands of years. Who were these people, and what message do they have for mankind, all these millennia later?

Dr. Carter shakes her head in disbelief. A tear slides down her cheek. The words are beautiful. She points out that no one has heard these sounds in such a long, long time. "It is as if the dead are speaking to us," she says quietly.

Dr. Carter says she needs the rest of the night to attempt any sort of translation. Meanwhile the PCs may do what they like on the ship. This is a time to rest, roleplay, and plan for their next move.

Early in the morning, just as the sun breaks over the horizon, Dr. Carter comes out of the commander's borrowed cabin and claims the language is *Rongorongo*. None of the team has any idea what that means.

She sighs in frustration. "*Rongorongo* script. Found on Easter Island. You know the *moai*? The big heads?"

Their next destination is that very mysterious island.

The USS Colorado is needed in the battle, but ASOCOM reassigns her to delivering the team to Easter Island. They may encounter Axis or SSU naval positions along the way, though ASOCOM deems this unlikely. Still, having a battleship helps. The commander is not happy about being called away from the Battle of the Philippines. During the trip he comes to resent Dr. Carter and the team. He is a naval man through and through. He has no time for archaeological mysteries or talk of aliens, but orders is orders.

It takes days to get to Easter Island, a tiny, remote isle in the South Pacific. The team is far away from civilization. They are also not alone.

EASTER ISLAND

Easter Island was named for the day on which the Dutch discovered it in 1722. Of course, like most colonial empires, the Dutch only "discovered" the island in the minds of Europeans. Rapa Nui, what the Polynesians who settled there in the First Century A.D. called their new home, was actually inhabited long, long before either group stumbled upon the island.

Easter Island happens to be the tip of a very large underground mountain well known by the human's who survived the Flood. Survivors made the long journey from the Middle East to Rapa Nui mostly by land. The trail the PCs have followed in this episode marks that passage. It ends on Easter Island.

Like many of the cultures that followed in the wake of the Flood, the Easter Island culture was but a dim reflection of the achievements of the Anunnaki. The survivors, expecting another attack at any time, tunnelled deep into the island where they made a permanent underground shelter. These first settlers had lost nearly all of their cultural memory by the time the Polynesians arrived. What remains is only the *Rongorongo* script and the great heads—or *moai*—for which the island is famous.

The Seal the characters seek is located underground.

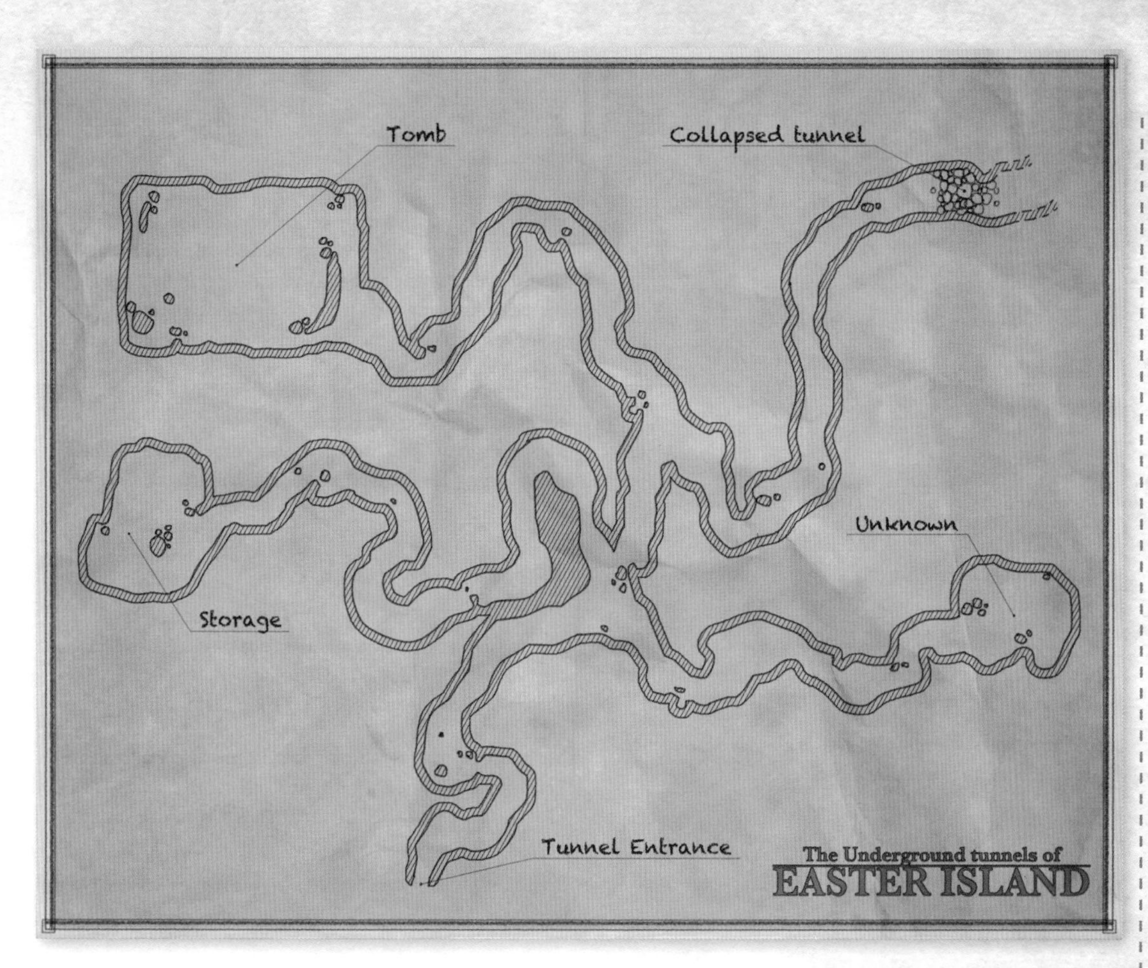

Novikova, should the GM decide that she makes a move against the team, must do so on the island, but there are other enemies here, including ones that might curl the toes of even *Blutkreuz* who deal with the *Untertoten*.

The island itself is a study in collapse and symbolizes the fall of the Anunnaki civilization as well as the curse of the current war. The islanders destroyed their environment, cutting down the last tree hundreds of years ago. Some resorted to cannibalism. Strange birdman cults grew at the end, anything that might fend off an apocalypse the Rapa Nui islanders had brought upon themselves. It seems the *moai* took precedence over all things, and the society that made them died caring for them.

Cycles of history repeat. The current war is, among other things, a war for the resources of VK left on planet earth. Are the great blocs re-enacting the fate of Rapa Nui? Of the Vrill and Anunnaki?

THE UNDERGROUND

The topside is mostly barren, as all the trees are gone. Scrub still exists, but little to persist on. The great *moai* loom along the shores, blank eyes staring out to sea for who knows what to return. A cave, which Dr. Carter found in her research on the way here, leads to the underground where she believes the Seal to be located. As the team descends, the natural cave leads to man-made tunnels.

Dr. Carter remarks that they look like a similar underground structure in Turkey called Derinkuyu. The team notes the tunnels look very much like a bunker built to withstand an aerial bombardment. As they move deeper underground, *Rongorongo* script begins to appear. The deeper they go, the more the script changes. What remains today is only a shadow of the original language. At the lower levels, this language looks like the script on the Seals. A couple of the symbols look like the squatting man from Episode 2.

This continues to foreshadow the backstory about the Vrill-Anunnaki War.

The lowest level holds great *moai* built by some of the original survivors and their immediate descendants. These are far superior to the ones above ground. Each looks like an Anunnaki, though the team has no way to confirm this having never seen one. Each face bears distinct features, though this is really only apparent on close examination.

Along the walls are catacombs on the upper levels. These become proper tombs as the journey descends. The Seal is in a central chamber where the kings of the survivors were buried. Each king dedicated his life, and his death, to protecting the Seal. The dead kings do not rest much longer. Each has been mummified (the bodies above are not), and each has a piece of the same crystal the Seals are made from embedded in its chest. This brings them back to life, reanimating them using the Seal as a power

source. The range therefore only extends to about 100 feet beyond the Seal, but the PCs have no way of knowing this.

The mummies wield curved swords and take half damage from automatic fire. In range of the Seal, they are incredibly powerful. There are 10 kings in all.

EASTER ISLAND KINGS (10)

EASTER ISLAND KINGS

Characteristics

MB 3	MD 0	PH 3	PR 0

Movement 7	Capacity 3	Initiative 3

Skills: Athletics 1, Attack: Melee 2 (Sword 1), Interaction: Intimidation 1, Special Ability 2 (Special Power 1, Damage Resilience 1), Special Power 1 (Zombie 1).

Special Abilities: Special Power (Zombie 1), Damage Resilience 2, Fast 1.

Special Powers: Zombie 2 (grants Damage Resilience 2, Fast 1 listed in Special Abilities).

Equipment

Weapon	Rng	Dam	Rank	Special
Sword	C	1	0	Penetrating 1

The Seal is set into a huge statue which functions like a machine. If the PCs remove the Seal, the mummies become lifeless once more. They are not, in fact, reanimated flesh as much as puppets propped up by alien technology. In this way, they are different than Axis zombies.

Once the team has the Seal, there is nothing stopping them from leaving the island. No doubt, they expect another turnaround, but that only comes if Novikova makes a play for the Seal now. That is up to the GM.

WRAPPING UP

This long trek ultimately led to a forgotten secret on Easter Island. The team emerges not only with the Seal but also with more clues as to what happened long ago. All of these point to the war between the Vrill and Anunnaki.

Since the team is as close to the United States as they have been in some time, they might stopover in Kansas at the Octagon. There, Dr. Schliemann has traced the Seventh Seal to Alexander the Great.

To: General Grander, ASOCOM and Dr. Schliemann, Clio

From: Dr. Jessa Carter, Clio

Subject: The Fifth Seal

The following summarizes the recovery of the fifth Seal under Operation: Apocalypse.

We began in Saigon, one of the last Free French holdings. As I related to Dr. Schliemann, the "experience" I had at Shambhala offered a host of information. He and his team at the Octagon were successful in turning this skein of data into viable intelligence. Thus were we led to Saigon in pursuit of alleged artefacts found in Cambodia. The artefacts were Persian coins, wildly out of place in this location. Through intelligence obtained by the communist resistance known as the Viet Minh, we traced the coins to Alexander the Great's eastern imperial expansion.

At this point in the operation, such inexplicable artefacts are almost mundane. The strange things that I have personally witnessed make these otherwise astounding archaeological discoveries pale, at least to the layman. We travelled to Cambodia where we encountered SSU Spetznaz under the command of Colonel Novikova.

We recovered an ancient journal that one of them carried. Said journal was written by a 15th Century Moslem explorer on the trail of Alexander the Great. That is a time gap of 1700 years. Novikova was already on the trail and we inserted into the SSU-controlled island of Sumatra by parachute. Stowing away on a Tupolev with Novikova herself. Before we reached our destination, the plane was shot down. Pirates recovered us in the open waters. With the help of Novikova and her men, we overpowered the pirates. A deal was struck. We traded intel. Novikova was headed for Nan Madol (a site built of ancient basalt megaliths). I approved the trading of intelligence. Any discipline for this should fall upon me not the Rangers.

On Nan Madol it became clear the Japanese had beaten us to our goal. However, in the tomb they had raided, enough clues were left for me to ascertain Novikova knew more than she was saying. This resulted in my cable to General Granger requesting she have access to the Allied side of the Philippines. It is not a bargain stuck lightly. However, given time constraints, and my dislike of certain interrogation methods, I deemed it the best choice. In return for access, Novikova revealed that the treasure we sought was taken by General Yamashita and hidden on the Island of El Nido.

We met Japanese resistance, but obtained the treasure we sought. This led directly to Rapa Nui (Easter Island). There, we fought something akin to Axis zombies, but far older. We obtained the Seal. Moreover, we obtained a final piece of information. I am now convinced that about 12,000 years ago, the Vrill and Anunnaki were at war. The Vrill sought to wipe out the Anunnaki on Earth (and their human servants). This attack resulted in what we know as the Great Deluge. We have been pursuing survivors of this Deluge for the entirety of our mission in one way or another.

Without lapsing into academic detail, the rise of civilization we know of around 5,000 years ago appears to be the second rise of civilization following a long Dark Age after the Flood.

Perhaps, it is that very weapon which the Seals ultimately unlock. The Bible speaks of the Seals as revealing (hence Revelations) Armageddon. Anything that could unleash that would no doubt win the war for whoever utilizes it first.

We continue our mission following the Arab's diary. I believe Alexander the Great possessed the last of the Seals that we seek. I shall send a cable when we arrive in Istanbul.

-- Dr. Jessa Carter, Captain, ASOCOM, Clio

CHAPTER 7: THE TOMB OF ALEXANDER

Alexander the Great was one of the greatest conquerors the world has ever known. At the time of his death at age 32 in 323 B.C., Alexander's empire stretched from ancient Greece across to India. His tomb has long been the subject of speculation. Rumours suggest he was buried in several different locations and at different times. For purposes of the adventure, we have established a pseudo-historical series of events.

Following his death in Babylon in 323 B.C., Alexander's closest advisors and generals debated what to do with his body. It was decided to return him to Macedon for a traditional burial. However, along the way, one of his general's, Ptolemy I (who would eventually found the Ptolemaic Dynasty in Egypt) hijacked Alexander's body. History records the corpse was entombed in the self-named city of Alexandria. Not an unlikely story.

However, Alexander's tomb was built in Alexandria and an account from Julius Caesar records visiting the tomb and making an offering. This document has emerged with enough clues to give Dr. Carter a location for the tomb itself. Following the reading of the full diary from the last episode, she reasoned that Alexander might have obtained one of the Seals.

Yet Alexander requested to be buried at the Siwa Oasis across the Great Sand Sea where he was told he was a pharaoh and a god. Ptolemy I followed Alexander's request and brought his body to that oasis in secret, so that he would never be found.

All of this would be merely a footnote in history were it not for the lid of the coffin Alexander was buried in. During his travels, as recounted in Musef's diary, Alexander happened upon legends of a lost civilization whose survivors had spread out across the world. Everywhere he conquered, Alexander sought remnants and myths of this civilization believing himself to be directly descended from their gods. Alexander was, if nothing else, a megalomaniac.

Ultimately, he died before he could uncover the truth of this civilization's alien origins. Yet he did recover one of the Seals while in Babylon. The text on this tablet was never translated, but Alexander wished to be buried with it, as it connected him to that lost civilization of "living gods." The Seal was installed in the lid for his sarcophagus. It currently resides, along with his body, outside the Siwa Oasis. Or so the theory goes.

It is this Seal that the PCs now seek. Of course, the route to the Seal does not follow a linear path.

ISTANBUL

A nest of spies, the neutral nation of Turkey is home to a Casablanca-like situation in the great city of Istanbul. Here, in the former heart of the Byzantine Empire (when it was named Constantinople), a document has emerged from the Roman Empire that records a visit by Julius Caesar to the tomb of Alexander the Great. This document is the first subject of the team's mission.

Dr. Schliemann informs the team by coded cable that this document has recently surfaced in the ancient city. A portion of the great Library of Constantinople (which is said to have housed books from the Library of Alexandria) was recently discovered. The renovator who discovered it sold the few scrolls he found to a local antiquities dealer. The document in question, recorded by an unnamed scribe, is currently the subject of a hunt by all three blocs, the *Ahnenerbe*, and the Sons of Belial.

Into this den of spies, killers, and war profiteers, the characters venture into what is their most cloak and dagger mission yet. This section bears some similarities to the Vladivostok episode. Rather than detailing a precise order of events, the GM is presented with notable NPCs and motivations surrounding the document. When the team arrives, they are thrust into the middle of this secret quest.

WHO WANTS THE DOCUMENT

Besides the Allies, as represented by the players and their Istanbul ASOCOM contact John Mies, five other distinct groups want the scroll. All are willing to bribe, cajole,

torture, and kill to obtain the document. Dr. Carter has heard of the existence of this unnamed scribe that recorded Alexander's life, but no proof of his existence has ever emerged… until now.

BLUTKREUZ

Colonel Orbst is after the document. Following their previous encounters with him, Orbst is more than eager to take out the PCs. As with all blocs, the Axis has a station and multiple safe houses in Istanbul. When Orbst arrives, he is under direct orders from Sigrid von Thaler. The entire apparatus of the Axis spy machine in the city is turned toward finding the book.

Blutkreuz knows about Jarvis Hancock, having had dealings with him in the past. However, Hancock has gone missing (see below). *Blutkreuz* knows that the man who found the documents, Coskun, sold them to Hancock. They know that Hancock is in trouble with a local gangster and suspect he has gone to ground.

In addition to Orbst, *Blutkreuz* has 20 agents at his disposal and six Axis gorillas kept in the city for "special circumstances." This search certainly qualifies.

SMERSH

The SSU is eager to acquire the document and knows that Rasputin is after it for his own purposes. Stalin's loyalists have therefore set themselves against Novikova. While she is technically their superior, they plot to get the document on their own. The Russians are thus divided in finding the book. Of course, Novikova has the advantage of Rasputin's clairvoyance and knows exactly who she is looking for. The rest of SMERSH only knows the man who sold the book, Coskun, but not to who. When they go to investigate, they find Coskun is dead, killed by an agent of the Sons of Belial.

SMERSH has 15 agents at their disposal for this mission and that includes any who might be working for Novikova directly. It is entirely possible the two factions come to blows over possession of the document. That is left to the GM's discretion.

RASPUTIN

Rasputin has more of an idea that the Biblical Seals lead to a great treasure in Babylon than perhaps anyone else does. He has Novikova acting as his personal agent. Depending on what occurred in the previous episode, Novikova might still be with the PCs, or she may have split from them and ventured off on her own to Istanbul. There is no way to determine for certain how events transpired. The GM must decide what her likely moves would have been following the mission to Easter Island.

Once in Istanbul, she proceeds to look for Jarvis Hancock.

THE ALLIES

John Mies is acting station chief for ASOCOM in Istanbul. His superior has been called away to the Octagon for unknown reasons. Mies has heard Hancock's name but has not connected him to the missing document. Agents who sought Coskun found him dead. This is one day before the characters arrive.

Mies knows very little about the PCs' mission but has ascertained that something big is going on worldwide relating to the Vrill. The fact that this involves the Anunnaki and not the Vrill is unknown to him. He has 10 agents he can "loan" to the characters should they request them. He is unwilling to give any more agents unless he hears from his superiors in Kansas.

THE SONS OF BELIAL

This ancient organization killed Coskun once they discovered he did not have the scribe's account. They tortured him beforehand, as evidenced by his broken body, and learned he sold it to Hancock. When the PCs arrive in Istanbul, they are up against 20 agents of the cult led by Dr. Carter's father. He is unwilling to hurt his daughter, but dispatches anyone else who stands in his way. Aside from Rasputin, he has the best understanding of the truth behind the Seals.

The Sons of Belial are well practiced at espionage. Over many thousands of years, they have existed in secret. They also have a man inside Black Murat's organization (see below). They are already planning to buy Hancock from the gang along with the book, though Hancock does not currently have the actual document.

BLACK MURAT

Murat is a gangster, smuggler, and otherwise most unsavoury character in Istanbul. He is large, dark-haired, and well dressed. Jarvis Hancock is in debt to him. Murat therefore had his men, 15 in number, scoop up Hancock. Hancock was going to be tortured and then killed as an example of what happens to those who do not pay their debts. Instead, Hancock offered the gangster the book as payment.

Murat was not about to hear any such thing, but he realized the book was valuable once the Sons of Belial offered money for Hancock. Murat knows when he has leverage, and now is such a time. He plans to take the money from the cult, but keep Hancock.

No one gets one over on Black Murat in his own city.

JARVIS HANCOCK

Jarvis has been a thief, an asset for various intelligence organizations, an antiquities forger, a smuggler, and just about anything else that could make him a few bucks. He spends that money as fast as he makes it. An English aristocrat by birth, Hancock's family lost their money during the Depression. He is, technically, royalty, but his family has long since moved to Canada.

Hancock is a well-bred gentleman. This gives him more credibility than he deserves. He is also a liar and a cheat, though not a wholly unredeemable character. He has been known to back up his friends. Hancock knows that the book is valuable. He also knows something of why it might be so. While he does not know details about the Vrill, he has inferred their existence in his antiquities dealings. Currently, he has the book hidden in a bathroom at the back of a cafe, but, as Hancock is slippery, this is little more than a forgery. He sent the actual book to a friend in Alexandria where he hoped to travel. He knew Murat was after him, and that the book was attracting the attention of the war. He planned to slip out of Turkey and make his way to Egypt.

Murat's men got to him before he could escape.

THE AHNENERBE

The Nazis have pursued the course of events since South America. Now, they use their agents in Istanbul to ferret out the book. The *Ahnenerbe* knows more about Babylon than anyone else does, as they possess the original documents from the Kvasir interview—see ***Operation: Babylon*** for details.

Leopold von Thaler conducted a series of extended interviews with Kvasir before the fall of the Reich. During these interviews, Kvasir revealed that the Vrill had been at war with the Anunnaki. They pushed the Anunnaki off Earth and secreted away some of their unique energy here. This is not what the Seals open, though the energy is related.

After the Nazis were purged, the *Ahnenerbe* kept these files. They want to obtain the energy for themselves but, more importantly to ***Operation: Apocalypse***, they want the Tower of Babel. Only they have pieced together what lies at the end of the quest. Dr. William Carter suspects as much, but he is not certain.

The *Ahnenerbe* play the role of observer in this chapter. They do not want to give themselves away, nor do they have near the number of agents as do the other factions. Their plan is to follow the winner of this secret battle for the book all the way to the end of the trail.

THINGS THAT MIGHT HAPPEN

The Sons of Belial "purchased" Hancock from Black Murat. Murat does not intend to keep his side of the deal. The transfer is supposed to happen at the Hagia Sophia, a magnificent mosque built during the reign of the Byzantine emperors. The place was selected because it is public and neither party felt the other would be bold enough to do anything rash. Regardless, Black Murat makes a move, and in response, the Sons of Belial attempt to grab Hancock.

Who winds up with Hancock is undecided. If the PCs spend too much time doing legwork, then the exchange already went down. While Murat is a clever gangster, the Sons of Belial are deadlier. If the PCs are not at the Hagia Sophia during the exchange, assume the cult has Hancock. Of course, everyone looking for the book knows about the resulting battle at the famous mosque.

It is also possible that Hancock escapes during the confusion. In this case, he tries to get out of Istanbul any way he can. Murat's men are on their way to the café to retrieve the book prior to selling Hancock. Blutkreuz tails them.

Blutkreuz, Novikova, and SMERSH all learn about Murat having Hancock right before the transfer, though no one finds out in time to do anything about it. Based on what happened at the Hagia Sophia, each faction acts to either find or rescue Hancock.

Outside the Hagia Sophia, the SSU makes a move to get the book. This too results in a shootout, which finds the ears of every faction. If the PCs miss Hancock at the Hagia Sophia, they might pick up the trail with the fake book. Dr. Carter immediately recognizes it as a forgery. The other factions are slightly slower to do so. This could give the team a head start to Alexandria.

Of course, without the actual text, they do not know they need to go to Alexandria. Carter knows it is one of the possible resting places of Alexander the Great, but it is only one among many.

RESOLVING ISTANBUL

Somehow or another, the PCs need to learn about the tomb's probable location in Alexandria. Remember, it is not there, but no one knows this yet. This can happen in a number of ways. The ideal scenario is the team recovers the actual book and/or Jarvis. Jarvis has a rough understanding of what the book says. He also knows where he sent it.

Another option involves the team following a faction to Istanbul. Certainly, this is a viable route so long as the team is cautious.

The SSU and *Blutkreuz* follow the same leads, and the PCs may, in turn, pursue them. Regardless, their next stop is supposed to be Alexandria, but there is an unplanned detour ahead.

OPERATION: KRAKEN

As detailed in ***Operation: Babylon***, the Axis has a submarine aircraft carrier. It is this awesome technology, made in partnership between Germany and Japan, that allowed the *Neue Deutsch Afrikakorps* (NDAK) to so quickly invade the Middle East.

All of this would be of no concern to the PCs except that they are about to run into this behemoth called the *Kraken*. However, the PCs decision to go from Istanbul to Alexandria involves crossing the Mediterranean. The *Kraken* is going to sink their boat or shoot down their plane and then capture the group. Anyone with them is also captured.

Orbst informs *Blutkreuz* what flight or ship they are on. Due to the extremely important nature of the mission, the *Kraken* surfaces, if necessary, and shoots down or sinks the PCs' transport.

Floating among the wreckage of your craft, you watch the flaming oil slick where you went down burn itself out. Again, you are stranded at sea. Perhaps it is the weariness this mission has brought upon you, but surely you must be hallucinating, for below, in the dark depths of the Mediterranean, a sea monster lurks.

Impossibly huge, the dark bulk of the beast seems to be rising up to you. This is perhaps not the strangest way to die after all that you have seen. The water all about you seethes as the beast breaks the surface, a monstrosity the size of a New York skyscraper looming overhead. A wall of steel. Yes, steel, for this is no creature, but somehow, a construct of welded metal.

Seawater pours from the bow, slipping over a giant Knight's Cross. This impossible vessel has a name painted along its side: "The Kraken." She is Axis, and you cannot swim out of her immense shadow fast enough.

Like Jonah and the whale, the submarine carrier literally opens up and swallows the team before retreating into the depths. Along with the team, anyone else (and a great amount of detritus) is scooped up. After the titanic doors snap shut like a jaw, the vast, cavernous chamber begins to drain. Truly, this room could swallow a battleship. It is that massive.

As the chamber drains, a whirlpool forms in the centre sucking the PCs toward it. A Swimming roll is necessary to avoid taking drowning damage. After a few minutes, the team finds themselves sprawled on the cold metal floor of the beast, gasping for air. It is then that an airlock door opens, allowing in a group of Naval *Sturmgrenadiere*. They surround the party and point their StG 47s at them. Once again, the team finds the hunter has become the hunted.

PULP FICTION

Operation: Apocalypse is a mix of military simulation and pulp-style adventure. In the pulps, the bad guys often capture characters—think about the Indiana Jones films. So, too, with this campaign. The delight in pulp is the roller coast ride of successes and losses. Indiana Jones often finds that luck gets him out of one situation while tossing him into an even worse dilemma.

Being captured can come off as a bit heavy-handed, depending on how it works. The instances here attempt to make it believable and epic, but the GM should not feel that the PCs need to be captured. If they figure a way around it, let them. If the GM simply wishes to cut the scenes where the PCs are captured, do so. You know your group best. Will they enjoy the turning fortunes of being at the enemy's mercy one moment and free the next? Would they prefer to chart their own course?

We cannot hope to write for every group's taste, but ***Operation: Apocalypse*** hopes to mix free-form gaming episodes with more linear sections as well. Like a symphony, the pace and nature of each movement varies. Good pulp adventures should too. We hope this one accomplishes that.

IN THE BELLY OF THE WHALE

While being swallowed by a huge submarine aircraft carrier is pretty epic, it is also an obvious reference to the events of the Book of Jonah. Biblical references are sprinkled throughout this campaign. This is not to imply any specific religious view, but rather to draw on the shared gravitas of Judeo-Christian culture for the purposes of adventure.

Dr. Carter mutters a passage from the Old Testament as the team is lead to the brig. "Now the Lord provided a huge fish to swallow Jonah, and Jonah was in the belly of the fish three days and three nights."

If Novikova is with the PCs, she says, "I think we will be here much longer than that, doctor."

In any event, the PCs are put into a secure brig. They are next to a group of Russian Naval *Spetznaz* who were also captured. They have been here for two weeks. An alliance may be in order. That is up to the PCs. If Novikova is with the heroes, it is simultaneously easier, and more dangerous, to partner with the *Spetznaz*.

As the PCs spend time in their cell, they note the guards shift from German to Japanese. Indeed, both German and Kanji is written on various pieces of equipment. No one can say precisely how far underwater they are.

Dr. Carter again exhibits some of her earlier impatience, expecting the team to figure a way out of this mess. That opportunity comes when they are led out of their cell by Japanese guards. They are brought to a lift that takes them up three decks to an interrogation room. Orbst is there waiting for them.

IF THE PCS ESCAPE NOW

This is an opportunity for the team to get away. There are six soldiers guarding them on the way up. The team is, of course, unarmed. The *Kraken* is a massive ship, and a fight in the elevator is not likely to attract attention until the bodies are found.

Once the soldiers are dead, the team may stop at any level they like. Most likely, they take one of the flight decks, as that appears to be their best chance of escape—assuming they are above water.

If they believe that they are underwater, the team might try to get out another way. One or more of the characters might have experience with the Japanese. Recently, Japan has been experimenting with manned torpedoes. Like the Kamikaze, these torpedoes are literally piloted by an occupant. One of the soldiers might be motivated to speak about these.

If none of the team has a reasonable chance of knowing this, Dr. Carter or Novikova does.

IF THE PCS ARE INTERROGATED

If the PCs ride the elevator all the way up, they are then led to an interrogation room. There is a porthole here which helps clarify whether or not the *Kraken* is surfaced (something entirely up to the GM).

Orbst is here along with a Japanese intelligence officer and three more guards. The six that brought the team here do not leave.

Orbst questions the team based on what has since transpired. Many scenarios are possible. The Axis may already possess one or more of the Seals, or they may possess none. Orbst wants to know what the team thinks they are used for. He uses any and all methods to extract this information. One such method, in order to avoid a grisly torture scene, involves the administering of a new drug. The character injected must roll against their Physique at Difficulty 2 or they tell Orbst the truth, as they know it.

Orbst is a skilled interrogator and reveals nothing. However, if the PCs escape at this point, there is some chance they might capture Orbst and use the serum on him. In this case, he fails his Physique roll as necessary. If the PCs need a leg up, Orbst now provides that. He can tell them the tomb is not in Alexandria but in the Siwa Oasis instead. This is true, as far as he knows.

ESCAPE

One way or another, the team needs to get off this boat. If not, they are not going to recover the last Seal and the Allies are likely to miss what happens in the final episode. Two methods are provided above for the team to escape, but they are only suggestions. The ship is colossal offering the team several options.

Any plan the GM deems reasonable ought to be given a chance for success. This includes the classic pulp trope of dressing up as enemy soldiers and walking out (of course, they cannot simply walk off a submarine at sea). Some of the team might pretend to be soldiers, while the rest play as captured prisoners.

Alternatively, the team could partner with the *Spetznaz*. Neither side trusts the other, but both must escape from the *Kraken*. However, once the team finds themselves free aboard ship, they now have to find a way off.

That means by air or by sea. If they launch themselves out in manned torpedoes, they could emerge anywhere in the Mediterranean. If they escape by plane, they are pursued by a host of Japanese and German fighters. Either proposition is dicey. Their best bet is to radio from the *Kraken* to alert either the SSU or Allied navy to the secret ship's location. This, of course, requires a stop by the radio room. That in itself should be quite a battle. Use the stats previously provided for German and Japanese soldiers. Ballpark how many you think your team can handle. After all, this should not be easy. In reality, they likely would never escape. Of course, in reality, ginormous submarine aircraft carriers don't exist, either!

Once they use the radio, the GM must decide who responds. The team can try one of the secret ASOCOM frequencies. Once it is clear to the Axis that their ship has been compromised, recapturing the PCs (if they are off the ship) is second priority to protecting the *Kraken*. The revelation of the *Kraken's* existence is quite a coup for the Allies or the SSU. It evens up ***Operation: Babylon*** just a little bit, but just because they now know the secret submarine carrier exists, does not mean they can find it. Its very existence gives the Axis supremacy in the Mediterranean for the time being.

ONE IF BY LAND, TWO IF BY SEA

The PCs are either flying away or being shot out of torpedo tubes. Either way, they have to find friendlies as soon as possible. If they did not think to radio previously, they are in for some trouble. The torpedoes are not designed for long-range undersea travel, and any plane they took would have had to be large enough to carry them—thus not very fast.

The plane has the advantage of being able to make it to land. The man-piloted torpedoes do not. If the team escaped by plane, three fighters are immediately on their tail. Once the Allies or the SSU show up, the planes may turn back. Certainly, the *Kraken* submerges. Having either the SSU or Allies show up is the only way the team can get away without a total suspension of disbelief. They really need to think of using the radio on the ship. If they wait to use the one on the plane, the GM may decide an allied carrier is within distance to intercept the enemy fighters.

Certainly, if the PCs alert the Allies from the ship, they have time to escape while the full power of the Allied navy and air corps in the Mediterranean begin to search for the *Kraken*. That at least keeps the *Kraken* busy.

In either case, the team finds a friendly ship or an area of land they can reach. Likely, they wind up on the coast of Egypt, as that is where the *Kraken* planned to launch a diversionary air assault while thrusting from Axis occupied territory in Egypt toward Cairo.

RABBI SHIMON BAR YOCHAI

Named for the alleged author of the Zohar, an ancient Jewish mystical text, Rabbi Shimon bar Yochai is an expert not only in that but also in the Kabbalah. He is a scholar of the Torah, and fears that man is seeking the power of God. His friend, a Christian archaeologist named Tudor, is an expert in the New Testament. The men are debating eschatology—the end of the world—when the PCs arrive at the cafe where they frequently meet. They are playing chess while sipping strong, black coffee from small cups.

Shimon can find the location of the tomb based on the notes in the account left by the scribe. Tudor is eager to come along. Dr. Carter actually knows Tudor, a dashing American. The two appear to have a history. If one of the PCs is already involved with Dr. Carter, jealousy should flare between him and Tudor.

ALEXANDRIA

Named for Alexander the Great, the city of Alexandria was the Hellenistic capital of the Roman (then Byzantine) Empire until the 7th century A.D. when the city fell to the Moslems. Founded circa 331 B.C., speculation has long held that Alexander's tomb is located somewhere inside, or beneath, the city. Currently, an Axis push has Alexandria's citizens worried. The Neue Deutsch Afrikakorps is determined to capture Egypt, and Alexandria, as the second largest city in the nation, is a prime target.

If the PCs did not bring Jarvis Hancock along with them from Istanbul, he may well have reached Alexandria on his own or via one of the other blocs. Everyone is looking for Alexander's tomb, and the account given by the scribe guides them all.

The GM needs to decide who has enough knowledge to make it to the tomb. Possibly, all factions have the requisite knowledge. Definitely, the Sons of Belial are already there. The rest is dependent on what happened in Istanbul. Upon arriving in Alexandria, still under the control of the Allies, the PCs meet with ASOCOM. ASOCOM informs them of the dangerous situation in the Middle East. Both the SSU and the Axis have made significant gains, and the Axis seems to appear wherever they like. This is, of course, because of the *Kraken*. The existence of this sub has not yet trickled down to the Alexandria station. The PCs know more than the spies do.

The GM needs to build tension. Make the sense of impending attack palpable. It will not come in Alexandria, but it will manifest in the final episode at Armageddon (Megiddo in Hebrew). Once the Axis has knowledge of where the Seals lead, they aim to take the entirety of that territory. To do so, they need to control the strip of land around the Sea of Galilee—Megiddo. According to Revelations, the greatest battle in the history of man is supposed to take place there.

For now, the team has to secure the tomb of Alexander, or so they think. In fact, as mentioned, the body is no longer located in Alexandria. That means the Seal is not there either. Of course, this is not revealed until the PCs find the empty tomb.

After meeting with ASOCOM, their next order of business is to speak with a rabbi located in the city. Alexandria was once the largest urban Jewish centre in the world. The rabbi traces his roots very far back indeed.

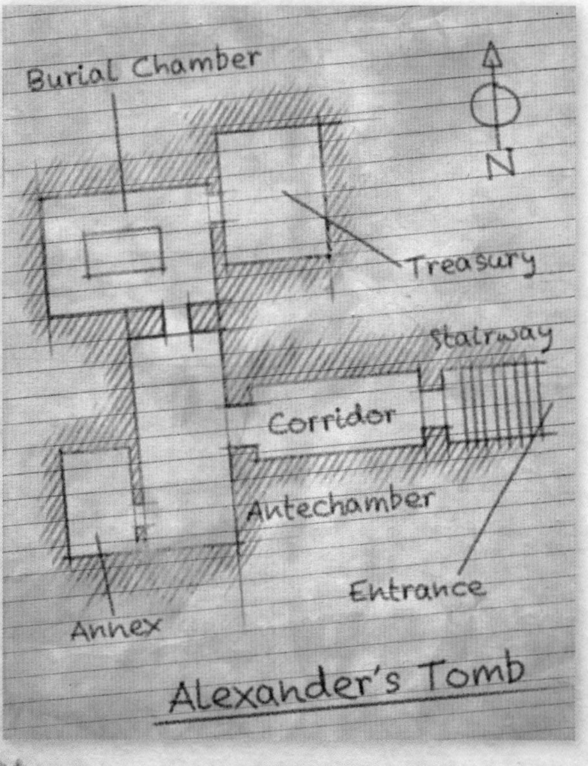

ALEXANDER'S TOMB

The tomb is located in an old section of the city accessible via Roman catacombs. As the team picks their way through the catacombs, the Sons of Belial wait to ambush them at the tomb itself. The tomb was sealed off from the catacombs long, long ago and all but forgotten.

Tudor provides pickaxes and sledgehammers once they determine the precise location of the tomb. The wall that seals off the tomb is so old as to appear the same as every other wall around it. The only thing of note is a "zipper"—a weak point created by masonry stacked atop each other rather than in a stronger, alternating pattern. This is where the team needs to break through. It is also where the Sons of Belial attack.

The catacombs provide a natural ambush spot. The PCs are situated in a location from which there are two exits. The Sons of Belial have both of these covered when they attack. Cover is only affordable once the wall is down or by actually climbing into one of the burial recesses. During this attack, Jessa's father reveals himself to her. He calls out for her, giving her one last chance to join him.

Acting only on instinct, and the rush of seeing her father, long thought dead, Jessa rushes to him. There is no stopping her, as the team is pinned down by the Sons of Belial. As soon as she reaches him, he takes her hand and pulls her deeper into the catacombs. The team must deal with any remaining Sons of Belial.

Burial Chamber
Treasury
Stairway
Corridor
Antechamber
Entrance
Annex
N
Alexander's Tomb

SONS OF BELIAL (8)

CULTIST OF BELIAL

Characteristics			
MB 2	**MD** 1	**PH** 1	**PR** 2
Movement 3	**Capacity** 3	**Initiative** 3	

Skills: Attack: Melee 1, Attack: Firearm 1, Awareness 1, Interaction 1, Radio 1, Knowledge: Occult 1, Survival 1.

Special Abilities: None

Special Powers: None

Equipment				
Weapon	Rng	Dam	Rank	Special
Knife	C	1	0	None
Heavy Pistol	5	2	0	Ammo 6
Light Pistol	5	1	0	Ammo 4
Sword	C	1	0	Penetrating 1
M1 Assault Rifle	15	2/1	0	Ammo 6, Rapid Fire

Once the battle is over, the team can either pursue Jessa or enter the tomb. They may, of course, split into two groups.

Inside the tomb, hidden among the cobwebs, the PCs find a number of potsherds, and a platform where once sat Alexander's sarcophagus. An inscription in Egyptian hieroglyphics and Greek shows his name along the edge of the dais. Faded murals, once no doubt glorious, depict his conquest of much of the then known world.

The tomb is otherwise empty. Neither Tudor nor the rabbi knows where the body might have gone. "It could be anywhere," Tudor says. "This city has seen more than one conqueror." In his zeal to discover something as great as Alexander, Tudor seems unconcerned with Jessa.

JESSA'S RESOLUTION

The PCs pursue Jessa and her father. As they do so, read the following aloud:

It is very hard to determine which way they may have gone down here. You stop and look for footprints in the dust or cobwebs ripped aside without care. All around you, the dead lay in their final places, skulls and bones held together with the slimmest of remaining fibres.

Then, suddenly, the tunnels reverberate with the sound of a single shot. This gives you the direction you need. Racing, hoping she is not dead, you come upon Jessa and her father. He looks quite surprised, clutching his chest as he sits, legs akimbo like a puppet with its strings cut.

Blood runs from his mouth as he manages a slight smile. "Thank you, Jessa." He coughs, blood misting the air in front of him. Jessa holds a smoking pistol in her hand. She looks at it as if she does not know what it is then drops it and backs away.

"He was going to.... He was going to..." She shakes. Tears well in her eyes.

Dr. William Carter slumps to the floor... dead.

Jessa killed her father. In the mad rush of emotion she felt on seeing him again, she followed him but, as they neared the exit to the catacombs, he explained his plan to call the Anunnaki back and she knew she had to stop him. They argued. He grabbed her wrist and she drew her service pistol and shot him. It happened so very quickly.

"I had to stop him, didn't I? Didn't I?!" she asks.

Jessa is in shock. The PCs need to get her somewhere safe. As her romantic interest holds her, Tudor and the rabbi come upon the scene. The rabbi says a prayer.

Tudor is less sensitive. "You shot him? Ah, hell, Jessa! You killed your own father!"

NEXT STEPS

It takes the rest of the night for Jessa to collect herself enough to assist the team. She needs something to think about besides her father. As they talk about where Alexander's body might be, she begins to pull out of her grief and process historical facts in her mind.

"A ruse. It must have been a ruse. Alexander was here, but he would have been moved. The Sons of Belial or Hancock, I don't know who, maybe both, wanted us to think he was still here. They would have directed us away... from..." here she pauses, having an epiphany. "They would have directed us away from the real location. Istanbul. I mean Constantinople. We have to go back!"

Jessa explains that the city of Alexandria fell to the Persians in 619 A.D., but was recaptured by the Byzantine Emperor Heraclitus in 629 only to fall to the Moslems some 12 years later. She believes the Byzantines would have moved the body to the most important city in Christendom—Constantinople. If she is right, Alexander was there for the last 1400 years.

The team is headed back to Istanbul, though Jessa is barely holding on.

ISTANBUL REDUX

How the PCs get back to Istanbul is up to them. They no doubt want to be careful given what happened en route to Alexandria. This time, their journey goes smoothly. Along the way, Jessa again retreats into her academic mind to push away the incident with her father. She mumbles to herself, tracking the history of Constantinople. Christian Crusaders and Moslems alike captured it, she says.

During excavations at Topkapi Palace late in the 19th century, both Roman and Byzantine sarcophagi were found. One, she remembers, was noted as being a Greek sarcophagus with an odd lid. No further mention was made of it. If she is right, Alexander's body remains in Topkapi Palace, which has since become a museum. No one found it, because it was in the last place anyone would expect—a museum.

TOPKAPI PALACE

The home of sultans up until the 15th century, Topkapi is now, as Jessa says, a museum. In the cellar, amongst things

Inside the cafe, a member of the Sons of Belial watches them. He is inconspicuous and difficult to spot (Difficulty 3). The Sons of Belial know the tomb is empty but plan to ambush the team there. They are also trying to kill off anyone else who comes looking.

The rabbi and Tudor need an evening to look over the book or notes. Dr. Carter helps them as they do so. The PCs can do nothing until the exact location of the tomb has been determined.

Rabbi Shimon bar Yochai serves another important narrative function—he illuminates the characters about the story of Enoch, Noah's grandfather.

According to the Old Testament, Enoch, too, was warned of a flood that would consume the world. His task was to build a series of nine vaults in which human knowledge would be preserved. In the final vault, he put the greatest secrets and a golden triangle on which was written the secret name of God. In fact, this is a Freemason legend, not a Biblical one, as such. However, for the purposes of the mission, it is Biblical. Again, the GM should lean on the gravitas of prophecy and the name Armageddon to give import to the final episode.

Enoch's nine vaults are located at Megiddo. If there is something to be done with the Seals, the knowledge will be found there, according to the rabbi.

ASOCOM can confirm troop movements appear to be headed toward Megiddo.

of little importance, lies Alexander's sarcophagus, or what remains of it. Of course, the team does not have permission to access the museum basement. Neutral Istanbul wants no official cooperation with Allied spies.

The team therefore needs to break into the museum. Guards are posted nightly. The outside of the building is scalable, and the upper windows do not have alarms attached to them. From one of the higher floors, the PCs make their way down to the cellar. There are no elevators. They are going to have to hoof it. Climbing the walls is at Difficulty 2.

Torch-carrying guards also patrol inside the museum. No one has any idea they guard such a valuable treasure, but many other, more mundane antiquities, are present. The factions that were after Alexander's body are still on the trail. It is up to the GM if they have traced it back to Topkapi Palace.

The Sons of Belial have been looking for the body here in Istanbul since the 13th century. They never dug under the palace and, by the time the body was found, no one thought it was anywhere near the palace. It became lost in the dust and files of history. Catalogued as "Item #337-A - Odd Greek Sarcophagus" and forgotten.

INSIDE TOPKAPI PALACE

Assuming the PCs enter on one of the upper floors. They find themselves in one of the exhibits, in this case one focused on the early Byzantine Empire. All manner of precious objects lie behind locked display cases. Goblets, jewels, and daggers twinkle in the light of the moon as the PCs creep through the exhibit toward the stairs.

A lone watchman, who happens to be a member of the Turkish Army, arrives on this floor just after the PCs enter.

WATCHMAN (1)

Use stats for Mercenary Troop on p. 155 of ***Dust Adventures***.

Avoiding the guard is a Difficulty 2 Stealth roll. As he is alone, it is not difficult to overcome him, but he has a police whistle around his neck. If he blows it, two more guards arrive in two rounds.

THE CELLARS

The basement of the museum is where actual researches do their work. It is also the warehouse for the great majority of artefacts housed here. Only a scant sliver of any museum's collection ever sees the public light. In basements like these, lies the greater history of humankind.

Dr. Carter is familiar with cataloguing methods and procedures. She needs about a half hour to find the information she seeks. Otherwise, the team must wander around aimlessly hoping to find the conqueror's body among the heaps and rows of history.

During that half hour, the GM should decide if any of the other factions, who have reliable knowledge on the location of Alexander, arrive at the museum. Whichever faction, if any, comes after the body, they enter through similar means as the team used. They are armed and, perhaps, expecting the team to be there depending on their intelligence.

The GM should select a small group (no more than 8 men) from one of the factions that arrive at the museum. The ideal time for their arrival is just after the team discovers Alexander.

Jessa writes a number down on a small slip of paper. The lamp-lit desk she is using is now scattered with journals and logbooks, each cataloguing items you can only imagine. She leads you through the maze of crates, shelves, and upright mummies until, at last, you stand before a plain wooden box. It looks old. "Help me with this," she says, grabbing a crowbar from a nearby shelf. Together, you pry off the lid. Inside lays pieces of a broken sarcophagus and a jumbled skeleton. The body wears no adornments. To one side of the crate lies the sarcophagus' lid. Inset into the basalt stone is the final tablet: The Seventh Seal.

Here, in a dusty museum lies the once great king. The conqueror. The man who once ruled the breadth of the known world has been consigned to a plain wooden crate stuffed with straw. To one side of the crate lies the sarcophagus' lid. Inset into the basalt stone is the final tablet: The Seventh Seal. Dr. Carter laughs, saying, "To what base uses we may return, Horatio. Why may not imagination trace the noble dust of Alexander till he find it stopping a bunghole?" She then begins to cry.

The tablet weighs the same as the others. After the PCs have a moment to appreciate the irony of the great king's final resting place, the faction with the best intel arrives on the scene. Naturally, a firefight ensues.

When the battle is over, the PCs need make haste for an ASOCOM safe house. There, they can examine the Seal. The previous Seals were taken to the Octagon—at least those the players obtained. Dr. Schliemann has been studying them along with "top men." He understands they collectively point to a spot in what is now disputed territory, but would once have been the land of Judea—Israel. Specifically... Megiddo, called in the Greek, "Armageddon."

LOST SEALS

Now is the final opportunity for the team to recover any Seals obtained by another faction. If they have not managed to gain all Seven Seals, see the **Lost Seals** chapter for mission notes on retrieving those tablets. Everything has led to the birthplace of civilization. That is where the team is headed next.

To: General Grander, ASOCOM and Dr. Schliemann, Clio

From: Lt. Darian Anderson, Rangers, Temporarily reassigned to Clio

Subject: The Final Seal

General and Doctor, I am assuming the responsibility for this report following events which have incapacitated Dr. Carter. She remains in shock from the experience, but she is very tough. I have grown to respect her greatly.

As you know by now, her father, the senior Dr. Carter, was alive long after his reported death. It is by his daughter's own hand that he met his end. A single gunshot wound was the cause. Jessa, that is Dr. Carter, is in no condition to lead right now. Therefore, I have assumed command.

It appears that her father faked his own death and joined the Sons of Belial. His reasoning has to do with a Vrill invasion he believed was imminent. I cannot confirm her father was correct. Certainly, he did horrible things in pursuit of what he saw as a greater goal. I see nothing but madness in him, but I am just a soldier in this war.

We spent a great deal of time and effort finding the last Seal. As I cabled earlier, we were briefly captured by the Axis. The submarine aircraft carrier in which we were imprisoned is probably how they invaded North Africa in Operation: Babylon, but, again, I leave it to the intel boys to sort that out.

I like to keep my reports brief because writing about missions is not my strong suit. The operation was successful. In the end, we found the Seal, and the body of Alexander the Great, in Istanbul where we began. We are now on our way to use the Seals to unlock what Jessa, sorry, Dr. Carter, says is the Tower of Babel. If either of you can make sense of that, you are well ahead of us on the ground.

Incidentally, the site that Jessa believes the Tower is in is called Megiddo. She said that translates into "Armageddon."

I have given up trying to understand any of this. I am just a grunt awaiting orders.

-- Lt. Anderson

12/3/47

I'm sorry, Dad. I don't know what else to say. I killed you. You raised me to do that in the end, didn't you? You grabbed my hand and dragged me down those catacombs because you wanted me to shoot you. You couldn't stop yourself, so you had me do it for you.

I must still be in shock. Nothing seems real. How could it, though, after one has murdered their own father? I am some latter-day Elektra. I have taken my father's life and looked in awe upon the face of Alexander the Great all in the span of just a few days. He, like you, met an ignominious end. To be conscripted to such a place after being the ruler of the world... Hamlet, Act V, Scene 1, right, Dad?: "To what base uses we may return, Horatio! Why may not imagination trace the noble dust of Alexander, till he find it stopping a bung-hole?"

No, you did not die ignominiously. You were a sacrifice. I see the truth in the ancient texts now. We are all of us called to sacrifice those we love in the name of those whose names we can never truly know. You were right. Had you lived, you would have brought those creatures back.

That is little comfort to me.

Why did you make me do this, Dad?

CHAPTER 8: ARMAGEDDON

MEGIDDO

It has all led to here and now. It has always been leading here, perhaps, for thousands upon thousands of years. Revelation is but one prophecy of the end of the world. Great world-consuming wars are the endings of so many cultural myths. This one, today, ends in Megiddo, also known as Armageddon, on the shore of the Sea of Galilee.

Glance at it for a moment through the lens of our all too brief lives—thousands of years ago, someone wrote about this location, foresaw the greatest battle of all time happen on this very spot. Today, the characters are going there. This is the climactic episode in a long campaign. This is everything the team has been striving for over several sessions. This is, for the characters, exactly what it advertises—the end of the world.

Or at least the end of this world's illusions. Apocalypse is, in Greek, the lifting of a veil so that one might see the truth. The truth is revealed to the characters here, at least part of it. Practically, the team must reach the Enochian vaults and use the Seven Seals to open them. From there, they learn of the location of the fabled Tower of Babel and learn of the actual structure that inspired the legend. It did reach the heavens. The Tower of Babel was a space elevator built by the Anunnaki. They are ten thousand years gone now, and their technology and their legends are all they have left behind.

The great mythologies of the world speak of wars of light against darkness. For a very long time, the cosmos has been divided into a Manichean duality, but which of the two is the force of light and which is the force of darkness? The characters now know that there were actually two alien civilisations that warred over Earth in the remote past. Can either be trusted? Can any of the blocs, including the Allies, be trusted with such technology?

PREPPING FOR ARMAGEDDON

By this point in the campaign, the players should fully expect a huge battle to take place in the Middle East. They have uncovered the existence of a second alien race—the Anunnaki—and their war with the Vrill. They have discovered that Earth was a battlefield for these two races, and their human subjects, long, long ago.

For the larger ***Dust*** story, a climax occurs when the Battle of Megiddo rages on Tel Megiddo. For the characters, another climax occurs in the depths of space. It has been a long, strange trip, and the GM should feel free to lay it on thick at the end. This is war through a pulp lens. This is adventure with gritty, military realism.

The point is, the GM should have the players champing at the bit to uncover the final mysteries in ***Operation: Apocalypse.*** For all of their troubles to have been worth it, they deserve a huge payoff at the end. This is it. It begins as the largest Battle of World War II (***Operation: Babylon***) is underway.

A harsh wind scrubs the hill called Megiddo. Through a tide of airborne sand, Axis planes appear from the Mediterranean. The SSU sweeps from the south; the Allies from the north. All converge at this point in former Judea. Beneath that soil, you will find the greatest treasure man has ever known…or you will die.

The first shells come in from the German 88s, ripping open the desert floor and shredding the poor men at the frontlines. They are some ways behind you. Here you are, a lone team of Rangers leading the way to God only knows what. Three armies about to clash over this spot in the desert, and you have to get there first.

This moment could come in several different ways. If the PCs obtained every Seal, they can access the Enochian vaults alone. If not, they are racing against the other two blocs (or factions) to get to the Tel Megiddo and open the vaults. Of course, this means each faction must capture any of the Seals they do not already have.

The team may have made a deal with Novikova, in which case she is sharing any Seals she obtained with the team. If the Axis possesses one or more Seals, they are ready to fight the team for the others. Because each bloc is fielding a huge army, it falls to smaller units—like the Rangers—to speed toward the vaults first. The Allies provide a recon platoon with fast walkers to get the team there. The Russians are using a helicopter, but it is having trouble with the intakes because of the swirling sands. The Axis has a four-legged "runner" which moves like a cheetah across the scrub plain floor toward Tel Megiddo.

As GM, you have two roles in the forthcoming battle. The first is to manage the battle from the player's point of view—the conflict around the hill itself. The GM runs this like a ***Dust*** miniatures game, if possible. If not, use tokens to represent the three forces.

Your second role is to provide the larger context for the massive battle that soon erupts around them. Imagine the flat desert floor with a hill at its centre. From surrounding hills, by sea, air, and land, comes the mighty blocs with all they can muster in the Middle East Theatre of Operations. This is bigger than D-Day, bigger than the Battle of the Bulge. Hundreds of thousands are going to die here.

Of course, the battle extends far beyond the hill. Tanks, walkers, and planes are moving against each other for miles and miles around. Still, the PCs are at the bloody heart of it, a calmer eye in a greater storm. The danger in that eye is Tel Megiddo and what lies beneath.

Below is the order of battle for the fight in which the PCs take part. Remember, this is a mere skirmish compared to the larger combat around them, but it is their little slice of the war. Describe what is happening to them as well as around them.

The following two battles are described using ***Dust Warfare*** and ***Tactics***. Simply substitute the appropriate NPCs if you do not wish to use those rules. The Battle of Megiddo may be run as an RPG. The GM may decide some of the battle happens abstractly, in the background, while the PCs star in the main show.

The Battle of Megiddo is divided into two battles. The first is The Enochian Vaults where the factions are actively engaged in gaining entrance to the vaults. The second is

Armageddon in Pure RPG Terms

As a pure RPG battle, potentially sans miniatures, the GM must rely on description and pace to suggest the larger battle surrounding these final events. More walkers and tanks than seen in history converge at this point. Planes scream across the sky. Explosions rip open the ground the fury of Lucifer himself.

Of course, you cannot make every roll, account for every unit. Thus, this penultimate moment plays out between smaller units at the eye of the storm.

Practically, the PCs should have ten extra men and two small, fast walkers. Their opponents have 20 men each and 3 fast walkers. Of course, not all necessarily try to kill the PCs. Depending on events, they fight each other as well as the allies.

Further, some detachment of the Sons of Belial or the Ahnenerbe may likewise race toward the prize. They have mercenaries with them—The Sisters of Demolition. Assume 10 Sisters, one captured walker and another ten each of the Sons or Ahnenerbe.

On a battlemat or piece of paper, draw approximate locations. Each turn, roll four Dust Dice per faction. The number of Faction Symbols determines the side that does best that round. For the winning faction, no losses occur. For the Second, two, the third, three and so on down. Walkers should be taken out by targeted attacks resolved as normal.

The above only applied to the Allied soldiers under the PCs command, not the PCs themselves.

In this way, the battle is large, but manageable. Remember, what the PCs do should ultimate determine the course of the battle. Ignore dice rolls where their actions should intervene.

War to End War, which is just a massive battle. Both battles are very similar in set up, but the objectives are different.

SCENARIO: BATTLE OF MEGIDDO (THE ENOCHIAN VAULTS)

For use with *Dust Tactics / Battlefield*

FORCES

The Allied forces begin play with 75 AP. They must purchase up to one light walker (Wildfire, Honey, or Blackhawk) per Player Character in the adventure.

The Allies are represented by using Soldier 1 USMC units (Choppers, Devil Dogs, Leathernecks, Mustangs, Mavericks, Saints, etc.). They may only have one Mustang squad.

The Allies may have one aircraft representing the RAF but it has the Delayed Reserves Scenario Special Rule.

The Axis forces begin play with 75 AP. They can choose any force composition they desire as long as there are more infantry units than vehicles and more vehicle units than aircraft and at least one infantry command squad. They must also have more Infantry 1 units than any other infantry units, but not combined. They may have more Infantry 2 and Infantry 3 combined than Infantry 1, but not more Infantry 2 than Infantry 1. They must also have at least one walker from the following: *Prinzluther*, *Sturmprinz*, or *Stummel*.

The SSU forces begin with 50 AP and must have at least one transport Helicopter.

All other force organization rules apply as normal.

SPECIAL RULES

See Forces, Deployment, and Winning the Game.

SETTING UP

The table should be set up to simulate Megiddo as best as possible. Therefore, the table should be barren with few scraps of terrain save the large hill in the middle. Most terrain is remnants of earlier conflicts. Each faction rolls one die, on a SHIELD they may place no terrain, on a TARGET they may place one piece of terrain, on a FACTION symbol they may place two pieces of terrain. Acceptable terrain is as follows: vehicle wrecks, craters, barricades, rocks/boulders, and so forth. No buildings, woods, or water-based terrain features.

At the centre of the table there is a single hill, roughly 8"x8"x8" (4 squares) in size. On this hill is the entrance to the Enochian Vaults. This is the goal. It follows all rules for objectives as normal, except for victory conditions.

DEPLOYMENT

The Allied player begins with all of their units (except aircraft) on the table. They must set up completely within 16" of the table edge.

All Axis forces are in reserve. They enter the table from the opposite long table edge as the Allied player sets up.

All SSU forces are in reserve. They enter the table from the two short table edges not used by the Allied and Axis players. The SSU must deploy with half their force on each side.

WINNING THE GAME

The game concludes when one player gains access to the vaults. This means the player must be the only bloc on the hill. If necessary, the game continues until only one faction occupies the hill.

SCENARIO: BATTLE OF MEGIDDO (THE ENOCHIAN VAULTS)

For use with *Dust Warfare*

FORCES

The Allied forces begin play with 200 AP. They must purchase up to one light walker (Wildfire, Honey, or Blackhawk) per PC in the adventure.

The Allies are represented by the USMC. Therefore, the first platoon in the force must be a USMC Expeditionary Platoon found in the ***Dust Warfare Babylon*** PDF. Any extra platoons must also be USMC Expeditionary Platoons or hero-led platoons.

The Allies may have one aircraft representing the RAF, but it has the Reserves Special Rule.

The Axis forces begin play with 225 AP. They must use the NDAK Platoon structure found in the ***Dust Warfare Babylon*** PDF. They must also have more Infantry 1 units than any other infantry units, but not combined. They may have more Infantry 2 and Infantry 3 combined than Infantry 1 but not more Infantry 2 than Infantry 1. They must also have at least one walker from the following: *Prinzluther*, *Sturmprinz*, or *Stummel*.

The SSU forces begin with 200 AP and must have at least one transport Helicopter, and use any platoon structure they desire including the *Spetznaz* found in the ***Dust Warfare Babylon*** PDF.

All other force organization rules apply as normal.

SETTING UP

The table should be set up to simulate Megiddo as best as possible. Therefore, the table should be barren with few scraps of terrain save the large hill in the middle. Most terrain is remnants of earlier conflicts. Each faction rolls one die, on a SHIELD they may place no terrain, on a TARGET they may place one piece of terrain, on a FACTION symbol they may place two pieces of terrain.

Acceptable terrain is as follows: vehicle wrecks, craters, barricades, rocks/boulders, and so forth. No buildings, woods, or water-based terrain features.

At the centre of the table there is a single hill, roughly 8"x8"x8" in size. On this hill is the entrance to the Enochian Vaults. This is the goal.

FORTIFICATIONS

None.

DEPLOYMENT

The Allied player begins with all of their units (except aircraft) on the table. They must set up completely within 9" of the table edge.

All Axis forces are in reserve and follow the rules for Unprepared Deployment (***Dust Warfare***, p. 66). They enter the table from the opposite long table edge from where the Allied player sets up.

All SSU forces are in reserve and follow the rules for Unprepared Deployment (***Dust Warfare***, p. 66). They enter the table from the two shot table edges.

The battlefield condition of Off Target Shelling is in effect for this battle (***Dust Warfare***, p. 67).

The field is also heavily bombarded as the battle begins. The Allied player suffers the effects of the Axis upgrade *Nebelwerfer* Barrage (***Dust Warfare***, p. 77), but resolve the *Nebelwerfer* Barrage at the beginning of the Allied player's first command phase instead of during the Axis player's first command phase.

INITIATIVE

Initiative is determined as if a normal three-player battle was being waged (***Dust Warfare Campaign Book Zverograd***, p. 22) during each game turn. Regardless of the initiative roll during the first command phase, the Allied player can decide to go first or second during the first turn only. After this, normal rules apply.

GAME LENGTH

The scenario lasts for six game turns.

VICTORY CONDITIONS

The game concludes when one player gains access to the vaults. This means the player must be the only bloc on the hill. If necessary, the game continues until only one faction occupies the hill.

LESS THAN SEVEN

If the Allies do not possess all Seven Seals, the PCs having failed at some stage or stages along the way, the GM must decide how to proceed. One scenario, though a bit *deus ex machina*, is that the Allies captured the Seals during battle before they were spirited back to secret SSU or Axis facilities. This certainly simplifies things for the PCs but deprives them of agency.

The better option is that the team must make a side-trek to recapture the lost Seals. Each of these missions could play out as mini-adventures. The team needs to locate the Seals and either intercept them before they arrive at the Kremlin, *Blutkreuz* HQ, or anywhere else the GM wishes, or they must break in to these facilities to steal the Seals after they have been delivered.

These adventures are outlined in the **Lost Seals** chapter, but they do not necessarily have to played through as written. Players have free will, and they love to throw monkey wrenches into the plotting of any campaign.

SCENARIO: BATTLE OF MEGIDDO (WAR TO END WAR)

For use with *Dust Tactics / Battlefield*

FORCES

The Allied forces begin play with 150 AP. They can choose any force composition they desire as long as there are more infantry units than vehicles, more vehicle units than aircraft, and at least one infantry command squad.

The Allies may bring any force they want to the battle, but at least one USMC platoon must be used.

The Axis forces begin play with 150 AP. They can choose any force composition they desire as long as there are more infantry units than vehicles, more vehicle units than aircraft, and at least one infantry command squad.

The SSU forces begin with 150 AP. They can choose any force composition they desire as long as there are more infantry units than vehicles, more vehicle units than aircraft, and at least one infantry command squad.

All other force organization rules apply as normal.

SPECIAL RULES

See Forces, Deployment, and Winning the Game. In addition, whether the game is fought using Tactics or Battlefield the special Reserves rules for Tactics (***Dust Tactics*** rulebook, p. 34) are in effect.

SETTING UP

The table should be set up to simulate Megiddo as best as possible. Therefore, the table should be barren with few scraps of terrain save the large hill in the middle. Most terrain is remnants of earlier conflicts. Each faction rolls one die, on a SHIELD they may place no terrain, on a TARGET they may place one piece of terrain, on a FACTION symbol they may place two pieces of terrain. Acceptable terrain is as follows: vehicle wrecks, craters, barricades, rocks/boulders, and so forth. No buildings, woods, or water-based terrain features.

Up to one large hill, roughly 8”x8”x8” (4 squares) in size can be placed.

DEPLOYMENT

The Allied player begins with all of their units (except aircraft) on the table. They must set up completely within 12” of the table edge. They may opt to use the reserves Battlefield rule (even if the battle is fought using Tactics) see ***Dust Tactics***, p. 64.

The Axis player begins with all of their units (except aircraft) on the table. They must set up completely within 12” of the table edge opposite of the allies. They may opt to use the reserves Battlefield rule (even if the battle is fought using Tactics) see ***Dust Tactics***, p. 64.

All SSU forces are in reserve (see ***Dust Tactics***, p. 64). They enter the table from the two short table edges not used by the Allied and Axis players. The SSU must deploy with half their force on each side.

WINNING THE GAME

The game ends after turn 8. The player that has destroyed the most enemy units wins.

SCENARIO: BATTLE OF MEGIDDO (WAR TO END WAR)

For use with *Dust Warfare*

FORCES

The Allied forces begin play with 500 AP. They can choose any force composition they desire as long as there are more infantry units than vehicles, more vehicle units than aircraft, and at least one infantry command squad.

The Allies may bring any force they want to the battle, but at least one USMC Expeditionary platoon must be used.

The Axis forces begin play with 500 AP. They can choose any force composition they desire as long as there are more infantry units than vehicles, more vehicle units than aircraft, and at least one infantry command squad.

The Axis may bring any force they want to the battle, but at least one NDAK platoon must be used.

The SSU forces begin with 500 AP. They can choose any force composition they desire as long as there are more infantry units than vehicles, more vehicle units than aircraft, and at least one infantry command squad. The SSU may bring any force they want to the battle, but at least one *Spetznaz* platoon must be used.

All other force organization rules apply as normal.

SETTING UP THE BATTLE

The table should be set up to simulate Megiddo as best as possible. Therefore, the table should be barren with few scraps of terrain save the large hill in the middle. Most terrain is remnants of earlier conflicts. Each faction rolls one die, on a SHIELD they may place no terrain, on a TARGET they may place one piece of terrain, on a FACTION symbol they may place two pieces of terrain. Acceptable terrain is as follows: vehicle wrecks, craters, barricades, rocks/boulders, and so forth. No buildings, woods, or water-based terrain features.

Up to one large hill, roughly 8”x8”x8” (4 squares) in size can be placed.

FORTIFICATIONS

None.

DEPLOYMENT

All forces are in reserve and follow the rules for Unprepared Deployment (***Dust Warfare Core Rules***, p. 66).

The battlefield condition of Off Target Shelling is in effect for this battle (***Dust Warfare***, p. 67).

The field is also heavily bombarded as the battle starts. Allied forces suffer the effects of the Axis upgrade *Nebelwerfer* Barrage (***Dust Warfare***, p. 77) but resolve the *Nebelwerfer* Barrage at the beginning of their first command phase instead of during the Axis player's first command phase.

INITIATIVE

Initiative is determined as if a normal three-player battle was being played (***Dust Warfare Campaign Book Zverograd***, p. 22) during each game turn. Regardless of the initiative roll during the first command phase, the Allied player can decide to go first or second during the first turn only. After this, normal rules apply.

GAME LENGTH

The scenario lasts for six game turns.

VICTORY CONDITIONS

The victory conditions are the same as if using the Battle Builder Objective of Eliminate the Enemy (***Dust Warfare Core Rules***, p. 65).

The GM may assume the outcome of the greater battle is a stalemate if they do not want to conduct the battle with miniatures. No side wins. It is thus the small units who enter the vaults, and then find the Tower of Babel, who really claim victory. In the end, much like the Battle of Megiddo, no one will win. The technology of the Anunnaki space elevator is beyond every bloc and, in the end, the elevator becomes another prize over which to war.

ENOCHIAN VAULTS

There are nine vaults in all; each tiered atop the next leading to the final vault that holds the golden triangle on which the secret name of God is written. The vaults are built of limestone but show evidence of precise cutting that would wow engineers today. Script similar to that found on the Seals marks the stairway entrance to each vault. When each vault is approached, a cyclopean stone door is encountered. These are round doors, designed to roll out of the way in the presence of an Anunnaki or one of their servants. The PCs are neither, and the doors do not open for them save the last.

The final door recognizes any one of the Seals and opens accordingly. The code is embedded into the Seal itself, though it appears rather magical to the characters. As the door rolls aside, the team experiences something akin to what Howard Carter must have felt when first opening the tomb of King Tutankhamun back in 1923. This stale air has not been breathed for over ten millennia. Inside, sitting on a simple stone dais, rests the triangle with the true name of God. That, too, is a code, one designed to activate the Tower of Babel.

When the golden triangle is held, images flood the character's mind. He sees the Great Deluge that wiped out the Anunnaki colonies. From space, a giant meteor is hurled at the Earth by a stragne weapon. This is the Vrill's final attack against the Anunnaki. The impact occurs in the Pacific and causes a tsunami so huge that it rolls deep into the continents surrounding it. Things are simply washed away.

As this occurs, the PCs view a giant tower that seems to grow from the city of Babylon itself. The tower is literally alive. Whether it is nanotechnology or some other form of advanced tech, it cascades upward from the sands until it reaches the very stratosphere and then space itself.

The entire scene plays out like an emergency evacuation—indeed, it was. The Anunnaki pile into the Tower, which is clearly a gigantic space elevator, and ride the whole thing up. From there, the PCs, as from the vantage point of Anunnaki survivors, watch the impossibly high waves wipe over the coast of South America, North America, Europe, and Africa. A ship has docked with the end of the Tower and the survivors flee the solar system. What happens after, one can only guess.

Because of the way in which the triangle stores data, it interfaces with the mind. This process is a bit dodgy being as it is designed primarily for an Anunnaki brain. Thus, there is more information encoded in the triangle, but it requires trial and error to access it.

Given that time, the team locates the exact location of the tower in the ruins of Babylon. Further, they watch this surreal recorded history of the Seals as they are divided among humans who serve the Anunnaki. These humans are then commanded to flee to the dry corners of the Earth. When they have rebuilt culture, the Seals will impel men to seek them out and bring them back to the tower. The Anunnaki shall then return.

Whatever backstory has not yet been revealed to the PCs can be revealed now. The triangle serves not only as a plot device to get the team to the final encounter, but also as a narrative device to fill in any holes in the team's understanding of the Vrill-Anunnaki war and its resulting fallout.

This should give players a full picture of what the history of ***Operation: Apocalypse*** entails. The PCs now possess as much knowledge of the Anunnaki as anyone in any bloc—but the Nazis know a great deal as well.

After the PCs emerge from the Enochian vaults, they may encounter some remnants of the forces above. The GM may rule that the Allies have prevailed and driven off the

two blocs from the immediate area. In any case, the greater Battle of Megiddo still rages around them.

The team finds conveyance via Allied transport off the battlefield and toward their final destination—Babylon.

THE TOWER OF BABEL

Not but a scant month or two ago you would have surveyed the ruins of Babylon and thought of the birth of civilization. Now, however, you know these broken Shedu, these ziggurats torn down by Alexander the Great, these monuments to the birth of cities are, in fact, but a second iteration of an older civilization of men ruled over by alien beings called the Anunnaki.

Here, in the desert of Iraq, where the wind whips through the time-lost ages of this once great city, you know that history once again plays out. It is cyclical, and ends where it began more than 12,000 years ago.

Under the tumbled pile of rocks that was the great ziggurat lies the entrance to the Tower. For so long, this legendary Biblical place has lurked under the noses of archaeologists and historians alike. And all of it, every last thread in the tapestry of man's history inextricably ties to those of two alien races. This war you fight in is, somehow, the extension of an intergalactic war the human mind is perhaps best off not trying to comprehend.

The team has come a long way. They have travelled the globe over the last two months hunting relics left by the Anunnaki long, long ago. It all leads to Babylon, the Fertile Crescent, and the (re)birth of civilisation. The SSU and Axis are not here. It is only the PCs, the ages... and the dread threat of the Nazis. For they have the full interviews with Kvasir and know, at least, where the Tower was, even if they do not possess all the Seals.

THE AHNENERBE

The *Ahnenerbe* has been playing the long game. As the other blocs sought the Seals, the Nazis waited in the shadowy corners like spiders, ready to pounce on the victor that emerged. That victor is the team. While they fought at Megiddo, the Nazis waited here to ambush them. While ASOCOM assigns men to come with the PCs, they do not have the luxury of assigning an entire company right now. That means the ensuing battle is skirmish scale. If the GM wants to include more forces, that certainly makes for an epic ending. Use the previous Megiddo Battle forces if you want to conduct a miniatures game. However, this encounter is designed to be played with the RPG rules.

For now, the Nazis do not reveal themselves. They want the team to access the underground before following them inside.

FIGHTING IN ZERO-G

None of the team is prepared to fight in an environment without gravity. Penalties to rolls must be applied as the characters, including the Germans, struggle to learn how to move and fire. Recoil bounces the shooter in the opposite direction and likely into a wall. One cannot "swim" though the air, but must use the walls, or weapon recoil, to manoeuvre. All actions suffer a -1 penalty.

THE NAZI PLAN

While the great blocs of the Earth have been striving to unlock the secret of the Seals, the Germans already knew what they were. Realizing, based on Kvasir's testimony, that the Anunnaki tech would take decades to unlock, the Germans settled on another plan.

During the fall of the Reich, many secrets were kept. Among them was the existence of a German space station in orbit above Earth. The Axis believes this was just a plan. No one knows the satellite was built and is operational.

UNDER THE ZIGGURAT

The PCs, and whomever the army sent along with them, must spend some time clearing debris and excavating. Dr. Carter laments that none of this is being done properly, but her eyes are wide with the promise of discovery ahead. Whatever equipment they need has been provided—cranes, bulldozers, and other earth-moving machinery. It isn't pretty, but it gets the job done.

Once the dig finds the entrance to the tower control base, it is clear they are no longer digging through human-made ruins. The entrance looks more like an airlock than a tomb entrance and it is forged from an unknown metal. Having any one of the Seals does not open the door. No explosives appear to affect it either, at least not those that humans currently have access to.

The name on the triangle is the code that opens the door. One only need speak it aloud. If the PCs do not realize this, Jessa Carter does. With a quiet swish, the door appears to literally collapse in on itself, as if it were being decomposed on fast forward. This sort of thing occurs often in the Tower. The Anunnaki mastered molecular construction and deconstruction on the nano-scale. This technology is far, far beyond anything the blocs could hope to understand in the coming decades.

An airlock system allows the PCs to enter the control room after an alien voice speaks, and a violet laser plays over them. This is a decontamination process. Anything inside the Tower might reach space and vice versa, so the Anunnaki were careful. The walls are smooth and curvilinear. There appear to be no interfaces or the like. A ridge circles the room at waist level. When approached, this "ridge" comes to life and reveals itself as the interface. Wherever a character interacts with the interface, a chair "grows" out of the floor for them. It fits that PC perfectly.

A dim red light comes on. There is no direct source—the walls themselves emit the light. On the ridge in front of the character, a kind of television screen appears from thin air. More alien text is visible on the screen in a kind of 1980s style, monochromatic green computer font. Dr. Carter can read the text. It is a request. The team need only speak the same word uttered previously. When they do, certain portions of the wall sink in on themselves, leaving recesses precisely in the shape of each of the Seven Seals.

Each Seal glows when it comes near the recess built for it. When all seven are in place, the Seals each deconstruct themselves much like the doors before them. In almost liquid fashion, the Seals pour into the moulds made in the wall. Once this process is complete, the walls seal behind them. The Seals are not merely code, but pieces of the grand machine—pieces the machine has lacked for 12,000 years. Jessa laments the loss of the knowledge on the Seals but what happens next is too much to miss.

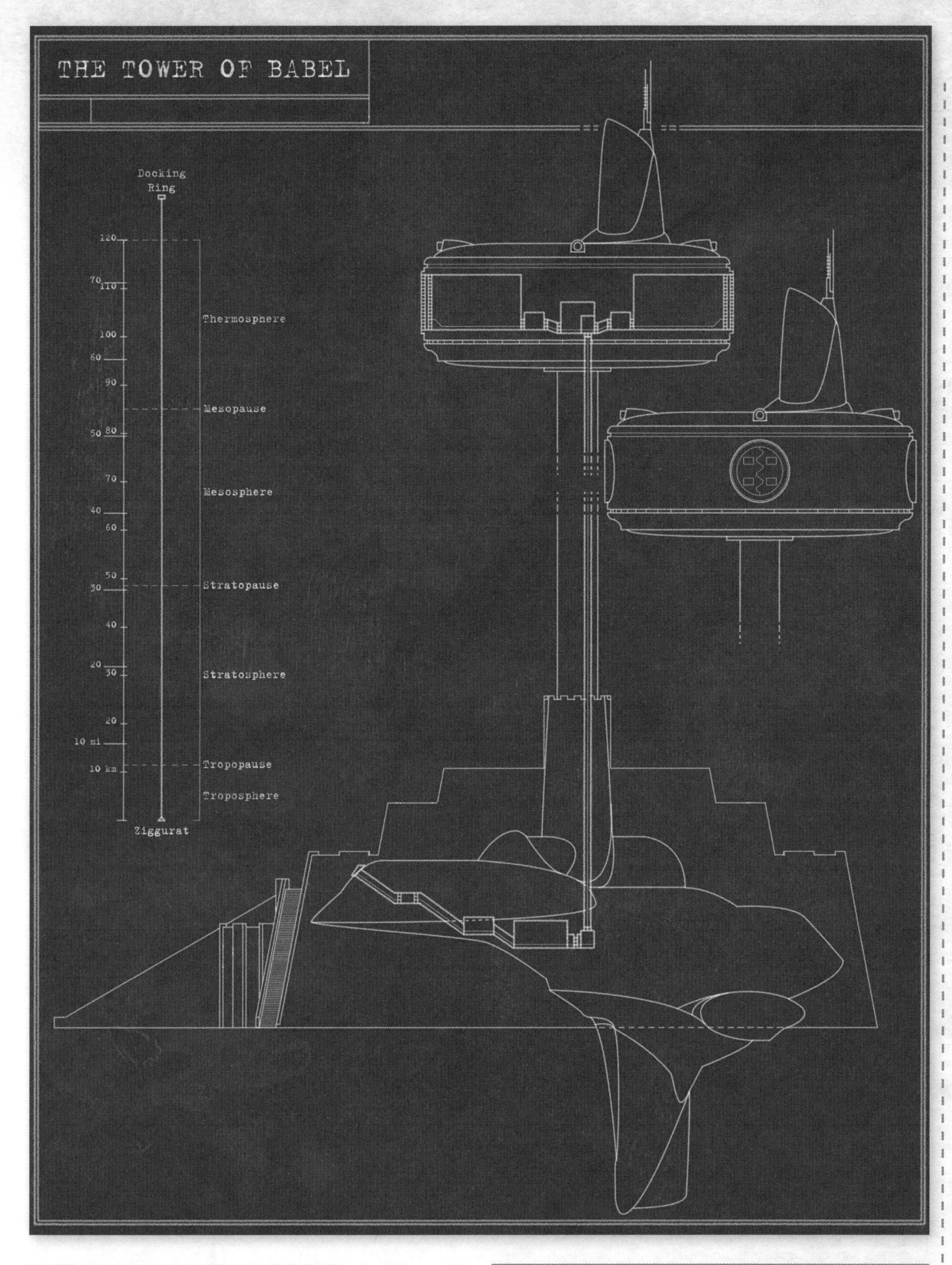

The Nazis destroyed the communications array used to speak with the station as they lost power. Being exiled in South America has stranded them from the resources they need to construct another communications array. These do not work on mere radio frequencies, but VK powered devices, which, while looking like radios, actually work along different wavelengths, entirely.

The Nazis were only able to build a small version and thus needed to get close to the satellite to reactivate it. This is why they needed to get into space and sought the Tower of Babel. They have since contacted the station and woken one of the *Kampfaffen* gorillas in cryo-storage there. These apes now pilot the V-6X to the Tower of Babel docking ring.

Who can say what the Nazis plan to do once they arrive on the station. Perhaps they have nuclear weapons poised to rain down on the blocs below. Hopefully the PCs prevent this from happening.

WHAT HAPPENS NEXT

The Nazis barge in, of course. With the path open before them, they storm the room and attempt to seize it from the characters. At this same instant, one of the walls of the room "unzips" itself, revealing an enormous cylindrical room beyond. This is the entrance to the elevator.

AHNENERBE (20)

Use stats for Axis Grenadiers on p. 144 of ***Dust Adventures***.

UBERMENSCH (3)

See p. 194 of ***Dust Adventures***.

The firefight is likely to drive the PCs into said elevator. As each enters, another laser, this time green, scans them. This is followed by an alien voice. Dr. Carter cannot understand the spoken form of this language. The voice is untranslatable at this time. What the team heard, but cannot understand, is "Vrill DNA detected. Proceed with termination sequence."

As The Tower of Babel was Anunnaki, it was designed to destroy itself in the event of being taken by the Vrill. The PCs, much to their surprise, possess Vrill DNA. Virtually everyone on Earth does, though none can say why. When this DNA is detected, the Tower believes them to be enemies who have gained access and it proceeds to cycle a destruct mechanism.

Meanwhile, when the PCs enter the elevator, the floor shoots up immediately.

The Earth falls away below you, the ruins of Babylon becoming an incomplete puzzle on the desert floor. Then, they are but spots, fading to a deeper topography of a high altitude point of view. That too recedes, as you simultaneously realize the floor and walls have become transport. An arc of light lies just above you and, even as you pass through it, you realize it is your world's atmosphere. Above, there is only the thick blanket of stars unoccluded by city lights.

Below, your enemy has likewise been thrust into the firmament.

The elevator arrives at a docking ring and stops mysteriously, without the characters experiencing any noticeable inertial effects. A red light shines and an alarm sounds, signalling the approach of the elevator below. The Nazis continue to pursue the team. One of them is wearing a personal radio pack that he takes off and begins to fiddle with. In German, they speak about the imminent arrival of the V-6X. The characters are no doubt familiar with earlier iterations of the "V" series rocket.

If that weren't enough, everyone suddenly finds himself or herself in zero gravity.

Everything in the docking ring is secured, and thus there is no "cover" floating in the air. While the two sides fight it out, two other events are underway—the V-6X is shuttling in from a Nazi satellite base hidden for years, and the Tower is about to decompress the docking ring and destroy itself. Both of these events are of some concern to the team.

Looking around in panic, the team spots suits of what look like armour hanging from the walls below. These are spacesuits. Some are clearly designed for non-human creatures, but others fit nicely on team members.

Meanwhile, the *Ahnenerbe* enact the final stage of their plan (see sidebar).

The alarm increases in timbre, auguring something no doubt unpleasant. The PCs do not need to be able to understand the alien voice to know this. The Germans are counting on the V-6X to arrive and dock with the Tower. The PCs are probably going to want to suit up. The Germans are doing so already. What follows is a chaotic scene in which the two sides dress for the cold vacuum of space, shoot at each other, and wait for the V-6X to arrive.

The suits are not easy to don correctly. Mind checks are needed to do so. Two total successes are required to put the suit on. There are, by now, five rounds until explosive decompression and three rounds until the arrival of the V-6X.

Fighting can, of course, continue in space. It is a very pulp set piece to be sure.

V-6X ARRIVES

Surviving Nazis board *The Hess*, named after its namesake's rogue mission to England. The PCs can see the Tower has begun to lose pieces, floating off into space. In fact, the entire Tower is designed so that it detaches from its base on Earth and, by force of the rotation of the planet, is shot into space where it then completely self-destructs. The Tower represents a technology the Anunnaki did not want the Vrill to possess. One way or another, the Tower of Babel meets its end here, some tens of thousands of years after it was built.

This means the team's only way back to Earth is in capturing, or being captured by, *The Hess*. As the surviving Nazis pile aboard, the team must follow them in.

Inside, the shuttle is not very big. One of the *Kampfaffen*, the co-pilot, unbuckles from his seat and takes on the team. Firing aboard the shuttle is extremely dangerous. Another explosive decompression would leave everyone stranded in space. The PCs should be aware of this as the Nazis pick up spanners or pull knives to fight them.

The next battle is hand-to-hand, fought in space as the Tower of Babel is flung from the Earth toward the sun or other self-destruction. Whoever is victorious has *The Hess*.

Of course, if the PCs win, they have to convince the remaining pilot and navigator to take them to Earth—hopefully to a destination of their choosing. The two gorillas have been in stasis for a long time, in which they dreamed repeatedly of being abandoned by their creators. They are therefore predisposed to listening to offers of defection and better treatment. They only speak German, of course.

And there before you, the whole of the Earth. A blue curve against darkest, eternal night. No one in your lifetime, in a thousand lifetimes, has seen your planet in this way. It is small, and terribly fragile from up here. More surprising, it is peaceful, the war so very far away.

Take a moment for the PCs to absorb the scene. They are, for the first time, off their home planet. This scene provides a metaphorical context for the larger, intergalactic war and the stakes involved in World War II. The team should get a hint at the broader scope of what that war really involves.

ENDING THE CAMPAIGN

The V-6X is designed to re-enter the atmosphere. The gorillas can land her. Presumably, this landing takes place somewhere in America. If the PCs lost, it does not happen at all. Instead, the team is brought to the satellite where they meet a cold death after being blasted out of the airlock.

ASOCOM takes great interest in the German rocket. While the Tower of Babel is destroyed, this rocket technology can put the Allies years ahead in the aerospace field. Regardless, the Allies now have as good an understanding of the Anunnaki, and the history of their interaction with man, as anyone does—perhaps more. While the Seals are gone, ASOCOM reveals that a very, very strong signal was emitted from the Tower before it was destroyed. That signal was not pointed at Earth but into the deeper reaches of outer space. The Anunnaki, for better or worse, are likely coming back. Dr. William Carter got his way in the end.

It remains unclear to everyone if the Anunnaki can be trusted or not. It is unlikely their designs on Earth were any more altruistic than the Vrill's were. The global conflict the PCs have been fighting for years just became interstellar.

The Allies now have some sense of why the Axis wants to unite the Earth under one flag besides their desire for dominance. The SSU and Rasputin do not forget being thwarted either, nor do the Nazis. The Sons of Belial, ironically, have seen their goal achieved by their own failure. For a continuing ***Dust Adventures*** campaign, ***Operation: Apocalypse*** expands the range of mission options available to the GM. There is yet a Nazi satellite somewhere in space that might be claimed by the Allies or by another bloc. Of course, the *Kampfaffen* who man it may decide they have other plans now that the Nazis are gone.

The PCs are heroes, but their medals cannot be officially awarded as their mission is deeply classified. While the

Dad, you are gone. You missed the end or, rather, what you thought would be the end. I do not know if I should hate myself for killing you or hate you for what you were about to do. I hate myself for having unwittingly made your crazy dream a reality.

I cannot begin to describe this day. It began on Earth and ended with me seeing my planet from the heavens above. The Tower of Babel fell for the final time. This is no longer the world I recognize. I know things about our history, and perhaps about our future, that upends everything.

Three great blocs waged war for technology as old as our species. In the end, I don't know if we won. I cannot say for sure. Perhaps none of us won. At least the technology isn't in the hands of our enemies. Enemies, I have heard that word so often during the war, but now it takes on new meaning. You, dad, turned out to be my enemy. Above, out there in the void, other enemies return for the treasure they left behind, the treasure we use to power this awful war.

I have fallen in love, killed my father, and thrown off the bonds of gravity to exit my planet. What does one say about that?

I have seen the Tower of Babel and I have touched the stars. There is nothing else to say.

I am sorry, dad, though for what I cannot say.

-- Jessa

scope of the war has been enlarged, the PCs still have the war itself to deal with. Simply because a potential alien threat to Earth exists does not in any way mean the blocs are going to set aside their differences. The greater enemy, whenever they arrive, will likely find a fractured, battle-scarred Earth. The war may very well still be grinding on...

Meanwhile, the Vrill no doubt have their own agenda. Kvasir was only the first Vrill that modern humans have met. Who is to say that others might, even now, be making their way back to Earth? There is VK on our planet and the secret store of Anunnaki energy as well. What else might have these two races left behind? And what is their deep, aeons old connection to Earth and humanity?

All these are answers left to future missions and future ***Dust*** products. ***Operation: Apocalypse*** is but one peek behind the curtain, and a brief one at that. There are still many mysteries, and many years of bitter war, ahead.

CHAPTER 9: OPTIONAL MISSION

THE SIXTH TESTAMENT
In addition to any specific answers the team came in search of, the Sixth Testament can, at the GM's discretion, include any information the team needs to get up to speed. If they've missed anything or failed to puzzle out part of the current plot of ancient backstory, the Testament serves as a fine plot device to get them back on track.

Whatever Seal the team currently seeks, its location is suggested in the text either directly or through conjecture on the part of Dr. Carter. Note, smuggling a woman into the archives arouses more than a little suspicion. Salvetti is reluctant to do so.

The book is a thin, vellum bound volume that recounts a story from the 6th century B.C., itself a copy of an even older text the book assumes no longer exists. The account is that of a previously unknown Old Testament prophet who, miraculously, is said to have lived more than ten thousand years ago.

THE ETERNAL CITY

As this is primarily a pulp/military campaign, many mission objectives are simply delivered to the players via superiors. While there is nothing wrong with this, some GMs and players may desire to uncover clues and do research on their own. Should this be the case, the following optional side mission is provided. Herein, the team must venture to recently liberated Rome, where they seek out a storied "missing" Biblical text recounting information on the Seven Seals. In addition, this mission can provide a red herring following the discovery of only one tablet inside the Ark of the Covenant.

OVERVIEW

Following the recovery of one of the Seals, the team comes up short on where to look for the next. Either Dr. Carter or Dr. Schliemann has both heard of a text called the Sixth Testament. This apocryphal account pre-dates what was left out of the Bible as arranged at the Council of Nicaea. It was likewise lost for many of thousands of years, supposedly having been mentioned by the Essenes in the Dead Sea Scrolls. Dusty rumours indicate Catholic priests found the Sixth Testament in whole or part. These priests brought the text to the secret Vatican archives.

Clio believes the Sixth Testament still resides somewhere in these archives. If the PCs need a clue to continue on, this text is the mostly likely source for such help. Of course, gaining access is easier said than done. While Rome itself was liberated, Vatican City is an independent nation. Mussolini declared it so, and the Allies have not violated that precedent. Certainly, the Allies possess the requisite power to take over the Vatican, but they aren't going to do so.

If asked, the Vatican denies possession of the text. Official Allied channels have already enquired. Perhaps one of the characters (Caleb Congrove if using the pre-generated characters) has a contact inside the Vatican?

THE CONTACT

Father Giorgio Salvetti is an acquaintance or even close friend of one of the PCs. In the case of Caleb Congrove, Salvetti taught a class in seminary while Congrove studied to become a priest. He speaks English. Father Salvetti is an academic within the Church. He enjoys a life of research and theological investigation, though he holds minimal power. See below for the current structure of the Vatican during wartime.

Father Salvetti specializes in Roman era research and thus is no expert on the Essenes or their texts. However, being a researcher inside Vatican archives, he's certainly heard of the Sixth Testament. He likewise knows it's a very touchy subject inside the Church, as it indicates the Vrill may have been mistaken for the "watchers" in the Book of Enoch. This casts some doubt on the divinity of Biblical accounts, something the Church refuses to let out.

Salvetti owes the PC a debt. The PC can call this favour in by expending an appropriate Expendable Resource. The debt in question is left up to the GM and the player whose PC has the contact. Salvetti is still a priest, however, and loyal to the Vatican. He also fears reprisal if his assistance is discovered.

A reasonable plan needs formation if the team is to get inside the archives. Father Salvetti refuses to smuggle the text out to them. That is asking too much. However, he eventually agrees to smuggle the PCs inside the Vatican archives. At the GM's discretion, any decent plan for getting inside—posing as priests, a side entrance, etc. works. It's what happens inside and, later, outside, that is at issue, for the Allies are not alone in seeking the Sixth Testament.

INSIDE THE VATICAN

Once inside the Vatican, Father Salvetti guides the team to the archives. An impressive steel door stands open. Assume Father Salvetti talks his way past the priest on duty at the entrance but make the scene tense by keeping

the PCs on guard. Any rolls the GM feels are appropriate to generate tension should be made.

As the two priests talk, the one guarding the door casually mentions that "the German" came to the archives again today with a War Cardinal's seal. Once out of earshot, the PCs can ask Salvetti about "the German." His description fits Orbst exactly. Fortunately for the team, Orbst was unable to smuggle the text out. He had to settle for copying. If asked, the priest admits that two others accompanied Orbst, including a woman, of all things. The woman's description is none other than that of Sigrid von Thaler.

The archives look rather like Roman catacombs, branching and forking in Borgesian complexity seemingly to infinity. Without Salvetti, the team has no chance of successfully navigating the maze. The book itself is kept unceremoniously on a shelf along with several similar volumes. It appears to date from the early 1st century A.D., a copy of a much older book. The text is in Latin. See sidebar for the contents of the Sixth Testament.

Orbst left nearly an hour before. If the team requires only one clue, Orbst vanished into Rome. The team can attempt to track him if they wish. If the team needs more than one clue, Orbst pursues the tablet allegedly secreted to Axum by King Solomon's son Menelik.

AFTER THE SIXTH TESTAMENT

Once the team secures the necessary information, the GM decides how it leads to the next Seal of which they are in pursuit. If the GM desires, that is as far as this section goes. However, there is another alternative. Should the GM wish to make ***Operation: Apocalypse*** more of a sandbox style adventure, the Sixth Testament may include leads to each of the major episodes in this book.

For example, rather than merely being ordered from one locale to the next, the team could opt to pursue each Seal in the order they desire. The outline presented in this book assumes a roughly geographical progression, but there is no reason your game need follow this path. The various NPCs, especially Jessa and her father, could alter the course of this adventure at any time.

The Sixth Testament can lead to any of the Seals as outlined in the individual episodes of this book. The order in which the PCs pursue these treasures is up to them. Perhaps they decide that one of the clues give them more to go on and, instead of proceeding directly to the American section of the adventure, they make for Russia or even the Holy Land. The final portion of the adventure should still climax in the Fertile Crescent from whence man's "first" civilisations sprung.

Putting this all together takes more work on the part of the GM. Simply having NPCs in Clio do the legwork, while the PCs focus on the action, can result in a perfectly fun adventure. That determination depends on both the style the GM wishes to impart and what the group of players enjoy. If the GM is up for a bit more preparation, he or she need only decide how moving around episodes affects the overall plot. In fairness, the GM might have to do this anyway if an NPC like Orbst is eliminated early in the adventure or if Dr. Jessa Carter herself is killed.

He was friend to Noah and witnessed the Great Deluge. The Deluge, as outlined in the background seen in Chapter One, is explained as a work of angels who thrust a mighty stone at Earth, which, upon landing in the ocean, raised such great waves that the world of man was smote.

The book further indicates that one of the tablets found in the Ark of the Covenant (there are allegedly two) found its way to the Kingdom of Axum in northern Ethiopia. If true, this gives the PCs a clue to yet another Seal's location. Should the PCs need only one clue, the GM may omit this thread.

If the GM preserves this plot thread, it leads to a deeper mystery the team need investigate. That side mission is outlined later in this section.

THE VATICAN IN WARTIME

The Vatican as we know it is not the Vatican of the ***Dust Universe.*** During eight long years of war, the Church has elected to restructure. The Pope, facing not only the loss of the Church in South America, but elsewhere around the world, felt beset on all sides. In this unprecedented time, he created five War Cardinals whose duty was to continue the power of the Church in the face of the war. Each Cardinal serves as best they can, and rumours of someone called the Shadow Cardinal have reached even the lower priestly ranks. Who that individual is, if real, is not known.

What is known, at least to the War Cardinals, is that the Sons of Belial infiltrated the Church long, long ago. In so doing, they have been able to monitor not only discoveries made by the Church but partially guide policy. An internal inquisition is now underway. While this might share the name of the dreaded capital "I" Inquisition, it has thus far not reached those depraved levels. One of the five War Cardinals is Chief Inquisitor, trying to ferret out members of the Sons of Belial within the Church.

For the PCs, this means the Sons of Belial might learn of their visit to the archive. That is up to the GM.

The Vatican is, for the first time in hundreds of years, at war once again. At stake, according to the Pope, is the very survival of the Church.

THE ETHIOPIAN CONNECTION

This is where the side mission gets more interesting. The Sixth Testament suggests King Solomon's son spirited one of the tablets in the Ark to Ethiopia and the legendary Queen of Sheba. While historical record makes the existence of Sheba, and the theft of the contents of the Ark, unlikely, it provides an interesting red herring for the adventure.

First, though, the team needs to find out what Orbst got up to after he left the Vatican.

WHEN IN ROME

Orbst only has an hour lead on the PCs after they reach the Vatican archives. As Rome was liberated by the Allies months ago, he is not in friendly territory. Of course, he also has a remnant network of Axis agents in the city on which to rely. His first stop is one of the remaining Italian safe houses located across from the Colosseum.

The Colosseum took further damage in the campaign to liberate Rome. The "eternal city" weathered yet another war, or at least a portion of one. Between the Seven Hills, this ancient metropolis has seen the feet of Romans, Visigoths, fascist Italians and, now, Americans in its ever-shifting history. The citizens are still in shock, though they welcome the Allies. They do not like the fascists in general, including the Germans.

Orbst is in a tenuous position, as the spy network he's leaning on for support is in danger of collapsing. With the Allies in Rome, most of the network wants to leave the city behind and head north into Axis-held Italian territory. They feel it is only a matter of time before the Italian Resistance ferrets them out and executes them. German members of the network often stand out but are more resolute. The Axis intends to retake Italy now that they have done so with France and have the Allies on the defensive in England.

Putting out word to the Italian Resistance or Allied intelligence in Rome that Orbst is there isn't going to uncover him immediately. The team needs to use Salvetti to get information from the Vatican. He is extremely reluctant to do this. During the fascist regime, members of the Church made questionable deals with the Axis. There are even rumours that these elements made arrangements with the Nazis and helped some get out of Europe. (If the GM decides to use this plot element, though a sensitive one, it can lead to Argentina should one of the Seals fall into Ahnenerbe hands).

Salvetti eventually bends under the PC's demands and asks after Orbst. He gets the location of the safe house but, after the PCs leave, word comes through ASOCOM that Father Salvetti has vanished. The PCs may have gotten him killed. That ought to weigh on them.

THE ITALIAN SAFE HOUSE

Orbst comes here to arrange transport out of Italy to Axum, Ethiopia. There, he hopes to recover the Seal. Records indicate that Mussolini displayed little interest in the rumour positing the Ark of the Covenant's location was Axum. He wanted territory, not religious artefacts. Of course, the Axis now wants both.

The "safe house" is a flat on the top story of a tenement building. Like many Italians, the three spies inside live poorly. A radio is secreted in a compartment carved out of the plaster wall. When the PCs arrive, they probably miss Orbst. However, the three spies left behind know where he was headed. Since Axum is no longer held by the Italians, and of low priority to the Allies, it isn't hard to access. Even now, the NDAK (Neue Deutsche Afrikakorps) plans to take Ethiopia back. Orbst can access troops from the NDAK for use in Axum.

3 ITALIAN SPIES

Use stats for Spy on pp. 145-146 of ***Dust Adventures.***

The spies do not want a fight and attempt to escape if found out. This leads, or can lead, to a scenic chase through the streets (and across rooftops) of Rome. Use the rules for chases on pp. 47-48 of ***Dust Adventures.*** Any of them, if caught, fess up to Orbst's destination if properly motivated. Suggesting that the team might turn them over to the Italian resistance is more than enough to compel them to betray Orbst.

This entire scene can be avoided if the GM wishes. Dr. Carter, or a qualified member of the team, might piece together the story of Solomon's son, Menelik, and his supposed journey to Ethiopia with the Ark of the Covenant. From there, they might remember that a church in Axum once claimed to possess the one, true Ark.

Should the PCs wish to track Orbst and take him out, he did not reveal exactly how he was getting to Axum. An alert might be directed to allies in the area but with ***Operation: Babylon*** in full force, reaching Axum with a significant force could be challenging. It's really the GM's decision if any Allied troops could get to Axum first. In any case, the PCs should have to do the brunt of the work.

ETHIOPIA

Operation: Babylon affects all of North Africa, including Ethiopia. The Allies nominally control Axum, but the team arrives at Addis Ababa. They take flak coming in to the airstrip there, but that's for effect rather than actual damage. The airfield itself was hastily patched, and artillery fire echoes in the distance. For all that, the city itself is relatively safe, at least for now.

ASOCOM arranges for the team to link up with a British team of "Desert Rats." These hardened men have been in one desert or another since the start of the war. The

Desert Rats are very close and don't like being imposed with a bunch of "Yanks."

Mostly, they've just seen too many people killed to get close to anyone new. The PCs themselves likely have similar defences. The transports the Desert Rats have are four souped-up jeeps, enough to carry both teams. There are 4 Desert Rats. Use stats for Rangers on p. 147 of ***Dust Adventures.***

It's a 14 hour ride to Axum. Nothing of note happens unless the GM wants to throw an encounter or two at the team.

AXUM

According to the Ethiopian book, the *Kebra Nagast* (*The Glory of the Kings*), the Ark resided for some years in Egypt before making its way down the Nile to Ethiopia. Menelik I, son of King Solomon and Queen Sheba, allegedly stole the Ark from the Temple of Solomon in antiquity. Various other theories surround this legend, but the Christian church in Ethiopia has claimed to possess the Ark for some time.

Axum is not fortified, or at least it is not anymore. Battle scars pockmark the walls of the town's buildings. Even the Church bears such scars. A tall, palisaded fence surrounds the Church. Men with automatic weapons guard the outside. Use the stats for Mercenary Troops in ***Dust Adventures*** if necessary. Hopefully, the team will not need to shoot their way into a church. However, Orbst has no such compunctions.

He has one Luther walker and 15 *Blutkreuz* Axis Grenadiers at his disposal.

AXIS GRENADIERS (15)

See p. 144 of ***Dust Adventures.***

LUTHER (1)

See p. 82 of ***Dust Adventures.***

It is up to the GM if Orbst is with the group or not. In any event, they lay siege to the small church not long after the PCs arrive. Give the team a chance to talk to the men outside. One of them speaks English and explains only the Guardian can look upon the Ark and, in so doing, slowly dies. No one else may enter the church, and certainly no one may view the Ark.

THE CHURCH OF ST. MARY OF ZION

Behind the palisaded fence lies a simple church; at least it appears simple on the outside. Once inside, one finds themselves in the tight, twisting corridors of a labyrinth. It is more symbolic than effective, as the building is not that large. The journey through the maze represents the journey toward the wisdom of God housed in the Ark. The team may lose a few turns navigating.

The Axis does not fire on the church at this time because they do not wish to destroy their prize, however, the prize is not there to claim. The Ark is not housed in Axum. Perhaps, once, long, long ago the Ark (or something like it) sat here, but it has since vanished. The Guardian is an old man. He tells the PCs, "This is the secret I guard. We have no Ark. I am the keeper of the worst of secrets."

He does possess a verbatim litany passed down from one Guardian to another. This litany leads the team back toward the Templars. It speaks of the Ark travelling from Jerusalem to Ethiopia as a ruse to fool those who might seek to possess it. Only one of true faith and heart can touch the Ark, says the Guardian, all others are destroyed.

He believes the PCs are true of heart, and so passes on his litany. He does this also because the Axis now threatens the church. He has seen Italian fascists invade Ethiopia. He would not have them know the secrets of the Ark. If the Axis looks unstoppable, he requests that the team kill him. "I shall be the last Guardian. So it was written long ago. The End of Days is at hand."

The players may choose to fulfil his request or not. In any case, there is neither Ark nor any Seal here. This entire trek has been a red herring, one set up by those trying to protect the Ark in antiquity. The Templars are but a later custodian of its secrets. Thousands of years before them, one of the Tribes of Israel was charged with this secret.

WRAPPING UP

The team has gone through quite a lot only to come up empty-handed. The Guardian's words may steer them on the correct path, but there is no getting around the fact that this mission was one of misinformation. Such misinformation is rampant in the search for lost treasures. Separating fact from fiction is harder and harder the further back a legend goes. The PCs get a taste of that here.

This red herring is not meant to frustrate players, but to remind them of the hazy stories that surround kernels of truth. With this firmly in mind, they may proceed to the next leg of their grand adventure.

CHAPTER 10: SEALS LOST

WHAT HAPPENS IF THE PCS FAIL ONE OF THEIR MISSIONS?

Sooner or later, the team may very well fail to acquire, or may lose, one of the Seven Seals. That could be a real problem completing the campaign since all seven are needed for the final episode. One way to get around this is to allow the various factions to negotiate a temporary truce to combine all Seven Seals. They'll duke it out after, of course, but not before you get to run the climax.

More satisfying, however, is allowing the PCs to get a second chance to recover lost Seals. Of course, we cannot predict exactly how your campaign will unfold, but this section provides mini scenarios detailing what each faction does once they capture one or more Seals. The GM needs to work these scenarios into his or her specific mission. There are simply too many permutations to cover here. As with the previously suggested sandbox-style mission, GMs can utilize these suggestions to weave a campaign that allows for more variation than any book can possibly provide.

WHO'S GOT WHAT?

Just because the PCs are heroes does not mean they win at every turn, just think of *Raiders of the Lost Ark*. Indiana Jones loses and regains possession of the Ark more than once. So too with the Seals, only the PCs aren't just racing against Nazis, they are up against cultists, the Axis, and the SSU as well. The adventure is relatively straightforward, but becomes more complex as the various factions interact. Perhaps the Sons of Belial have one Seal and the Axis has another? Or, maybe the SSU gains two and the other factions come up short? Many possibilities exist. Each mini scenario below details a series of events, which could lead the PCs to recovering one or more Seals from a single faction. Afterwards, more suggestions are provided allowing the GM to align factions for simplicity. Of course, there's no reason you need to make it easier on the PCs. They may very well need to recover multiple Seals from multiple factions.

As the campaign progresses, note which Seals escape the PC's grasp, and introduce the possibility of their recovery at a time of your choosing. ASOCOM has assets in every other intelligence network (no doubt the reverse is also true), and they use these assets for situations just like this.

A BRIEF SYNOPSIS OF POTENTIAL EVENTS

Each faction wants the Seals as much as the Allies, but not every faction has the resources of the major blocs. The Sons of Belial are an old organization, but they do not have the funds or the manpower of the SSU. Below are briefings related to each faction. Three of the briefings are designed for location neutrality. That way, the GM can set them in any appropriate corresponding location such as an island, at sea, etc. Only Argentina is location-specific.

THE AXIS

The Axis thinks they've made a clean getaway, but Majestic has been on the trail of the Seal as well. Hughes makes his play at sea, sinking the ship the Axis was using to transport the Seal. Unfortunately for Hughes, the Seal, in the hands of some surviving crew members, made it safely to a small island, but an island with a strange history...

THE SSU

SMERSH acquires one of the Seals, but Rasputin intervenes. A mercenary company hired by Rasputin ambushes the SMERSH agents trying to get the artefact back into the USSR. The PCs have a chance to take the mercs out and grab their prize.

THE SONS OF BELIAL

This cult is dedicated to the return of their Gods. Having obtained one of the Seals, they make for an impossibly ancient stronghold, one carved out of the Earth in pre-history. The team intercepts them before they can reach their redoubt, but both groups find themselves fighting against an angry, revolutionary group tired of the three blocs and looking to kill anyone involved in the war.

THE AHNENERBE

The *Ahnenerbe* brings the Seal to a secret location in Argentina. In a daring raid, the team must capture the Seal, but the old Reich has more secrets than anyone knows.

THE QUIET ISLAND— THE AXIS

ASOCOM INTELLIGENCE

Understandably, the Axis has kept their eyes on ASOCOM, but they did not have their eye on Majestic during this operation. That means they missed a would-be player in this ancient game—Howard Hughes. The billionaire made his move by rerouting an Allied submarine, which then sank the Axis ship ferrying the Seal (or Seals) back toward Germany. This could have happened in any ocean or sea. Circumstances dictate where the mission takes place. A mole inside ASOCOM revealed the attack, the location, and the odd nature of the area. The mole had no further details. Hughes intercepted a coded Axis transmission about the Seal, and the mole relayed that as well as the subsequent sinking of the Axis ship to ASOCOM.

Hughes chose this point to attack the Axis ship for a reason—he has an abandoned research facility nearby. The survivors of the Axis ship, along with the Seal, have made it to a small island, which appears on no chart. This island, called only Quiet Island, was used by Majestic because it has strange properties—namely, no sound is heard on the island. Further, once within a mile of the island, any compass or other navigational equipment goes haywire. While one can see the island with their eyes, it does not appear on any technological method of detection. Cameras, for example, cannot photograph it.

ASOCOM knows the area is a kind of "dead zone" on the globe. A mission to explore the island did not return. In fact, the issue is one of reliance on technology. The island emits a powerful electromagnetic field that causes all electronics to malfunction. Ships crash onto the rocks and planes drop out of the sky. ASOCOM doesn't know this, and they're likely sending the PCs by plane...

GETTING THERE

ASOCOM provides the latest, fastest cargo aircraft to get the PCs to the area. Once there, they have to spot the German lifeboat. It's a big area, and other planes are sent to assist. Of course the plane crashes, either into the sea or on the island. The Axis washes up on the shore, as well. Meanwhile, Majestic, who have a much better idea of the island's mysterious effects, dispatches their own team to recover the Seal.

THE OPERATION

The mission really begins with the plane crashing. While the team is bumped around, the crash is survivable. Whether the pilots or crew survive is up to the GM. The island is littered with wrecks. They lay along the rocky shores, derelicts and rusting hulks corroded by the sea. Some of these predate the war by nearly a century, indicating that the effects of the island are not solely the result of Majestic's experiments.

Once the team makes it ashore, they find an island appropriate to the global location. If they are in the tropics, a jungle exists. If they are in the Arctic, they find a cold, tundra-like land. Remnants of previous survivors exist further inland. The team might find the remains of Dutch sailors, or World War I soldiers. The latter could very well still be alive. Getting off the island is difficult, because the mysterious properties seem to inevitably draw would-be escapees back to the island, an effect of the electromagnetic field. No doubt some few have escaped, but they haven't returned to tell anyone else how to do so. Majestic 12 obviously has the means to come and go from the island.

The team needs to find the Axis and fight them for the Seal. Alternatively, they might bargain with the Axis once Majestic 12 arrives. They have greater numbers, and knowledge of the island, to use to their advantage. The research facility is a series of concrete buildings with a small underground complex. Various scientific devices and an array of radar-like antennas are present. Any appropriate Science roll affords the character an idea that Majestic was trying to control the island's magnetic field.

Many of the remaining equipment is stamped or plated with the Majestic logo. They *are* a capitalist organization after all. The surest method for getting off the island lies with the men Majestic sends to kill both teams. Interrogation reveals how those men intended to escape the magnetic field. A special device, rather like a compass, allows them to navigate and avoid the pull of the island.

The remaining population of the island is left up to the GM's imagination.

The oddest, and perhaps most formidable obstacle, is the silence. While it makes ambushes easier, it also means normal communication is impossible. Not only do radios fail, speech fails as well. The team must rely on notes and hand signals. This makes things slow and, in combat, nearly impossible. Mind tests need be made to convey information between team members. In play, the GM needs to enforce this at the gaming table. Players love to talk about plans at length, but here, the usual back and forth isn't possible. Having to write notes or, when paper runs out, draw lines in the dirt, makes that back and forth very, very slow. Whether the team suspects that Majestic is on their way remains up to the GM.

AFTERMATH

The precise nature of the island, and how it may or may not relate to the Vrill or Anunnaki, is up to the GM. As a side mission, we do not cover it here. Certainly, the island is of interest to the Allies and, now that they know how to get there and back, other units are no doubt going to be assigned to explore it. The PCs, however, have to worry about the Seal. Exploring the full mystery of Quiet Island must wait for another day.

THE ENEMY OF MY ENEMY — SONS OF BELIAL

ASOCOM INTELLIGENCE

This side mission requires the team to intercept the cultists taking the Seal (or Seals) to a secret location in the French town of Troyes. The mission itself does not need to occur in France, though it suits Europe best. The territory the Sons of Belial are moving the Seal through is currently disputed—no side has total control. In occupied territory, this might be a region the prevailing bloc has yet to pacify.

The team must access the region and lay an ambush for the Sons of Belial. Unfortunately, the ASOCOM asset who turned on the Sons of Belial knows nothing of the current regional situation. ASOCOM only has limited information. The revolutionary group could well come as a complete surprise.

GETTING THERE

If the team needs to get inside occupied territory, ASOCOM preps them for a combat jump. If the GM wishes, another method may get the team to their target. If the target is in neutral or disputed territory, the team selects the method of approach. Depending on where the team is when they receive the intel, they may need to hurry. The GM should indicate the clock is counting down but should not allow them to miss their opportunity.

THE OPERATION

The team inserts into the target zone to mount an ambush on the Sons of Belial. The location of the ambush determines the method by which the cult travels. Most likely, they are moving the object by truck or small, unassuming, convoy. GMs can repurpose the ambush found in the core book intro adventure, ***Operation: Apocalypse***, for such a scenario.

The actual threat isn't so much the Sons of Belial as the revolutionaries occupying the area. These are desperate men and women who, sick of being the victims, have taken up arms and decided to kill *any* soldiers they encounter. If the war is going to pound them, they are damn well going to pound back.

These are radicals, people pushed to the limits of human endurance, and beyond. They have watched loved ones die, their homes burn, and bombers reduce their towns and cities to smouldering ash. They have snapped, and their ideology is now one of extremes. If captured by this group, the PCs are slated for execution, as are any members of the cult. The group doesn't care who is who. They know only that this operation relates to the war. They take the Seal if they can.

The GM should play up the sheer hatred these citizens have for the war and the soldiers fighting it. They have had enough. Reasoning with them is not possible. The PCs must escape or kill them to a man.

AFTERMATH

The team needs to acquire the tablet. Apart from that, many outcomes are possible. The main take away should be emotional rather than merely plot related. Citizens have grown to hate all sides in his war. Men and women are taking up arms not in defence of their nation, but for purposes of revenge. Eight years of escalating, unending war have driven these poor people mad.

INTO THE LION'S DEN — THE AHNENERBE

Though they lack the resources of the Axis themselves, the *Ahnenerbe* still control a vast supply of gold and money secreted in Argentina, free from Allied or Axis interference. Argentina herself is a Neutral Nation, but high-ranking Nazis fled there after the assassination of Adolf Hitler.

Former SS pull strings in local and national elections. All intelligence agencies are aware that the fugitive Nazis fled to Argentina but in the middle of the greatest war mankind has ever seen, they cannot spare adequate resources to catch them. There is a tacit agreement between each bloc that the Nazi problem will have to wait until after the war. However, Russia has not forgotten what the Nazis did to their people, and do spare resources from time to time to kill or capture such fugitives.

BUENOS AIRES

The capital of Argentina was often the first stop for Nazis fleeing to the country. Some stayed on, but the vast majority were redistributed under Odessa. The *Ahnenerbe* handled assignments for soldiers, officers, and their families. The *Ahnenerbe* continue to monitor arrivals in the city, as they know the SSU is actively hunting them.

A secret sub pen is located along the coast near the city. The *Ahnenerbe* possess U-Boats.

BARILOCHE

When one imagines fugitives, one thinks of desperate men hiding in root cellars and attics. This is not the case with the *Ahnenerbe*. The Nazi elites have headquartered themselves in the ski-resort town of Bariloche. Located on the slope of an Andes mountain, the town could understandably be mistaken for German resorts once enjoyed by these butchers before they were deposed.

It boils the blood to see such monsters enjoy a fine life not so very different from the height of their power. Bariloche citizens are largely silent, though it remains an open secret that the town is home to some former top-ranking members of the Third Reich.

Not all the high-ranking officers are here, however. The *Ahnenerbe* doesn't want to make it too easy to round up their leaders. Men of power and influence have spread

like a cancer throughout many small towns in Argentina. Bariloche is only one.

It is, however, very close to a secret facility built with looted gold. This facility, which has no name lest word get out, is built into the Andes, a cavernous complex hiding the greatest secrets the *Ahnenerbe* brought with them. Among these secrets is the mad plan to somehow resurrect their dead *Führer*. Only a handful of men even know about this project.

ASOCOM INTELLIGENCE

ASOCOM is very aware of the threat in Argentina. At the same time, they are focused on the war. ASOCOM does not consider the *Ahnenerbe* a top threat. In this, they underestimate the group. This allows the *Ahnenerbe* an advantage—they have moles working inside ASOCOM. This is one way they stay in the race for the Seals. It also gives them a heads-up when the team comes to retrieve any Seals the *Ahnenerbe* possesses.

The *Ahnenerbe* take the Seal to the secret facility outside Bariloche for study. The Seal spends several nights in the home of an *Ahnenerbe* leader before it is moved. The precisely scheduled war machine the Third Reich enjoyed previously is no more.

GETTING THERE

ASOCOM isn't aware of the *Ahnenerbe* presence in Buenos Aires. They assume that, it being the capital, the Nazis spread out from there. It seems rather obvious they wouldn't stay in the most obvious location, right? Further, Argentina, as a signatory of the Neutral Nations Organization, demands all foreign travellers be processed through a central city.

This means the PCs walk right into a situation carefully observed by *Ahnenerbe* assets. Relaying the arrival of the Rangers to an *Ahnenerbe* hit squad, the PCs are now the target of assassins.

THE OPERATION

The team must move fast to reach the Seal before it is moved to the secure underground facility. This means not only defeating the German killers but also finding quick transport to Bariloche. Fortunately, ASOCOM has assets in the country as well and has arranged transport. A bush pilot on ASOCOM's payroll flies supplies, and sometimes passengers, to Bariloche. He has agreed to let the PCs complete a low altitude jump from his plane. Once they land, they have to hump it into the town.

At Bariloche, the team likely waits until nightfall before making their move. The Seal is located in the home of *Ahnenerbe* SS-Sturmbannführer Albrecht Steintz. His home lies along one of the ski slopes in the resort town. The Seal has a detachment of soldiers guarding it.

Assuming the team gains stealthy access to the resort, they must enter the house and take the Seal. The resort is guarded by crack troops. Ten are there right now on duty, with another ten sleeping. The GM should make the mission seem harder than it is. Remember, the team already failed to get this Seal once; it isn't fun if they fail again. Any reasonable plan of getting in works...up until the team has the Seal. Then the firefight breaks out, as firefights are wont to do.

GUARDS (20)

Use stats for Axis Grenadiers on p. 144 of ***Dust Adventures***.

The main purpose of the firefight is to push the PCs toward an epic chase down the mountain. They need to get the Seal to an exfiltration point and the Nazis want to stop them. The quickest route for both parties is on skis. This should play out like the opening teaser in a James Bond or Indiana Jones film. The Rangers are flying down the mountain while the Nazis are in hot pursuit. Bullets are whizzing by in the air, jumps are made, and the possibility of running into a tree or going over a cliff is very real. Have a lot of fun with this chase. It's supposed to be hair-raising and crazy.

AFTERMATH

Once the PCs have outrun or dispatched the *Ahnenerbe*, they need to get to an exfil spot and get out of Argentina. However the GM wishes to arrange this is fine. The climax was the ski chase. Don't waste too much time or detail on the dénouement. The main point is that the team got the Seal they failed to retrieve earlier. Pick up wherever you left off in the quest for all Seven Seals.

Depending on where they are in the adventure, the team might have a long journey to their next lead. If so, the GM can run another encounter with *Ahnenerbe* agents attempting to get the Seal back. This could take place on a ship, a train, in cars, or even in the skies. It's more a diversion than a real threat, so don't let it get out of control. If the PCs look like they might lose, fudge some die rolls or call in a *deus ex machina*.

CHAPTER 11: NON-PLAYER CHARACTERS

GENERAL LESLIE GRANGER, COMMANDER ASOCOM, ENGLAND

General Granger finds himself in an unenviable position. After many successful operations, England is on the precipice of falling. Already having had to leave London for Glasgow, General Granger is in no mood to move again even though he sees the tide turning in the Axis' favour. Current plans are to move British Operations to Ireland, but Granger is convinced this is just another delay against the inevitable.

Time and again, he finds himself at odds with the Octagon, which has moved various ASOCOM resources to the defence of the United States in Alaska and Florida. General Granger feels left out in the cold. He is seriously considering relinquishing his command and forming a guerrilla force inside of England to help fight the Nazis. While such plans exist in tentative stages, General Granger has had a plan in reserve for some time. ASOCOM does not want to lose him.

Characteristics

MB 2 **MD** 2 **PH** 2 **PR** 3

Movement 4 **Capacity** 5 **Initiative** 3

Skills: Athletics 2, Attack: Melee 1, Attack: Firearms 2, Knowledge: Language 3 (English, French, German), Awareness 1, Knowledge: Military Strategy 3, Knowledge: United Kingdom 3, Interaction 5 (Command 2), Willpower 2, Radio 2, Special Ability 1 (Rank 3).

Special Abilities: Rank 3

Special Powers: None

Equipment

Weapon	Rng	Dam	Rank	Special
Knife	C	1	0	None
45 Auto Colt Pistol	5	2	0	Ammo 5

Description

General Granger is a man in his early 50s with iron-grey hair kept neatly trimmed. He wears his uniform with the crispness of the day it came off the rack. He shuns his medals and has none of what the Americans call "spaghetti" dangling from his breast. A simple set of two general's stars is all he wears to identify himself.

He has a moustache the colour of new-fallen snow, which he also keeps trimmed. He is in excellent shape for his age, and one can see the powerful muscles that yet lurk beneath his uniform.

LIEUTENANT COLONEL A. WALLACE STONE, COMMANDER, CLIO

Lt. Col. Stone previously worked on the Manhattan Project under General Leslie Grove. Stone's tremendous organizational abilities, coupled with his natural ability to deal with the inflated egos of various academics, made him a natural choice to command Clio.

While Lt. Col. Stone is not himself a historian or archaeologist, he has made it his business to learn as much as he can about the various disciplines under his command. He is wise, well-spoken, and difficult to anger. Stone believes that technology will win the war, and that the Allies have pushed the alien tech as far as they can for the immediate future. He therefore concluded that gaining more of the Vrill tech is the key to victory. While his academics are given many indulgences, Stone always makes sure their top priority is the weaponization of Vrill tech. This often brings complaints from the civilians under his command. Stone handles these deftly, and ruffles as few feathers as possible.

He is not accustomed to women serving in the armed forces in an equal way with the men and, if he has any fault, it is a paternal sexism that seeks to protect women working for Clio. He believes sexual and racial integration of the Armed Forces was necessary, but he is an old school solider who has trouble imagining women on the front lines. This often causes tension between him and Dr. Carter.

Characteristics

MB 2	MD 2	PH 2	PR 2
Movement 4	Capacity 4	Initiative 4	

Skills: Athletics 2, Attack: Melee 1, Attack: Firearms 2, Knowledge: Language 2 (English, German), Awareness 1, Knowledge: Military Strategy 1, Knowledge: Technology 3, Interaction 3 (Command 2), Willpower 2 (In Control 1), Radio 2, Special Ability 1 (Rank 2).

Special Abilities: Rank 2

Special Powers: None

Equipment

Weapon	Rng	Dam	Rank	Special
Knife	C	1	0	None
45 Auto Colt Pistol	5	2	0	Ammo 5

Special Disadvantage

Paternal Sexism: Lt. Col. Stone has problems accepting women in the military in combat and other life-threatening roles. Any attempt to use character interaction against Stone that relates to women endangering their lives suffers a penalty of 2.

Description

Lt. Col. Stone is a black-haired man of 40 years of age. His eyes are clear blue. He wears no facial hair and discourages it in men under his command. He wears full regalia only on his dress uniform, preferring to wear simple fatigues with small rank insignia. He doesn't look like a civilian, but he looks, to them, less military than many of those around him.

DR. (CAPTAIN) JESSA CARTER

Jessa is a force of nature anywhere she goes. Her intellect is greater than almost anyone she meets, and she presupposes this when interacting with others. She does not strive to be haughty or entitled, but she projects an arrogance her peers find off-putting.

That said, she is usually right. It is a rare day when Dr. Carter isn't the brightest mind in the room. She gives orders as if her honorary rank of captain were earned in battle. This causes many soldiers to dislike her. She makes a lousy first impression, and it is only her beauty which saves most first encounters at all. She is aware of her good looks but considers it an irrelevance compared to her keen mind.

It is widely believed that Dr. Carter's father killed himself two years ago after pursuing occult scripts and artefacts related to the Vrill. This was before the Vrill presence was widely known. His colleagues began to shun him. In truth, her father is still alive, but she does not find this out until well into the campaign.

Characteristics

MB 1	MD 3	PH 1	PR 2
Movement 2	Capacity 3	Initiative 4	

Skills: Knowledge: Archaeology 4, Knowledge: Language 2 (English, German), Awareness 2, Knowledge: Science 3, Knowledge: Technology 3, Knowledge: Invention 2, Knowledge: Occult 1, Interaction 2 (Command 2), Radio 3, Special Ability 1 (Rank 1).

Special Abilities: Rank 1

Special Powers: None

Equipment

Weapon	Rng	Dam	Rank	Special
Knife	C	1	0	None

Description

Jet-black hair and piercing blue eyes, Jessa Carter could easily be a pin-up girl for the American war effort. However, she does little to accentuate her beauty. She wears conservatively cut dresses and suits, bordering on being out of fashion. She smokes habitually with none of the grace most women display when doing so.

HAUPTMANN KLAUS ORBST

A former member of the SS, Orbst narrowly escaped the purges that followed the overthrow of the Nazis. His fortune is due to Sigrid von Thaler herself, who recognized in Orbst a certain mercenary sensibility. While von Thaler is loyal to the Fatherland and her father's memory, Orbst is loyal to himself. He is not, however, a traitor.

Orbst was a Nazi in name only. Being a member of the party, and then the *Waffen-SS*, was the quickest route to the top. He disavowed the Nazi ideology and did not die in the mass hangings.

Orbst is an arrogant man, but one who also knows his limitations. He has his overconfident moments, but always tempers them with good judgment. An excellent solider and leader, Orbst has served in every theatre of the war. His newest assignment in *Blutkreuz* provides him with what he sees as the best shortcut to the power he craves. While those around him loot for gold and silver, Orbst knows it is in the war's aftermath that real power will be wielded. Who you know may be more valuable than how much wealth you possess.

While he is not a traitor, a suitable opportunity might sway him. First, though, he would have to be made to believe the Axis will lose the war, something he disbelieves.

Characteristics

MB 2	MD 2	PH 2	PR 2
Movement 4	Capacity 4	Initiative 4	

Skills: Athletics 2, Attack: Melee 3 (Knife 1), Attack: Firearms 3 (Pistol 1), Knowledge: Language 2 (English, French), Awareness 2, Black Ops 2, Knowledge: Military Strategy 1, Knowledge: Ahnenerbe 1, Knowledge: Blutkreuz 1, Interaction 2 (Command 1, Intimidation 1), Willpower 2 (Bad Ass 1), Radio 2, Survival 3, Special Ability 1 (Rank 1).

Special Abilities: Rank 1

Special Powers: None

Equipment

Weapon	Rng	Dam	Rank	Special
Knife	C	1	0	None
Luger	5	2	0	Ammo 7
Mauser	5	1	0	Ammo 5
StG 47	15	2/1	0	Ammo5, Rapid Fire

Description

Slicked back blonde hair and grey eyes, this finely-featured man looks almost effeminate in his beauty. He is not, but his features are like those of a finely rendered Grecian statue. He wears his *Blutkreuz* uniform with all the deserved regalia, having redesigned his own outfit to his tastes. Looking at him, a solider often dismisses him as a dandy. This is a dangerous mistake to make.

DR. WILLIAM CARTER

Supposedly, Dr. William Carter killed himself after being ostracized by mainstream archaeology for his theories on ancient aliens. In reality, Dr. William Carter still lives. He is a man consumed with obsessions. First it was archaeology, then the Vrill, then the Sons of Belial. William is something of a narcissist and a megalomaniac. He truly believes he is destined to save the planet from both the war and the aliens who visited it so long ago.

While the Sons of Belial are dedicated to the return of the Anunnaki, William instead devotes his energy to uncovering their secrets. He does not believe either race has good intentions for man, but he thinks the return of the Anunnaki is the lesser of two evils. He is willing to give the Earth to them if it means the Vrill do not win.

William's theory is that the Anunnaki and Vrill are related, the latter having been a slave race to the former. He still loves his daughter, Jessa, very much, but his obsession with being a saviour for the human race has eclipsed this. He yet hopes he can draw her to his cause, and helps engineer her discovery of the tablets before the other blocs wherever he can. His ultimate intent is to use them, with his daughter by his side, to unlock what he believes is a powerful weapon that could end the war and bring back the Anunnaki.

Characteristics

MB 1	MD 3	PH 1	PR 1
Movement 2	Capacity 2	Initiative 4	

Skills: Knowledge: Language 2 (English, German), Awareness 2, Knowledge: Science 4, Knowledge: Technology 3, Knowledge: Invention 3, Knowledge: Occult 2, Knowledge: Vrill 3, Interaction 2, Radio 3, Repair 3.

Special Abilities: None

Special Powers: None

Equipment

Weapon	Rng	Dam	Rank	Special
Knife	C	1	0	None

Description

Thin faced, William is handsome in a ghoulish sort of way. His lips are almost non-existent, as if a slit was made across his face by something sharp. High cheekbones and square features offer a classically handsome male face, but his eyes betray a certain feverish zealotry.

ROBBIE "MAD DOG" CORRIGAN

An East End gangster through and through, Robbie inherited his position from his father. He's always been a bit of a criminal, even as a lad. Robbie's father tried to get him to stay in one boarding school after another, but the boy just would not conform. His father was secretly proud of him for refusing to do so.

Robbie gleaned enough classical literature and maths at places like Eton before being kicked out. Under his hard-ass demeanour is a man with a brain in his head. Maybe that's why he rose to be the top gangster in East London.

As a criminal, he looks out for himself first and his crew second; at least he did until the bloody Germans came across the Channel. He's still a crook, willing to loot the British Museum while the city is under siege, but he plans to use his ill-gotten gains to fund an insurrection. No one is taking Robbie's London without a fight.

Characteristics

MB 2	MD 3	PH 2	PR 2
Movement 3	Capacity 3	Initiative 5	

Skills: Athletics 2, Attack: Firearms 2 (Pistol 1), Attack: Melee 2 (Unarmed 2), Knowledge: Language 2 (English, German), Awareness 3, Black Ops 3, Knowledge: London Underworld 4, Knowledge: London City 3, Knowledge: London Underground 3, Interaction 2 (Command 1, Intimidation 2), Pilot 1, Radio 2, Repair 1 (Vehicles 1).

Special Abilities: None

Special Powers: None

Equipment				
Weapon	**Rng**	**Dam**	**Rank**	**Special**
Knife	C	1	0	None
Heavy Pistol	5	2	0	Ammo 6

Description

A pockmarked, wide faced man with unruly ginger hair, Robbie would not be considered classically handsome. His nose has been broken twice and he has a few scars here and there. Powerfully built, he stands at 6' 2". He wears pinstripe suits and quality fedoras. He once owned a prized Duesenberg, but the bloody Jerries blew it up. When he smiles, he shows straight white teeth, a product of his father's money. He speaks with a Cockney accent, though he can turn it off and go the full "high Londoner" at will.

SIMCHA GOLAN—ANTIQUITIES DEALER

Golan has a reputation for being able to find any illicit antiquity for a price. He also has a reputation for having faked a few. Prior to the war, British authorities in the Middle East wanted him. Now that they are focused elsewhere, Golan has made the most of their diverted attention. He has few scruples, but he keeps them well-hidden in the pockets of the light coloured linen suits he favours.

Golan has dealt mostly in Middle Eastern artefacts, but dabbles in anything he can get his hands on which might turn a profit. He is a thorough coward, and has no creed or ethos that he venerates. Religion is just another way to make connections for him. Many natives of Jerusalem do not like him, but he is low on their list of priorities.

Characteristics

MB 2 **MD** 2 **PH** 1 **PR** 2

Movement 4 **Capacity** 5 **Initiative** 5

Skills: Athletics 1, Attack: Firearms 1, Attack: Melee 2, Knowledge: Language 3 (English, Hebrew*, Arabic), Awareness 2, Black Ops 1 (Counterfeit 3), Knowledge: Antiquities 4, Knowledge: Jerusalem 3, Knowledge: Religion 1, Interaction 2 (Negotiation 2), Repair 1 (Antiques 2).

Special Abilities: None

Special Powers: None

Equipment				
Weapon	**Rng**	**Dam**	**Rank**	**Special**
Knife	C	1	0	None
Light Pistol	5	1	0	Ammo 4

Description

A short, rotund man with thinning hair pasted across his perpetually sweaty scalp, Golan favours wearing a bright flower in his lapel. He smells of cologne and takes care to present himself in a pleasing manner. He always has a handkerchief at hand ready to mop his brow in the subtropical heat.

COMMANDER DONOVAN BONNEVILLE

A member of the SOE, Bonneville was tasked with reconnoitring the Forbidden Zone when it first appeared. Prior to that, he had been a reliable agent and excellent saboteur. The recapture of France was, in part, due to his organization of the Resistance in the south of France.

All that changed when he entered the Zone. Whether he has gone mad or really does communicate with the Zone is unclear. He believes the Zone is an alien intelligence that is trapped on Earth. There is no proof for this, though he does seem to understand the Zone's patterns like no one else.

He does not wish to leave the Zone, believing it has yet to reveal his purpose in being there.

Characteristics

MB 2 **MD** 2 **PH** 1 **PR** 2

Movement 3 **Capacity** 3 **Initiative** 4

Skills: Athletics 1, Attack: Melee 3, Attack: Firearms 2 Knowledge: Language 2 (English, French), Awareness 2, Black Ops 2, Knowledge: Military Strategy 1, Knowledge: The Zone 2, Knowledge: France 1, Interaction 2 (Command 1), Willpower 1 (In Control 3), Radio 2, Survival 1, Special Ability 2 (Special Power 1, Rank 1), Special Power 1 (Zone Sensitive 2).

Special Abilities: Rank 1, Special Power 1 (Zone Sensitive 2)

Special Powers: Zone Sensitive 2

Special Power

Zone Sensitive: Bonneville has a unique connection with the Zone. Any action that involves the Zone (navigating it, finding it, manipulating it, survival in it) gains a 2 dice bonus.

Equipment				
Weapon	**Rng**	**Dam**	**Rank**	**Special**
Knife	C	1	0	None
Webley Revolver	5	2	0	Ammo 6

Description

A short man with brown hair and brown eyes, Bonneville has a coarse beard and long hair. He hasn't cut or shaved since being in the Zone. He washes daily, but his clothes have an almost sulphurous odour to them which he picked up from a certain area inside the Zone. His eyes are keen but inflected by madness.

DR. MELI SANCHEZ

Meli Sanchez is a Zuni Native American. She is the first in her family to not only leave the reservation but also complete a college degree. University was tough for her in New Mexico, being a "redskin" in the late 1930s and early 1940s. She took this more as a challenge than a deficit and excelled in her class.

Meli specializes in the Clovis people who are believed to be the first Americans. She can trace the history of her people all the way to this culture that crossed the Bering Strait Land Bridge during the last Ice Age.

While she is a scientist, Meli also believes (to some degree) many of the traditional stories about star beings that her people keep alive. While she has no direct knowledge of the Vrill, she has inferred their existence from the massive leap in current technology. Some of her colleagues, with a little too much alcohol in their blood, have revealed that they have seen evidence of these aliens inside the Octagon. Meli keeps this knowledge to herself, but she is very curious to uncover the truth.

Characteristics

MB 2	**MD** 2	**PH** 1	**PR** 2
Movement 3	**Capacity** 3	**Initiative** 4	

Skills: Athletics 2, Attack: Melee 2, Knowledge: Language 3 (Various Native American Dialects), Awareness 2, Knowledge: Clovis People 3, Knowledge: Native American Lore 3, Knowledge: Science 2, Interaction 2, Willpower 1, Radio 1, Survival 2.

Special Abilities: None

Special Powers: None

Equipment

None.

Description

Meli is a dark-skinned, raven-haired beauty. Her eyes are intense and inquisitive. She only stands just over five feet tall, but her personality makes people think she's much bigger. She wears flannel shirts, blue jeans, and work boots

along with some traditional Zuni jewellery. If she owns a dress, she hasn't worn it in a long time. There's not much to celebrate on the reservation these days.

DR. THACKERY SCHLIEMANN, DIRECTOR OF CLIO

Of German descent, Schliemann received considerable hassle from his peers during the outbreak of the war. He himself is not a German immigrant, but his father is. Were it not for Lt. Col. Stone handpicking him to lead Clio, it is unlikely he would be in the organization at all.

Schliemann thinks the prejudice against him absurd, but he is not the sort to make a passion out of it. He is far too interested in the Vrill and how they relate to ancient human history than he is to righting any slights.

His fascination with the Vrill and ancient history often come up against the immediate needs of Clio and ASOCOM, but Stone has come to trust his impulses. Schliemann has single-handedly convinced Stone that the history of the Vrill and the human race is the key to finding, and exploiting, their technology.

As director of Clio, he answers only to Lt. Col. Stone. Mostly, Schliemann handles the scientists and academics, while Stone gives military direction for the organization.

Characteristics

MB 1 **MD** 3 **PH** 1 **PR** 2

Movement 2 **Capacity** 3 **Initiative** 4

Skills: Athletics 1, Awareness 2, Knowledge: Bureaucratic Red Tape 3, Knowledge: History 3, Knowledge: Science 4, Knowledge: Vrill 3, Interaction 2, Special Ability 1 (Rank 1).

Special Abilities: Rank 1

Special Powers: None

Equipment

None.

Description

A thin man in his late 50s, Schliemann wears spectacles to assist his aging eyes. He sports a white lab coat over a uniform that is rarely squared away. His hair is going gray, and his thick curls bounce as he walks. His lanky form is stooped from hours and hours spent poring over books and specimens under microscopes. He looks every part the absent-minded professor, though his intellect could buy and sell most people's idea of "smart."

DR. LANCE PEREAU

Dr. Pereau is a specialist in the physics of plasma. He has been working on a theory that posits that early petrolgyphic art is representative of plasma phenomena seen in the sky by prehistoric man. Pereau is also something of a communist, though not in the same way the Soviets are. Sadly, America makes little distinction in 1947.

All in all, Pereau is actually an idealist. He believes a cohesive communal society constructed around Marx's principles is the future of mankind. He ignores the many refutations of this that the current war offers. If an academic can be accused of living in the ivory tower, it is Pereau.

Characteristics

MB 1 **MD** 3 **PH** 1 **PR** 1

Movement 2 **Capacity** 2 **Initiative** 4

Skills: Awareness 3, Knowledge: Marx 1, Knowledge: Art History 2 (Petrolgyphic Art 2), Knowledge: Science 2 (Physics of Plasma 3), Interaction 2.

Special Abilities: None

Special Powers: None

Equipment

None.

Description

Pereau favours plain suits and hats. He smokes a pipe and has it shoved in one side of his mouth as if an afterthought. He isn't unattractive, but he isn't handsome either. His hair is brown and his eyes a gem-like green.

COLONEL NATASHA NOVIKOVA

Novikova is a loyal Rasputin supporter, but more out of logic rather than zeal. While the "mad monk" has a reputation for teetering on the edge of sanity, Novikova believes him to be far more stable than Stalin. Rasputin craves a power not of this Earth, and she hardly sees how his desires could lead to the sort of mass killings undertaken by Stalin.

She is likewise logical in most of her affairs. Novikova believes in Mother Russia and its people far more than any cult of personality. It is her desire to see the SSU dominate the globe. In equality, shall all people be united. She believes in the communist ideal, not the regime that has claimed that ideology.

Because she is no zealot, Novikova can make a valuable, if temporary, ally. She has no special desire to see the Allies hurt at this point, seeing their betrayal of the Soviet Union as a logical choice given the course of the war. She neither hates nor likes the Allies. Germans on the other hand are a lifelong enemy after having fought in Stalingrad.

While Novikova is not dishonourable, she is practical. Any alliance she enters is only good so long as it is advantageous to her. She expects other parties to behave the same.

Characteristics

MB 2 **MD** 2 **PH** 1 **PR** 2

Movement 4 **Capacity** 4 **Initiative** 4

Skills: Athletics 2, Attack: Firearms 2, Attack: Melee 1, Awareness 3, Black Ops 3, Knowledge: Language 3 (English, German, Chinese), Knowledge: Military Strategy 2, Knowledge: Rasputin's Plan 1, Knowledge: Sacred Dawn 2, Interaction 3, Survival 1, Special Ability 1 (Rank 2).

Special Abilities: Rank 2

Special Powers: None

Equipment

Weapon	Rng	Dam	Rank	Special
Knife	C	1	0	None
TT-46	5	2	0	Ammo 47

Description

A beautiful, blonde Russian woman, Novikova's face could be a propaganda icon for the future of the SSU. Her brown eyes are sharp, revealing levels of intelligence and logical evaluation to those they look upon.

RABBI SHIMON BAR YOCHAI

Rabbi Yochai is a dedicated theologian and occult Kabbalist. He believes the *Biblia Hebraica*, and the cosmos, are infused with the word and mind of God. In this code, one finds the true meaning of the universe. God creates masks to reveal himself to man so that God might thereby know himself.

To Yochai, this war has been a long time coming and was written of in Judaic texts long predating the New Testament's Book of Revelation. An apocalypse is coming, though whether it is one of revealing or destroying, the rabbi cannot say. The Anunnaki and Vrill are not aliens in Rabbi Yochai's view, but angels of different stripes. These are not the angels of Frank Capra movies, rather those of the Old Testament—warriors and avengers of the Lord.

Characteristics

MB 1 **MD** 2 **PH** 1 **PR** 3

Movement 2 **Capacity** 3 **Initiative** 4

Skills: Awareness 3, Knowledge: Language 3 (English, Arabic, Hebrew), Knowledge: Theology 3, Knowledge: Occult 2 (Jewish Kabbalah 2), Knowledge: Vrill 1, Interaction 2, Survival 1.

Special Abilities: None

Special Powers: None

Equipment

None.

Description

The rabbi is a thin man with close-cropped dark hair. He favors dark clothes, a tallit (prayer shawl) and yarmulke. He habitually carries several books around with him and wears rimless spectacles. Inquisitive eyes also reflect an inherent kindness.

DR. TUDOR

A dandy who uses his academic credentials for fame and renown, Tudor is less the bow tie-wearing academic and more the playboy. British by birth, he spent time in America studying archaeology at the University of Chicago where he met Dr. Carter. The two were an item for three years, but neither was truly happy with the other. Tudor has a fickle heart, and Jessa knew this prior to becoming involved with him.

Tudor is always after the next big discovery but has yet to achieve one. He really needs a significant find to secure his reputation in the field. He wishes he had been considered for Clio but pretends such an assignment is beneath a "real archaeologist."

Characteristics

MB 2 **MD** 2 **PH** 1 **PR** 2

Movement 4 **Capacity** 4 **Initiative** 4

Skills: Athletics 2, Awareness 2, Knowledge: Science 2 (Archaeology 2), Interaction 1 (Charm 2).

Special Abilities: Rank 2

Special Powers: None

Equipment

None.

Description

Tudor favors white linen suits with the occasional safari outfit and pith helmet to impress the ladies. He dresses the way he looks, freshly molded from a divine press. His face might appear on film posters—he is that good looking. Sadly, his attitude shows that he knows it.

INDEX

ACHTUNG! Cthulhu™

CORE GUIDES TO THE SECRET WAR

- Investigator's Guide
- Keeper's Guide
- Limited Edition Secret War Combined Volume

SUPPLEMENTAL SECRET WAR GUIDES

- North Africa
- Eastern Front
- Pacific Front
- Terrors of the Secret War

CAMPAIGNS & ADVENTURES

- Shadows of Atlantis Campaign
- Assault on the Mountains of Madness Campaign
- Zero Point Series
- Adventure Series

The Secret War Has Begun!